THE CLAIMING OF ALEC CALDWELL

Casey K. Cox lives and works in the South West of the United Kingdom. Known for popular titles such as *Be My Boy* and *Finding King*, Casey has been writing for many years, finally delving into the world of homoerotic fiction and gay romance back in 2010. Works include fan fiction for classics *Special Forces* and *The Administration Series* as well as some popular TV Shows. A number of free short stories are available on the author's page at Goodreads.com.

Casey K. Cox

The Claiming of Alec Caldwell

Erotic Adventures of a Young Businessman

BRUNO GMÜNDER

The following is a work of homoerotic fiction. The Order of Gentlemen is a fictitious institution that exists only in this work of fiction. All characters are fictional. Any similarities with living or deceased people are completely coincidental. In case of real life events, creative license has been applied.

1st edition
© 2016 Bruno Gmünder GmbH
Kleiststraße 23-26, D-10787 Berlin
info@brunogmuender.com

© 2016 Casey K. Cox
Cover design: Matthias Panitz
Cover photo: © CockyBoys.com (Model: Levi Karter)
Printed in Germany

ISBN 978-3-95985-195-4

Mehr über unsere Bücher und Autoren:
www.brunogmuender.com

For Roger, and Olie, and Angelo.

Thank you, to all those who continue to follow Alec's adventures.

You continue to inspire me and keep Alec's voice at the forefront of my musings so please enjoy the latest offering from my little office boy.

Long may the adventures continue

Always Expect the Unexpected

Lazy Sunday mornings at Hamilton's. Alec loved them. He'd checked in with his house boys, Sebastian and Brad, at home. They were happy to amuse themselves for the day and to keep Hamilton's boy, Dylan, still hiding from Brendan's pouting, for company. Alec translated that to mean they were enjoying the opportunity for a master-less fuck fest. Brendan, never wanting to be far from his master, fussed in the kitchen and Alec lounged in his favorite place, naked over Hamilton on the sofa.

"We should change these bands," said Hamilton, thumbing the one at Alec's left wrist.

"Why?"

"They're too thick for your new position at work. You need something that isn't so obvious to those in the know."

"Yeah, even my fourteen-year-old sister told my mom I was a sex slave."

"I would suggest to your mother she limit your sister's internet access," Hamilton said with a wry smile. "Seriously though, it could make life difficult for you."

"I didn't have any problems at the Davenports."

"I know, but gentlemen are always more relaxed away from the City."

Alec kissed Hamilton's hand. "Whatever you think is best, Master."

"I have an idea of what I'd like for you. I'm sure Maurice will be able to have them in time for Harrison's party if it isn't in stock."

"Do you want to go today?"

"Would you mind?"

Alec put Hamilton's hand on his cock and took up a gyrating movement. "I can think of other things to do but I don't want you worrying about it."

"I will worry. I'm sorry to eat into our time together."

"Rick, we'll be shopping together."

Hamilton smiled. It sent a ripple of need through Alec and he pushed his hips toward Hamilton's hand, still resting on his cock.

"Go and get dressed then."

Alec stood and headed for the bedroom. He looked back and puffed out his ass. "Sure you don't want to fuck me first?"

"You little tease." Hamilton dived after him and they soon tumbled into a cacophony of moans and gasps that settled, if not sated, Alec's hunger.

The Underground station was surprisingly busy for a Sunday. Taking in the crowd on the platform, Alec guessed a good percentage were tourists or people visiting London for the weekend. He attempted a spot of people-watching but lacked focus. Alec felt sleepy after his unscheduled morning fuck and thoughts weren't staying long enough in his mind to develop interesting stories.

His belly was full of Brendan's exquisite cooking and for the moment the rumble in his body for sex had quieted. He let the thoughts of those around him fall away. There was only one person of any importance today. Stepping in close behind Hamilton, Alec wrapped his arms around Hamilton's waist and rested his chin on the broad shoulder in front of him. A contented sigh slipped out.

"You've spent too much time with Sebastian," Hamilton said, turning to kiss Alec's cheek.

"No, I just need to hold you." Alec kissed Hamilton's neck and squeezed a little. "You make me happy. My life was rubbish before you."

Hamilton turned in his arms and kissed him. Passionately. With full tongue. On the fucking platform waiting for the tube. On a Sunday afternoon. Alec stepped back a few paces and leaned against the wall, letting Hamilton crush against his body. Never before in public like this.

The rush of wind announcing the approaching train roused Hamilton and he broke away leaving Alec staring open-mouthed after him.

"You'll miss it." Hamilton winked as he stepped toward the slowing carriages.

The bell tinkled as they entered the shop. There were two men in the far corner near the back room where Marcus had fucked Sebastian, looking at chains. A couple near the dildos, the woman's clothes folded neatly at her feet, and a soft grunting coming from the dressing rooms. Business as usual. Alec browsed over a nearby rack of rubber shorts and remembered with a smile his first pair: skimpy and white. Maurice appeared a moment later looking a little flushed.

"Oh, wonderful to see you. Alec, you're positively glowing."

"Thank you, Maurice."

"How is Sebastian?"

"Very well, thank you. I have a new boy I'll be bringing in for bands this week."

"Wonderful, wonderful. And you sir, you're looking very well. How are Dylan and Brendan?"

"Defiant." Hamilton smiled.

"Oh, you tease. They're wonderful boys. What can I do for you today?"

"We're looking to change Alec's bands. Something lighter. I was thinking of a fine chain and instead of bracelets, a ring."

Alec's breath caught in his chest. Hamilton wanted to buy him a ring.

"Oh, how wonderful." Maurice clapped his hands. "I have just the thing."

"A ring?" Alec whispered, as Maurice disappeared.

"You don't like the idea?"

"I ... it's just ..." Alec's thoughts stalled.

Hamilton took hold of Alec's left hand. Alec couldn't hide the light trembling that assailed his body. A knot formed in his chest. A sea of uncertainty and excitement swelled in his stomach.

"I want you to wear it here." Hamilton stroked Alec's wedding finger. "To remind you of me. If you want."

A ringing noise started in Alec's ears. "Rick, what are you saying?"

"I'm saying that I want people to know you're spoken for long term. Not as property, Alec, you're my lover. My partner." He traced Alec's finger again, stroking his palm at the same time. "You have my heart, Alec. I'd make it official if I could. I want you to know how much you mean to me."

"So it's …" *Fuck, fuck, fuck.* "… an engagement ring?"

"If you'll have it." Hamilton's voice was so quiet, unsure for the first time in Alec's memory. "If you'll have me. I can't lose you. Ever."

Fuckity, fuck, fuck.

Alec couldn't say anything, just gaped and struggled to breathe. Hamilton patted his hand and let it drop. "You don't have to tell me now. We'll get the chain today."

"Shut up."

"I beg your pardon?"

Alec grabbed Hamilton off his feet and hugged. "You stupid man. Of course I'll wear it. Of course, I'll have you."

"Alec, I can't breathe. Put me down."

"No. I don't have to, ever again. You're mine."

Hamilton tried to wriggle free. "I think we've known that for a while."

"I didn't. I hoped, but it wasn't real. This makes it real and everyone will know." Alec dropped Hamilton on his feet and fell to his knees, wrapping his arms around Hamilton's waist and nuzzling against his stomach. "I love you. God, I love you. I think I'm going to cry."

"Alec, darling." Hamilton stroked Alec's hair and a tear escaped, streaking over his cheek.

"Oh, how sweet," Maurice cooed, as he appeared with several boxes. "I've found just the thing."

"Alec, sweetheart, stand up."

Alec shook his head. He couldn't. This couldn't be real. Too many emotions crowded for attention and Alec felt dizzy. He tried to follow a logical path through the words Hamilton had said but he couldn't find one. Hamilton had claimed him before, why did this feel different? It was different, wasn't it? *Not as property—as a lover, a partner.* That's what Hamilton had said. A partner. A fiancé? That would one day be … a husband? Living together, just the two of them. Every day of every week and into forever. Alec swayed on his knees.

"I'll get him a chair." Maurice was back a moment later and Hamilton helped Alec off his knees and sat him down.

"Are you okay, Alec? You look pale."

The room started to spin and Hamilton's voice seemed to be getting farther away. Alec closed his eyes to try to focus. When he opened them again, he was lying on the floor with his legs on the seat of the chair.

"What on earth?" He tried to sit up but a strong hand pinned him to the floor.

"Just lie there for a moment." Alec looked up into a stranger's face. A stethoscope pressed against his chest. "I think he's fine," the stranger said. Alec followed the man's line of sight to a worried looking Hamilton. "Just overwhelmed. Make an appointment for him to have a medical." A blood pressure cuff Alec hadn't realized he'd been wearing was removed from his arm.

"What happened?" Alec asked nobody in particular.

"You fainted." The stranger smiled at him and brushed his hair away from his forehead. "It was lucky Maurice caught you or you'd have a hell of a headache."

"Thank you, Maurice. Can I get up now?"

"Just swing your legs down and sit slowly. Don't try to stand." Alec looked at the guy. Not a paramedic. He'd been in the shop. He smiled at Alec again. "I'm a GP. I had the kit in the car just outside."

"Am I okay? I feel okay."

"Stressed? Exhausted perhaps, you've got some impressive bags under your eyes."

"Haven't had much sleep lately." Alec smiled, looking directly at Hamilton.

"Don't blame me. You've been away all week."

"Well, congratulations anyway," the man said.

"Sorry?"

He helped Alec sit up. "On your engagement."

Alec felt his face flush and he reached for Hamilton's hand. "Thank you." Engagement. *Fucking hells bells.* He'd just got back from introducing his parents to Sebastian and now he was engaged to another man. Alec blinked a few times trying to clear the vision of his mother forcing Hamilton to eat biscuits and drink tea from a mug.

"Okay, do you want to try for this chair again?" the GP said, gripping Alec's arm.

They helped Alec to his feet and sat him on the chair. "I feel okay now. It was just the shock of it." Alec reached for Hamilton's hand and looked up into the perfect blue eyes that still looked so worried. "You should have told me before we came."

"I wasn't sure I could go through with it," Hamilton said. "But after what you said on the way here …"

"How could you think I wouldn't want to?"

"You're a young man, Alec."

"So are you."

"Exactly. We're both young men, maybe too young. I don't know. Everything's messed up with you."

"That's how I feel with you."

"And that's love," the doctor said. "Pure and simple. It doesn't make sense, confusing as hell and you have to take it a day at a time. Sounds to me like you'll be very happy."

With that, Maurice opened a small ring box and held it out to Alec. "What do you think of this one?"

Alec looked up at Hamilton. He wasn't sure what he was searching for. Some sign that this wasn't all an elaborate dream, a trick his mind was playing on him after the Patrick fiasco. Hamilton liked to play games. Usually to find answers to very simple questions he could have just asked, but Alec was learning it was Hamilton's style. Like pretending to give Alec to their neighbour, Patrick, for discipline and to do with as he pleased until such time as Alec … well, Alec hadn't figured that part out before Hamilton had called time and revealed the trick.

"Do you like it?" Hamilton asked.

Alec took a proper look at the open box. The gold band was slightly thicker at the front at about half a centimetre. He picked it up. Embedded into the band was a rectangular cushion-cut diamond, almost as deep as the band itself and about half a centimetre wide.

"Rick, it's incredible. I don't know what to say."

"Try it on."

Alec handed the ring to Hamilton and smiled as he slipped it onto Alec's finger. It was a little loose. A rush of emotion washed over Alec as he looked down at his hand sporting the diamond. He'd never thought of himself as sensitive or girlie, but right now, he could happily skip through flowery meadows singing along with fat little birds that circled his shoulders.

"I'm going to cry again," Alec said, grabbing at Hamilton's hand and wrapping his other arm around Hamilton's waist."

"My sweet boy." Hamilton squeezed Alec just a little.

"What am I going to tell Sebastian? He'll be so upset."

"I'm sure he'll settle. It's not as if he's losing you."

And it wasn't as though Alec could tell Hamilton about the plan to elope in a few years. That wouldn't happen now. Or would it? Hamilton did say it wasn't official, couldn't be. Maybe he would still tire of Alec after a few years. Until then Alec would wear his ring and be happy for every day.

Alec smiled through the tears threatening to fall. "I love it."

"I'll have it altered for you," Maurice said. "Make it a little smaller."

"And an engraving, Maurice," Hamilton added. "My surname on the inside."

"Of course, sir."

Alec's thoughts faltered. No loving message or anniversary date. A brand. A seal of ownership. Just a fancy slave band after all. But for what purpose? To keep Alec loyal and less likely to fuck around, perhaps? Did he care? No. None of that mattered. From the last week's experience, Alec already knew he was unlikely to keep up his open-ass policy. And besides, it was still a ring to wear on *that* finger.

Maurice produced another box, long this time. A fine two-tone omega chain, completely smooth, lay inside. It looked short enough to be visible in an open collar.

"Perfect again, Maurice," Hamilton said. He reached around to remove Alec's choker and bracelets and Alec resisted the urge to hold on to them. Too many lines were blurring in Alec's mind. The bands carried a set of rules, a code. Where would he be without them?

Taking the new chain, Hamilton stepped behind Alec and placed it around his neck. "I think this is much more suitable," he said, kissing Alec's neck.

Alec could barely hear his own voice. The overwhelming elation had passed and Alec's mood was crashing with great force. "Thank you."

"Given Alec's current condition, I think we'll have to forgo the usual service reward Maurice. I should get him home. Perhaps a taxi would be appropriate?"

"I'll call one for you now, sir."

Service. Something Alec recognized but accompanied by a feeling in Alec's gut that he didn't. Lover, partner, yet still given out in service. Definitely new boundaries that needed to be reconciled in Alec's head. Hamilton's worldview was so fucked up it followed that his ideas of engagement, marriage, and partnership would be too. Maybe it was Alec who was out of touch, holding too tight to his parents' ideas of the sanctity of marriage. *Oh, god.* Alec baulked at the thought. Was he really stupid enough to think a ring equaled monogamy? From a man like Hamilton? Alec wasn't sure he wanted that for himself. He certainly didn't want to give up Sebastian. Or Brad. Or Harrison. Alec felt sick. Everything was messed up again and after such a fulfilling morning.

Hamilton wandered off to chat to the doctor while Alec sat, still a little stunned by the proceedings. He fingered the new band at his neck. It looked like an ordinary chain that anyone would wear. An expensive chain admittedly. Nothing in the shop ever had price tags. But even those who were aware of what his other bands had meant wouldn't think twice about this one. Alec realized he felt naked without the heavy chain and his bracelets.

And a diamond. To wear on his wedding finger. No wonder he was light headed. But there was another conversation to be had before he put that ring on his finger for good. He needed to own up to Hamilton, be honest about how many people had fucked him and who. He'd have to speak to Harrison.

"Are you okay, darling?"

Alec smiled up at Hamilton. "I'm great. Should I thank the doctor?"

"Not today. I've invited him to the apartment for a light supper on Tuesday. If you're still unwell, Brendan will service him."

"Thank you, Master. Just, so much happening."

"I know. And I did give you a fright with Patrick. I'm sorry it upset you so."

"I needed it. It's brought me to a good place." A good place threatened by uncertainty right now.

"I hope I'm there with you."

Alec reached for Hamilton's hand. "You are."

"I think you should take tomorrow off. Have some tests and rest up. I've been working you too hard."

"But I move upstairs tomorrow."

"It can wait. We'll announce it anyway. You can supervise the movers with Sebastian. Bradley can stay home with you as well."

"And you, can you stay with me?" *I so need you to stay with me right now.*

"Tonight." Hamilton kissed Alec's forehead. "I'll stay with you tonight."

Alec ran a finger over his naked wrist, trying to fight the leaden weight in his stomach. It was all for show. Nothing had really changed. He'd still service the doctor and Maurice. He'd still have to live in his own house, with his own boys. Stupid dreams. They always had a way of misrepresenting reality, even when they sort of came true.

"Alec?"

He looked up and smiled. "I'm okay, really."

When the taxi pulled up, the doctor came to say goodbye. He kissed Alec on the cheek and squeezed his ass. "I look forward to seeing you Tuesday, Alec."

"Thank you again. I'll be happy to show my gratitude."

"I know you will."

Alec tried to smile but his heart wasn't in it. He felt cheated somehow. Everything had lost its shine against the backdrop of his weird-ass life.

The taxi journey was quiet. Alec leaned his head back and closed his eyes. He was supposed to be deliriously happy. He had been, for all of five minutes.

"Something's troubling you."

"Yes," he said, turning to Hamilton. "I don't think now is the time to discuss it."

"As you wish."

So quickly dismissed. Pushed under the carpet where it wouldn't notice and everything could be 'business as usual.' Alec's new necklace felt tight and his head pounded. A good night's sleep would set things straight.

Alec's legs were heavy as the door to the apartment closed behind them.

"Go straight to bed, Alec. I'll bring you some tea."

No celebrations. No calling friends and family. No announcing their purchase to Brendan. Alec didn't say anything. Just obeyed his orders.

Once Hamilton had stopped fussing, he left Alec alone to phone Sebastian. Alec rang Harrison instead.

"Alec, my boy. Lovely to hear from you."

"Hey, Edward. I have something I wanted to talk to you about, but Hamilton wants me to stay at home tomorrow."

"Is everything okay?"

"I passed out today. Stress I think. He's buying me a ring, Teddy. Taken off my bands. How can I wear his ring if I don't tell him about us?"

"He did miss you terribly. He's been a pain all week. I'll pick you up tomorrow and take you to Giles. Old friend of the family, excellent doctor. Rest up and we'll talk then."

"Thank you."

"I've told you I'll always take care of you. Everything will be fine."

Alec couldn't tell Sebastian about the ring over the phone. He needed to be there in person so Sebastian could see the bittersweet edge to the fairy tale. They had a brief catch up and Alec settled back and closed his eyes. He probably wouldn't sleep but he couldn't stand staring at the ceiling anymore. His breathing slowed, the pillows seemed to soften around him and he drifted off to sleep before he had a chance to think things through.

Belonging

Alec shouldn't have been surprised at the Daimler, complete with chauffeur wearing a cap, which arrived to take him to the doctor. Despite a reasonably good sleep, he hadn't managed to shake the gloomy mood that had taken over his mind after Hamilton's surprise. He took a quick look around to ground himself in the bustle of the London streets as the chauffeur bowed slightly and opened the car door for him.

"Come on, Romeo," Harrison teased as Alec got into the car beside him. "How are you feeling today?"

"There's nothing wrong with me. I was just overwhelmed. It's not every day you're offered an engagement ring in a sex shop."

Harrison patted Alec's leg and sighed. "Alec, I'm not sure how much you should read into what Hamilton is doing."

"I know," Alec said, trying to curb his bad mood. "I was stupid enough at the time to think he was actually proposing to me. It's all just a show. He's engraving the inside of the ring with his name. It's a mark, a band the same as the bracelets and so is this." Alec tugged on his new necklace.

"Let me see."

Alec moved closer and lifted his chin. Harrison moved in, but rather than look at the chain, he kissed a line along Alec's throat and pulled him into a kiss. Alec let the touch melt through him and kissed with everything he had, climbing astride Harrison's lap and rocking over his hardening cock.

"It's lucky I have privacy glass," Harrison chuckled, breaking away. Alec rested against Harrison's chest and Harrison just held him close. "Talk to me, Alec."

Talk. About what? So much had happened since the last time he'd seen Harrison and Alec's thoughts were less than ordered about any of it. Where would he start? The old man took up a slow stroking motion over Alec's back and he started to relax. There was one thing at least—Alec knew he didn't have to filter his thoughts from Harrison. He could tell him anything, everything, and still have a safe place nestled under the old man's wing.

"I told Hamilton when I got home that I'd let someone else fuck me. He… well, I chose not to tell the whole truth. I told him one guy, a stranger, when in fact I've had a busy week."

"I expected no less when I heard you'd found the Davenports."

Alec smiled. It had been an experience. A high-society family, well respected within the Order and with social calendar in full-swing, had provided plentiful entertainment during Alec's break. "I had fun."

"Good. That was the intention of your trip, after all." Harrison's hand slipped lower, smoothing over Alec's hips. Alec shifted a little as his cock perked up but kept his head resting on Harrison's shoulder.

"I was so sure when I got back that my bands, Hamilton's bands, were what I needed. But then he said they were too obvious." Alec told him the rest of the story, fighting the urge to let the rising tide of passion in his balls take over the conversation. "He's invited the doctor around tomorrow so I can thank him. For all I know Hamilton's going to offer him my ass."

"And?"

"And I don't know." He really didn't. Too many confusing thoughts warred in his head. He'd been ready to accept Patrick at Hamilton's will but did that mean he'd let go of their one rule and become another boy to hand out to anyone? "So far, the only people who've fucked me have been people I've chosen. I won't know what to do if he hands me out, Teddy."

"How many, Alec?"

"Six. You were number three." Alec smiled, reaching up to kiss Harrison's cheek. "Sebastian fucked me before you. We were going to run away together in a few years."

Harrison chuckled. "You are so lovely. You know you remind me of me. When I was your age, I wanted to run away with my cousin William. I didn't want the wife, and the children, and the Gentleman's Club."

"And now?"

"And now I'm glad we had our dreams and our fun but that I stayed on track with what was important."

"And what's important?"

Harrison's hand slipped lower again, massaging the globes of Alec's ass cheeks. "Making a life that will last. I wouldn't be without my children or my wife."

"Are you saying I should get married and have babies?"

"Not if you don't want to. I had family obligations. You, at least, are free of those."

Alec moved into the touch of Harrison's hands, relished hot breath coursing over his neck. "You're getting hard."

"What do you expect with you sitting on my lap?"

"Do I have time to suck you?"

Harrison's massage stopped dead. "Absolutely not. I'm taking you to the doctor. It wouldn't surprise me if too much cock is exactly your problem, young man."

Alec sat back and stared into Harrison's bright blue eyes. There was so much wisdom there, and mischief, and that sparkle of wit and cheekiness that Alec was beginning to love. "But it's the job you gave me," he said, with a touch of indignation.

"Yes, but with your additional after-hours timetable it seems to have left you rather run down. You were a virgin a year ago, Alec. Now you fuck all day. You're probably dehydrated."

"I may have been a virgin, but I have hands," he said, waving them in the air.

"Delightful." Harrison pulled Alec into a brief kiss. "Now sit next to me properly and give me time to calm down."

Alec huffed and sat back on the seat. Why did he feel so comfortable on the old man's lap? It was weird. Before the GC, Alec hadn't been aware of having a thing for older men, especially not as old as Harrison. So much of his life was opening up to directions he'd never dreamed of. Alec watched the world out the window. So many people rushing around, each with their own story. Could any of them be as odd, or exciting, as his own?

"Vaughn wants me to remind you that you have a date."

"Yes," Alec smiled. "A real one."

"Don't let him get you drunk. He'll play rotten tricks on you. I know this from experience. He shaved my eyebrows off once you know."

"You must really love him."

Alec watched the contented little smile play across Harrison's lips. "I do. He's part of the family. Even comes for Christmas."

"That's nice. Does he wear your bands?"

"No, he never has. Not his thing."

"It is my thing. I'm just not sure…"

"Not sure of what?"

Alec met Harrison's gaze and his heart skipped, just a little. "I'm not sure who I belong to."

Harrison's smile was kind, empathic, but it felt like a punch to the gut. "You don't belong to me." Harrison said, patting Alec's knee.

But what if I want to? Alec dropped his gaze to Harrison's hand. The old man squeezed.

"I don't need to *own* you, Alec, to enjoy your company."

Alec watched the hand slip away and wanted to reach out and grab hold of it. But Harrison's attention was already elsewhere.

"Ah, we're here," he said, straightening his tie. The car pulled to a stop and the door soon opened for them. There was so much more Alec wanted to say, to own up to, but the moment had passed. As he stepped from the car, his earlier gloom descended again. Time to be poked and prodded in all the wrong ways just to be told his only problem was an inability to make decisions and manage his life. Alec was more than aware of that already. He sighed and followed Harrison through the commanding Harley Street door.

An hour later, and what felt like a few pints of blood less, Alec and Harrison were having tea at a very exclusive Gentleman's Club dining room. Alec was impressed. Not by the grandeur but by the fact it was so much like the films and TV shows that he always thought exaggerated such things. Harrison had just clasped a hand on Alec's thigh and started to trace his way up to somewhere more promising when a voice boomed from the other side of the room.

"Teddy. Just the man I wanted to see."

"Oh, lord. The man can talk for hours. This may be a good time to faint for me." Harrison winked at Alec and stood to face the intruder. "Moody, how are you? This is Alec Caldwell, one of our new managers."

Moody took a seat at their table and Harrison sat back down and waved for the waiter. "Caldwell, ah yes, you were at the Davenports last week. Running through the halls naked with young Charles, if I remember correctly."

Harrison raised an eyebrow at Alec as he flushed scarlet. "He certainly does seem to be settling in."

"Lovely boy, Charles. Best of the bunch wouldn't you say, Teddy?"

"Toby's very fond of him."

Alec listened intently as the men discussed things he knew he shouldn't be hearing, about things that shouldn't be discussed in tearooms. It all seemed very natural to them. Moody was younger than Harrison, an odd-looking man with sandy hair and round glasses. He wasn't much more than five foot eight and very round. Alec realized it was only a matter of time until he'd be on his knees sucking the man's cock. He wondered if he should get it over with and just do it now. It couldn't be as bad as some of the ones he'd already wrapped his lips around. *Funny thing really, sucking cock.*

"What do you think, Alec?" Moody asked.

Alec looked up, startled out of his wandering thoughts. "I'm so sorry, gentlemen, I thought perhaps it wasn't my place to—"

"Don't worry, Alec," Harrison said, squeezing his thigh. "You don't need to have been listening. Alec has just come from Giles," Harrison said to Moody. "He's taking a few days' rest."

Alec tuned out again as the men continued talking. Few days now? Chloe would be phoning him from the office today then, to find out what was going on. He hadn't taken a sick day since she'd known him, and the rumour mill would be cranked to full speed if he didn't stop it in its tracks. His mind drifted and he wondered how Sebastian and Brad were getting on with the move. At least there was an excuse for Harrison to be dropping by his house all the time. Alec became faintly aware that Harrison was now stroking his thigh with more intention. On the upward stroke, his hand ghosted over Alec's crotch. He stared at Harrison, but he was laughing and joking with Moody. On the next stroke, Harrisons hand stayed at Alec's crotch and started to knead his swelling appendage. Alec shifted slightly in his chair.

"Are you okay, Alexander?" Harrison grinned.

"Oh, I'm just great. Thank you."

The old man's fingers wriggled down Alec's zip and slipped inside. Luckily, most of Alec's blood was rushing to his cock, so his face didn't flush too badly.

Harrison flipped Alec's cock out and wrapped his fingers around it. Alec choked on a quick inward breath. "I think I need to use the bathroom," he said, just as Harrison squeezed the head and slipped back Alec's foreskin. *Fuck.*

"That's our cue, Moody. I should see Alec home."

"Of course. It's been a pleasure, young man. I hope to see much more of you." Alec knew exactly what that meant: *I hope to see you naked, on your knees in front of me.* The men said their goodbyes and Alec fought against his unruly cock, tucking it away and zipping up.

"Would you really like to use the bathroom?" Harrison said, stepping in close as they stood to leave. "Or would my offices be more appropriate?"

Offices? Ah, sex. "Offices, yes." Alec strode from the room, the slow rumble of passion bubbling in his gut. He was tired of the cotton wool and the eggshells. What Alec really needed, he knew Harrison could give him—to be fucked into oblivion—a place where the world and this state of confusion no longer existed and Alec could just be, free-floating on a sea of orgasmic bliss.

And Alec had thought the fourteenth floor of his office building was plush. Harrison's office suite, located on the twentieth floor of a far more impressive building a few blocks away from Alec's own, was more like a penthouse apartment. Admittedly, the reception area and first room had a business-like air but stepping through the double doors to the rear of the wood-paneled office left Alec with his mouth open.

A large open plan living space unfolded before them with floor to ceiling windows along one side and what looked like several rooms leading off in either direction. Alec stayed in the doorway and watched Harrison walk to the sideboard.

"Make yourself at home." Harrison gestured to the seating area marked out by several large over-upholstered sofas in a rich plum color that contrasted with the ginger flooring. Alec forced himself to walk forward trying not to think about how much the things around him were worth. The mix of antiques, modern furniture, and art was perfect, obviously put together by a very skilled and expensive consultant. Alec frequently forgot the affluence of the circles he moved in these days, particularly when associated with regular clients. He studied Harrison for a moment and how well he fit in with his surroundings. Not just Alec's old man after all.

Harrison poured himself a whiskey from the selection of crystal decanters on display. "Would you like one?"

"No, thank you." Alec settled himself onto the sofa facing Harrison and tried not to think of the reality presenting itself to him, that maybe he'd wandered into a world he wasn't cut out for, where he'd never truly belong.

"You're very easy to be with, Alec. It's a pleasant change from many of the people I meet. You don't have an agenda. It's refreshing."

"I've always been happy just doing what I was doing and being who I am rather than trying to get somewhere else." Not that Alec was sure who he was right now or even where Harrison fit in the bigger picture. He sat next to Alec on the long sofa and loosened his tie. Alec took it as his cue; putting all thoughts of wealth and power behind him, he sat astride Harrison's lap and took the tie off completely, leaning in to kiss as his fingers worked on the buttons of his shirt.

"I'm not sure I should fuck you, Alexander."

"You bloody well will. I've been looking forward to this." Harrison chuckled, shaking his head, but Alec held it still. "I want you, Teddy." *I need to forget you're too important to be interested in me.* "Don't play games with me."

Harrison grabbed him and threw him on the sofa, crawling over him with a wicked grin. "In that case, Alexander. I think you should take off this god damned awful suit." He ground his hips against Alec, licking his neck and face, fumbling with their clothes. Alec captured his mouth, drinking in the taste of whiskey and tea and a zest for life Alec hoped he still had at sixty.

As Harrison moved inside him, Alec thought he heard singing. It was the sweetest sound, much like the drilling he was getting that pressured his sweet spot over and over. Harrison rested balls-deep in Alec and looked down into his face. "I've never taken any of my boys in this position, Alec. You are a first for so many things. What is it about you?"

Alec rested his legs over Harrison's shoulders and rocked himself, settling lower, pushing the cock even deeper. "I like to answer people's need, Teddy. You didn't know it but you lacked someone that would fuck you for you, rather than your name or your monster cock. Take you as they would any lover."

"And what did you want from me?"

Alec shrugged. "I wanted to give you something you didn't have, for the care and kindness you constantly show to others."

"And that's what you're doing for Hamilton?"

"Maybe it is."

"And Sebastian and Bradley." Harrison stroked Alec's face, holding his gaze. "What about what you need, Alec?"

Harrison resumed the slow steady fucking that felt like it was caressing Alec's heart. "I like to see people happy. It makes me happy."

"There has to be more. Search inside yourself, lad. Find out who you are."

"All there is inside me is you."

They chuckled together for a few moments and Harrison picked up the pace. Alec felt so full he couldn't think straight. He let his legs fall open to the side and groaned as Harrison's monster cock threatened to split him in two. Over and over, the relentless thrusting building the heat in his body, the pooling in his guts, the sweat over every inch of skin, the flush of desire spiraling onward and upward, the slow steady burn giving way to the endless feeling of bliss. The orgasm washed over him in waves, his ass trying to clench around the massive intrusion pushing the spasms up through his body instead, rocking him with a throaty cry. Harrison let go, his body going rigid against Alec's, filling Alec more than he ever knew possible.

The sweat started to chill against their bodies and Alec shifted to find more breathing room.

"Beautiful," Harrison whispered. He lay over Alec's chest, kissed his neck. "Sweet, sweet boy."

They rested together. Dozed a little. Showered, washing each other with tenderness. And then it was time to leave. The journey home was peaceful and perfect. Harrison threaded his fingers through Alec's and Alec held on to that moment.

When the car slipped out of the traffic and pulled up outside the apartment he didn't feel ready to let go, but the gloom from before was well and truly banished.

"Tell Hamilton about the others, Alec." Harrison said, squeezing Alec's hand. "But don't tell him about me. It's too soon. When you prepare to move to the fourteenth we'll take it in hand."

"Okay, Edward." Alec kissed, teased with his tongue to pull a chuckle out of his old man and then stepped from his blanket of protection and watched the Daimler pull away. The few steps to the entrance reminded him of the afternoon's delights. It brought a smile to his lips. He wasn't particularly sore this time, just pleasantly stretched and a little achy. All in all, a very good day.

Testing, Testing...

Alec felt nervous waiting for the doctor to arrive. Hamilton hadn't really said anything about the plan for the evening but Brendan wasn't around so any servicing would fall squarely on Alec's shoulders unless he was allowed to call in Sebastian or Brad from down the hall.

He had a sick feeling in his stomach that Hamilton was going to test his commitment and Alec wasn't sure how it would go. He still felt fragile, unsure about his position in Hamilton's world. The new apartment had been more stressful than he'd thought. It felt like an obligation hanging around his neck, like he owed the men of the Order for it and the only payment he could offer was his body for them to do with as they pleased. At least he was dressed. That was a good start at least.

Hamilton looked at his watch for the hundredth time. He was definitely nervous too. "I think we have some time yet, Alec. Suck my cock, there's a good boy."

"Of course, Master."

Hamilton sat down on the sofa and Alec immediately went to his feet and took out his cock. The taste settled his nerves. The stroking of his hair soothed his mind. Hamilton had known once again how to make things right in Alec's troubled world. Was there ever reason to doubt any decision he made for him? No. He'd never put him wrong. Sucking down the last of Hamilton's cum, Alec smiled. "Thank you." He kissed Hamilton's cock before putting it away. "You always know don't you?"

"I would hope we know each other well enough by now that I can read when you need focus."

"You know me better than I know myself. I trust that even if I forget sometimes."

"You're very dear to me. I want what's right for you, even if it's wrong for me."

"What do you mean?"

"What I mean to say is, you are the one who's important, Alec."

The doorbell chimed and Hamilton stood.

"Should I answer it for you, Master?"

"Yes, thank you."

Alec tried not to over think what Hamilton had said. When the door opened the doctor smiled. "You're looking much better, Alec."

"I'm very well, thank you. My master is in the living room." He took the doctor's coat and showed him through.

Hamilton poured drinks for the three of them and Alec served the food Sebastian had prepared earlier. It was pleasant conversation and Alec relaxed into the company. After he'd cleared away the dishes he joined the two men in the living room.

"Strip, Alec, please." Alec took a step toward the bedroom. "No, here is fine." Alec removed his clothes and sat at Hamilton's feet. "Good boy." The men continued to chat for a while and Alec let himself zone out to the soft stroking of his hair Hamilton had taken up.

"I'm ready for Alec now, Hamilton."

Hamilton's hand paused and a ripple of nervousness ran through Alec's body, bringing him out in goose bumps. "Of course," Hamilton smiled at Alec, meeting his gaze. "Alec." He gestured toward the doctor and sat back in his seat.

Alec knelt before the visitor. He'd never been so unsure in what were usually very capable hands. "Sir," he said, touching his forehead to the man's knee.

"You didn't say if there were any restrictions, Hamilton."

"No pain, no permanent markings."

"I can fuck him?"

"Certainly. He's well broken."

Alec spun round to look at Hamilton. "Is there a problem, Alec?"

"You said …" Alec fought around the sudden dryness of his mouth but the words wouldn't come out.

"I said?"

Alec bit back the insults that threatened at the back of his throat and swallowed, strengthening his resolve. If this was what Hamilton wanted, to see him pimped out, *well broken* for any of his friends to fuck, so be it. For now, at least. "No, Master, there is no problem." Alec turned back to the doctor. "How would you like me sir?"

"Once you've sucked me hard you can sit astride me and fuck yourself on my cock. I'd like to see your face while I'm inside you."

Alec stood to get a condom and lube from the draw and set it on the arm of the chair. He returned to his knees and helped the man unzip his pants. It was a nice enough cock. Alec started to suck. He licked and teased but his heart wasn't in it. How could it be? It had just been smashed to pieces and thrown in the trash. All those promises, the confessed love, all lies. Alec was a whore and the sooner he got used to it the better. He put in a little more effort, trying to focus on the job in hand but tears pricked his eyes. A few more vigorous sucks and they started to fall over his cheeks.

"I say, Hamilton. Your boy is crying."

Alec stopped and wiped his face. "I'm not, sir. I'm fine. Are you hard enough to fuck or would you like me to continue?"

"I think I'm ready."

"Would you like to prepare me or shall I prepare myself?" Alec ripped open the condom. His hands were shaking as he tried to roll it over the man's cock.

"Alec," Hamilton said, touching his shoulder.

"I can do it," he said, pulling away. But the damn thing kept flipping out from his fingers. He felt sick to his stomach. He just had to sit on the thing and be done with it.

"Alec, darling. Stop."

"No," he screamed, spinning round to face Hamilton. "You wanted to hand me out to be fucked, I'm going to do it. It doesn't matter that you broke your promise. It doesn't matter that you lie every time you tell me

I'm special or that you love me. I'm just your whore and I'll bend over for whoever you tell me to because whether I like it or not I *do* fucking love you, you rotten, filthy bastard." Hamilton held Alec tight against his chest, crushing him close, but Alec fought to get away, out of the treacherous arms that threatened to break him again.

"I needed to know," Hamilton said.

"Know what? That I'm a stupid fuck who'll do anything you tell me too? I thought you knew that already. I have a client, *Master*, let me go."

"No baby, you don't. Poor Dr. Keen didn't even want a blowjob. I think you may have traumatized him for life with your tears."

"What are you *saying*? Why can't you ever just say what you mean? You're always tricking me. I hate you." Alec sobbed against Hamilton's shoulder. "I hate you so much but I can't stop loving you."

"I know about them all, Alec. I know you were trying to tell me. News travels fast and you were busy while you were away."

"You told me to. You said I should be sure." Alec shivered. Everything felt wrong. Everything except Hamilton's breath against his neck driving out his anger. Not this time. This time Alec was prepared to fight it.

"And I had to know if you really needed to keep the one boundary we have with our arrangement."

"You could have fucking asked me. Is that what I am, an arrangement? I thought I was special. You wanted me to wear your ring."

"I still do."

"Then why, why hand me out like I'm nothing. Not like the boys who love it, but against what we've always agreed. Against my will."

"I thought you'd given your will to me, darling."

Alec pulled back to glare at Hamilton. He always twisted everything to make himself out to be the innocent party. "I have. With trust, Rick. Trust in you to do what's right for me, and this isn't it. But I'm here aren't I, with a fucking condom in my hand and I'm going to do it anyway. For you. So you can fuck me over once and for all."

"Alec, enough. Look around. The doctor is gone. He would never have fucked you."

"You're a lying bastard."

Hamilton slapped him. Alec held his face not sure if it was the shock or the sting that hurt the most. He let his body slip down the wall, slumping into a little heap.

"I made a mistake, Alec. I shouldn't have played games with you. I'm sorry. I'm not perfect. I get scared and do stupid things the same as you or anyone else."

The rush of blood through Alec's ears quietened and he looked up, seeing Hamilton's expression for the first time. "What have you got to be scared of?"

"You stupid, stupid boy." Hamilton sat next to him and pulled his knees up to his chest. He dropped his head and sighed. Such a ragged fretful sigh that it tugged at Alec's conscience. It was enough to shake him loose of his temper tantrum.

What the fuck am I supposed to do now? "Rick, what's wrong?"

"I'm afraid I'm losing you, Alec, and I'm tired. I'm tired of always being strong, of always making the decisions. I'm tired of being the focus for everyone. I made a mistake." He reached out, his fingertips grazing Alec's cheek. "Please, forgive me?"

This time it was Alec who held Hamilton as he cried. It was an odd feeling, playing the role for Hamilton he usually played for Sebastian. Yet it comforted Alec that he wasn't the only one whose life had been turned upside down, who had lost sight of who he was. It seemed Hamilton didn't have all the answers after all, wasn't the superhuman iceman he often appeared to be. He was as lost with Alec as Alec was with him.

"I'll do whatever you need me to, Rick."

"No, Alec. I can't do this with you anymore."

"You don't want me?"

"For goodness sake. Don't you understand anything that's going on here?" Hamilton relaxed back against the wall with a sigh, letting his legs slip out straight in front of him. "With the boys I've always had a sense of what they need. It's been a natural process of growth between us and each stage has followed a set of unspoken rules."

"The way you prepared Sebastian for the pool?"

"To an extent. But you… I can't find the rulebook. You have to understand, Alec, the role I play with them is all I've ever known. I'm twenty-nine and I haven't had a boyfriend since I was fifteen."

"You had a boyfriend?"

Hamilton chuckled and leaned against Alec's shoulder. "Mostyn Harvey. My first blowjob. My first fuck. Well, almost. We came pretty damned close."

"What happened?"

"He dumped me when my father gave me my first boy at sixteen. Refused to compete with a sex slave for my affections. His words not mine. I didn't understand that I was being groomed for this life. If I had, maybe I would have fought against it."

"I'm sorry. I forget things have been different for you."

"So do I, and I forget the rules I've always fallen back on to handle boys won't work with you. Be patient with me, Alec. I know it's new for you, but it's new for me too. I do love you. I just don't know how to work it in with everything else sometimes."

"I'm not ready." Alec took Hamilton's hand and kissed it but he couldn't meet the gaze he felt burning his skin. "To be handed out. It doesn't work for me."

Hamilton shifted closer. "I'm sorry I couldn't just discuss it with you. Stupid really. I won't push it. It was as much a test for me as for you."

"What do you mean?"

"Whether I could watch it. The thought of you … I don't know if I like the idea of someone else inside you. Less so if it's not at my hand. Pretty fucked up, I know."

"You don't want me to have sex with other people?"

"Alec, I'm not going to ask that of you. I can't offer it of myself. It wouldn't be fair."

"But I thought only I fucked you."

"That's true but there's still a lot about the GC you don't know. It's complicated."

"Do you have to give service?" Alec couldn't imagine it. Hamilton on his knees servicing a client. Harrison, maybe? Surely not his family.

"You enjoy your job, don't you? You like having Brad and Sebastian around?"

"Yes, I—"

"Then I don't want you to give that up."

Alec couldn't stop the word tumbling from his mouth. "Harrison." He looked at Hamilton, the questioning in his eyes. "I'm fucking Harrison."

"Are you joking?"

"I'm sorry, Rick. I didn't know how to tell you. Only a couple of times. He's such a sweet guy."

Hamilton stared. Alec felt uncomfortable with the fact he was naked with Hamilton's eyes boring into him. He was about to get up when Hamilton's lip quirked. "You can actually take that thing? I should get you a bigger dildo."

"You're not angry?"

"I'm surprised. Surprised I didn't notice something was going on, but not angry. I told you, I want you to have your freedom." He was quiet for a moment. "Doesn't it hurt?"

"I was a bit sore the first time, but he's very careful."

They looked at each other for a moment and the laughter started. The tension dissipated and Alec nuzzled into Hamilton's neck, tracing the line of his jaw, searching out his mouth. The resulting kiss sent tingles over every inch of skin. Gentle, reassuring touches left them breathless and smiling.

"Are we good?" Hamilton asked, still holding Alec's face in his hand. "I promise we'll talk. No more pushing boundaries without discussing it."

"I don't mind the blowjobs. I like it, you know I do. But I can't ..."

"You don't have to. I know my promises don't mean much at the moment but at least know that you always have the last say."

Alec nodded. "It's just ... I love you, Rick. You have to understand what that means."

"You think I don't?"

"I know you don't. I'd do anything to see you happy. Anything. I'd have fucked that guy tonight and then hated myself for it, hated you."

"I understand. Your love gives me power over you that I don't have over the boys."

"I don't always see when it's right to say no. Not when all I want is to please you."

"We'll find the way. I won't lose you, Alec. Now, let's get you dressed. A cup of tea is in order, I think."

An hour later, after a cup of tea and a sweet, passionate session that was more about love and appreciation than fucking, they installed themselves onto the couch with a blanket to ward off the non-existent chill that still lingered in Alec's bones. He sighed contentedly at the soft stroking of Hamilton's fingertips over his shoulder.

"That poor doctor," he said, hooking his leg over Hamilton's.

"I'll invite him again. He only wanted to make sure you were okay. I talked him into our little charade against his better judgment."

"It would be better if he came to mine. So he can see you're not manipulating me."

"That's a very good idea, though I doubt he'll be intending to touch you."

Companionable silence followed. Just being together. Alec was feeling sleepy when Hamilton spoke.

"Alec, we still can't tell people at work about us."

"I know," he kissed Hamilton's cheek. "They'll think it's Sebastian's ring anyway."

"Have they met Sebastian?"

"Hell no. You know what he's like. It's his fault the whole Davenport thing happened. I only raised my voice slightly and he fell to his knees in the park, next to the ice cream van." Hamilton laughed. "That's how Danny Merrimont spotted us."

"Right place, right time. Well, I wouldn't let on that he works part time if you want them to think the ring is his."

"Why?"

"I know he earns good money..."

"I've no idea, we never talk about money."

"He does, but I still don't think they'd believe he'd go for a sixteen-thousand-pound engagement ring."

"*How much?*"

"It's a four carat diamond. I thought it was a bargain."

"What if I lose it?"

"I'll buy you another one." Hamilton kissed Alec's neck lazily. "One day, perhaps when you've had another promotion or two, we can tell people."

"Tell them what?"

"That I love you. That you're mine. And that you've given meaning to my life I didn't know I wanted."

"I'd like that very much." Alec felt a twinge of guilt. "It'll break Sebastian's heart, you know." Sebastian was counting on him, waiting for him, but for what? Alec had no idea what kind of life he wanted now, let alone in a few years.

"No it won't. He'll see it as the gentlemen that already know us will. Just another band to show who you belong to."

"Isn't that what an engagement ring, a wedding ring, is for everyone?"

"I suppose it is. Your love with Sebastian is different. He'll be good for you. Remind you there's an alternative to my crazy world. I told you in the very beginning there are few who choose this life for more than a few years."

"I thought you were talking about the boys."

"The managers too. They may avail themselves of the services occasionally, but there aren't many of us who stay on recruitment and less still who live the life outside of business hours."

"How long have you been doing it?"

"This is my fifth year at the office but I took the role because I was already part of the life. Brendan has been with me seven years. And before that I had Eric and Jesse. I was sixteen, remember, when my father gave me my first house boy."

Father. What kind of man gives their son a live sex toy at sixteen? "Will I meet him?"

"My father?"

"Your family."

"Some of them you know. The Merrimonts, Wessex. My immediate family live in Australia. They grew tired of the politics. I haven't seen them for a long time."

"Would you like to?" Hamilton looked at Alec with interest. "We said we'd take a vacation. If you want to go and see them ..."

"You'd really want to meet my parents? I have a twin brother you know. And don't get any ideas. He's never been the slightest bit interested in boys. Father was very upset."

34

"Don't people have house girls?"

"Not that I know of. I'm sure there's an alternate scene. The clients would know. Very few of them are considered gay. They've just been brought up to fuck boys. It's a power rush. A leftover glitch from pre-war private schools. And for some reason they keep inducting their boys into the ritual. And the girls these days. I know a few young ladies in the family who make use of boys for entertainment."

"No office girls?"

"There are some but the recruitment process is very different. The girls are selected outside and trained for roles within the company rather than internal promotion."

"And that's because?"

"Sexual harassment laws make coworkers more aware of changes in a woman's behavior. Our girls are already in service when they start work, there's nothing to detect. It's also far more likely for rumors to start if a woman is suddenly visiting the boss's office more than usual. Our laws ensure we aren't gender prejudiced, unfortunately society's preconceptions remain. With a man they assume preparation for promotion."

"Which it is." Alec smiled.

"Yes it is," Hamilton chuckled. "And I am so glad I decided to promote you."

Back to Work

Alec still couldn't get his head around the new apartment. Bradley and Sebastian were taking it in their stride but Alec felt ... wrong. He'd always paid his own way in life. It was the way his parents had raised him. Sure, the last year had seen a whirlwind of unusual activity but apart from the debatable morality of his promiscuity, he'd pushed toward better things. All except for this. He longed for the freedom of his little flat even if it was too small for the three of them.

Alec looked again around the living room. Contemporary lived-in, just as he'd asked for. Comfy sofas in bright colors, deep armchairs in abstract prints, light wood floors with wool rugs and just enough accents to make it look as though they'd lived here a while. It was perfect. Massive TV hanging over a modern open fire, state of the art sound system, even down to the photos and the books that lined several niches along one wall. Vaughn had thoroughly spoiled him. Not a shred of his old apartment remained. Here, or anywhere else. He wasn't sure many of his clothes had survived the move either, though he put that down to Harrison or maybe Sebastian. A conspiracy was also possible.

"Are you brooding again?" Sebastian said, slipping an arm around his neck and kissing his cheek.

"Don't you think it's ... I don't know, seedy?"

"There is nothing seedy about this place. Believe me, I know. I've lived in a cardboard box and sucked cock for food."

"Fuck, I'm sorry, baby." Alec pulled Sebastian onto his lap and squeezed. Now he felt guilty for forgetting Sebastian's past and like an idiot for not being able to make the best of his new situation.

"Forget it. Look, we aren't whores. No more than any woman that stays at home to look after the house while hubby goes out to work."

"That covers you, Sebastian, but I get paid to fuck. I've been given this place so I can fuck important people without them visiting the office."

They both looked up as Bradley walked through from the kitchen. "Actually that's not true," he said. "You have this place so you can keep me and my client happy. If you want to assign labels, I'm the whore." Brad flashed his best smile. "And I don't give a fuck. Or rather I do, which is the point." He laid the breakfast tray on the overlarge Perspex coffee table and sat in the chair opposite. "Brunch is served, Master." He winked and reached for a piece of toast.

"It doesn't rest heavy with you at all?"

"Nope. Why should it? They get what they want. I get what I want. It's a life choice, nobody's forcing my hand."

"And your family?"

"Nothing to do with them. As far as they know, I'm a PA for an investment manager. Which I am, and I earned that position through hard work. To me, the sex is a perk of the job." He took a moment to bite and crunch on his toast. "You achieved your position through being a good account manager, Alec. Don't devalue that just because you've taken on some extra-curricula activities."

"Not this last promotion."

Brad shrugged. "So your boyfriend got you a pay rise, big deal. Happens all the time. They still wouldn't have given you the job if you weren't capable. Now eat."

Alec took the toast Sebastian handed him and smiled. He did like the company he was keeping these days and the upgrade from his old flat was pretty amazing. Who needed dog-eared furniture and chipped floor tiles? Perhaps it was time to stop fretting and enjoy it just as he enjoyed Harrison's cock up his ass.

Sebastian squirmed on Alec's lap as the thought of fucking Harrison caused a swell to his nether regions. Not only should he enjoy it, he should make the most of it. How many others had exquisite sex on-tap at home and at work? It wasn't as though he had to bend over and be fucked by anyone and if there was one thing Alec was pretty sure of by now it was that he liked to put on a show.

"Master." Sebastian's hot whispered breath sent shivers through Alec's body as he continued to wriggle over the growing appendage.

"Breakfast," Bradley reminded them with a chuckle. "If we don't eat regularly there's no energy for fucking."

"Food first, Sebastian." Alec smiled at Sebastian's beautiful little pout and rubbed a thumb over his bottom lip. "Eat, baby, then I can fuck you into next week. How's that?"

"Will you tie me up?"

"You betcha."

"Blindfold?"

"You're really getting a taste for the kinky stuff aren't you?"

Sebastian wrapped his arms around Alec's neck. "Only when it's you, Master. I like the way it feels to be completely at your mercy."

"Breakfast," Bradley said again. "He's got you well and truly whipped, that boy."

Sebastian turned to glare at Bradley but the mood was short lived when Bradley handed Sebastian a glass. "I made your favorite fruit smoothie."

"Now who's whipped?" Alec slapped Sebastian's butt cheek and moved him onto the seat. "Me? I just like a quiet life."

"I beg to differ, Master," Bradley said. "With the noise Sebastian makes I'd say the quiet life is out of reach for you. Unless you go for a gag along with the blindfold and cuffs."

"Gag it is then. I'll shove your cock in his mouth, that way we all win."

There was a pause for thought before they all concentrated on clearing the tray of its contents.

Chloe flopped into a chair opposite Alec. It was the first time Alec had been in the break room since starting back to work. He felt much more at home here than in his shiny new office on the twelfth floor. Up there, everything was uncertain. He didn't even have a job description. Soaking up the familiar atmosphere, friendly faces and Chloe's indifference seemed to be doing wonders for Alec's self-esteem. He relaxed into his chair and watched as Chloe kicked off her heels and put her feet on the chair next to him.

"So, how did your date with Brad go?" he said, slumping a little further into his seat.

"He's so cool. A bit of a gentleman too. You and all your promises of first-date sex," she said, pulling a face. "Great kisser though. But you knew that already."

"Did you go anywhere nice?" Alec had heard the story from Bradley already, but he was intrigued to hear it from the other side. Brad had been more than a little disturbed by how little Chloe seemed to think of herself. He was all for an intervention, anything to get Chloe to accept that she was a wonderful girl with real prospects.

"It was so great, Alec. We went for dinner and he sat through all my whinging and moaning over Josh, which I felt a bit guilty about afterward. But then we went on to the Monroe for some dancing. He's a great dancer, but you probably knew that already too."

"Actually, I didn't."

"Everyone stopped to look when I walked in with him. It felt great. Josh was there with his new bit of fluff."

"Not his wife then?"

"Don't be silly, he'd never take his wife to a dance club. She's the free babysitter for his precious son. Anyway, he took one look at Brad and came right over, left his date on her own."

"What a bastard."

"Brad played a great role. I thought Josh was going to punch him."

"So you and Brad are an item now then?"

"No. He's a lovely guy, but … well you know."

"No, I don't know."

"He's just … too nice. All that holding the door open, taking my coat, paying for everything when he had no intention of fucking my brains out, it's kind of creepy don't you think?"

"Brad treating you with respect is creepy?" No wonder Brad was pissed off.

"No, I don't know. He just seemed like a bit of a doormat. I need somebody who can stand up to me."

"Knock you around and tell you you're a whore?"

"Yeah, sort of. I know, I know, I need to see a shrink. But I like my men to be men, Alec."

"You mean you like your men to be animals who think women are breeding machines and sex toys."

"I guess it does sound like that." She shrugged. "But Josh is great once you take the time to get to know him."

"Change it now, Chloe, or you'll end up the free babysitter while your husband is out finding something to shag."

She stared into her coffee mug for a few moments. "Do you know what? You're right. It's about time I had a bloke to myself. It still wouldn't be me and Brad though. You should ask him out again, he still has the hots for you. I was hoping to get a bit of gossip but he clammed up as soon as I mentioned you, and his blush is so pretty."

"Hmm, what do you know?" Alec smiled imaging Brad getting flustered at Chloe's persistent questioning. She had a way of prising information from you whether you were willing to say anything or not.

"Would Sebastian mind if you were fucking someone else on the side?"

"Chloe, I'm not going to discuss my sex life with you."

"Just give me a hint. Have you slept with many people, any women, do you bottom or top? I think you top. Brad is definitely a bottom. I can't imagine him fucking anyone. It's weird, I always used to think he was such a blokey-bloke until you said he played both sides."

"I've slept with a few—no women though—and I do both. Now leave poor Brad alone."

"Yes, sir. Hey, am I supposed to call you, Mr. Caldwell, now?"

"Don't be so daft."

"Now we work in different teams, can I ask you out? I could be your first girl." She winked and Alec tried not to shudder at the thought.

"Step too far, sweetie. No offense, but women just don't do it for me. Besides, you're my friend. It would be weird, like going out with Tom." *Good job she doesn't know I've fucked Tom. Several times.*

"You are so funny. Hey, have you met Fraser, the guy who's replacing you? He's cute. Hayley has her eye on him. She was saying he's been doing one of the big boss ladies on the tenth. He's always up there when he has no need to be."

"Well, good for him."

"Good for her, you mean. Okay, coffee break is over." She gave Alec a quick hug. "Good to see you, sweetcheeks, and don't forget I want to meet this Sebastian at some point."

"Yes, ma'am."

Alec made his way back to his new office on the twelfth floor. It didn't feel right just yet, and no real clients had been passed to him so far. He sat back in the deep-red, leather executive's chair and spun round to look out the window. It was a great view. Not the best, by a long shot, but for a guy his age, it was a hell of an office. A matching leather sofa and two chairs took up one side of the room around a low, wide coffee table, the ideal height for fucking over. A large painting hung on the wall above it in shades of rust, black and gunmetal gray with flecks of the cherry colored wood woven through it. On the other side of the office was a long cabinet with a bar and a music center. The lighting could be subdued or work-bright. It was so obvious some of the offices were built for entertaining rather than work; he wondered why more people weren't aware of what really went on behind the scenes. Off the main office to one side was a bathroom with a shower large enough for three men. Not as big as the shower in Rushton, but still big. To the other side was a kitchen area, complete with a state-of-the-art coffee maker and a small dining area. Alec planned on fucking Brad over that table in the very near future.

He turned back to the massive six-foot-wide cherry desk that could comfortably accommodate two men lying across it and started to scroll through his calendar on the built-in touch screen. Harrison was scheduled for one appointment a week for the next two months, which made him smile. Brad had highlighted his own weekly meetings with Harrison. He was just thinking about whether to schedule time with Hamilton officially when a soft knock at his door preceded Bradley.

"Mr. Worthington is here to see you, Alec. Would you like me to arrange refreshments?"

"Show him in Brad, and wait a while." The old geezer could want anything.

"Alec, my boy." Alec stood to greet him with a handshake. Worthington pulled him in to kiss his cheek. "I had a free half an hour. I thought I'd call in as you're just along the corridor."

"Of course, sir. Would you like anything in particular? Bradley can bring coffee or we can service you in the more conventional way."

"Call me Peter, Alec, and coffee would be wonderful. I wouldn't have thought you were still offering to suck cock, but if it's on the menu it's a definite yes."

Brad left for the kitchen. "New office, Peter, but as far as I know, my duties haven't changed. Of course you're welcome to fuck Bradley, if you prefer."

"The little hotrod that's gone for the coffee is an office boy?"

"Sure. He used to be with Davis on the second, but he works with me now."

"Well I never. I've often seen him around and thought he'd be a nice little fuck. I've always arranged my boys through Hamilton."

"Bradley is more than a nice little fuck, Peter. You're in for a treat. He's one of my houseboys as well."

"I've never seen him offered before. I'll take that fuck, young one, and save your blowjob for another day."

Bradley returned with a tray, setting it on the table. "Would you like me to pour, sir?"

"I'll take care of it. Lock the door, Bradley, and take off your clothes. Peter would like to fuck you."

"Yes, sir. Thank you."

Alec sat back in his chair sipping coffee as Worthington fucked a naked Bradley over the arm of the sofa. They were both very vocal and Bradley seemed to be hitting a particular spot for Worthington. Alec hadn't seen him quite so caught up in his fucking before, it had always seemed a clinical thing that he did because it was required of him. But Bradley pulled out the magic and Worthington clasped Bradley's hand as he shot his load. Bradley did his usual little trick for the older men and played the helpless puppy needing to be hugged and cossetted after monumental sex. It reminded Alec of Sebastian and brought a smile to his lips. Bradley curled into Worthington's chest as Alec passed them fresh coffee.

"This boy is pure gold, Alec."

"I'm very pleased with him."

"I wouldn't offer him at Hamilton's parties. He should be savored in a more intimate setting."

Alec noticed Bradley's attention perk up. That was Brad, always on the lookout for the next opportunity. Alec returned his attention to Worthington. "What do you suggest?"

"I'll filter those interested your way. I'd offer full day getaways or weekend packages. Let the boy travel the world with the rich and idle."

"Is that safe?"

"He'll be in no danger from those I recommend to you. But you should meet them to discuss the arrangements and make up your own mind. He's your boy, after all."

"Thank you for the suggestion, Peter. I'll certainly consider it."

Bradley was kissing and sucking Worthington's chest, his erection looked painful as he wriggled over Worthington's spent cock. "I can't take you again, boy, as much as I'd like to. Speak to your master for me, and I'll take you to Bermuda with me next month."

Bradley slithered over Worthington's body and caught the man's groan in his mouth. It seemed Bradley was getting a little too comfortable. It irked to see him so caught up in someone else.

"Bradley, get dressed and wait outside."

He didn't need to be told twice. He pulled away from Worthington and knelt before Alec to kiss his cock through his pants before slipping into his clothes and disappearing.

"You're angry with him," Worthington said. "I'm sorry. I should have asked you first."

"It's okay, Peter. We're still finding our feet. I've been away for a few days and Bradley has had a free run and been rather spoiled in my absence."

"Nip it in the bud with a firm punishment." Worthington tucked himself in and straightened his suit.

"I'm rather new to that too, other than seeing Hamilton punish his boys."

"Speak to, Maurice. There isn't a thing the man doesn't know about keeping boys, or girls for that matter. I notice Bradley isn't wearing bands."

"It's on the to-do list."

"The boy has no boundaries without his bands, Alec. As a man who wears them yourself, you should understand that."

"You're right, Peter. You've always been so good to me."

"That's because I see potential. It's our job to encourage those who are capable of greater things, Alec. That's what the Order is."

"And Bradley?"

"Bradley is a nice little fuck. You're right, more than a nice little fuck, but he's an office boy. You on the other hand, while you've carried the same title, have always been one of us. The sooner you realize it, the easier your job will be."

One of us. Fuckity fuck. The hug Alec gave Worthington was heartfelt and Worthington kissed him tenderly on the lips, lingering to stroke his face. "Punish the boy, but only if you're ready to set boundaries, Alec. You don't want to confuse him."

"I'll take him to get bands."

"One of these days, young man, I'd like to spend some quality time with you."

"So you can take my ass?" Alec chuckled.

"Ah, I should be so lucky. I'd like to share more with you, of my experiences, set you on the right path."

"I'd like that, Peter. And you can, of course, take Bradley to Bermuda. Have him schedule the dates and book cover for his absence."

"Thank you. I'll look forward to that."

Bradley knocked as always before entering the office. He knelt at Alec's feet and rested his head on Alec's knee. "I'm sorry I've upset you, Master."

"Bradley, we need to talk about boundaries." Alec ran his fingers through Bradley's golden locks and lifted his chin. "We need to think about how we fit together."

"Can I speak, freely, Alec?"

"I need you to do exactly that."

Bradley blinked a few times and rested his head again. "I've been an office boy for a while, sure, and Davis told me who to fuck and when to get naked. He owned my ass while I was at work and it's been such a turn on. But everyone who's touched me was just getting a kick out of fucking the hot guy who had no say in it."

"Are you saying you've had enough?"

"No." Bradley grinned. "Far from it. With Sebastian, Harrison, even Worthington just now, I feel as though they're having sex with me, not just some piece of ass. And you, Alec, I'd never wanted to belong to someone, until I met you. The way you've taken me in, made me part of your life. I love being with you."

Alec opened his mouth to respond but Bradley put a finger against his lips.

"You don't have to say anything. You've got Hamilton and Sebastian. I don't need you to say you love having me because I know you want to take care of me. But I'm not used to having people expect me to behave in certain ways."

"What do you need from me to make this work?"

"Tell me why you're upset. And then be patient with me while I figure it out."

"Okay. The patience thing works both ways. I've never trained a houseboy before. Sebastian came readymade." They both smiled and Alec reached down to kiss. Bradley had super soft lips and always tasted so sweet. A slow rumble started in Alec's gut but there had to be more talking or they'd never get anywhere. He broke off the kiss and ran his hand again through Bradley's hair. "We should take it in stages. Review it every few weeks; make sure the boundaries are working for us both."

"And Worthington?"

"You enjoyed him fucking you, and I'm happy with that. You should enjoy it."

"But?"

"When he invited you away with him, it was as though I didn't matter."

"What should I have done?"

"The first time it happened to me, I said it would be at my master's discretion. I didn't fawn all over the guy for being nice to me."

"Am I like that with Harrison too?"

Alec nodded. It was surprisingly easy to talk about, far easier than discussing anything with Hamilton or Sebastian. "If I'm going to be your master, Bradley, you need to treat me like one. That means having me as your first priority, unless I give you leave."

"I can do that, Master."

Bradley was nothing if not sincere, but it wasn't enough. Alec thought about what had really pissed him off about the theatrics. "What worries me, Brad, is that I have to tell you. For me it was natural. Every cock I sucked, I sucked for Hamilton. You fuck for yourself because you like it. You want to be controlled, owned, but I don't think it bothers you who by."

"Are you saying you don't think we're compatible?"

"I'm saying we need to work at this and make it right. I'll be your master, but you have to be my slave, not a slave to your monstrous sex drive."

Bradley snuggled in closer and rested his head in Alec's lap. "I'd like that, Alec. We'll find a balance. I trust you to do what needs to be done."

"Good. The first step is bands. Do we have anything on this afternoon?"

"Nothing until tomorrow at noon."

"In that case, we're going shopping. Time for you to meet Maurice."

Time for Tea

Bradley was subdued on the Underground and Alec wondered if it was too soon for bands, too soon for Brad to be a houseboy. Nevertheless, he understood the problem Brad had described, not having to answer to anyone before now. Alec also understood Bradley's more subtle request for Alec to take over the reins and bring him under control. To an extent, it was where Alec found himself, although on a different level. Alec recognized he needed Hamilton to take a firmer control of who fucked him. Not to the extent of handing him out, and Hamilton thankfully understood that now, but Alec had a hankering for the days of simple rules—'nobody fucks you but me'—easy, risk free and blissfully uncomplicated.

"Alec?"

He looked across to Brad. It was the first time, other than when he'd thought Sebastian didn't want him at the apartment, that Alec had seen him even remotely sad. "Hey, it's okay." Alec moved to sit next to him and pulled Bradley against him. *Please don't cry on the tube.*

"It does matter," Bradley said, looking up at Alec. "Who I belong to. It has to be you, Alec. Don't give me away, please. I feel strong with you, worth something."

"You're worth more than something, Bradley. I do care about you. In a strange way I don't understand perhaps, but I feel responsible for making you happy."

"I'll be what you need me to be, Alec."

"I know." Alec kissed Bradley's forehead, ignoring the stares of the couple of teenage hoodies at the end of the row. One of them opened his mouth to say something, but closed it again. Alec smiled at him and the lad came and sat opposite them.

"Is he okay?"

"Just needs a bit of reassurance. We don't have all the answers just because we wear a suit."

"Ain't that right. You don't look very old."

"I'm twenty-five. Bradley is twenty-six. What about you?"

"Twenty. H is nineteen."

"H your boyfriend?"

"No, mate. I don't … we aren't … I just wanted to know if he was okay."

Bradley touched a hand to the youngster's face. "I'm okay, kid, thanks for asking."

They sat in silence for a while, rocked and jostled by the hurtling car. When the kid made no attempt to move back to his friend, Alec reached into his pocket and handed him a business card. "Call me, if you need anything."

"Thanks. I'm Gareth, My friends call me Gee." He smiled, lingering as though wanting to ask something. After another moment, he went back to his friend.

"What did you take the card for?" Hushed words from H and a shove to Gee's shoulder.

"I dunno."

"He'll end up kidnapping you and selling you into slavery or something stupid."

"You're bloody stupid, you mean."

"Our stop," Alec said, untangling himself from Bradley's arms. "See you, Gee." Alec waved at Gareth, who raised his hand. There was something about him that reminded Alec of Dylan. His manner maybe, the way he looked through you. Alec had a feeling he'd be hearing from him soon enough though the reason was unclear. He didn't get a gay vibe from him, not really, but definitely curious about something.

It was a short walk from the tube station. The street was busy and the weather blustery but it helped clear Alec's head of some of the worry that had started to plague him with the business of boys. Sebastian was easy. He and Alec had a natural rhythm together that didn't need much in the way of discussion. The dynamic seemed to feed itself, born of their desire to see one another happy. It had blossomed from being together at Hamilton's, the odd boys. Bradley was something new, not just a houseboy and so different in temperament to Sebastian in his orderly little world. Bradley was so laid back about everything most of the time that if he hadn't been so fanatical about his skin and his body Alec would conclude chemical assistance. Left to their own devices they would probably find their way but with the extra pressure of working together, of Brad being an office boy handed out on a platter most days and to men Alec didn't know himself, everything seemed bigger. More complicated. And it was only the beginning. 'Start you off with one boy,' Harrison had said. 'One of us,' Worthington had said. Oh yes, Alec had to find a way of easing new boys into a framework he could cope with as their manager, carer, master—whatever he would end up being—a catchall to tweak for each new addition as they came along. God, he was turning into Hamilton. How was it possible to be so clinical about such things?

The familiar tinkle of the shop bell over the door made Alec shiver. He felt as though he'd traveled a million miles and a thousand years since the first time he stepped over the threshold with Hamilton. It was empty this time, though he noted one of the doors at the far end of the shop had an engaged sign. Alec breathed in the smell of leather and chains, that faint metallic tang in the air of well cared for equipment. He noticed Bradley's jaw drop and followed his gaze to a rack of oversized dildos. They'd had so little time to play with each other Alec didn't know if it was something Bradley would want. Alec's mind was always on Sebastian or Hamilton. He wasn't sure where Brad fitted into the bigger picture.

"Alec," Maurice purred. "How wonderful to see you. And who do we have here?"

It amazed Alec that Maurice remembered everyone's names, and when not to use names depending on who was in the shop.

"This is Bradley, my new boy. We're here for bands."

"Oh, how lovely. And may I say, you are just beautiful." Maurice pinched Brad's cheek and he beamed. The slightest attention and Bradley just glowed and he got so much of it. Not a surprise he was usually so contented.

"Bradley, why don't you have a look around, I'd like to speak to Maurice."

Once Brad was out of earshot, Alec turned to Maurice wondering where to begin. He should have known he wouldn't need to say anything. "Oh my, Alec, what on earth is wrong?"

"Peter Worthington suggested I speak to you. I'm a bit lost at how to deal with discipline."

"Lovely man, Peter. Discipline. With this new boy or in general?"

"Both. Sebastian runs rings around me, not that it's ever a problem, he doesn't misbehave as such, but Bradley is new to the whole thing. He's been something of a freelancer up to now. I don't know the best way to deal with his transition."

"I think we need a cup of tea," Maurice said with a smile. "Let me show you through to a private room."

Alec was feeling much better after his cuppa. Maurice listened as he attempted to explain what he thought were the issues at hand. Bradley knelt obediently at Alec's feet with his head bowed and his hands folded in his lap. Something he must have picked up from Sebastian, unless Davis had run a tight ship on the second.

"I have an idea, Alec, but I'm not sure either of you are going to like it."

"Bradley, would you leave us for a moment?" Brad kissed Alec's shoe and left the small conference room. "I trust your judgment of the situation, Maurice."

"He's a lovely boy and I can see he wants to please. At the moment however, he has no real understanding of what it means to belong. He wants it, craves it, but it isn't real for him yet."

"And so?"

"You say the thing he loves most is sex."

"When I first met him, he told me he wasn't happy unless he was being fucked every few hours. He's been at it since he was twelve."

Maurice nodded as though the information had confirmed his theory. "You need to enforce a period of abstinence."

"Abstinence?"

"He needs to stop fucking for himself and realize he belongs to you. Not for sex, but completely."

"Right." Fuck.

"I told you, you wouldn't like it."

"It's not that, Maurice. He's an office boy."

"You are his master and an Order manager. For him your will comes first. I would also suggest you use abstinence as a form of discipline with Bradley once he's settled. Reduce him to oral service only for example."

"Any other forms of discipline?"

"You should take a paddle for Sebastian, it's something he's used to and not fond of." Maurice topped up Alec's cup of tea and sat back to regard him. Alec felt the weight of his inspection. He smiled briefly. "The problem with corporal punishment is that you have to be comfortable giving it. I'm not sure you are."

Am I that transparent? "You're right about that. I wouldn't know where to start."

"Treating them as a parent does a child may be your better option. Removing privileges, giving them chores they don't like. Not all punishments have to be physical."

Alec let out a relieved sigh. He hadn't considered how heavily the thought of wielding a paddle had been weighing on him. "Peter said you'd know what to do."

"We go back a very long way," Maurice smiled. "Ask him to come and visit me soon. Now, I have just the bands for your boy. Something a little more bohemian to match that lovely long hair of his."

"They're perfect," Alec said, looking over Bradley in his new bands. Bradley was grinning widely as he twirled the wristbands. He looked like a surfer with the Balinese crafted silverwork ropes. The necklace had three tiger's-eye beads that sat in the hollow of his throat. "Do you like them?"

"They're great, Alec, and I love the feel of them."

Alec kissed his cheek. He wanted to do a lot more but that would have to wait for later. "Good, because I like seeing them on you. Maurice, may I offer you Bradley's service?"

"I'd be delighted, Alec, thank you. Do remember my suggestion though."

Alec had his bag of carefully selected items to help him install order at Castle Caldwell. "I'll get straight on it, once we're home. Bradley remove your clothes, Maurice is going to fuck you."

"A full service? Why, I'm honored, Alec. Thank you."

"You more than deserve it, Maurice, truly."

Alec watched as Maurice pounded away at Bradley. He was a funny little man but from the look on Bradley's faced very skilled in the fucking department. But then every time Alec had been in the shop over the last year Maurice had been involved in some kind of sexual activity. He wondered if it was a daily thing for him, whether it was a duty rather than something he actually wanted to do. Perhaps it was in his job-description much like being part of the Order.

Alec thought back to his bag of goodies. A plan was forming in his mind as he tuned out the grunts and groans. Bradley wasn't going to be happy. Mutiny was a possibility. He'd start with dinner, a few hours of great sex and a hot bath. Once Brad was nice and compliant and a little sleepy Alec would hit him with the proposal. Not that it was a proposal, as such, but not quite an order either. They could discuss the details. The hardest part would be telling Harrison, but he'd deal with that tomorrow.

He focused back on the action and discovered it was a much better experience watching Bradley being fucked wearing bands. His bands. A mark of what—ownership, respect, control? Sure, it was a turn on having a private sex show, but there was more to it. A light thrumming ran over Alec's skin accompanying the usual rumble deep in his stomach. It was something he'd have to think more about, get to the bottom of why it made a difference. He fingered the band at his throat and thought of Hamilton. Soon, Alec would be wearing a band on his wedding finger. Would that change anything? Would it stop Alec's hunger for new fucks, shore up his need to belong to just one man? So many changes and he'd soon be twenty-six. Still young enough that if he made a wrong turn he could put it right.

Maurice came with a grunt and pulled out, tying off the condom and throwing it in the small, lidded waste bin in the corner of the room. "Wonderful," he smiled, pulling on his pants. "I do love my job. Let me prepare your bill. I'll see you shortly."

Alec admired his recovery time; he wasn't even short of breath. Likely from needing to head straight back to customers during busy periods. Bradley sat heavily in the chair looking dazed but content and stroked his cock a few times.

"You don't touch that, unless I give you permission."

"Oh, okay. You seem happier." Bradley was obviously unsure of what to do with his hands. His weepy erection bobbed in his lap and his body shuddered. The temptation to finish him, provide some wet suction over the length and a firm hand to his tight sack had Alec licking his lips. Better to wait until later.

"Maurice has a lot of experience in dealing with … issues. He's helped me to see a way forward. We'll discuss it later. Get dressed."

"Thank you, Master." He started pulling on his clothes. "Maurice has a lot of experience in a lot of things, I'd say."

"Good fuck?"

"Very. Had to fight the rising tide." He winced as he packed his still hard cock back into his pants. "Alec?"

"Yes, babe."

"I really love the bands. They make me feel …" he shrugged.

"I know, Brad. I wear bands too, remember?"

"I forget. You're such a good master; it's hard to remember you're a houseboy."

"I'm Hamilton's houseboy first and foremost, but as your master, it's not for you to see that side of me."

"Can I kiss you, Master?"

Alec straightened Brad's tie and smiled. "I'd like that."

There was definitely a new edge to the depth of their kiss. Alec allowed himself to let go of the worry and stress of how things would work out and relaxed into it. His cock was rock solid by the time he pulled away.

"Do you want me to see to that for you?"

"Later. I'll stop off at Hamilton's, put in some time as a boy myself. You can deal with it after. Let's get back to the office."

53

Alec sent a quick text to Hamilton to see if he was free. He ached to spend time alone with him, a leisurely evening, just the two of them. He hated that they both had other commitments. Other men who needed attention. Relief washed over him with the invitation for a late afternoon tea break in Hamilton's office. Alec had to try not to run along the corridor.

He managed to avoid stopping to talk as he crossed the open office and knocked on the door before entering. His heart sank when he saw what he presumed to be Fraser standing before the desk. Alec hated the guy for no other reason than he'd taken a place in the Hamilton daily fucking rota.

"Alec, I'd like to formerly introduce you to Fraser."

"Mr. Caldwell," Fraser said, bowing his head a touch and offering his hand.

Alec forced a smile. "Fraser, nice to meet. I've heard good things."

"Thank you, sir."

Alec wondered if he'd seemed as green around the gills when he started on the eighth. The poor man looked terrified and Alec felt guilty for disliking him for no other reason than his own pride. Chloe was right. He was cute. How had Alec missed him in the building before now? Dark, smoky eyes in a baby face. A mop of unruly curls cut short into the nape of his neck. Mixed heritage, for sure, but Alec couldn't begin to guess the genetic contribution responsible for the amazingly silky glow to his bronzed skin. And tall. A good inch taller than Alec. For some reason Alec had expected him to be little, like Sebastian. Young though.

"You can leave us, Fraser."

He nodded briefly in Hamilton's direction, caught Alec's gaze for a second and scuttled out.

Despite the obvious attraction—and the fact he was now intrigued to find out more about him—Alec was relieved to see him go. "Thank you," he said, settling at Hamilton's feet and resting his head in Hamilton's lap. "Can I suck your cock, Master? I need to taste you."

"I've been saving myself for you." Hamilton smiled as Alec looked up at him. "It's true. I haven't come since our quickie in the shower this morning."

"Rick, I love you so much. I've been having visions of that kid with your cock down his throat every five minutes and I hate it." Alec opened Hamilton's pants and took his prize, already semi-erect, into his mouth with a groan. It was like coming home. Alec took his time, savoring every moan and whimper from Hamilton until the warm salty flavor flowed over his tongue. He spent a little extra time, licking and cleaning his favorite cock, before stowing it away and resting his head again in Hamilton's lap. The simple things in life were undeniably the best.

"Maurice called." Hamilton ran his soft manicured hands over Alec's cheek and paused to massage his earlobe. "Your ring is ready."

"I've just come from there, he didn't say. I bought Bradley's bands."

"Maurice is very good at keeping the lines drawn."

"That's true. I asked his advice on a few things. He's worth his weight, that one."

"Problems?"

Alec relaxed into the caresses, a light sleepiness enveloping him. "Nothing serious or I'd have discussed it with you. I recognized this morning that I need to assert myself more as Bradley's master."

"And you've found a solution?"

"Mm, I think so. That feels so good, Master."

"We'll call in for your ring tomorrow if you're free."

"I have a meeting at noon so early morning or late afternoon would be best."

"Perhaps after work then and we'll go on for a bite to eat."

"Can I stay with you tomorrow night?" Alec looked up to meet Hamilton's gaze, searching for the reassurance he needed that his heart, at least, was in the right hands.

"Darling, you know you don't need to ask. I miss you just as much, you know that."

"I wish it was just the two of us." A pipedream, but one Alec was determined to hold onto for as long as possible.

"Soon," Hamilton said. Alec detected a touch of excitement in his voice. "I've looked at our schedules. We can have a month together to visit my family in Australia."

Alec sat up. "A month?" *Too good to be true. Surely, too good to be true.*

"Too long?"

"Hell no," Alec grinned. "When do we leave?"

Hamilton looked relieved. He even chuckled. "Not for a while yet, sweet. Another few weeks or so. It's a lot to arrange, us both being away for that long. We have the boys to think about and I'll need to contact my father."

"Sebastian is going to stay with Jasper and Charles Davenport for a while. Not sure he can go for a month though. I guess Bradley will stay with Harrison's boys."

"Harrison won't be able to take him. We'll think of something."

Bradley alone for a whole month. That didn't bear thinking about right now. Alec would have to make sure they found their place with each other before hand or he wouldn't have a boy to come back to.

"Are you sure everything's okay, Alec?"

"Yeah, just need to carve some boundaries."

"It takes time. Don't rush it."

"I'm going to take Bradley out of the work pool for a couple of weeks."

"Is he okay?"

"Well, he isn't going to like it, but yes, he's fine."

"Use Fraser or Mehmet to cover his duties. Whatever you're planning I trust it's for the best. I'll support you, Alec, without question."

"Thanks, Rick. I needed to hear that."

Hamilton lifted Alec's chin and smiled. "So, do I get to suck your cock or do you have to run off?"

"I'm yours, Master, to do with as you wish," Alec grinned.

"Good. Lock the door and take off your pants. It's too long since I've had the pleasure of your cock in my mouth."

There was no arguing with that. Alec almost tripped over his own feet, scrambling to get to the door. He folded his pants and stretched out on the sofa. Absolutely and without doubt, the perfect afternoon at work.

Claiming Bradley

Alec let Sebastian fuss over them as usual. He took their shoes, helped them shuck their stuffy suits, brought drinks and had dinner ready to serve. Alec found a moment to pull him to one side and explain what was going to be happening. He was shocked for all of five minutes and then shrugged and got back to the kitchen. Maybe Brad would have much the same reaction, though Alec wasn't really counting on it.

Dinner was light and entertaining. They talked about bands, service and the things they loved about sex. Maurice had really hit on something. As Bradley talked about what sex was for him, it became apparent he was using it as a crutch for a lack of meaningful relationships in his life. It gave Alec more confidence to move forward with his plan.

The three of them slipped into sex, a very free flow, whatever felt right session that left them sleepy and sated. Alec ran a bath, another blessing of the new apartment—a huge tub, big enough for the three of them to stretch out in all manner of interesting positions—and they stroked and sponged each other. Once dry, Alec tucked Sebastian into his own bed. It still made Alec smile that he'd gone for something as romantic as a four-poster complete with drapes, even with the contemporary feel of cool white linen against the dark wood of the frame. Sebastian wished him luck with a last hug and a lingering kiss that left Alec wanting to curl up with him rather than face the conversation that beckoned. But he pulled himself together and took a deep breath before heading back to the living room.

Bradley sat cross-legged on the sofa fingering his wristbands. He looked up with a smile. "I really like it, Alec. I had no idea how good it would feel."

"I'm glad. It will make this next bit easier."

"You're going to punish me for the way I was with Worthington, aren't you? I understand why you need to and I want it. I want to show you I'm serious about this."

"Bradley, I'm taking you out of the office pool for two weeks."

"I don't know what that means, Master."

"It means you won't be required for service other than your contractual PA duties."

"No sex at work?" He didn't look convinced that was what it meant, his fingers had stilled against the band at his wrist.

"No sex full stop." Brad's mouth fell open and his hands dropped into his lap. "I need to break this cycle you have and instil some order into your life, Bradley. Order that comes from me as your master and not from your need for constant sexual activity."

"But Harrison?"

"Will understand my need to exert authority at the beginning of our relationship."

"I don't know what to say."

"There's nothing to say, Bradley. I'm your master, and this is my requirement of you. You will not have sex or touch another person sexually, or allow them to touch you, until I give you the order to do so. That includes masturbation."

"I can't come for two weeks?"

"You can't come until I give you permission. It may be two weeks, it may be a month. That is not your concern. Your only thought should be pleasing me and right now it pleases me for you to refrain from any kind of sexual activity."

"Fucking hells-bells. I didn't know you could be so cruel."

"It isn't a punishment, Bradley. It's a line in the sand. But I should warn you that in your case future punishments will include terms of abstinence. I'm not really one for wielding canes, though if it's appropriate I can."

"It easy for me to say I trust you right now and that everything is great. I'm not sure I'll be as amiable in a day or so."

"I know it isn't going to be easy for you. It won't be easy for me to see you miserable but we need to do this, Brad, or this whole setup isn't going to work."

"Whatever it takes, Alec. I'll do it."

"Good. You can sleep in my bed tonight."

"To make sure I don't stroke my morning wood?"

"Bradley, I'm not going to keep an eye on you every moment of the day. I trust you not to need a locking chastity device overnight."

"A what?"

The final nail that could make or break the plan, or Bradley, or both. "I have a chastity brace for you to wear when I'm not with you. It prevents erection and penetration."

"You don't trust me?"

"It's nothing to do with that. It's part of the expression of authority. Think of it as an extension of the bands."

It was impossible to read the expression on Brad's face but he definitely had the air of a man accepting things he didn't understand. "Thank you, Master, for taking the time to see what needs to be done."

He didn't understand and Alec wouldn't be able to explain it in words. Best to get on with it and see what developed over the next few days. If it all crashed and burned, they'd find another way. Alec felt drained. He didn't mind managing or implementing difficult strategies but he usually preferred to keep those concepts away from home and firmly in the office. His worlds had been on a collision path for a while but today they had mushed together into a huge bowl of stress and the one thing that would help was now off the menu. "Let's go to bed," Alec said, reaching for Brad's hand. "I don't know about you, but I need a hug."

Morning wood was indeed a problem. Alec woke up with Brad's erection pressed against his hip. Time to move quickly before he gave in and let Brad have his morning shower relief. Alec pushed a sleepy Brad into a cold shower, laughing at the curses flying in his direction. A swift rub down and a few padlocks later everything was in order. The silicone chastity device was much easier to put on than Alec had anticipated though with a bit of thought he was pretty sure Brad could still manage to get a cock up his ass. There had to be some trust however, so Alec left it at that.

Breakfast was already set by the time they made it through to the kitchen. A day for Sebastian to go to work. Alec never tired of seeing him in a suit and tie. It transformed him from timid houseboy to power executive. A heady rush indeed, but it wouldn't be fair for Alec to indulge his needs so blatantly in front of Bradley.

"What about kissing?" Brad said, his toast half way to his mouth. "Can I still kiss people?"

"Me, when I ask it of you. Nobody else."

"Not Sebastian?"

"Nobody else."

"Harrison always greets me with a kiss."

"Not in the open office he doesn't. Bradley, if you're going to be difficult—"

"Please, Alec, I'm not being difficult. I'm worried I'll end up breaking the rules because I can't stop people groping me."

"Everyone will know you're not available. They won't know why. For all they know you could be mourning a family member. They won't touch you."

"Or nursing an STD."

"They know better than that."

"And I really have to wear this thing all day for—"

"Bradley!"

Bradley's head dropped. "You're right," he said, throwing his half-eaten toast back on the plate. "I'm such a crap slave."

Alec crouched next to him and lifted his chin. "No you're not. You're in training. Now stop sulking and finish your breakfast. You're going to make me late."

By morning coffee, Bradley was looking pale. He hadn't had his ass pinched or been winked at by any of his regulars and he was finding it difficult.

"I hadn't noticed how much I need their attention," he said to Alec as he stared into his mochaccino. "It's like I feel ... I don't know, wrong."

"It's just as much about you finding yourself as it is about me owning you."

"Yeah, I see that now."

"Harrison will be here soon. I'll lock the door, just in case you need to attend to anything." Bradley nodded but kept his eyes down. "Bradley?"

"I'm okay, Master. It's just giving me a lot to think about."

"Good boy. You can follow up Worthington's dates for your Bermuda trip. That should cheer you up."

"Thanks, by the way, for letting me go with him."

"You're welcome. You are a good boy, Bradley, and you'll be rewarded as such."

That put a smile on his face—finally. Alec kissed his cheek and sent him back to work.

"Hello, beautiful," Harrison said to Alec as Bradley showed him into the office. "You look like you're settling in."

Alec stood to greet him in a hug and smiled as Harrison squeezed his ass. "Hey, Edward. It's good to see you." He took the few steps to lock the door.

"What's the story with young Bradley out of the pool?"

Alec spent the next half an hour discussing technicalities related to being a master. Harrison supported Alec's decision, which was a relief. He didn't think he'd be able to stand up to the old boy if he'd pushed to be excluded from Alec's ban.

"I'll fill in Bradley's time with you, Teddy." Alec rocked over Harrison's lap, nipping at his lips.

"Good. And the first thing I'm going to do is take you to my tailor and get you a proper suit."

"This is a Brioni."

"It's off the rack and it's awful. Now take it off before I rip it off you. I need to bury my cock inside that sweet little ass of yours."

"Yes, sir. Can I undress you too?"

"Why on earth would you want me naked?"

"I love feeling you against me, Teddy, you know that."

Harrison wasn't kidding when he said he wanted to bury himself but Alec loved the new edge to sex with him. He really let go now, taking Alec as deep and rough as he wanted. Alec leaned back against Harrison's chest as the old man erupted inside him just as Alec sprayed over the floor.

"Good boy, Alec." Harrison was panting, stroking Alec's chest. "God, I love that feeling I get with you." Alec reveled in Harrison's attention. Tender kisses and cuddles, the mingling of their sweat as their bodies cooled. "If I was twenty years younger, I'd make you mine."

"Would you?"

Harrison's arms tightened around him. "Just mine and you'd be the only boy I'd want."

"Now you're teasing, Edward."

Harrison nuzzled against Alec's neck. "I'm serious, Alexander. I've never felt possessive of any of my boys, not even Vaughn. But you... the thought of you with other people burns me." He pulled back, loosening his grip around Alec's waist but leaving his softening cock inside him. "I want to lock you away and have you all to myself and this," he said, tugging at Alec's necklace, "I hate it."

Alec disengaged himself and turned to face Harrison. He did look troubled and it left Alec with an uneasy feeling in his gut. "We're collecting my ring this evening."

"I wish I could claim you, Alexander, I really do."

"You have no idea, how much it means to me that you feel that way."

Harrison grabbed a towel from the desk and sat on the sofa. "I'm just a silly old man with a high school crush," he said, wiping himself down.

"I love you too, Teddy." Alec kissed over his face and climbed back on to his lap. There wasn't much sign of life in the monster, but they took their fill of sexy, soul tugging kisses before heading to the shower. Alec loved the attention, loved knowing finally that Harrison had a soft spot for him. It helped him categorize things in his head, where each of his regular fucks sat in relation to Hamilton. Hamilton sat at the top as lover, partner, fiancé, master. Sebastian, where-oh-where did he fit into anything? Beloved friend, houseboy, secret lover, single-handed support system. He was a foundation. Bradley, currently a one-way street. Too soon to know if he'd be rooted anywhere permanently but a pleasant regular addition to the festivities so far. And Harrison—the old man—fast becoming something special, though Alec didn't know what. A crush, like Harrison had said he had for Alec, a phase, maybe, of needing to be coddled, a power rush of having the boss's boss wrapped around his finger. Could be any or all of the above. Not that Hamilton was his boss anymore. Technically Alec reported directly to Harrison now.

Dressed and looking respectable again, Harrison pulled Alec into a slow, sexy kiss. A welcome addition to the regular menu, for sure.

"I'll see you at the party tomorrow night, Alec. I should have thought about getting you a suit beforehand."

"I have a Savile Row suit, Edward. I'll wear it especially for you."

"And a dark blue shirt? I like you in navy."

"As you wish."

"Wear a tie, so I don't have to see that blasted thing around your neck."

"Teddy—"

"I know, Alec, I know. Stupid old man." Harrison took out his wallet and handed Alec a credit card with his name on it. "I had Vaughn order it for you. Make sure you use it."

"For what? I seem to have more money than time to spend it these days."

"Buy your mother something nice."

"Seriously?"

"Send your parents on a dream vacation as a thank you for bringing you into the world." Harrison reached in to steal another kiss. "You're right, I do love you. It's damn annoying at my age to have something so young and beautiful claim my heart, but you have it. What will you do with it, young one?"

"Treasure it, Teddy, for as long as it's mine."

Alec spent the rest of the afternoon shoring up Bradley's self-esteem. He was completely lost without the underlying flow of sex in his life. They were from opposite ends of the spectrum. Alec had been sex-free for far too long whereas Bradley had lived the extreme of an over-sexed life. As Alec found the balance in his own relationships, hopefully he could help Bradley find more of himself.

No sooner was the apartment door closed than they were both stripping off. Brad grabbed the cloths from the floor and Alec followed him to the walk-in-wardrobe that held all of their clothes and the laundry hamper.

"I should take that off you now," he said, pointing to the chastity device. "I'll be staying at Hamilton's tonight."

"I'd prefer to keep it on if you aren't with me, Alec. It's good for reminding me what we're working toward."

"Okay. I'm only along the hall if there are any problems. I understand the first few nights can be difficult. I'm really sorry I can't be here with you."

"The space is a good thing too. It gives me time to think things through."

"Is it comfortable?"

"It's not uncomfortable. Just weird. But oddly reassuring too."

Alec kissed his cheek. The urge to fall into the usual routine of a quick grope and snog was overwhelming but he stepped back and let Bradley carry on sorting the laundry. Seeing as though he was going to be busy for a while, Alec sought out Sebastian.

"Hey, you."

Sebastian looked up from his book and grinned. "I didn't think greeting you at the door would be a good move this evening, Master. I hope that was the right thing."

Alec sat next to him on the sofa at the end of his bed and Sebastian dropped his book to the floor and climbed onto Alec's lap.

"Perfect as always, baby." He groaned at the hot trail of kisses Sebastian laid over his neck, working his way down his shoulder to suckle on a nipple. The light graze of teeth made Alec hiss. Sebastian. His foundation. Home was where he knew Sebastian was waiting for him. Was that true love or the reality of having a houseboy? But Sebastian was so much more. Alec arched his back, wanting more connection between their bodies, wanting to feel everything at once. "Fuck me, Sebastian. I need you inside me, baby."

"Anything you want, Master. Anything at all."

Long, slow strokes tormented every cell of Alec's body. He tried desperately to keep quiet so Brad wouldn't hear them but it was so difficult. Sebastian rocked into him with precision, his fingertips blazing a trail over Alec's stomach. Hot lips pressed against his, breath mingling, and the slip of tongue against his own. *Fuck, fuck, so close.* But not fucking. Not fucking. So much more. Alec wrapped arms and legs around his lover and Sebastian continued to take him apart, piece by piece until there was nothing left but the rush of heat and ecstasy as his climax washed through him. Alec heard his own strangled cry as Sebastian kept up the pace, thrusting into the heat, stretching out the orgasm. Just as he thought he could take no more, Sebastian stilled, his body rigid, his breath heavy.

He slumped over Alec's chest. "God, I love you." A wet sloppy kiss landed on Alec's cheek. A contented sigh shook his body. "Wake me in the morning. Shattered."

Alec smiled to himself, stroking Sebastian's back as a soft snore escaped his sated body. As much as Alec would have liked to stay snuggled up with his little slave boy, he had to get moving. A shower was in order and then an evening out with Hamilton. A ring, dinner, and more monumental sex. If there was a better life, Alec couldn't think of it.

The Ring

Butterflies danced annoyingly in Alec's stomach. He had no reason to be scared of a ring, or overly excited. Not really. It didn't stop the fluttering or cure his slightly sweaty palms. Hamilton chided him playfully but Alec could sense the edge of tension radiating from him just the same. Was this really such a big step for both of them?

The car pulled to a stop outside what was becoming a familiar doorway. He fumbled with the car door and in the end, the driver got there first to open it for him. Alec had never envisioned himself as a chauffeured executive but being with Hamilton had made it another commonplace extravagance in his life. Weak knees. In fact, his whole body was trembling as he waited for Hamilton to get out the car.

"Are you okay, darling?"

"Yeah, just ... I don't know."

Hamilton took his hand and kissed it lightly. "Me too," he smiled. "A day at a time?"

Alec nodded, squaring his shoulders to the shop door. "I'm ready."

A light buzz of activity filtered through to Alec's senses as they walked in. He'd never seen the shop so busy. Several groups, in various states of dress, filled the corners and a further gathering took center stage. Alec's cock twitched at the sight of three naked men on their knees, weepy erections skyward, before what Alec could only describe as a god of Olympian proportions, chiseled to perfection in skin-tight leather pants. His broad chest was smooth and golden, biceps bulging, focus completely with his boys.

"See something you like?" Hamilton brushed a hand over Alec's growing crotch and he flinched.

Alec turned to Hamilton, his face flushed. "Sorry, Master. I didn't mean to stare."

"I've seen people stare at you that way. What thrills you most, the boys or their master?"

Alec swallowed, his mouth dry. Was this a trick question? One that would earn him a slap for stepping out of line? "Both, equally. The boys look so devoted and their master has eyes only for them."

"Good answer." Hamilton smiled. "While we're here I'd like to buy you a larger plug. Now I know you can comfortably accommodate Harrison, I think it only fair I get to push you beyond those limits."

"As you wish, Master."

"Mr. Hamilton, Alec." Maurice greeted them with a handshake and his usual knowing smile. "How are things with Bradley?"

"First day but he seems to be holding up."

"Excellent. I understand business is booming, Mr. Hamilton."

"It is indeed. A very busy time."

Interesting. Alec had no idea to what Maurice was referring but he noticed the new tension in Hamilton's shoulders.

"I have your ring right here." Maurice disappeared behind the counter. A jingle of keys later and he slipped a small box onto the glass surface. He opened the box and held it out to Hamilton. "The engraving is very nice."

Alec felt faint seeing Hamilton take the ring from the box and inspect it. This was it, the moment they became officially engaged. If that's what it really was. Hamilton's smile was blazing as he turned to Alec and every ounce of uncertainty and fear melted away. He reached for Alec's hand and held it before him. "Alec, darling, I love you with all my heart. Please do me the honour of wearing this ring as a token of our love and a sign of our commitment to one another."

Alec's mouth opened but he couldn't say anything. Heat flushed through his body, his eyes pricked with tears. *Fuckity fuck fuck. Don't pass out again.*

"Will you?" Hamilton prompted, squeezing Alec's hand.

"Yes. Yes, yes, and bloody yes."

Hamilton's hand shook as he pushed the ring onto Alec's finger. They both stared at it for a few moments.

"Oh, congratulations." Maurice clapped, pulling them from their daydream. "Such a lovely couple."

Hamilton kissed the ring and looked up into Alec's eyes. There was a glint of something. Something magical. Something dangerous. Alec's heart skipped. "Now you're mine," Hamilton said in a low growly tone.

"I always have been, Master." Alec thought back to the days when he prayed Hamilton would notice him. "Long before you knew it."

"Maurice, do you have time this evening for Alec's service?"

"Oh, how lovely. I'm sure Missy can deal with things alone for a short time."

"Good. Alec, into the changing rooms with you. No need to undress."

Alec hung his jacket on the hook and got to his knees, sitting back on his heels, hands in his lap. Maurice slipped through the curtain and stroked Alec's cheek. "You don't have to do this, Alec. I can tell your master that I'm busy, or wait a few minutes and say you were wonderful as always."

"I want to, Maurice." Alec reached for Maurice's zipper and dropped his pants. He licked the head and shaft of the semi-erect cock. "It pleases me to follow my master's commands." Before Maurice could respond, Alec sucked him in, relishing the gasp from the man who probably had more blowjobs than he did. It took a while to find a rhythm. Definitely out of practice sucking strangers. Not that Maurice was a stranger, but it was still different to getting off Hamilton, or the boys. It'd been nearly two weeks since he'd sucked cock for account holders, something he'd have to address with Hamilton, find out if there were new rules of service.

It wasn't too long before Alec received his reward with the bath of warm liquid over his tonsils. He looked up to find Maurice flushed and breathy. Impressive, considering.

"Wonderful." Maurice leaned down to kiss Alec's lips. "Such a beautiful boy. You've come a long way in the time I've known you."

"Thank you, sir."

Maurice started as he pulled back the curtain to find Hamilton leaning against the wall. "Perfect, as always," he said, before scuttling away.

Alec stayed on his knees. Hamilton stepped into the cubicle and smoothed a hand over Alec's hair. "Maurice has grown very fond of you."

"Not fond of me, Master. He appreciates you thinking of him."

"He was willing to lie for you."

"But there was no need. I'm always happy to be of service for you. I'm out of practice though." Alec moved into Hamilton's touch, aware of the thrum of irritation running through his body. "He was being kind when he said it was perfect."

"Maybe I should find you some more cocks to suck."

"If it pleases you, Master. I want to be the very best for you."

Hamilton smiled. Another good answer by the looks of it. Alec was out of practice for this too—being a boy. The last weeks had seen little time for their private dynamic and Alec missed it. Missed being at his master's feet. Missed the look in Hamilton's eye when Alec opened his mouth to suck cock at his master's command. Hamilton was his lover but also his safety net and he wanted more of it to balance the change in job title.

"It's tempting. There are plenty of candidates through that door. But not tonight." Hamilton held out his hand and pulled Alec to his feet. "Come, it's time for dinner."

Now Alec felt pampered. The restaurant wasn't a restaurant at all, not really. The highly ornate room still managed to exude an intimate atmosphere. Soft lighting, just two tables, a large round affair set for six and their own tucked in the corner complete with flowers, candles and a bucket of chilling champagne.

"Looks as though we'll have company later," Hamilton said, sitting as an attendant pulled out his chair. A second attendant pulled out Alec's chair for him and he sat, slightly dazed and watched Hamilton order wine and request the champagne opened.

"A toast," Hamilton said, raising his glass. "To many more years of love and companionship. I never imagined I'd want to grow old with someone, Alec. Until I met you."

The clinking of their glasses had a dreamy quality. Alec wondered if pinching himself would be in order. He sipped the champagne and tried not to stare around at the room. "This place must have cost a fortune, Rick."

"You're worth it. But don't fret; it's an Order meetinghouse. Exclusive, yes, the food is exquisite but the price, surprisingly reasonable."

"Is it appropriate for us to discuss business this evening?"

The attendant returned with appetizers. "I pre-ordered to save time. And we can discuss anything you'd like."

"My new role. I'm not clear what it is. Do I still offer personal service to clients or just use of the boys? My calendar is filling up and I don't know what to say to these guys."

Hamilton put his fork down and took a sip of champagne. "Your official title is still Service Level One but you hold the qualifier Manager in Training. That means you're only required to offer personal service if another service officer is not available or it is specifically requested of you by a high ranking member."

"And the restrictions to my service?"

"Still stand. You won't be required to bend over." Hamilton smirked. "Unless you want to, of course."

That was very good news indeed. Alec relaxed a little. "And once I'm finished with my training?"

"Then the rules change and for the most part are dependent on your line manager. Officially, you are always available for service to Order members of a certain standing."

"Do you still give service?"

"On occasion. Only a handful of times since we've been together."

"You've never said."

"I didn't think you'd be concerned with the details of my job description. It happens very rarely. One or two members like to keep me in my place. Especially since father left the City. Just politics."

"I'm sorry."

"Alec, you know me well enough. I enjoy sucking cock as much as you do and have serviced every one of the boys that work with me. It's hardly a chore."

That was true. But Hamilton wasn't like Alec to the extent he'd enjoy a command to do anything. He wasn't a switch.

"Unofficially, members will respect your manager's handling instructions. You should discuss it with Harrison. He'll be the one to decide whether you can be called on for personal service."

"Oh, in that case, none of them will touch me. The old man hates that—" The words dried up. Fuck. Alec took in the flaring nostrils, the shallow breathing and knew he'd stepped over the line. He grabbed Hamilton's hand and pressed it to his face. "I'm sorry, Master. I've let my mouth run away. Forgive me?"

It could go either way. He'd either feel those knuckles embedded across his cheek or they'd get back to dinner. Seconds felt like hours but eventually Hamilton smiled.

"It's okay, darling. I love that you feel at ease with me enough to ramble. I'm not so impressed that Harrison has opinions about who should and shouldn't touch you. But that isn't your fault."

Alec refrained from the bubbling need to defend his old man. "Thank you, Master."

Dinner continued in a light, airy mood. The food was incredible, the wine flowing and Alec felt more than a little tipsy. Tipsy and horny.

"Is there something you want to ask me?" Hamilton said, a slight quirk to his lips. "You've been staring." He pushed back his chair and gestured to the floor before his feet. Alec took up his favorite position and rested his head on Hamilton's knees. "You have no idea what it does to me, seeing you like this."

Alec grinned, running his hands along Hamilton's thighs to his hardening cock. "Oh, I do, Master, and I love it." He made the move for Hamilton's zipper just as the door opened and the room filled with boisterous voices.

Hamilton cursed under his breath as they both looked at the newcomers. "Of all the bloody people. Alec, speak only if you're spoken to and choose your words carefully."

Alec nodded once and sat back on his heels. Carefully chosen words after the amount of alcohol he'd consumed were unlikely. Hamilton stood and greeted the party.

"Philip."

"Richard Hamilton," the loudest of them exclaimed. "And friend." The man devoured Alec in that single glance. Brown eyes, angular features, average build but commanding presence. Definitely in his thirties. The rest of the party consisted of average looking men all slightly the worse for wear from alcohol by the looks of it. Two of them were snogging against the wall, one fumbling for cock access. "Looks like we have our entertainment for the evening, gentlemen. Tell me your boy is part of the Order, Hamilton. He looks so appealing on his knees and I need something warm to wrap around my cock."

"You're drunk and your behavior is inappropriate." Hamilton stepped in front of Alec to shield him from the advancing Philips.

"Poppycock. What are service boys for if not to service? Strip him off and set him over the table. You can fuck him first if you must, but why you feel the need to wine them and dine them I don't know."

"Alexander is not a service boy, he's my partner."

Philip seemed to consider this for a moment before he started laughing. "You, with a boyfriend? Unlikely. Now hand over that boy's ass before I take your mouth instead."

Alec could see the anger rising off Hamilton in what he imagined as little puffs of steam. He also noted that cock access had been granted against the wall and two men had slipped to their knees to suck and kiss the exposed member. Alec's own thoughts seemed to be caught up in a slow motion play of the surrounding action.

"Alec, it's time for us to leave."

Alec rose quickly, pleased his body responded despite his mind's meandering, and took Hamilton's hand. Philip grabbed at his other and stared, open-mouthed at the ring on his finger. "Well, blow me down. Why didn't you say he was your fiancé? It would have saved all this unpleasantness." Philip turned to his friends. "Boys, boys, young Richard is tying the knot. To a man, no less. A pretty one, at that."

There was little to no response from the collected men groping and fawning over each other in various states of undress. Were they really going to fuck over their food?

"Now, if you'll excuse us." Hamilton started for the door.

"Wait, join us for a drink. I promise I'll keep my hands to myself."

"Thank you, but no. This was our celebratory dinner. We have further plans at home."

"I bet you do." Philip grabbed Hamilton by the shoulders. "I miss you, Ricky. I suppose it's inappropriate to ask you to suck my cock for old times' sake?"

"Very."

"Darn and blast. I've been meaning to call you for the last month. Ah well. Happy nuptials and all that." Philip took another all-consuming look over Alec. "I'll be in touch."

Hamilton practically dragged Alec out the room. Once they'd put a reasonable distance between themselves and the sex-crazed horde, he pulled to a stop and leaned against the wall. "Fuck, fuck, fuck."

"I could have just serviced them for you."

"You will *never* service that man, do you understand? Never. My will as your master overrides all Order requests. I can't bear the thought of him touching you."

"Who is he?"

"An old school friend. One that likes to keep me in my place."

"Important then?"

"Dangerous. And when he discovers you are, in fact, a service boy, he's going to be furious."

Alec pressed himself against Hamilton's tense frame. "I love you, Rick." He kissed a line along Hamilton's jaw; let his hands wander across the planes of his taught stomach. "Thank you for defending my honor." Alec slipped to his knees. Keeping his eyes locked with Hamilton's, he unzipped and retrieved Hamilton's cock, licking the length. Hamilton splayed his hands against the wall for support. On his knees in the hall of an exclusive gentlemen's club. There was something very right about it. Alec played with the head before sucking it into the wet heat of his mouth, worshiping his favorite cock and reveling in the knowledge only he could make Hamilton lose control. Alec pulled off, an idea racing through his head. A risky one.

"Alec, please," Hamilton whimpered.

"Turn around. I'm going to fuck you."

"What?"

"Just do it."

To his surprise, Hamilton turned and dropped his pants, leaning against the wall with his ass out. *Fuckadoodle.* Alec pressed between Hamilton's butt cheeks with his tongue, wetting his hole, adding two fingers and plenty of spit.

"Hurry, Alec, I need you."

Damn, the man was stupidly sexy when he pleaded. So much for Alec spending time as a boy. He pressed himself over Hamilton's body, wrapped a hand around his cock and guided it to butt against the pucker that belonged just to him. Nobody else fucked this hole. The power rush pushed him forward and they groaned in unison with the penetration. A few thrusts was all it took to have Alec shooting his load, he withdrew and spun Hamilton around sucking down hard over his cock. The sound Hamilton made when he came was half whimper, half muffled-cry. Alec rested his head against Hamilton's hips trying to gather his thoughts.

"We should go." Hamilton pulled up his pants. "You're a bad boy, Alec. Delicious," he chuckled, "but naughty. And I love you for it."

"As long as I'm *your* bad boy, I'll always be happy."

"We're not going home?" Alec watched unfamiliar streets whizz past the window. Despite the quick sex in the hall, he was still hankering after something long and leisurely. Preferably, with Hamilton spending a lot of time balls deep in his ass and a little reciprocation here and there on Alec's part.

"I've booked a suite at the Dorchester. I wanted tonight to be special." Hamilton moved closer and rested his head on Alec's shoulder. "We don't have to be in until lunchtime tomorrow. The Terrace Suite has an amazing tub."

"Rick, you've thought of everything and I don't have anything for you."

"You're here. That's enough. Besides, it's the only chance we'll have to celebrate. Everything is still unofficial as far as the office is concerned but tonight we can make it real."

"Whenever we're together it is real."

Slow, sensual kissing followed, gradually working its way into steamy sliding bodies. Too many clothes. Not far enough to go to get any car action. Alec's cock throbbed. He hissed at the friction over his sensitive cockhead from the fabric of his boxers. "How much farther?"

"Not far. Don't stop." Hamilton pulled Alec on top of him and into another deep, teeth-clashing kiss. After all the sex he'd had so far today, how was it possible that this made him more desperate, needier than anything else? At the time, Harrison had rocked his world; Sebastian had taken him apart, but this? Every touch burned his skin, the brush of tongue brought forth a moan—more, he wanted more. Now, tomorrow, the next day and every day into forever.

"It'll never be enough," Alec spluttered, gasping for breath and pulling away from Hamilton's grip on his neck. A small chuckle escaped him and he looked down at a confused Hamilton still reaching for him. "We can take it fast, slow, it doesn't matter."

Hamilton frowned, sitting up and straightening his jacket. "What are you going on about?"

"This. Us. It's what's different."

"You're not making sense. Are you breaking up with me?"

Alec put his arm around Hamilton's troubled shoulders. He looked so vulnerable in his lust-addled state, as open as Alec had ever seen him. "No, Rick. It's just that it doesn't matter how much of you I have—I'll always want more. One more kiss, one more touch, one more moment alone. It's you I want, first and foremost."

"That's good because I've never wanted anyone else."

The statement was so matter of fact. "Never?"

"I told you before you're my first love. I've had a lot of sex in my life. Much of it very good sex. I've desired bodies, been taken with wanting to provide and care for individuals. But you, Alec … from that very first day in my office you've consumed my thoughts and taken over my life. I may be your master but make no mistake—I am yours completely."

If the car hadn't pulled to a stop, Alec would have taken him right there. Stripped him off and impaled himself over the perfect member made specifically to drive him to the edge. It was possible alcohol had a part to play in the construction of Alec's thoughts but damn, the man — *this* man—was everything. Hamilton had stepped out the car before Alec could come up with a response. The only thing left was to follow him to the room and show him exactly what it was he would never have enough of.

It's My Party and
I'll Cry If I Want To...

"If you continue to flirt like a common whore, I'll hand you out like one."

Alec spun round to look at Hamilton. He was deadly serious. "Master, I didn't know I was flirting. Crap. Am I really?"

Hamilton dragged him across the hall and into a quiet anteroom. "You are incorrigible. Half of the men you've spoken to so far are expecting your ass on a plate in the near future because you find them so fascinating. I know these people Alec, believe me, you are flirting."

Alec fell to his knees and hugged Hamilton around the waist. After such an amazing night and the best part of the morning indulging each other's every whim, the last thing he wanted to do was fuck it up and make Hamilton grouchy. "Fuck, I'm so sorry. I'll be better, behave better."

"You expect me to believe it's your naivety that's at play?"

"Master, it is. Please forgive me and let me try again." Hamilton relaxed and Alec smiled. A definite thaw going on. Maybe a slow, sloppy blowjob would take him back to the docile kitten he'd been after an hour in the bath this morning.

"Problem gentlemen?" They both looked up to see Harrison in the doorway. "Is everything okay, Alexander?"

Alec felt Hamilton's body tense. *Oh fuckeroo, I am in trouble now.* Alec was pretty sure he could feel Hamilton prickling.

"I'm perfectly well, Edward. We're just taking a private moment."

"As long as you're sure."

"I am, thank you."

Alec sank back onto his feet as the door pulled to, but didn't close completely. He was prepared for the backhander as it crashed across his cheekbone. The second and third were a bit more of a surprise and the fourth left him sprawled across the floor. He scurried to get back to Hamilton's feet.

"You belong to *me*."

"I do, Master. Only you."

"Drop you pants and bend over the chair."

Alec didn't even think, he just did it. If Hamilton fed a string of men through the door to fuck him, he didn't care, as long as Hamilton wasn't mad with him anymore. Why did Harrison have to spoil it? But Hamilton didn't do anything of the kind. He fucked Alec hard, but it was claiming, possessive. Exactly what Alec needed to center himself in the unfolding drama. It reminded him Hamilton wasn't used to the fact other men fucked him regularly. Alec reached back to grasp Hamilton's hip and pull him close as he came inside him, not wanting it to end just yet.

"Don't remind me too often that I have to share you, Alec."

"Then don't, Master. Tell me to stop."

Hamilton moved away leaving Alec cold and empty. "It has to be your decision. But you should also understand the consequences. That's my ring you wear, my band around your neck. Remember who you belong to, Alec, or I will make sure you know it."

"Thank you, Master. For giving me the chance to make things right."

"Get dressed. You have to meet a few more people before the bruise starts to show on your face."

"Master?" Alec knelt at Hamilton's feet.

"Now is not the time to creep, Alec. I'm on the verge of making your ass open season."

"I was just going to say, that I'll wear your bruises like your bands. I'm proud of them, not because I've been bad, but because it means you care."

Hamilton grabbed Alec by both arms and shook him. "Don't be so *stupid*. It means I'm not thinking straight, that I've tipped over from confident master into jealous boyfriend. *Don't* be proud of them Alec, I'm certainly not."

"They aren't punishment?" Alec had too much alcohol coursing through him again and felt a bit woozy from Hamilton slapping him silly.

"It's a loss of control. Punishment… Oh, Alec." Hamilton pulled him into a hug and kissed over his sore face. "I can't believe you have boys of your own when you've so much to learn. Come and sit with me."

They settled onto the sofa and Hamilton pulled Alec in close, letting him snuggle into his side. He traced circles over Alec's arm. "When I punish you, Alec, properly, it will always be in a controlled way, at home. Loss of privileges, as you're exercising with Bradley, or a few rounds with the paddle. If I strike you in anger, it's something very different. Don't confuse the two."

"I think I understand."

"You're the only one who makes me lose control. So many firsts with you. It's just one more thing that shows me I love you, but it doesn't mean I should allow it to happen. You're my first love, Alec; I'm going to make mistakes. But abuse is just that, abuse, and I'm not proud of myself."

"You're my first love too."

Hamilton chuckled and squeezed him. The moment fell away as Hamilton sighed heavily. "Harrison has really fallen for you, hasn't he?"

"I didn't try to make it happen, Master."

"I know. You're such a sweet thing. It's so rare for us to come across someone so genuine. We can't help it. There will be more, Alec. Rich and powerful men that promise you the world."

"I don't need them. I have you."

"Thank you, darling." Hamilton kissed him tenderly and Alec sighed contentedly. Never enough. He wanted to stay here, safe in Hamilton's arms. Away from everyone else that made trouble for him. But there was no point putting off the inevitable.

"So, do I look as though I've slipped away to have make-up applied, or am I going to get away with it?"

Hamilton lifted his chin and turned it from side to side. "The skin's a little pink, but if you don't stay too late we should escape the obvious. I should get you to the kitchens really and find you some steak. Ice at the least. Does it sting?"

"Like a hell-burning fire."

"Shall we go home?"

"No. I have a job to do. Besides, it'll make me more mindful of my reactions. I really don't mean to lead these guys on."

"I know. The rational part of my brain deactivates when I see the way they look at you. And Harrison and I are going to have a falling out if he's going to start running to your rescue every five minutes."

"I should go and speak to him. He's probably worried."

"I agree, but no sex. I've been saving myself for you again and once is not enough. I intend to fuck you senseless for the rest of the night and into tomorrow."

"Mmm, much like last night then. Perhaps we should head home."

"I do love you, Alec."

Alec savored a tender kiss. Love hurts. Someone had told him that. Wasn't it the fucking truth? He felt amazing and torn in two at the same time and his face was on fire. But the kiss was so soothing and full of everything Alec craved. His life had been so simple, nothing ever happened. Now it was rich and full and complicated as hell. A very strange state of affairs indeed.

Hamilton left the room. Before Alec had gathered his thoughts to follow, Harrison came in and shut the door, locking it behind him.

"Edward..."

"Alec, shut up." Harrison was on him in a moment, turning his chin to look at his face. "That bastard. I can't believe he'd have the audacity to lay a finger on you here."

"He has every right."

"It doesn't mean he should. I want you to leave him."

Alec stepped back and stared. "I will *not*. You've no right to ask that of me."

"Why did he strike you?"

"Edwa—"

"Why, god dammit?"

"Because *you* came to see if I was okay."

"Because of me?"

"He's in love, Teddy. He was jealous. I'm supposed to be his and yet I've spent all evening being over-familiar with strangers. When he pulls me up on it, and I was doing very nicely on my own thank you, you come charging in to save me from the big bad boyfriend. What did you expect?"

"Not that, obviously."

"Well, it doesn't matter now."

"How can you say that? I've never raised a hand to my boys or my children for that matter."

"Good for you, Edward. Rick isn't so perfect, so what? He's still mine, and I still love him and every moment you keep me locked in this room with you is going to piss him off even more."

"You're angry with *me*?"

"Teddy, no." Alec hugged Harrison and nuzzled into his neck. "I'm not mad with you. I love that you care for me."

"Love you, Alec. I love you."

"And I love you, but I have a partner, other priorities, the same as you do. We should celebrate the fact we have the time we do together. Let's not make it difficult."

"If that man lays another finger on you..."

"You'll do nothing at all, Edward. Let me deal with it in my own way. You've known Rick for years. Don't let this change the way you feel about him."

"I don't know about that."

"For me, Teddy. I don't want any tension between you two. Don't make it any harder for me. I'm already fucking my boyfriend's boss; let that be enough for us to deal with."

"When you put it like that."

Alec kissed his forehead. "Good, now you have to let me go. I've work to do. This party is for me to meet everyone and you have me locked in a room."

"Your face..."

"Your guests are too polite to ask me about it. Now let's get going."

Alec was all talked out and had settled into a very soft chair in one of the quieter rooms. He watched as the men around him conducted business of a sort. You couldn't see the underlying rumble of sex, but it was there, you could feel it. Men would come back into the room adjusting themselves and would receive a pat on the back. Another would disappear. Much as at the Davenports, the sex was going on behind the scenes and for once Alec wasn't part of it… other than Hamilton telling him off. His face still burned, but after catching a glimpse of himself in one of the huge gilded mirrors, he thought he'd gotten away with it pretty well. He just looked a little flushed.

What he really wanted now was one of Hamilton's pamper baths and a big fluffy dressing gown. He stared into his whiskey glass. Anymore and he'd be snoring where he sat.

"You look like you're searching for the meaning of life in there."

Alec started. He looked up to see Worthington smiling down at him. "Hey, Peter," He stood to greet the man with a kiss to the cheek. "Have you had a good evening?"

"As always. You've made a very good impression."

"Have I?"

"You seem a little flat, Alec. Is everything okay?"

Alec smiled. Genuine concern and from a man that hadn't even fucked him. He'd have to remedy that at some point. "It's just been a long day. The timing isn't ideal. I should really be with Bradley."

"Ah yes, did you find a solution?"

"We're working on something. He's looking forward to his break with you. Make sure you have a family size box of condoms. He's very hungry."

Worthington's laugh was wonderfully healing and the touch as he clapped him on the back reassuring. "Make sure you give me his handling instructions before we leave. Perhaps we could have an afternoon together?"

"I'd like that, Peter."

"Wonderful, I'll have my secretary schedule some time."

"Do you have a moment now? I could honor that blowjob I owe you. I haven't touched a single cock all night. It's very strange."

"You're the other side of the fence now, Alec. You should be sampling the goodies on offer, and there are some beautiful boys here this evening."

"Ah, they beat me to it. Maybe next time then." Something familiar would have been nice about now to blast through the whiskey blues that were descending around him.

"You really haven't been through the rooms?"

"This is the first moment I've had to myself all evening."

"Let me take you on a tour. You need to be able to recognize the boys anyway."

Peter took Alec's hand and led him to a long corridor that ran central to the west wing of the house. He took Alec's glass and placed it on a nearby table.

"The first two rooms on either side are girls. It's always the same with Harrison's parties."

Worthington opened the first door for Alec to walk through. Sure enough, a young woman who could have been anything from eighteen to twenty-five was bouncing over what was a faceless cock from Alec's angle. The smell of sex nearly knocked him off his feet. She smiled at Alec, clearly enjoying herself. "If you'd like to wait," she said.

"Just giving him the tour, Penny. He isn't one of yours."

"That's a shame." She chuckled and gave Alec a wink.

Worthington took him through the rest of the rooms on that side, each interconnected. When they came out into the corridor at the far end, Alec was rock hard. "That's certainly something."

"You've seen nothing yet. This side of the hall is a little more risqué. If you want to try something kinky, you'll find it here." Alec remembered Patrick's room and shuddered. "Not your thing?"

"Can't say I've ever been introduced to it properly. I play with Sebastian a little, but nothing heavy. Some light bondage, nothing more."

They walked through a series of rooms with various props. A St. Andrews Cross, a fucking horse, and some kind of rack device that just looked painful. The groans coming from the guy strapped into it suggested it was anything but. Alec thought he'd seen it all, until they entered the next room. Chains from the ceiling suspended a man about Alec's height and build, his feet barely touching the floor. *His naked body trembled between each stroke of the lash against his back.* He was hard, and in an obvious state of ecstasy but the thing that threw Alec, that made him grasp Worthington's arm for support was the man wielding the flogger.

Hamilton.

He was so caught up in his scene, he hadn't even registered them enter the room. 'Saved myself for you', he'd said, but the naked man beating the crap out of the helpless sub bore no resemblance to Alec's Hamilton at all. Not his boss, not his master, and certainly not his lover. This man's face looked distorted, there was an odd glaze to his eyes—he looked fierce, scary. Alec watched Hamilton's cock bounce with every strike and it made him dizzy.

"I'm going to be sick." Alec dashed from the room and just about made it to the bathroom before emptying the contents of his stomach into the fine porcelain toilet bowl. The mirrored walls and gold accented lights threw his horror-stricken face back at him. The pain in his chest spread through his body until he wanted to scream and break something. Instead, he washed his hands, splashed his face with water and, because neither made him feel better, slumped into a heap on the floor in the hope that if he closed his eyes for long enough everything would go numb.

"Alec?" Worthington came in and closed the door. He sat next to Alec on the marbled floor and pulled him into a hug. "I didn't know he was in there. I've never known him use those rooms. I'm so sorry."

Maybe it was too much whiskey or the stress of the last few days but Alec cried. He curled into Worthington's chest and sobbed like a child who'd just discovered there was no Father Christmas. Worthington rocked and soothed and cuddled until everything calmed.

"I looked a picture before, I must be a disaster now," Alec said, dabbing at his eyes.

"You're still beautiful." Worthington pulled him tighter and kissed his forehead.

Beautiful. Alec needed to feel beautiful, cared for, cherished. Needed to distance himself from the monster along the hall. "Fuck me, Peter? I want to feel good and I want you t—"

"Alec, sweetheart, that isn't the answer. Don't do anything rash, you need to speak to him first." He petted and stroked but Alec wanted more than token comfort.

"But I want to … with you."

"You're upset, not thinking clearly. Speak to Hamilton. Clear the air with him."

No point pushing it. Worthington wanted nothing from him and yet there he was offering support, standing up for Hamilton. Alec held his stomach but the real pain was further up. A deep, ragged pain in his chest that refused to budge. "You're so good to me."

"I don't want to see you make a mistake. We've got years to fuck if it's really what you want, but not now."

Alec stood and helped Worthington to his feet. "Oh god, look at the state of me." His eyes were red and puffy, his left cheek slightly swollen and a shade darker than his right. "Definitely time I headed home."

"Why don't you stay here? Harrison would be happy to have you. I'll settle you in for a nice bath and send Hamilton up. How does that sound?"

"Perfect, Peter, as always."

"Come on, we'll use the back stairs. Boys on the run," he grinned.

Worthington started the bath and came through to the large, overly furnished room. He started to undress Alec, folding his clothes as he went. It was nice—being cared for with no expectations—Alec wasn't sure any of the men in his life had given him this, not even Sebastian. "What's your story, Peter? Were you born to this?"

"Heavens no. I started out much the same as you." He checked the bath, turned off the taps and pulled a naked Alec to sit on his lap on the long sofa at the end of the bed. "Very few people know this, Alec, I'm going to tell you because I want you to know you can always trust me, come to me with anything."

"I already do trust you, Peter."

"Maurice is my cousin. He's the one who arranged the job in the City. One of his regular clients had complained there were no new candidates for the dwindling office pool. At the time I was stuck in a very bad relationship with a female domme that abused, rather than cared for me."

"You were a slave?"

"The worst kind of slave. I didn't know the difference between submission and oppression. Maurice was desperate for me to see sense. He set up the interview. My mistress had trained me for anal penetration so the idea of sex with men wasn't a problem. The job transformed my life. I walked away from her and into the hands of the Order. My manager taught me to have respect for myself and to recognize that to serve was my choice and an act of strength not weakness."

The soft stroke of fingertips on Alec's back was making him sleepy and he nestled in closer. "I've learned a lot from my time as a boy," Alec said. "Or I thought I had."

"And you have to be ready to move on. A kind old gentleman took me under his wing. He showed me it was possible to move on from being a boy to being one of the men. That I had the potential to do it just as you have."

"All that man-sex, Peter, and you're not gay?"

"I've always had bisexual tendencies. Fucking boys or being fucked has never been a hardship for me. Not like some of the boys."

"Like?"

"Young Michael, from the second. He has a beautiful girlfriend. Very good actor, but not in the slightest interested in men of his own accord."

"No way," Alec sat up for a moment trying to gauge whether Worthington was joking. *Michael? Hell's bells.* Alec hadn't seen him much lately. "He was the first guy I fucked, ever."

"He'll be leaving the pool next year when he's married. I've never known a straight guy as committed as he is. I'm trying to get him a good promotion and a nice lump sum."

"God, I'll miss him."

"He'll still be in the building. He may even pop in for one of your boys now and then."

"Every function I spent on my knees he was there getting fucked, repeatedly."

"The man's a machine." Worthington patted his knee. "Now how about that bath? I'll find Hamilton. He's probably frantic downstairs searching for you."

"He's going to be so angry." Alec grasped at Worthington's jacket. The tears were threatening again. "That boy, Peter, he looked like me. Rick was pretending to whip me."

"That's what you need to discuss with him. Now, I'll stay with you if you need me to, but it's really between the two of you to work out alone. I know from experience, Alec. Don't leave anything unsaid."

Alec nodded but still didn't let go. Too many things were upside down. The look on Hamilton's face as he dished out those lashes seemed permanently etched in his mind and it hurt like fuck. More than the bruising on his face. More than the threat of being offered out like a toy. The lie burned more than all of it together. *Saving myself for you. Fucking bastard.* How many times had he said that this last week and then gone to fuck something else?

"Alec, time to get in the bath."

"Stay with me? Once I'm out you can go and get him."

"Come on then."

Worthington sponged and soaped, massaging away the tension. Alec kissed him full on the mouth a few times, but Worthington pulled back after a few moments. Alec moved Worthington's hand to his cock and Worthington stroked and eased it to hardness. "You're a beautiful boy, Alec." He reached over and kissed Alec's cock, tonguing the head.

"Please, Peter, make love to me. Make everything right."

"Not tonight, sweetheart." Worthington sucked on the head of Alec's cock, just tasting, not to finish him. "One day, maybe. Let's get you dried off."

Worthington spent a little more time, sucking and tasting Alec's body and Alec relaxed into the experienced hands hoping he'd keep going, purge the images that hovered every time he closed his eyes. He licked over Alec's pucker and slipped in his tongue just the once before kissing his way back to Alec's ear. "I'll send Hamilton along. He loves you, very much. Give him a chance to explain."

"Thank you, Peter."

Give As Good
As You Get

Soft kisses on his shoulders roused Alec from sleep. For a moment, he couldn't think where he was. "How are you feeling, darling? Peter said you were taken ill."

Alec rolled over and sat up, pulling a cover over his naked body. "Did he tell you why?"

"Would you rather I slept in another room?"

"Don't be ridiculous. I just want to know what the fuck is going on with you. You beat the crap out of me, fuck me and tell me you can't wait to be with me, and the next thing, I find you whipping the skin off a guy that looks like me. Was he a good fuck, Rick, as sweet as me?"

"I deserve that."

"Too bloody right." Alec flinched away as Hamilton reached for his arm. "How could you *lie* to me? That hurts more than anything else. I know you fuck other people and I don't care but don't tell me you're saving yourself for me if it's not true."

"I didn't fuck him." The matter of fact tone in Hamilton's voice threw Alec for a moment. It wasn't a retort or an excuse. It was a statement, delivered as he would a quarterly report in a meeting. Alec's temper fizzed. *The fucking hypocrite.*

"I *saw* how hard you were. It turned you on whipping his ass. You expect me to believe you left it at a beating?" Alec wanted to punch him. That would get rid of the smug look on his face.

Hamilton shrugged. "It's the truth."

Alec stared at him for a long moment but the coolness in Hamilton's eyes, his lack of comeback at Alec's accusations bled the heat from Alec's mood.

"I didn't fuck him," Hamilton repeated. "I haven't fucked anyone today, other than you."

"Oh." Alec relaxed his defensive position and Hamilton climbed onto the bed properly and sat next to him, leaving a respectful gap.

"I was touring the rooms. I had to do something, I was still annoyed at Harrison, at the fact everyone loves you so much. It messes with my head but I didn't want to take it out on you. Braithwaite was flogging the boy; I don't even know his name. He said I looked like I could use a time out."

"A time out, is that what they call it?"

"I've never been into the S&M scene. Master, slave, I get that. Well, you know how I run my ship. We don't do pain for pleasure. He offered me the flogger. Said the boy was ready to take it hard, no warm up needed. So I did."

"And you liked it."

"The release was immediate, like using a firing range at the gun club. All that anger just drained away from me. Then I was interested. You can't just thrash someone, I know that much at least. Braithwaite showed me how to move over the skin so as not to cause lasting damage and to maximize the boy's pleasure. He stripped off my clothes, said it was easier to focus."

"You imagined he was me?"

"No." Hamilton at least had the decency to look horrified at the suggestion. "I promise you, Alec, the thought never entered my head. I was concentrating on delivering each stroke, waiting to hear in the boy's breathing if I'd placed it correctly. Braithwaite took the boy down when he was ready and fucked him. I didn't even know you'd been in the room."

"It made me sick. The look on your face. You were a monster trying to rip the flesh off my back."

"Alec, I don't know what to say." Hamilton held out his hand and looked at Alec with big, sad eyes. Alec wound his fingers in Hamilton's and they both relaxed a little more. "When I couldn't find you, I was angry. I thought you were in one of the rooms or had gone off with Harrison. I played holy hell with him."

"You didn't?"

"Oh, yes, in front of his wife too. She slapped me." Hamilton rubbed his cheek.

Alec snorted. "I'd have liked to see that."

"Yes, well it was Symons that saved me from making an ever bigger fool of myself. Said you'd been taken unwell and Worthington was looking after you."

"Peter was with me. In the room. He was giving me a tour."

"I assumed of course, he'd stolen you away to fuck you."

Alec sighed. "For fuck's sake, Rick, how could you think that?"

"Don't you see how badly he wants you?"

Alec pulled his hand away and turned to face Hamilton. "I begged him to fuck me tonight and he wouldn't."

"What?"

"You'd become this huge, frightening monster in my head and I wanted to get rid of it. He was there for me, holding me. I cried all over him and he just sat there. He even bathed me for fuck's sake and I wanted him to make me feel good but every time I made a move, he stopped me. Told me to wait for you. Talk things over. He's not like you."

"What the hell's that supposed to mean?"

"How the fuck do I know?" Alec slumped back into the pillows. "I'm angry, nothing makes sense right now."

"Alec, all I can do is apologize. But to be honest, apart from being a prick with Harrison, I don't know what I'm apologizing for. I didn't fuck anyone, I haven't lied to you, and I didn't beat that boy imagining it was you. You've jumped to the wrong conclusion, the same as I did and let's face it—you were actually going to fuck someone. I need to be extra nice to Peter when I see him again. I may even give him your ass."

The words cut deep and Alec swung his hand and caught Hamilton across the cheekbone.

"Fucking *hell*, what was that for?"

"Don't you make light of this. *That* is exactly what I mean when I say he isn't like you. You use your position to mock me, play on my insecurities. It's not fair."

"Really? Is that how you see me?"

Hamilton reached for the chain and ripped it from Alec's neck, throwing it across the room.

"No!" Alec scrambled off the bed to get it. "You've broken it. You stupid, rotten, jealous bastard. Isn't it enough that I'm yours? I can't stop people wanting me." Alec dropped to his knees, as though from a punch to the gut. "All I've ever done is love you, why would you be so cruel?"

"You're bleeding." Hamilton crouched at his side and ran a hand over the back of Alec's neck. "The chain must be sharp at the end."

"I don't care, get the fuck off me." Alec tried to shrug him off but Hamilton held tighter. "Leave me *alone*." Alec took off the ring and threw it on the floor. Hamilton had said a day at a time. They'd made it a whole twenty-four hours. "There, I'm not yours anymore. Now *fuck* off."

"Alec, please. I'm sorry. I'm cruel *because* I love you. I know I've done wrong but we can work this out. Please, let's try at least."

"Why? So you can threaten to offer my ass to anyone next time I do something you don't like? I can't live like that, Rick. Punish me if you have to, but don't make jokes like that, it fucking hurts."

"Alec, look at me." Hamilton shook him. "*Look* at me, damn it." Alec could see the raw emotion and desperate power in those beautiful blue eyes and it set them on fire. So beautiful, Alec's breath caught in his chest. So dangerous. "You are everything to me. Don't let me lose you because I'm an idiot. Please, you have to hold on for me. Hold on 'til I get it right."

Alec reached in to touch those perfect lips, the softest touch and a world of passion and desire crashed down around them. Alec ripped at Hamilton's clothes, his hands desperate to feel everywhere at once, teeth and tongues clashing, nipping, tasting. Alec's cock felt raw and needy as it battled with Hamilton's, their bodies pressed together. "Take me, Rick. Not as your boy, as your lover."

"You've always been my lover, Alec, from the very first time. I was just too afraid to tell you." A quick slick of spit and Hamilton was pushing inside. "No one feels like you, Alec. I'm here body and soul with you."

"Yes, I want everything."

"You have it. Only for you."

The fucking was frantic. Hamilton came quickly and Alec rolled them over and penetrated him, taking up a hard, deep fuck he knew Hamilton would feel for days with only a bit of spit to help them along. Hamilton's name was on Alec's lips as he came. Hamilton searched around and finally slipped the ring back onto Alec's finger. "My lover," he whispered. "My life."

Alec awoke with a thumping headache, his face felt like a pumpkin, his neck was stinging and his ass was raw. He sat up and looked around the room with one eye still shut. "Rick?" He shoved the lump of snoring man next to him. "Rick, I think we need to go home."

"What?" Hamilton sat up and rubbed his face, wincing as he touched his cheek. "You hit me." He looked at Alec. "Holy hell, your face is a mess."

Alec fell back into the soft pillows and pulled the covers over his head.

"Why have you got blood all over you?"

"Because you're a fucking psycho."

"Alec, I'm not kidding. Let me see."

Alec sat up. "It's just a scratch, from the chain you ripped off me, remember?"

"I'm such a fucking asshole. Why are you still here?"

"Because I love you, idiot."

Hamilton grinned, leaning over him. "That's right, I remember now. That's why I've got a sore ass. No more sex without lube."

"I'll fuck you as often, and however I like."

"Okay, darling. Anything for you." Soft, healing kisses soothed the sore skin of his face and teased his lips. "Shall I bring you breakfast, or are you ready to see me get the dressing down from hell."

"Oh, I'm looking forward to that. But I'm not sure you have any buttons left on your shirt."

Hamilton reached for the phone at the side of the bed. "Hi, this is Hamilton. I don't suppose you could send me a couple of fresh shirts? And maybe a couple of glasses of Alka-Seltzer. Yes, we'll be long for breakfast, oh, for brunch then, shortly. Fuck," he said, hanging up the phone. "It's nearly eleven. I bet Harrison is prowling the halls waiting for us."

"At least everyone else will be gone."

"True. And we're both late for work. Did you have anything on this morning?"

"My schedule's still light. It kicks off toward the end of next week."

"Okay, shower first. Damn, I didn't think I was drinking heavily last night, why do I have a hangover?"

"As long as you're in pain, I don't care."

Hamilton sighed, his look serious. "You aren't going to forgive me?"

"After a shower and the killer blowjob you're going to give me, all will be forgiven and forgotten."

"Deal. Get your delectable ass out of bed and into the bathroom."

"Carry me." Alec grinned, raising his arms.

"You're pushing it, my sweet. But I guess I can try."

They were like a pair of naughty schoolboys by the time they made it to the breakfast room. A slow leisurely shower fuck, a killer blowjob and wrestling for the best shirt would do that to you. The look on Harrison's face was sobering to say the least.

"Never in all my years have I had to deal with such behavior. For goodness sake, Hamilton, look at his face. Look at *yours*. Did you slip out to a bare knuckle boxing match I wasn't aware of?"

"Sir—"

"Shut up and sit down." They both sat quickly and Alec winced from the discomfort in his ass. He was pretty sure Hamilton would have the same problem. Alec didn't want to look anywhere but at his hands on the table in front of him, but Harrison's temper was really something to behold. "You're lucky I'm so fond of you both. Alec, don't say a word. Just eat. And you, *Mr.* Hamilton, need to apologize to my wife."

"Oh, hell. I don't know what to say. It all sort of got away from me."

"You're lucky she can tell a man in love or she'd have had your innards on a plate."

"Thank you, sir, I mean … I'll just shut up."

"You should have put ice on that face last night, Alec. Remember that for the next time he takes his temper out on you."

Hamilton bristled. "Now wait one minute."

"Rick," Alec said, placing a hand on Hamilton's arm. "It's okay. Thank you, Edward. I know you're worried about me, but there's no need, really."

"I guess I'll have to trust your judgment on that."

Harrison's attitude had Alec's hackles rising. It was one thing to be angry that his wife had been on the end of Hamilton's temper and their petty squabbles but Alec couldn't sit by and let him run Hamilton into the ground. "Teddy, how long have you known Rick? Do you really think I'm in danger?"

"Honestly, I have no idea what to think anymore. I've never seen such a carry on."

"Are you sure you aren't being hard on Rick for another reason?"

"Of course, I'm jealous, Alec. But it's more than that. You should be with someone that knows how to respect you. You're not a punch bag. The things he said last night, accused me of in front of my wife, my friends, and did the same to poor Peter. Tell me, how is that the voice of a healthy man?"

Alec kept a grip on Hamilton's arm, and for once he stayed quiet. "Sometimes love isn't healthy," Alec said to Harrison. "I slapped him too. Don't think I'm the weaker party in this relationship, Teddy. It just takes more to get me angry. I can handle myself."

Harrison looked between the two of them and shook his head. "It's why I took a wife. All that testosterone flying around. It's a recipe for disaster."

"Rick has a new outlet for his tension, haven't you, baby?"

"I have? Oh, I have, yes." Hamilton took hold of Alec's hand. Possibly for reassurance. Alec was thankful for the touch. It was almost as bad as facing his mother with a bad school report. "Braithwaite is going to train me to use one of his boys."

"Very well, but if I hear, or see evidence that you have raised a whip to *this* boy, I will personally see to it that you are flogged by a professional. Do I make myself clear?"

"Crystal, Edward," Hamilton said, the color draining from his face. "I do love him you know."

"That much is clear. It's the only thing that addles a man's brains so." Harrison stood and walked to the door. "I'm off to work. Alec, I suggest you take the rest of the week off. Hamilton, stay out of my way for a few days."

"Teddy, are you okay?"

"I won't see you tomorrow, Alec. I can't fuck you with bruises. Don't forget Vaughn is waiting to hear from you about his date."

Alec went to him and stroked his cheek. "It's okay, Teddy."

"It's not okay, Alec. I abhor violence. It shows weakness of character. You are both better men."

Alec kissed him, trying to rouse him from his somber mood but he wasn't very enthusiastic. "I'll be a better man, I promise."

"I didn't want to love you, Alec. But I do. I can't bear to see you unhappy."

"I'm not unhappy. Please let me see you tomorrow. If for no other reason than for you to check I'm okay."

"Very well. I'll see you at home."

"Now will you kiss me properly?" Harrison surrendered to one of their sexy, all-out kisses that stirred the monster in his pants. "Do you want me to see to that?"

"Your fiancé is sat at the table, Alexander. You would do well to remember his whereabouts before turning those charms of yours on others. Vaughn will deal with it at the office."

Still pissed off but already thawing. Alec smiled, stroking Harrison's cheek. "I love you too, Edward."

"Hamilton." He nodded once and was gone.

"Wow, now I'm really pissed. I have to share my fiancé with the boss who thinks I'm a giant loser and you use the 'l' word. *And* with a cock like that he has to be better in the sack than I am."

"It's *your* ring I have on my finger." Alec draped himself over Hamilton's lap and took a little time to kiss and reassure and kiss some more.

"I'm sorry about your necklace. I'll replace it."

"Thank you. I feel naked without it."

"How about we head straight for the shop and I'll get you naked to put on the new one."

Alec wrapped his arms around Hamilton's neck and kissed the end of his nose. "You're such a tease."

"I think Maurice might enjoy one of your blowjobs while I fuck you from behind."

"Mmm, let's go, Master. Before the bruising develops anymore and I can't suck properly." Alec rubbed his jaw. It hadn't hurt last night but this morning it was starting to stiffen up.

"Alec, you know I'd never purposely hurt you, don't you?"

"It's forgotten already. Come on." Alec dragged Hamilton to his feet. It had to be forgotten because if Alec thought too much about what was really going on he'd be faced with decisions he wasn't strong enough to make. Not now, not ever.

The Games People Play

Alec cuddled Bradley against him as they watched the movie. One of the definite benefits of the house move was the change of furniture. Gone was his two-seater threadbare sofa and in its place, stretched out elegantly to one side of the room, was a four-seater leather couch, deep enough to make out on without the risk of falling on the floor. The softest leather, in some designer shade he couldn't remember the name of that looked like a field of wheat at the height of summer. It contrasted with its blue-green brother and rusty-red sister to make the room warm and just a little bit fun. But most of all it was ridiculously comfortable and very sexy. Alec didn't know furniture could be sensual, but this sofa was. Add a naked man to the mix and Alec always wanted sex when he sat on it. Always.

Sebastian curled over Alec's feet on the floor. He looked cosy and content on the thick wool rug, completely absorbed by the TV, stroking Alec's calf absent-mindedly. A strange dynamic had developed between the three of them but it worked. It eased Alec's mind about the things that went on outside his front door. A safety net of sorts. It seemed sensible to have times like this, where the pressures of work and the GC stayed away but Alec wasn't sure it was appropriate to have a haven from Hamilton too and yet that's what this was.

Alec stroked his jaw, the bruising just a light shadow after last week's antics. He wished he could say the same for his apprehension, though about what he couldn't be sure. Hamilton had been the perfect boyfriend over the past week. So much so, Alec felt smothered. The master/slave lifestyle had slipped into a regularity that was frightening—the occasional dinner, pleasant conversation, and far too much sweet and alarmingly vanilla sex. Alec almost preferred the fists, disturbing in itself, but right now he was happy to be free of Hamilton altogether which was a much bigger worry. A weekend escape into his own little master/slave world, one he was getting far too comfortable with.

It'd also been just over a week since Alec put the chastity device on Brad and he was holding up well. He was even wearing it to bed. Alec found he actually had more to talk about now that his days didn't consist of just sex. But Alec was horny, thanks to the sofa, and he wasn't just horny, he was horny for Brad.

He kissed Bradley's neck and shoulders and made his way down to suck on a nipple.

"Are you trying to make me uncomfortable, Master? Because this thing does pinch if I start to get hard."

"Do you still think about sex?"

"All the time."

"You don't hate me for making you wear it?"

"No way. I can't believe how much of my daily communication was about sex. I'm learning so much about myself and other people."

Alec didn't want to talk, but he felt he owed it to Brad to be able to follow his new thoughts to their conclusion, to express himself in words rather than actions. Something else Alec had discovered about Brad with sex out of the equation, he was a talker. Alec felt more than a little guilty for wishing he could take the option of shoving his cock in Brad's mouth to shut him up now and then. "What have you learned about other people?"

"That people don't have to fuck me to like me." Brad squirmed a little under Alec's ministrations. "I didn't expect to see any of my regulars. But they stop by, the same as they always did, just without whisking me off to the bathrooms for a blowjob. They actually ask about my work now and how I am."

"That's a good thing." Alec let his lips brush gently over Brad's skin leaving a trail of goose bumps. Brad tried to slither away but Alec kept his course, letting his tongue slip out to wet the path.

"I'm more confident too." Brad's voice was notably higher as he continued to fidget. "Climbing the walls mind you, but that's okay, because I'm doing it for you."

"Are you?"

Bradley smiled. A sweet, wholesome smile that made his eyes sparkle. "I'm certainly not doing it for me, cupcake."

"Well, as your master I think you deserve a treat."

Brad snorted: half laugh, half indignation. "I get to watch you fuck Sebastian? Or do I have to listen to you both again? This apartment might be big, but it ain't big enough for Mr. Squealer down there."

Sebastian gave Brad the finger without even looking around, and Brad clipped his ear.

"Actually," Alec said, wriggling around so that he could press more fully against Brad's body. "I thought I'd fuck you, while Sebastian sucks you off, but if you're not interested." Alec stopped the motion and sat up straight, waiting for the words to sink in.

"Huh?"

He shrugged, trying to hide his grin. "Doesn't matter. Watch the end of the film."

"Why would you tease like that? Didn't you slap Hamilton for teasing like that?"

Alec considered his response carefully. He didn't want to spoil the moment with the irritation that was threatening at the mention of the unmentionable. Best brush it away and get on with his evening plans. He kissed Brad's shoulder and smiled. "You're right, Sebastian shouldn't suck you off. It wouldn't fit with the training plan. But, I'm still going to unlock you and take you to bed."

"You're serious?"

"You've been a good boy and you deserve a reward. I'm so proud of you Brad, the way you're just getting on with it. I want to show you I've noticed and that it's worth it."

"Thank you, Master."

"Sebastian, lock up, babe. We'll see you in the morning."

"No worries, I'm on it."

Alec kissed the top of Sebastian's head and led Bradley through to the bedroom. Brad's cock started swelling as soon as Alec took off the silicon chastity device and threw it on the floor. "We'll sterilize it tomorrow and put it back on. Tonight I want you," Alec pulled Brad close and whispered against his neck, "... all night."

Brad let go of a groan. "Fucking hell, Master, could you be any more sexy?"

Alec took Brad for a shower and watched him tremble as Alec sucked in his cock and gave a quick swirl of his tongue. He let the cock slip from his lips and looked up into Brad's already blissed out face. "I'm going to fuck you over and over so you know you're mine."

"I am yours, Master."

It was a long, lazy session full of tension and teasing. Bradley came so hard, he cried real tears as he grasped Alec's shoulders and he kissed and kissed. Desperate, hungry kisses that stirred Alec's need for him all over again. Alec woke him in the night for a hard, fast fuck and again a few hours later. But it was Alec who woke with morning wood pressed against his butt cheek. What he wanted more than anything was to slide that cock up his ass and ride it 'til they both blew. Instead, he sucked Brad awake and swallowed his load.

"How are you feeling this morning, sunshine?"

"Oh, baby, you have no idea." Brad stretched out; his tanned skin looking a shade darker than usual against the crisp white sheets, and gave a killer grin. "I'm on top of the world."

"Good. That thing takes ten minutes in the sterilizer and then I'm buckling you back up."

"That's okay, Alec. I like being just for you. Last night was so special. Do you know we've never had sex with just the two of us before? I like being the center of your attention, and you are definitely mine."

They kissed and cuddled and kissed some more. Holding Brad's chastity key was working better than Alec could have hoped. He'd have to call in to see Maurice, give him a thank you blowjob, or let him fuck Sebastian. Maybe he'd even let him be Brad's first service fuck once training was over.

Alec left Brad to shower and make breakfast while he gave Sebastian a quick morning service all his own. They never seemed to have much time alone lately but Sebastian didn't seem to mind. It had been a while since Alec had handed him out to anyone too. He'd have to think about that. Perhaps Tristan would have a party coming up. For now, he needed to concentrate on Bradley. Another few days and he should be ready for the pool and business as usual. One boy at a time.

By the time the two of them made the kitchen, Bradley was waiting with the padlock in his hand, the chastity device already on. "It's your privilege, Master," he said, handing it to Alec with the key.

"Yes is it, thank you, sweetheart."

Alec locked him up and sat him on his lap at the table to feed him breakfast. It was something he liked to do. It always scratched a particular itch when Hamilton did it for him. It was an interesting ritual Alec spent a lot of time daydreaming about when he was bored at work. Sensual yet commanding, compliant yet suggestive, it ticked plenty of boxes on his list of needs. He shuddered, trying to put his Hamilton kink out of his mind. He'd have to figure out a way to coax the old Hamilton out to play. But not right now. He had other things to do, like find a way to be a better master to his own boys. One master at a time.

"So what are you boys up to today?" Brad sucked the grapefruit juice from Alec's fingers and he stifled a moan. His cock was all played out but it still twitched hopefully.

"We're cleaning out the rest of the old apartment," Sebastian said from somewhere behind his paper. It was almost as big as he was. "There will be tenants moving in next week."

"Oh, okay. They didn't sell the place then?"

"No, Master," Sebastian said, looking over the top of the huge broadsheet at Alec. "It's still yours."

Strange they'd decide to keep it when it was supposed to go toward the upkeep of the new apartment. Alec was only just getting used to the fact he was a kept man. It grated that the powers that be wouldn't have cashed in his contribution. Unless …"Who does this place belong to?"

"It belongs to you as well," Sebastian said, finally folding the paper and placing it on the table. "I hope you don't mind but Vaughn has been showing me how to keep your accounts together. GC regulations and stuff. You own both properties and …" He paused, biting on his lower lip as though he'd said too much already. If Alec hadn't just fucked him, he'd have dragged him to the floor and taken him right there. His cock stirred again but it was too soon even for Alec to manage another round. He'd fuck himself into an early grave if he wasn't careful.

"And?"

"You have a cottage in the country."

"I do?" *A what?*

"It came with the deeds to the apartment. I thought we could go and see it one weekend; see if it needs any work."

Cottage in the country. Hells bells, what a gentleman he was becoming. "Where is it?"

"Somewhere in Wiltshire or Somerset. I looked it up on Google Maps. It's cute. I thought you could use it as a vacation let, like a pension property."

Another whole house for him to rattle around in. It didn't seem right. And just when he was coming to terms with the multimillion-pound gift horse. "Right, well, next weekend then. Book a car."

"You have one of those too."

Alec looked at Sebastian, but this time he smiled. "Don't tell me, it came with the apartment?"

"No, actually Harrison bought it for you. They delivered it yesterday. I forgot to tell you. I'm sorry, Master. Should I get him on the phone for you?"

A car. From Harrison. Was the old man mad? How the hell was that supposed to stop Hamilton jumping back on the crazy boyfriend merry-go-round? "I'll have a look at it first. What is it? No, wait. Please tell me it has more than two seats and a solid roof."

Sebastian and Brad chuckled. "Don't look at me," Brad said. "I haven't seen it."

"Yes and yes," Sebastian said. He patted Alec's hand. "I took a peek while you were at work yesterday." He stood and walked to the dresser where he fished a large envelop from the drawer.

"And?"

"You're going to love it. I have all the documents. He even insured it for you."

Sebastian rummaged in the envelope and handed Alec the key fob. Alec stared at it for a moment. "What am I going to do, guys?" He turned over the Audi fob as though he'd find the answer stuck to the bottom.

"Just let him love you," Brad said, stroking his arm.

Sebastian shrugged. "He must have ordered it ages ago. It's an RS5."

He couldn't have ordered it ages ago. It'd only been a few weeks since the relationship had slipped into the potential 'I've bought you a car' category. "Probably pulled a few strings and jumped the queue, more like." Alec flipped the key over a few more times. Was Harrison trying to prove a point, hoping expensive gifts would cause Hamilton to lose the plot altogether so he could say 'I told you so'? No, that wasn't his style. He was nothing if not genuine in his affections.

"You want to drop us at the old place on your way to get Vaughn?" Sebastian leaned against Alec's shoulder and Alec drew some strength from his touch. Alec loved the comfortable moments; they held the promise of being there long after the fairy tale was over. He was lost in the midst of the fairy tale right now. Alec knew it was this, the little touches from Sebastian, that kept him grounded in the madness. Even the closeness he was developing with Hamilton, outside of the current vanilla sugar coating, had the air of the unreal about it. There was always the feeling it could just float away and have all been a dream. Brad was an unknown, though slowly making his mark, but Sebastian was solid. A foundation in Alec's shaky world.

"Lift?" he said, running a hand through Alec's hair.

Alec looked up from the car key and smiled at Sebastian's concerned expression. "Yeah, why not. I was going to take him to Covent Garden. I guess we can head out of the city now."

"Will you be back tonight?"

"Not sure." Vaughn had asked for a real date and Alec needed to get away from the circus for a while and straighten out his head. Coming home was something he could do without. Even his haven of five minutes ago was starting to feel tainted.

"Do you mind if we order pizza?"

"Sebastian, when have you ever asked me what food you're allowed to eat?"

"I never eat takeout unless you say to order it, Master. I always cook."

Alec shuddered. How was it possible to feel so grounded with some-one one minute and completely uncomfortable the next? "You guys, or-der pizza, drink beer, do whatever you want. Just no sex or touchy feely for Brad."

"Can we cuddle?"

"As long as it doesn't lead to snogging and a blowjob for you, mister." Alec poked Sebastian in the chest.

Sebastian actually bristled. Alec felt it, and the ground shifted beneath him like quicksand. Brad moved off Alec's lap and sat on the chair next to him.

"Fine." Sebastian grabbed Alec's plate from the table and stomped to-ward the sink. "Just remember I'm not the one with the bloody chastity belt." The plate clattered into the sink but sounded as though it had sur-vived intact—unlike Alec's understanding of the current situation.

"What's that supposed to mean?"

"How many times have you fucked me this week?"

Alec was falling through the looking glass. Talk about mood swings. The guy had been practically purring over cars and cottages a minute ago. "I don't know. Not enough, obviously."

"You've got *that* right. You've been out most of the time and I've been stuck with Mr. Don't-touch-me-I'm-a-sex-free-zone."

"Sebastian, why didn't you *say* something?"

"I *am* saying something and it's not fair. I'm left out all the time. When did you last spend all night in my bed or let me sleep with you?"

Brad slipped from the kitchen and Alec made his way to Sebastian. He pulled him into a hug and let him cry. It was more of a snivel, no real tears, but he was obviously upset. Upset enough to put Alec firmly in his place. If he couldn't look after Sebastian when the guy did so much for him then Alec did not deserve the title master. "Tomorrow, I'm all yours. I promise."

"It doesn't matter."

"Yes, it does. We'll go out. Stay in a fancy hotel if you like and you can fuck me too. How does that sound?"

Sebastian shrugged, his head still buried against Alec's shoulder.

"Come on, babe, don't be sad. I need you. You're the one that keeps me sane around here."

"I just miss you. A couple of weeks ago I had you all to myself. I've barely seen you since."

"I'll tell you what, when Brad goes away with Worthington, we'll head off to this cottage for a few days."

"That would be nice." He ventured a look up at Alec, his eyes big and sad with a hint of mischief returning. "Can we go to a club?"

"Sure, or I'll pimp you on street corners if we can't find one." Sebastian smiled and Alec relaxed, keeping a tight hold of his little-boy-lost.

"We could see if Jack is free. He emailed a couple of days ago to see how the move went."

"It's a plan." Alec kissed his forehead. "A weekend in the country with our very own fantastic-fuck coach driver."

"Just me and you?"

The hope in Sebastian's voice cut Alec to the bone. He really had hurt him, and he hadn't even noticed. What the fuck kind of master—*friend*—was he? "And Jack."

"Thank you, Master. I don't want to be a pain. I just need you to remember I'm here now and then."

Alec needed to remember lots of things about lots of people. He also needed to remember to do things for himself occasionally, not that he could ever make a decision about what that would be. "You could go to the club with the boys tonight, I heard Hamilton say he was going."

"I'll stay with Brad. It's no fun fucking if it's not you giving my ass away."

"Okay, babe. But I do know you're here and I still love you."

Alec watched the boys climb out of the car and waved before pulling away. And what a car it was. Black leather, chrome, and wood, with so many gadgets it was going to take him a week to read the manual. The smell alone was enough to make him splurge all over the seats. Heady leather scents mixed with the aroma of newness and polish. He turned the corner and pulled up at the curb, taking out his phone to make the call.

"Alec, is everything okay?"

"Everything is great, Teddy, I love it. You know you shouldn't have."

"Ah, the car."

"I'm just on my way to pick up Vaughn. I wanted to check in first."

"Have a lovely time. I'm pleased you like it, there was a debate over the color."

"It's awesome really. I feel like a movie star or something, especially with the tinted glass."

Harrison chuckled. "That's so you can fuck in it, and people can't see you."

"That would be hard work in these seats."

"Alec, you're a young man, you'll find a way. Oh, did you look in the glove compartment?"

"What have you done?"

"It's just a little something to remind you of me."

"On top of the sixty grand car, you mean?"

"Have a look."

Alec popped his phone on loudspeaker and placed it on the dash so he could keep talking while he opened the glove compartment. It was a square package and he knew straight away what it was. "Teddy, are you trying to stir trouble?"

"Just open it."

Alec pulled the heavy black box out from the carton and opened the lid. Inside was another smaller case with a flip lid that he pushed back. "Fuck, Teddy, it's amazing."

"I thought it matched the interior of the car."

Alec pulled out the Breitling Blackbird, slid it off its little cushion and turned it over. He was expecting to see Harrison's name engraved on the back but instead there were two words nestled around the edge of the inner brand circle under the Breitling wings—*For Alexander*. "It's perfect." Alec could barely get the words past the lump in his throat. "Just like you."

"Have a nice day with Vaughn, Alec. I'll see you next week."

"I love you, Edward."

"And that's all the gift I need right there."

Alec wiped a stray tear as he disconnected the call. A godammed sports coupe and limited edition watch. He hadn't worn a watch since university, always kept time by the phone in his pocket. With Hamilton's bands, he'd never thought about getting one, but it had crossed his mind when the bracelets came off because his wrists felt so bare. Harrison was one step ahead. It wasn't even claiming him, it was his own name, and yet in a way just as powerful as Hamilton's name engraved inside of Alec's ring. *The games men play.* He put the watch on and stowed the box back in the glove compartment. He'd have to ask Vaughn to take him shopping for clothes that Harrison would like to see him in, and a little something for the man himself from Alec, to say thank you. But today he would focus on Vaughn. Alec was determined to make it a real date. No GC, no common acquaintances, no City gossip. The purr of the engine made his heart flutter as he touched the gas and eased out into the Saturday traffic.

A Taste of Real Life

Vaughn was waiting outside his building smoking a cigarette. He looked ageless in dark denims, a casual sweater and a fitted leather jacket. He looked good. When he saw Alec, he stubbed out the cigarette and popped something in his mouth, a breath mint hopefully; Alec had never liked kissing smokers. Alec pulled up alongside and lowered the window. "Hey, sexy, need a ride?"

"Cheeky, beggar." Vaughn's smile was a full-on grin as he climbed in. He reached across to kiss Alec's cheek. "How are you liking the wheels?"

"Excuse me, I'm your date. I expect more than a kiss on the bloody cheek after driving through traffic for you."

Vaughn slapped his knee. "Don't be silly. That comes later, and only *if* you turn out to have been worth the effort of getting ready. Now what do you think of the color?"

Vaughn stroked the edge of his seat suggestively and winked at Alec. Trying to ignore the twitch of interest in his cock, Alec pulled out into the steady stream of traffic. "I love it."

"Darn. I had you down as a gunmetal gray kinda guy. Harrison insisted on the red."

"It's true I'm not usually into flashy and any other car I'd have said the gray but *this* car ... it's like an Alfa Romeo or a Ferrari—if you're under thirty, the *only* color is red."

"I could see that with the R8, but not this one."

"Granted, this is more conservative in styling, which I like. The color reminds you it's a beast in disguise which I really, really like."

"Hmm, a bit like you then."

"Exactly." Alec wiggled his eyebrows and reached out a hand to squeeze Vaughn's knee. He was rewarded with a killer smile.

"Where are you taking me, then?"

"It's a surprise, but it'll take a while, so get comfortable."

"Do you have music?"

"Didn't have a chance to think about it, sorry."

"Lucky I have." Vaughn fished his iPhone from his pocket and attached it to the car stereo. A few moments later George Michael's dulcet tones seeped from the speakers.

"Could you be any more stereotypical, and you brought your iPhone adapter on a date?"

"I always have it. Harrison's taste in music is appalling. And don't diss the George. Nice watch by the way, I haven't seen you wear it before." *Oh, fuckadoodle.* A gift from Harrison that Vaughn hadn't arranged. "Which of your sugar daddies bought you that?"

"Does it matter?"

"Not really."

The earlier kerfuffle repeated through Alec's mind. Mostly his inability to notice when something he did, or didn't do, grated people unnecessarily. He needed to clear it before the date went any further and for his own peace of mind however delicate the subject matter. Add to that the likelihood of Alec letting slip at some point during the course of their time-out the fact his new watch was from Harrison and he decided the right time was now. "Vaughn, I'm sorry if it hurts you ... me with Harrison."

Vaughn stroked Alec's thigh and leaned his head back against the seat. "It doesn't, sweetie," he said, closing his eyes and letting out a sigh. "It's actually a relief. With you and Bradley around, I have time for a life of my own. It's been a long time coming, Alec, and I'm ready to let go."

"You're not leaving?"

"Lord, no. I love my job and I love Teddy. I'm just getting older, like time to myself. I've been able to disconnect a little without Teddy noticing. I have to ask a favor of you though, Alec."

"Go on."

"He's fallen hard for you, I don't want him hurt."

"There's only so much I can do on that front, Vaughn. Know that I do care for him a great deal but I can't be his."

"I know that, but he worries about you constantly. A phone call each morning just so he knows Hamilton hasn't battered you to death in your bed. Can you do that?"

Alec sighed. "He's only hit me a few times and it's only ever when I—"

"You tell me you deserve it and I'll thump you myself."

Alec could feel the weight of Vaughn's glare. "I'm not always the perfect boy."

"None of us is but there is no cause or excuse for violence in anger. Punishment under agreed conditions is one thing; domestic violence is another. Don't let it escalate and never confuse the two. So, a phone call a day, yes?"

"That's easy. I've been wanting to do that anyway, but didn't want to be a pest."

"Call him whenever you want. I swear he'd put the Prime Minister on hold for you."

"He knows the Prime Minister?"

Vaughn's chuckle was delightful and welcomed after the sudden intensity of the conversation. "How do you survive in our business when you're so naïve? Do you even know what the company does?"

"I don't think I do, to be honest." Alec wasn't sure he *wanted* to know.

"Just know the term *investment* covers a lot more than money. You'll figure it out."

"Okay, well that kind of talk is banned for the rest of the day from now."

Vaughn chuckled again, and closed his eyes, his hand stroking Alec's thigh. "You are such a sweetheart."

"I have a cottage, did you know?"

"Yeah, we found the deeds with the apartment stuff. Sebastian is really good with paperwork. You should remember that. I wouldn't have spotted it. It makes me wonder if Harrison has houses stashed away that I haven't picked up on. The man's inherited a ton of stuff since I've known him."

"Sebastian wants to make it a vacation let and then perhaps a retirement property. We're going to have a look at it next weekend."

Vaughn sat forward and fiddled with the aircon. "It's in the right location. Somerville, Somerton, something like that. Not far from Glastonbury. You can become wand-waving, circle-dancing, tree-hugging hippies when you retire. I think I'd like it there."

Alec laughed. Right now, Vaughn looked more the suave European Casanova. Tie-die and kaftans were the last thing Alec could picture him in. "Once it's ready, you can use it whenever you like. Just get Sebastian to book out the time."

"Are you sure?"

"Vaughn, you're a godsend and well, lovely. You can make use of anything of mine, whenever you need it."

"Even your car?"

"Even the car."

"And your boys?"

"Both of them yours, just let me know when."

"And what about you, Alec?"

"I'm here aren't I? At your request."

Vaughn's predatory gaze sent a shudder through Alec's body. "So where are you taking me? I have to know."

"Well, I may have been a virgin when Hamilton picked me up but believe me, I have dating down to a fine art. I just lacked the follow through."

"I'm still not sure I believe that story of virginity, but carry on."

"I was going to take you to Covent Garden."

"I love it there. A stroll through Apple Market and lunch at the Canteen. I knew you'd be a great date."

"But, what with the wheels, I thought we'd get out of the city, forget all that stuff back there and just be us. So ... I'm taking you to Portsmouth for the day."

"Portsmouth ... sailors?" Vaughn grinned. "How well you know me."

"Sailors, historic dockyards, the sea and me."

"It sounds delightful. Perfect, in fact. Lead the way my beautiful captain." Vaughn leaned back and closed his eyes again and Alec let the comfortable silence between them fill with the weaving sounds of George.

It was the best day. Alec held Vaughn close on the observation decks of the Spinnaker Tower when it turned out he was queasy with heights; they could see all the way across the Solent to the Isle of Wight. The Historic Dockyards led to some interesting stolen kisses, Alec thought much like the days when the ships were a sail on the world's oceans with an all-male crew. Lunch on a floating restaurant, a long walk hand-in-hand along the front at Southsea, followed by a trip to the castle and the Blue Reef Aquarium to see the sharks filled the afternoon. Last stop was shopping at Gunwarf to pick up some overnight essentials before checking in to a little bed and breakfast where the only luxury was an *ensuite* bathroom so small they could barely squeeze in it together.

A candlelit dinner in a small restaurant a short walk from the guest-house rounded off the day. Alec watched the shadows flicker over Vaughn's face. He looked peaceful and younger away from the hustle and bustle of the City. "What are you thinking about?" Alec asked, reaching for his hand across the table.

Vaughn gave a coy smile, not looking up from his hand in Alec's. "How different life could have been." He caught Alec's gaze. "I don't regret my life and I'm thankful for many things." He sighed. "Just mid-life ramblings."

"What about the future?"

"Still waiting to be written. What about you, what's your five-year plan?"

"Not sure I have one at the moment. So much has changed over the last year; my old one is null and void. I've already passed where I would have seen myself back in the days before … Hey, I said no business talk."

"Okay, what did you want to be when you were a kid?"

"Fireman. But before that I wanted to be a dancer."

"Wow, what happened to that dream?"

"I was four." Alec smiled. "And in love with Johnny Castle from *Dirty Dancing*. My mom used to watch it when she was ironing."

"Interesting. No doubts about sexuality for you then?"

"I remember a time, preteen, before my first boyfriend when I realized I wasn't like my friends, but I was lucky. My family have always believed we are who we are and nothing can change it so it's best not to fight or try to be anything else. I'm proud of them for that now. I know what some kids go through. I still had kids call me names but it never really got to me. I had worse at uni for being a scholarship brat with a country accent. I worked hard to get rid of it."

Vaughn nodded. "My dad kicked me out when I was sixteen."

"Because you were gay?"

"Said it was a defect from my mother's side of the family. It wasn't his fault. His parents were the same. Besides, if I'd stayed at home I'd hate to think where I'd be now. If I was anywhere at all. I was still better off than most of the kids I met working the streets. I was never abused at home. I think my dad even loved me. He just couldn't understand that I didn't want to change, as if it was somehow a choice I was making just to piss him off."

"Sebastian had a rough time of it. He feels the same as you. It's amazing you guys can be so calm about it."

"What's the point of staying angry? Angry didn't feed me or put a roof over my head. Getting on with it the best I could did that. And brought me Edward. He stepped in and gave me a life I couldn't imagine. A reworking of the old Cinderella story."

The light brush of Vaughn's fingers drawing circles over the back of Alec's hand kept pulling at the edge of his mind, pooling heat deep in his guts. "And now?"

A small smile crept over his face. The candlelight picked up a sparkle in his dark eyes. "Now, I think I'd like to go to bed."

Alec slipped an arm around Vaughn's waist as they headed up the stairs to their room. "So, was I worth getting ready for this morning?"

"You have no idea. You're such a breath of fresh air, Alec. I can't tell you how lovely today has been."

"You let me book a double room, so I thought I must be doing something right." Alec unlocked the door and held it open for Vaughn to walk through. With it safely locked behind them, he turned to Vaughn and held out his hand. Alec pulled him close for a sweet kiss that tasted of lemon and wine and the sea air.

A gentle tugging of clothes followed until they were naked on the bed, writhing in each other's arms with a deep-seated passion, the heady kisses Vaughn was so good at stole Alec's thoughts and pushed blood south to his hardening cock.

"You're so beautiful, Alec," Vaughn whispered. "I want to make love to you so much, I'll understand if you say no."

"It's just us here. We can do whatever we want. You can make love to me and I'll make love to you all night long."

"Like a real date."

"This is *our* real date."

Vaughn lay between Alec's legs trying to get his cock to stand up.

"You've worn me out again, mister," Alec said, running a hand through Vaughn's graying hair. "But if you keep playing with that it will get hard again."

Vaughn let it drop to the side, he kissed Alec's hip and crawled over his body to rest his chin on his hands over Alec's chest. "I can see why they love you."

"Come here." Alec pulled Vaughn higher to kiss his lips. There was something so tender about him, innocent despite his years and the things he'd seen. "I can see why the old man loves you, too."

"I'll take you up on the offer of using the cottage when it's ready. I'd like a place of my own near there and it'll be a good base to find one."

"Vacation home or something more?"

"I'll be reducing my hours soon to three days a week. I'll want to be out of the City on my days off. I want a partner and a dog and a real life to relax into."

"You sound like Sebastian."

"Give it another few years, Alec, you'll be looking for the same."

"I don't doubt it at all. Even now the buzz gets wearing, the constant pressure of so many people needing me for something. This has been the best day, Vaughn. A real day, in the real world."

"You have that with Sebastian though don't you?"

"Sometimes. We had a great time in Cornwall, until Daniel Merrimont discovered us, at least. Then everything got weird again. It's harder to find it in the City."

"But you like the life?"

"I love it. It's the strangest thing. I love the craziness and then in moments like this, I love the normality."

"I love that I actually wanted to fuck someone for the first time in so long. I hope I find someone like you to share my life with."

"I'll always be here for you, Vaughn. My first real date sex, it's like you took my virginity all over again."

"Now there's a thought that turns me on." Vaughn ground his hips against Alec's. "How about I fuck you again just for good measure?"

"I'm all yours, baby."

Alec wrapped his legs around Vaughn's hips and Vaughn guided his already hardening cock to Alec's pucker. "You need some more lube, sweetie?"

"With the amount of cum you've shot up my ass, I don't think I'll be needing any for a while."

"Such sexy talk," Vaughn chuckled, as he eased his way into Alec's body. "Can I just rest here a while?"

Alec moaned at a particularly clever wiggle of Vaughn's hips. "Stay as long as you want."

Vaughn draped himself over Alec's chest. "I don't want Harrison to know I fucked you, Alec," he said seriously. "He won't mind but I need some privacy in my life."

"Then it'll be our secret." Kisses were light and tender. Just enough to keep the passion on simmer without pushing it forward.

"I don't mind if you want to tell Sebastian, I know you guys are real together, but not Hamilton. Is that okay?"

"That's fine as long as you and Sebastian aren't going to sit discussing my ass over coffee."

"He fucks you?"

"I did say I wasn't always the perfect boy."

"Is that why Hamilton hits you, because you fuck around?"

The sigh that escaped Alec's chest was heavy. With Vaughn balls deep in his ass he could think of better things to talk about. "It's a bit more complicated than that."

"Another time then." Vaughn kissed the end of Alec's nose and smiled. "Let me get this show on the road." Vaughn started to move slowly, re-awakening the fire in the pit of Alec's stomach. The sounds of their passion filled the air as they moved together and Alec forgot once more all the other demands on his time and his heart and was there, in that moment, just for Vaughn.

Ups and Downs

Monday morning hadn't felt as good in a long time. An all-night sexfest with Sebastian did that to a man. After returning early Sunday afternoon from his date with Vaughn, Alec had lavished attention on his little slave boy and been carried away on yet more clouds of sexual ecstasy. His body ached in the very best way, inside and out, and his mind was sated. Seeing Hamilton waiting for him topped off his perfect mood.

Alec savored the kiss that greeted him from Hamilton after he climbed into the car. "What's that for?"

"Because I love you." Hamilton threaded their fingers together and Alec noticed Bradley sigh at the gesture.

"Good morning, Mr. Hamilton."

"Good morning, Bradley. How are you enjoying the twelfth so far?"

"It's been very quiet," Bradley smiled. "I'm sure things will pick up soon."

"I'd forgotten you aren't on full duties. I do apologize." Alec squeezed Hamilton's hand hoping he'd leave it at that.

"It's okay. I understand the reason and it's really helping me find a base."

"Excellent. Alec you should spend more time with Fraser today. He can take some of Bradley's work load for the next few weeks."

Alec felt Bradley's heavy sigh and tried not to feel guilty. Hamilton wasn't the most tactful and his timing was rubbish. Since Alec had returned from his date with Vaughn, blissed out and starry eyed, Bradley had been quiet. Alec had every intention of finding out what was going on once they made the privacy of their office. Somehow, he doubted an open conversation about Fraser would help smooth the path.

"I can pop in for coffee this morning." Alec squeezed Hamilton's hand again hoping he'd take the hint.

"Good, I miss our morning coffee rendezvous." Hamilton let his head fall on Alec's shoulder. "I miss having you outside the door."

They traveled the rest of the way in silence but Alec was aware of a light buzz of sexual tension in the air. Hamilton wanted him. Normally he would have had Alec sucking his cock in the car when this particular mood struck. He was obviously behaving for Bradley's sake.

In the lift, Hamilton stood in front of Alec, hand behind his back fondling Alec's cock. "Don't forget morning coffee," he said, getting out on the eighth floor without looking back.

Alec was relieved to make it behind closed doors. Bradley went straight to the coffee machine. "You didn't have to refrain from your usual activities for me, Alec."

"Is something wrong, Brad?"

"I'm not looking forward to another week without much going on, but I'm okay with it."

"Yeah, I don't have much admin for you to take care of yet. What about a training course? There's always something going on in the building."

"I'll have a look." Bradley handed Alec his coffee. Brazilian blend, black, no sugar. "You had a nice time with Vaughn. Is he going to be a regular now?"

"Ah, is that what this is about, why you've been so quiet?"

Bradley sat in one of the tub chairs, carefully schooling his features. It was an old trick and one Alec hoped he'd grow out of becoming a houseboy, but the shields were definitely in place this morning. "Am I quiet?"

"Don't lie to me Bradley. I know we're friends, but I'm also your master. I won't tolerate it."

Bradley stared into his coffee cup and took a deep breath. "I guess I feel a bit jealous."

"Of Vaughn?"

"Sort of."

"Spit it out before I decide to paddle your ass."

"*You* with Vaughn." Bradley's gaze was confrontational to say the least when he raised his eyes. "I know he fucked you. I can always tell when you've been fucked; it shows on your face."

"You what?"

"When you fuck around you get a glaze to your eyes. When you're on the end of the fucking, your eyes sparkle. You were well and truly sparkling when you got home yesterday and it just, I don't know, hurt I guess, that you'd let this guy you've known all of five minutes touch you but you don't let me."

Alec's brain stalled. He blinked a few times but couldn't think of anything to say.

"It's stupid. Ignore me. You're the master for fuck's sake." Bradley almost dropped his coffee shoving it on the table. "I'll go and see about some training."

"Stay right there."

Brad sat back down in slow motion and locked his hands in his lap. He looked worried. "Alec, I'm sorry. I shouldn't have said anything."

"I told you not to lie. It's good that you didn't."

"But now you're angry with me."

"I'm not. I... you caught me off guard. I'm torn between worrying how transparent I am and what you're saying about you. Does Sebastian know?"

"That I want to fuck you? I would think so. Not that we've discussed it."

"About Vaughn."

"If he figured it out, he didn't say anything. But he's good like that. He doesn't gossip."

"I won't lie, Vaughn did fuck me but it's not something we want to be common knowledge." *And none of your, or anyone else's, damn business.* Alec clamped down on the words, determined not to show how pissed he was. He didn't want Brad retreating any further. "Vaughn isn't an office boy and he likes his privacy. Only Harrison knows we went on a date and even he'll never know the extent of it. Do you understand?"

"It's a private thing that I'm not supposed to know. I get it. You can trust me, Alec."

"I'm just making sure you understand how important it is that nobody else knows. I don't want everyone knowing the ins and outs of my ass either." Alec sipped his coffee, trying to steady his nerves. "So am I really that obvious?"

Bradley smiled, just a little. "To me you are."

"That is so, not good." Alec stared into his cup. If everyone could tell every time he'd had a good seeing to, well, it was embarrassing and it certainly wouldn't do anything for Hamilton's delicate state.

"I should leave you to it." Brad seemed pissed but what was there to say to a sex-free-zone—here's a free pass for when you're back on the road?

"Bradley, it's not that I don't want you to."

"You don't have to explain anything to me, Master." The syllables in the title sounded forced. If ever there was a time Brad was going to rethink the setup, Alec guessed it would be sometime around now. Certainly during a period of forced celibacy.

"We need boundaries," Alec said, trying to draw him back into the conversation. "To establish boundaries first..."

"Thank you, for seeing I needed to talk."

A polite dismissal. Alec stared at the closed door for a while after Bradley left. What a mess. If Brad fucked him now it would seem like Alec felt obligated. He'd missed the perfect opportunity during Bradley's reward day. It would happen again at some point and Alec would make sure it was extra special. An evening alone, definitely. A chance for them to spend time together outside of the bedroom and the office, get to know each other better. Bit like his day out with Vaughn. A plan was emerging, a structure for balancing his life and his boys—all of them. He was lucky enough to have his weekends free. It would be easy to schedule a full day one to one with Sebastian and Bradley once a month. Hamilton was a full weekend and Harrison—he wouldn't want to see Alec on a weekend. As much as they cared for each other, it was all about the sex in that particular pairing. But Sebastian and Bradley deserved more and Alec was determined to give it to them.

Still lost to his thoughts, he jumped when his com chimed. "Alec, Mr. Worthington is here to see you."

Another opportunity he wouldn't miss again. Time to turn on the charm and take off his pants. "Send him in, Brad. Thanks."

One of the best things about Alec's new office was the exceptionally comfortable seating for every occasion. The large sofa and handful of chairs gave Rushton a run for its money. Admittedly, the carpet wasn't as sumptuous, the room not so big, and the view not so far-reaching but when it came to seduction-style comfort, this office had it in droves. Alec steered the greeting toward the sofa and made a point of sitting next to Worthington, placing a hand his knee. "Thanks again for taking such good care of me at Harrison's, Peter. You have no idea how much it meant to have you there."

"You're always welcome. I thought I'd stop by to see how things are balancing out. You haven't been around much lately."

Alec touched the mark on his cheek from where Hamilton had belted him. It was all but gone, though still smarted if he caught it unexpectedly. "Everything worked out great. We're in a good place thanks to you." *A boring vanilla place.*

"I'm relieved. I've never seen Hamilton in such a state."

"Peter, I meant what I said." Alec left a pause for effect and locked eyes with Worthington, edging just a little closer. "About wanting *you.*" Alec brushed his hand over Worthington's cock and leaned in to meet his slightly open lips.

"Alec, wait."

But Alec was already unzipping Worthington's pants, fondling his nicely swelling cock, and imagining it slipping into his ass. Alec wanted the tenderness, the care and attention, but more than that, he wanted to see Worthington lose it and fall into the depths of fierce passion. Alec wanted to take him to all the places he never seemed to go with the usual boys, beyond the place Bradley had touched into all out ecstasy.

"Alec, please. Not here."

"Why? No one will come in."

"Because you're not an office boy. Not to me."

It was enough to stop Alec in his tracks. Worthington was right. Damn and blast the man. This wasn't an office fuck. Alec just wanted him. He'd spent many years wanting and not being able to reach out, had grown used to wanting and knowing he'd never have. The last year had changed that. The last month had changed him even more. He'd lost his stop button, his pause to think about the consequences button somewhere along the way. Alec sat back and took in the man in front of him, really looked at him. Funny how time changes your perception. Worthington was still short, still balding and still slightly rounded but now his features were familiar. He represented warmth and safety, a place to find comfort and good advice. Alec was also on very good terms with Worthington's cock. That had started out as business and morphed into habit. There was a time when Worthington would have joined the queue to fuck Alec senseless. What had changed for him? Was it time to let this habit go or push into a new phase?

"Tell me what you want, Peter, and it's yours."

"An evening out. Dinner, a show maybe."

Alec smiled, such a sweet guy, and kissed his neck and chin, up to his ear. "As long as I get to suck you off in a very inappropriate place like the bad boy I am."

"You'll make me come, talking like that."

"Good. But before you do, I want you to fuck me until I beg and then fuck me some more."

"Oh, hell, Alec." Worthington squirmed and Alec slipped to the floor and sucked in the hardening cock, reveling in the groan that fell from Worthington's lips. He may not get his fuck today but he could still send Worthington into orbit. Alec swallowed, taking the head into his throat and Worthington shot his load earning him the quickest blowjob Alec had ever given. Alec grabbed the moist tissues and cleaned him up before tucking him away.

Worthington's breath was still evening out. His eyes slightly glazed. "You're very good at being bad."

"It's a new thing for me," Alec grinned. "But I think I might get to like it." He sat back on the sofa and leaned against Worthington's shoulder. "So, when are you taking me out?"

"You were being serious?"

Alec's sensitivities prickled. "Peter, do you honestly think I would tease you like that if I had no intention of following through? But if it's not something you want, don't feel obliged. I know Bradley is more your type."

"Now you're being silly."

Alec's temper slipped. "Do you want to fuck me or not? I can't make my come-ons any more obvious. Stop messing about and give me a straight yes or no."

Worthington stared for a moment. "I can't imagine anyone ever saying no to you, Alec. Maybe I should."

"*Again*, you mean. It's not the first time you've knocked me back. I suppose I should take the hint." Alec stood and walked to the window, his good mood well and truly scuppered. "Thanks for stopping by, Peter. I appreciate your concern."

"Alec…"

"You don't have to explain. Everything is good." Alec fought the huge knot in his stomach and willed away the heat of embarrassment flushing his cheeks. He wanted the stupid old git so much and yet it wasn't enough. And what was it with his soft spot for the fatherly types? He'd made a complete idiot of himself. *Daniel Merrimont all over again. When are you going to accept you're not god's gift, dickhead?* He jumped at the touch of Worthington's hand on his shoulder. "It's better if you leave, Peter."

"Not until you listen to me. Come and sit down." Worthington's hand slipped off Alec's shoulder and took hold of his hand. "Please."

Alec sighed and followed like the good boy he really was. Worthington sat him on the sofa, taking up a perch next to him and keeping hold of his hand. "Alec, I think I made it clear at the party that I'm very fond of you, so don't think for one minute I'm not interested in what you're offering me."

"Then what? Why don't you want me?"

"You don't know what you want at the moment. You're bouncing off the walls and jumping in and out of so many beds, men telling you how wonderful you are, but what's it doing for you?"

"What's wrong with having some fun?"

"Nothing. You should. But it's not my thing."

"Rubbish. You fuck around all the time. I met you at a bloody sex party, Peter. I've been sucking your cock for the best part of a year. Don't tell me it's not your *thing*."

"There's fucking for the sake of it, or as obligation, and there's fucking because you want to. You aren't an office boy anymore, Alec. You're not on my list of obligatory fucks I have to work through to keep my name in the running for company perks."

"I don't understand what you're saying to me."

"If I … it would mean something, Alec, to me. You know my history. I can't do it unless I know for sure you're in a place where it means something real to you too. Call me old fashioned, or just plain stupid, but I don't want to take advantage of you when you have so much going on. I'll always be here for you, you can talk to me about anything, ask me anything, but if you really want me to have sex with you, you need to give me time."

"I don't let just anyone, you know."

"I do, and I'm flattered. I can't believe I'm not just doing it but please, wait a while for your life to settle down and then we can see where we are. Okay?"

Alec knew he was pouting but he didn't care. "Can we still go out?"

Worthington chuckled and pulled Alec into a hug. "You are so lovely, but you know that. Yes, I'll take you out. One evening next week."

"I'm sorry I'm such a basket case at the moment. And you're right, after so many years of being useless in the sex department I'm in this strange world where nobody says no to me, at least not often. So thank you, for saying no, twice."

"You aren't going to let me forget it, are you?"

"Nope."

Alec relaxed against Worthington's chest. Warmth, safety and good advice. He wanted something else but the package as it stood was more than satisfactory. They both jumped as the door to the office opened and a rabid Hamilton flew in. "What happened to morning coffee? Too busy to see me, are you?"

"Rick, what on earth?"

Bradley appeared at the door, closing it and apologizing for not being able to stop the intrusion. Worthington was on his feet and holding back a furious Hamilton who looked set to pummel Alec into the ground. Alec could only stare, the stream of obscenities falling from Hamilton's lips turning the air blue. He ran out of steam, his breathing heavy. "Mine, Alec, you're *mine.*"

"Rick, you have to calm down. Peter was just leaving. Another ten minutes and I'd have been with you."

"I haven't seen you all weekend and now you're more interested in entertaining in your fancy new office than keeping your meetings with me."

"Peter, I'll talk to you later. It's better if we deal with this on our own. Bradley, make sure we're not disturbed."

Alec wrapped his arms around Hamilton. He watched the two men leave and rubbed a hand over Hamilton's back to calm him. "I am yours. If you want me to give up this job, I will. Just say it, Rick. Whatever you need."

Hamilton buried his head in Alec's shoulder. "I feel as though everything is falling apart."

"A few more weeks and we have a whole month together away from everyone. Can you hold it together until then?"

Hamilton's shoulders slumped and he let out a heavy sigh. "I don't know what happened. I'm sorry. The thought of you up here with someone else's cock in your mouth, or worse."

"I did give Peter a blowjob, but it's not why he dropped by. He wanted to make sure everything was okay with us."

"And I fucked it up again. The man must think I'm having a breakdown."

"I think he thinks we both are. He'd just finished talking me down from a tantrum and you burst into the office having one of your own."

"What was yours about?"

"Not getting my own way and likely brought on by the thought of you having Fraser at your beck and call when it should be me."

"Alec, what are we going to do? They'll fire both of us if we can't keep it together."

"Deep breathing for a few weeks. By the time we get back from Australia it won't be a problem."

"And you think we'll make it 'til then?"

"I hope so," Alec said, rubbing his hands over Hamilton's upper arms. "I'm starting to get used to the apartment. It would be a shame to have to move again."

They spent an hour cuddled together, chatting and laughing about the craziness of their overactive minds. No sex, just reassurance. It felt good. It felt right. Away from everything else they were getting to know each other in a new way. It brought out a craving in Alec for just this, one partner, one love to spend all day, every day thinking about. If Hamilton was his alone, no fucking at work, no sex parties, Alec was sure he wouldn't be constantly adding to his own list of conquests. He wouldn't need to. And there he was, back to square one wanting something he couldn't have. Would monogamy be so different? Regardless, it didn't seem possible in their world.

The day was ticking on. Alec didn't want to interrupt their time for Fraser but he knew it was a necessity. He had meetings over the next few days that would need a sweetener. With Bradley out of action, he'd need to call on Fraser to entertain his clients. He needed to know Fraser's preferences before he made any decisions regarding contractual benefits.

"Are you sure Fraser doesn't mind working for me this week?"

Hamilton chuckled. "Fraser has been crushing on you for months, so my sources tell me. He's desperate to get up here in the hope you'll spend plenty of time with your cock up his ass."

"Oh." Alec certainly hadn't picked up that vibe from anyone on the office grapevine. "Are you sure?"

"Well, I haven't asked him directly, but he does blush when I mention you."

"I've only met him once or twice."

"You obviously have a reputation." Hamilton sat up and patted Alec's knee. "Anyway, I have to get back to work. I'll send him up."

"Okay. Just me and you tonight and I'll stay at yours. All night."

"Perfect. I'll apologize to Peter when I see him, *again*."

So many "agains" with Worthington for both of them. Hamilton's outburst would have put back by months any hope Alec had of getting Worthington into bed, but that was probably for the best. What Alec needed more than fuck buddies were friends. Like Tristan and Freddie and yes, Worthington, a man that offered advice and support wanting nothing in return. "I think he's getting used to us now."

"It's lucky it was him, anyone else wouldn't have thought to hold me back and you'd be nursing another black eye." Alec squeezed Hamilton's shoulder. "Alec, do you think I should see someone?"

"What do you mean?"

"Anger management or some such thing. I've never been a violent man. I don't know why I keep lashing out at you."

"I guess it's something we shouldn't get used to or allow to escalate but I wouldn't know where to start."

"I'll see what I can find. I love you, you know that, right?"

Alec accepted the kiss. He did know it, sort of. In the moments Hamilton looked at him through murderous eyes, not so much, but right now he knew it was true.

Alec saved the files he was preparing for the next day's meetings and swiveled his seat to stare out the window. Complications were part of life, he didn't mind dealing with stuff but things were taking a dangerous turn. It wasn't that Hamilton had found an itch for domestic violence as much as Alec's ability to explain it away. Rationalizing the irrational and unacceptable was just as much of a problem as the problem itself. His mother had taught him that one. Maybe he needed to see somebody too, find out why his need for ownership had slipped into thinking it was okay to be a victim because the truth of it was, after such a weird week with Stepford Hamilton, part of Alec had been relieved at the potential beating. Just seeing some real emotion in him had been exhilarating. His master was back. The wrong master, for sure, but a master none the less. However, the thought of having a professional sorting through his cock-eyed life sent shivers through his body and Alec pressed it firmly to the back of his mind. A problem for another day.

The comm chimed and Bradley announced Fraser's arrival. The meeting could go several ways. Alec would either like the guy on a variable scale or hate him. Only one way to find out.

Alec stood to greet Fraser. He looked terrified. "Hello again, Fraser."

"Mr. Caldwell, sir."

"Please, take a seat." Alec sat on the sofa and gestured to one of the tub chairs. He had no idea how to handle the situation. Fraser looked as uncomfortable as Alec felt as he sat down. He blushed when he looked up and met Alec's gaze. "Do you know why you're here?"

"Yes, sir. Mr. Hamilton said you need an extra service person for your meetings this week."

"How long have you been an office boy?"

"Just over a year now, sir. I've plenty of experience."

"Then why are you so nervous?"

"I don't know. Because it's you, I think."

Late afternoon sun picked up the auburn highlights in Fraser's hair that had always looked jet black until now. Exquisite bone structure and large, dark eyes gave him an otherworldly glow. Spending the afternoon with his cock buried in Fraser's shapely ass didn't seem like such a chore after all. Alec leaned forward on his knees and watched Fraser's breathing ratchet up a notch. Alec held his gaze. The color blossomed deeper across Fraser's cheeks. Definite crush, just how Alec used to be with Hamilton. What a turn up for the books. The kid would be useless with clients like this. Alec would have to fuck him to ease the tension. On the other hand, he didn't look like he had a reaction in his pants, not the fight Alec used to have around Hamilton and the days of saying his timetables backward to keep his mind on the job. "Do you fancy me, Fraser?"

"I'm sorry?"

"The blushing and heavy breathing you've got going on there. Is it because you find me attractive?"

Fraser looked at his hands and gripped his knees a little tighter.

"You can tell me the truth. I need to know if you're going to be like this whenever we're together."

"You are ... I mean, it is ... oh shit." Fraser took a deep breath and looked up. "I've heard so much about you, that's all, and Hamilton, *Mister* Hamilton is always saying how great you are and ... it's intimidating."

"Hamilton has a very biased opinion." Alec sat back and grinned. "I'm no different to anyone else. Do you fuck?"

"Yes, sir."

"There you go then. You're already better at the job than I was. I

126

only ever gave oral service and believe me, some of the clients were not happy about it."

"I didn't know that was an option."

"Would you have taken it, if it was?"

Dimples creased Fraser's cheeks as he smiled. "Probably not."

"So, what can we do to ease you into your time with me? I have three clients tomorrow who will expect some kind of service to seal the deal and several scattered across the remaining days this week including a small syndicate meeting. You should tell me what you like so I know what to offer."

"What I like?"

"Are there things you don't do, a certain type of man you don't like? Is three in a day too many to fuck? We need to work together."

After a little shuffling to get more comfortable, Fraser shrugged. "No one's ever asked me before."

"In an ideal world then, what would you be doing for me? Or the client, rather." Alec returned Fraser's cheeky smile. *Warming up nicely.*

"I guess I'm not a fan of oral with strangers. Regulars are okay but if it's a new client or a one off I'd rather they just fuck me." He shrugged, showing the dimples again with a grin. "I get more out of it that way. Other than that, three is probably my limit. Hamilton has had me take more but I'd rather not, if that's okay?"

"I'd prefer to stay within your comfort zone." Cute kid. Though in reality he was probably older than Alec. The dimples were a knockout, the hair longer on top than it should be but it suited him, added to the exotic look. There wouldn't be many clients refusing such a pretty package; he'd definitely be good for business. "So, do you like sucking off Hamilton?"

"Huh?"

"Does he suck you too?"

"I'm not sure I'm supposed to discuss those things with you, Mr. Caldwell."

"Come on, I used to be in your shoes. Don't think of me as a manager, I'm just another office boy that made good. How do you like being fucked by Hamilton?"

"Honestly?" Fraser looked at his hands again and tapped his knees before looking back at Alec. "Mr. Hamilton has only fucked me once, when I first started with him the other week. He hasn't touched me since, or asked for service."

Well, fucking hells bells. Alec sat with his mouth open. Right now, he could kiss Fraser from head to toe and give him the blowjob of his life for sharing that information.

"Will you be fucking me, sir? Or I could service you."

"I'm okay at the moment, thank you, Fraser. But don't worry; I'm sure the opportunity will arise." *Just not while I'm basking in the glow of my fiancé's ability to resist the temptation of your charms. And your charming ass.*

"Can I ask you a personal question, Mr. Caldwell?"

"You can ask, I won't guarantee to answer it."

"It's just that you still see Mr. Hamilton quite a bit." Fraser looked down and started picking a fingernail. "Is it because he doesn't like me?"

"He speaks very highly of you, Fraser. You wouldn't be here otherwise. You should smile more often," Alec said, grinning himself. "Those dimples are sexy as hell."

Fraser flushed a glorious shade of pink that contrasted his olive skin beautifully and Alec leaned back in his seat with a chuckle. Happy man. Despite his earlier hiccups with Bradley, Worthington and Hamilton, Alec was a very happy man indeed.

Stallions and Sweethearts

A very successful outcome. Alec sat back on the sofa and watched a rather embarrassed, very well-spoken Earl attempt to spear a naked Fraser. Fraser stretched out on his back, legs in the air, obviously enjoying the attention. He made the most endearing noises with a cock up his ass and it was driving this particular member of the nobility very close to the edge, very quickly. His business associates jibed him about his lack of stamina and he blushed even more. Fraser had been a rock star all week. Perfect service, an amazing ability to pick up on what clients wanted and a very successful negotiator in his own right around the table. Alec was in half a mind to ask Hamilton to transfer him permanently. His dark dusky coloring contrasted so well with Brad's blond summer surfer look, Alec would be able to cover most bases as far as clients' tastes were concerned between them.

Alec glanced around to see one of the syndicate members sit next to him. Dark, brooding looks, tall and well built. A very nice package all on his own. "Is everything to your satisfaction Mr. Viera?"

"Please, call me Sal." The husky Spanish accent caressed Alec's ears and made him sigh. "Your boy is very beautiful and I don't doubt your proposals will make us a lot of money."

"I can bring in another boy if you'd rather not wait."

"I let my colleagues play." Viera flicked his hand in the direction of the performance. "It's not for me."

Darn. Alec had never come across a client that didn't want the incentive. Should he offer a girl or would that be too pushy, and then where would he get one if Viera said yes? Viera stroked his hand along

Alec's thigh in a way that suggested a woman wouldn't be necessary after all.

"I don't go in for the public displays of virility. They tease me about it all the time," he shrugged, "but, it's just not my thing."

"That certainly places you in a select group." A non-existent group in the Order up to this point in Alec's experience.

A smile lit up Viera's face and made his eyes sparkle. "Just the way I like it. Tell me about yourself, Alexander. Do you indulge? I notice you're wearing a wedding ring."

"It's an engagement ring." Alec ran his fingers over the diamond and smiled. "My partner and I both indulge a little when the mood takes us."

"An open relationship? Very modern. And you don't have a problem with other men tasting your woman?"

"My man, actually." Alec smirked at the look on Viera's face. "And no, I don't mind. He always comes home to me."

"Is yours a business indulgence," he said, leaning closer to Alec and sliding his arm along the back of the sofa. "Or do you play privately?"

Alec squared up to him. "Are you asking me on a *date*?"

Viera laughed. "If that's what it takes to get an evening alone with you, then yes. Dinner perhaps? Or will I need to whisk you away for an exotic weekend on my private jet?"

Hot breath rolled over Alec's neck and nose-dived straight to his cock. Smooth, very smooth indeed. *He's just going to fuck you and throw you away*, the angel on his shoulder screamed. *So fucking what* said the devil.

"I've bamboozled you," Viera said, twisting a finger in Alec's hair. "Surely you must have men coming on to you all the time. You are far more enticing than your little office boy and I would imagine a far rarer prize."

"You're the first." Alec didn't let on this was technically only his second week in such high-riding circles.

"Oh, I do love to be first. Name your price, Alexander, and I will gladly pay it. Lunch in Paris, dinner in Rome, a car?" Viera let his lips trail over Alec's neck and he shivered. Serious cock swell. "A diamond grander than the one on your finger? Anything at all for an evening of your undivided attention."

Fraser let out a particularly loud groan that broke Viera's spell. Alec straightened in his seat. "I'm flattered, really. But it's not the kind of entertaining I take care of."

"Forget business. The deal is signed and sealed already. This is purely for pleasure." Viera stroked Alec's crotch, kneading his cock. "Your pleasure, Alexander, as well as mine."

It was a miracle Alec hadn't already dropped his pants and spread his cheeks. Viera's voice was hypnotic. Would it be so bad to bend over for a slap of luxury? Alec gasped as Viera's nimble fingers jacked him through his pants. *Fucking hell.* The comm chimed and Alec startled out of his daze.

"Excuse me." He jumped to his feet and took refuge behind his desk taking the headset to minimize any background noise from Fraser. "Caldwell."

"Alec, sorry to bother you in the middle of your meeting," Bradley said sheepishly, "but Hamilton wants to know if you're free for dinner this evening. He insisted I interrupt you."

A saving grace. "No problem, Bradley. Tell him I'll be leaving at the usual time. We can share the car."

"That Spanish guy is gorgeous. I'm so jealous Fraser gets to do him and not me."

"Never say never." Alec replaced the headset and debated his next move. The last of the men was still fucking Fraser so he couldn't end the meeting. It would be rude not to return to the sofa; on the other hand, if he sat next to that man again he'd be well and truly fucked in every which way. Alec met Viera's questioning gaze and smiled. *Backbone of steel, backbone of steel.* Despite his own warning flags, he took up his seat next to the Spanish stallion. Alec didn't need this man's indulgence. He was earning more money than he had time to spend, had an unlimited credit card he didn't have to pay off, a very nice car, and a multimillion-pound apartment. What else did he need? Not that he wasn't enjoying the attention but he wouldn't be bought. Any more than he already was. And not by a stranger.

"So, Alexander, do we have a date?" The guy's smile curved suggestively and he leaned in again to kiss along Alec's neck.

"Why don't I give you my business card?"

Viera paused for a moment then moved closer to whisper. "Is it not appropriate to arrange such a meeting in front of your colleague?"

Alec shook his head once and Viera sat back, smiling in acknowledgment. They waited out the rest of the show with general conversation. When Fraser headed into the shower, Viera asked his associates to wait for him in the lobby. He hovered for a moment then stepped in close to Alec, slipped one hand around his waist and let the other ride the crack of Alec's ass. "Tell me you want me as much as I want you."

"Sal, I—"

Viera spun Alec around and pushed him over the desk. He pressed over the full length of Alec's body and ground his hips. Viera forced a hand underneath Alec's body and squeezed his traitor cock, swelling with every shuddery breath.

"Yes, I feel it too," Viera purred. "The adrenaline. The excitement. We will be so hot together. You like it rough, yes? I sense that in you."

Alec could only groan in answer. The weight of Viera was driving him toward the edge, the inability to move, to fight against his bulk. God the man was pure sex. Every breath on Alec's neck pushed him closer, every thrust against his ass increased his need to feel Viera wedged as far into his body as Alec could take him and then a little further. Alec only cottoned on that his pants were around his ankles and his ass spread when Viera slipped to his knees and licked Alec's pucker. He kissed and licked Alec's balls, tongued his hole and stepped back. Alec was waiting for the breach, the stallion's rock hard member skewering him to the desk, but Viera hauled him up and pulled up his pants.

"You are my choice, Alexander." He kept Alec against his chest and reached around to tuck in Alec's shirt. "I hope one day soon, I will be yours. Say you want me."

"I want you, fuck, do I want you."

"Good boy. Go and play your little domestic game at home with your husband. The fire in your soul belongs to me." He squeezed Alec's cock and let go. When he stepped away, Alec felt cold. He hoped to god Hamilton was on form tonight or he'd never get this super smooth fucker out of his head. Alec turned to look at Viera. The passion blazed in the man's eyes and Alec's knees wobbled. "Remember, anything you want. I will pay you any price."

"I don't need anything."

"We all want something, Alexander. Have needs and desires we try to ignore. If you don't tell me what you want I will find out for myself and surprise you."

And didn't *that* sound promising. "I'll think about it."

"Do that." Viera handed him a card. "My private cell. I can collect you within a few hours of your call. Don't leave it too long or I'll come to collect on that promise and I won't be gentle."

Alec was still looking at the card, his hand trembling, when Fraser appeared looking very clean and shiny. Viera was already gone.

Sweat pooled at the base of Alec's spine and he stretched out lazily, rolling onto his back to let the linen sheets take up the excess moisture from his skin. Hamilton was on form and then some. No vanilla on the menu so far this evening and boy, did it feel good. No one came close to reading Alec's body like Hamilton, especially when they unplugged from the rest of the world. Sure, Viera had spun a little magic, fanned a few sparks, made Alec lose track of his thoughts for a few minutes but he'd just lost an hour or more at the hands of his master and he was still feeling light headed.

Alec smiled at the slow sensual slide of Hamilton's foot along the inside line of his arm. "You seem troubled, Alec."

"Not troubled, just thinking." *Thinking how much better you are than a certain Spanish someone.* Alec turned over and returned a stroking motion along Hamilton's thigh, ending with his fingers twisting in the damp curls along the base of his cock. "Do you know Sal Viera?"

"Ah, you've met the real life Casanova? I've given you my everything and your mind is spinning fantasies of Mister Tall, Dark and Extremely Handsome. I should be offended but I'm too exhausted to care."

Alec crawled over Hamilton's body, tracing a line with his tongue over the perfect torso, along his neck and finishing with a slow, sloppy kiss. "Mmm, nothing compares to that." Alec settled comfortably to the side and traced lines over Hamilton's chest. "I don't need to spin fantasies. I have everything I need right here."

"Then why do you ask?"

"I met him today. He got a little frisky. Promised me the world if he could have me. Sexy as hell but I was thinking he has nothing on you."

"I'm sure I'll be relieved when I have the energy."

"I fell for practically every one of his cheesy lines. I'm annoyed with myself for being so easy."

Hamilton lifted onto his elbows. "He fucked you already?"

"No, of course not." Alec pushed him back down into the pillows. "I'm not a complete slut you know."

"But you want him to."

"I did at the time. I don't *now*."

Hamilton chuckled. "The man with the silver tongue strikes again."

In oh, so many ways. "He said he'd give me anything for a night alone together."

"Did he promise the private jet?"

It was Alec's turn for a little indignation. "Has he come on to you as well?" That was something he couldn't bear to think about. Surely Hamilton couldn't be won over by such cheesy moves.

"I've never had the pleasure but I've heard the rumors and the warnings."

"Warnings?"

Hamilton nestled closer. "Sweet young things having their hearts broken. He wines and dines, promises the world, fucks them into heaven and never calls."

"That's a good thing." Alec stretched to let Hamilton's kisses work further along his neck. "Who'd want that sleaze around fulltime?" A one-time fuck would be more than enough for Alec, and even that was looking less appetizing by the moment. There was nothing worse in Alec's mind than being just another notch on a player's bedpost. He'd thought that's what he was to Hamilton at one point and he knew he didn't want to go there again. Fucking around was one thing, but it had to be for his own victory dance. Or Hamilton's. Maybe. Likely at some point. Alec noted the interest his cock had in the thought of Hamilton handing him over to a stranger. Not friends or business associates. Someone anonymous. He'd thought about it before. Definite cock swell happening. Undeniably more arousing right now than Mr. Viera and his silver tongue.

"Am I not exciting enough for you anymore, darling?"

"You know very well it's nothing of the sort." Alec pushed his current train of thought from his head and reached over to stroke Hamilton's cock. Still his favorite. "What would you do?"

"Turn the tables. Ask for the most extravagant thing you can think of and shrug it off when he gives it to you. Fuck him into tomorrow and then walk away before he does."

Alec pondered for a moment. "You mean ask for his ass?"

Hamilton laughed. "Not quite what I had in mind. But you could have any ass you wanted, darling. You took mine after all. You have no idea how many have begged me for it over the years."

"And I love that I have it. You want me to give it a good pounding for you right now?"

Hamilton rolled them over and settled between Alec's legs. "I think I should be the one pounding. Just to make sure you remember me over your Spanish sweetheart."

Alec squirmed as Hamilton brushed light lips over his ticklish spot. "He may be a smooth talking stallion but you are my only sweetheart, sweetheart."

"Let's hope for my sanity, that remains so for the foreseeable future."

"'Til death us do part, Rick, and on into forever."

Saturday's were so much more relaxing living just down the hall. Brendan and Dylan had gone to Alec's for brunch with Sebastian and Bradley while Alec remained at Hamilton's for a little one-on-one. There had been some debate over how long to leave Viera on hold but now seemed like the perfect opportunity to court a response. It could go either way, but if Alec was collected for a night of Spanish passion, Hamilton would at least have his hands full with the boys. Hamilton tried to sneak out of the bedroom but Alec dragged him back and sat him at the head of the bed so he'd hear the full conversation.

"Just remember not to laugh," he said, poking Hamilton in the ribs.

The phone only rang twice. "Alexander, you are free today?"

"I know what I want."

Silence.

"How much does it cost to fly one of your dates to some place exotic, wine and dine them and lavish them with gifts?"

"Twenty thousand, thirty. The cost doesn't matter. It is the time that is precious."

"Then I want you to donate forty thousand pounds to the charity of my choice plus, and this is the deal clincher ..."

"Go on, it is yours, whatever you ask of me."

"I want you."

"You have me."

"No, you don't understand. I want to fuck you first." Alec leaned forward and placed a finger against Hamilton's lips when he looked as though he'd say something. Hamilton smiled and opened his mouth to suck it in, stumbling Alec's train of thought.

Viera laughed bringing Alec back to the task in hand and then went quiet. Alec let the silence hang in the air. After a long pause Viera spoke. "You're serious?"

"Very. I'm not interested in your wealth. If you want me, you have to give something real. I want the man not the money."

"Out of the question."

A quick enough response to know it wasn't worth trying persuasion. Alec was bored with this game already, especially when someone much more enticing was currently wrapping his tongue around Alec's finger. "Then my next call will be to update you on the progress of your portfolio. Have a pleasant day, Mr. Viera."

Alec hung up the phone and took a deep breath. *Fuck.* He'd never played it cool in his life. It felt good. He turned back to Hamilton who'd let go of Alec's finger and was grinning like an idiot. "My Spanish sweetheart doesn't want me after all. Looks like I'll have to settle for something a little more domesticated."

Hamilton rolled onto his stomach and wriggled his ass. "It's all yours, darling, to take as you please."

Alec reached down and bit Hamilton's butt cheek, letting his hands massage the firm globes of flesh. "It had better damned well stay that way," he murmured, more to himself than to Hamilton. Hamilton rocked back into Alec's hands.

"I'll never be anyone else's, Alec."

God, Alec wanted to carve his name in that ass, so perfect, so completely his. The words repeated over and over in his head—*never be anyone else's*—and he wouldn't. Alec wouldn't allow it, *couldn't* allow it. The one thing that was his and his alone. The priceless gift of his master's body and he wanted it. Wanted to bury himself so deep Hamilton would feel him for the rest of the week. For the rest of forever. He spread Hamilton's cheeks and added a little spit, tongued around his rim and added some more. A few tugs of Alec's cock brought him to full hardness and he nestled between Hamilton's strong thighs and prepared to ride him all the way to heaven and back. They groaned together with the breach, one firm stroke to the hilt, relishing the drag and burn from spit alone. Alec rested over Hamilton's back. "This is where I always want to be," he whispered. "Don't ever let anyone take my place."

Hamilton writhed beneath him, pushing for more depth, rocking into the bed. "Only you."

Alec felt the shift. A deepening—a loosening—a breaking down of another layer that had previously held them in established roles. "That's it, sweetheart," Alec whispered. "*Now* you're mine." Hamilton's body unfolded beneath him and they fell into each other losing the world and everything around them to their passions.

Turning Tables

The weekend finally began. A long, hot shower and clothes—shock, horror—so rare at home for so long, but Alec wanted to check on the boys and the new neighbors who had moved in the week before. They were an unknown quantity and he had temporarily suspended nakedness in the hall.

"I like you in that color," Hamilton said, handing him a cup of coffee.

"Mom always said I looked good in lilac." Alec brushed the front of his polo shirt. Some designer label or other. "Sebastian bought this one. At least I think he did. New clothes seem to turn up randomly in my wardrobe."

"Ah, our little fashionista." Hamilton followed the same path over the front of the shirt and ended by squeezing Alec's hand. "He should be a personal stylist."

"I'm going over there now. I'll be spending the day with Brad and then I think it's time to release him back into the world."

"Send the others over, Sebastian too if you want some alone time with Bradley. I'm going to the club this evening if you want him to join us."

"He does need a work out. I'll let you know later." Alec handed his empty cup back to Hamilton. "Thanks, sugar." He winked and had to jump out the way of Hamilton's playful lunge to slap his ass.

"I think you need to be reminded of who the master is in this relationship, young man."

"I'll look forward to that." Alec kissed Hamilton's cheek, grabbed a piece of toast from the counter, and headed out the door.

Clothes had been a very good choice. He barreled headlong into a tall slender woman, all six foot and the rest of her, who squeaked with surprise. "I'm so sorry," Alec said, dropping his toast and sending the packet she'd been carrying flying. He reached for the parcel and handed it back. "Not the best way to meet. I'm Alec. 3B."

"Tessa." She held out her hand, a shy smile spreading across her face. "3A. You know 3E by the looks of it."

"Oh. That's Rick." Too soon to say whether it was safe to add details. "And Patrick lives in 3F."

"That's a lot of boys on the floor." She chuckled and flushed a fraction of a shade darker. There were no determinable age references in Tessa's appearance. She could have been eighteen, or thirty with a good skin care routine. Immaculately presented in an expensive looking skirt suit, cut tastefully to the knee in an odd shade of brown that made her red hair look redder, Alec thought she was probably on her way to work. With her heels, she was a good three inches taller than he was. "Do you live alone?"

"Me? No there are three of us."

"Three? Sounds complicated."

"Oh, not like that, well, actually it is ... but ..." Alec finally gave up and shrugged. "Yeah, it's complicated."

Tessa chuckled. "Well, I have to go. Maybe you can introduce me to the neighbors later? Daddy said to make sure I knew everyone just in case I need help at some point."

Ah, obviously a GC daddy. Real father or sugar daddy was the question. Alec studied her again but couldn't place any kind of resemblance. "Would I know your father?"

"I think you know him very well, Alec." She flushed again, but smiled. "I'm Tessa Harrison. My father is Edward."

"Oh, hell." Alec's turn to blush.

"I'm looking forward to meeting Bradley. I think he must be one of your 'three'?"

Alec couldn't think of anything else to say. She pinched his cheek and left. "Don't forget your toast," she called out, waving a hand over her head.

"Damn, that's embarrassing." Alec picked up his breakfast and scuffed the butter stain into the carpet. No doubt Bradley would find it hilarious.

"Hey, Brad. Where is everyone?"

Brad smiled and came over to greet Alec with a kiss. "Good morning, Master. The boys are torturing Sebastian."

"Oh, okay. You'll never guess who's moved in next door." Brad shrugged. "Harrison's daughter, or one of 'em anyway. Real beauty too."

"I guess naked in the hall is back on the menu then."

"I dunno, she looks pretty young. Anyway, time for you to get dressed, I'm taking you out for the day."

"Anywhere in particular?"

"Haven't decided yet. I thought we needed some quality time. You get ready, I'll check on the boys."

Oh, yes. That was Sebastian's squeal all right. But as soon as Alec opened the door, he wished he hadn't. His jaw dropped as he took in the sight of Dylan plowing into Sebastian and Sebastian shooting a trail of pearly cum over Brendan's face.

"Sebastian!"

"Oh fuck." Possibly Dylan's voice, Alec was too stunned to distinguish.

Sebastian untangled himself from the action and threw himself on the floor at Alec's feet, arms stretched over his head to grab Alec's ankle. "I'm sorry, Master. Please, *please*, forgive me."

"Alec—"

"Shut the *fuck* up." Alec glared at Brendan. "You come into *my* house, with *my* boy and push him beyond the rules laid down by his master. Don't you dare, speak to me. I'll see to it that Hamilton deals with you later."

Alec was shaking with rage. Of all the people to shaft him, Sebastian was the last on the list he'd come up with. The fucking he could deal with, the boys were only stepping in where Bradley had left off, but coming without Alec's permission, and on a day when he was around—that was a step too far. That was breaking their only contract. It's not as if the cheating little wretch had gone for days without any attention. Alec had only fucked him the day before. "How many times?"

"Master, I'm sorry."

"How many *times*, Sebastian, have you been unfaithful to me?" Alec grabbed Sebastian's hair and lifted his head so he would look at him but he refused to meet Alec's gaze. "Look at me before I throw you out!"

Sebastian's eyes shot to Alec's. The fear and uncertainty in them cut through Alec but he wouldn't back down, not for this. Alec waited for an answer but instead he got tears. Sebastian broke into huge wracking sobs and Alec let him go. He looked back to Dylan and Brendan cowering on the bed. "Get out, both of you. And don't you *ever* touch him again without my permission. Do you understand?"

They answered together in the affirmative and left quickly.

"You *will* stay in your room for the rest of the day and think about what you've done."

"Please, don't leave me here on my own."

"You will stay on your own because I can't trust you to be with company. I'll decide on your punishment when I can stand to look at you again."

Alec closed the door and left Sebastian to his tears. He turned away but found he couldn't move. His feet stayed glued in place, his heart shattered. Everything had seemed so real with Sebastian, not just a game of master and slave, they loved each other, lived it day to day. What the fuck had gone wrong?

"Hey." Alec let Bradley wrap him in his arms. "I didn't know they'd push him that far."

"It's my fault. He's obviously unhappy and I didn't see it." Alec rubbed his forehead on Bradley's shoulder. "Why didn't he ask me? I wouldn't have said no if he wanted to have some free time."

"Perhaps it just happened. You know how hard it is sometimes to hold back."

"That was premeditated. He couldn't look at me, Brad. I bet he's been fucking at work too."

"He wouldn't do that."

"And how do I know? It's not as if I can believe what he says."

"Alec, it was one mistake."

"I have to see Hamilton. Come on, grab some clothes."

Hamilton was looking more than a little perplexed. Dylan and Brendan were on their knees, heads to the floor. "They won't tell me what's happened," he said. "I don't know whether to be angry or worried."

"*I'm* angry with them. You shouldn't necessarily be. It's Sebastian who's in the wrong."

"No," Brendan said before Dylan pushed him. "I made him." Dylan shoved Brendan again. "Please, Alec, don't punish him. It was my fault."

"Will someone tell me what the *hell* is going on?" Hamilton demanded.

Alec choked back the emotions clogging his throat and took a deep breath. "I walked in on the three of them fucking, no surprise there, but Sebastian isn't allowed to come without my permission under *any* circumstances unless he's given leave, which he didn't have. The flaky remnants of love-paint over Brendan's face belong to Sebastian."

"And you're angry with the boys for …?"

"They weren't necessarily to know Sebastian's rules, Rick. But I don't expect to be interrupted or challenged when I deal with insubordination on my own ground."

"Dylan, what happened? You, at least, have the sense to tell the unadulterated version of events."

"Master, I did ask Sebastian if he was sure it was okay for me to fuck him without asking Alec. He said it was."

"It's fine, Dylan, really," Alec said. "That part I understand. Sebastian doesn't have permission to fuck anyone other than Brad, but the lines are blurred with you guys especially with Brad being out of the picture. I'm not angry at you or Sebastian for that."

"Thank you, Alec. I'm still sorry though, for not checking first."

"And Sebastian came by accident?" Hamilton asked hopefully.

"No, Master." Dylan hung his head. "We didn't think Alec would find out."

"So you encouraged it?"

"We both did, Master, and Sebastian gave in to us. We are the ones who should be punished, for embarrassing you with our bad behavior in another master's house when we've been trusted with his boy."

"I was teasing him." Brendan barely got the words out. "I said Alec didn't need him anymore, now he had his new job and Bradley."

"For fuck's sake, Brendan. You know how sensitive he is about being given away." Alec cringed inwardly remembering his own words—*before I throw you out.*

"I'm so sorry, Alec, you know how my mouth runs away with me. I don't know why I'm so mean to Sebastian."

"Okay," Hamilton said, stroking Alec's arm. "Do you want me to speak to Sebastian?"

"No, I'll deal with it."

Hamilton smiled. "Very well. But I'm here if you need me. As for you two," he said, turning back to the boys, "you'll go to your room and await your punishment."

The boys scattered. Alec let go of a heavy breath that shuddered through his chest. He was close to tears himself. From anger, disappointment and now guilt. Guilt for turning the knife Brendan had so kindly stabbed through Sebastian's heart.

"Alec," Hamilton lifted his chin. "What else is bothering you?"

"He's done it before. I saw it in his face. He couldn't look at me, Rick. How could he be so unhappy and not say anything?"

"I've known Sebastian a very long time. It's unlikely this is a regular thing. If it were Brendan, I'd believe you, but not Sebastian."

"How will I be able to trust him again?"

"Come now, are you honestly saying you've never stepped over the lines I've given you?"

"I've never ..." Alec paused. He had broken the rules. With Sebastian. With Harrison. Great, now he was a hypocrite too. He met Hamilton's gaze and felt the stab of guilt twist deeper at the understanding he saw there.

Hamilton stroked his cheek. "And yet we still have trust and love, do we not?"

Alec nodded. Right now he could do with a little boy time of his own. He wanted Hamilton to hold him and reassure him that he was still a good boy despite his indiscretions.

"Go and calm Sebastian down, he's probably climbing the walls over there on his own. Give him the time and space to tell his own side of the story. You'll both feel much better."

"I'm not cut out for this." Alec leaned against Hamilton, taking comfort as Hamilton slipped an arm around his waist and pulled him close. "It's always something. Today was supposed to be for Brad."

"It still can be." Hamilton kissed the tip of Alec's nose. "Go and speak to Sebastian. Bradley can help me punish the boys."

Alec looked at Bradley.

"Go, Alec. I'll be fine."

The few steps along the hall felt like miles. Alec knew what he needed to do but he'd rather peel off his own skin than punish Sebastian, especially after the ribbing Brendan had put him through. But it still hurt. That Sebastian would let them get to him like that, make him break his vows as Alec's boy to be just for him.

He closed the front door quietly. As he walked along the hall, he could hear Sebastian still sobbing and the last of his anger drained away. He knocked on Sebastian's door.

"You can't come in. I have to stay on my own."

"It's Alec. Can I come in?"

The door flew open and Sebastian threw himself into Alec's arms. "You have to forgive me. I've never done it before, I promise, never. I don't know why I did. I *am* happy. I love you. Please, don't make me leave." He stopped for a deep breath, the tears subsiding but his body still trembling.

"Let's go and sit down."

Alec sat on the sofa at the end of Sebastian's bed and pulled the shaking little heap of bones onto his lap. It was definitely time to address Sebastian's weight as part of their new deal, the guy was looking jagged all folded in on himself. "It was the shock," Alec said, stroking Sebastian's back. "I'm sorry I shouted. You have to know I'd never throw you out, sweetheart. Nothing you do would ever make me throw you out. Do you understand?"

Sebastian nodded, snuggling closer.

"We're going to sit here until you feel better and then you can tell me what happened, okay?"

"Thank you, Master. I just... need a... minute." Sebastian pulled Alec's arm tighter around him, his fingers played with the buttons on his shirt. "I like you... in this color," he said, choking back a snivel.

"Baby, I'm so sorry. I don't know what I was thinking getting you in such a state."

"It's okay. I know better... than to listen to Brendan. I just..." He stopped with a particularly strong shudder. "I wanted to. It was my choice. I don't know why, but in the middle of it... I wanted to be bad, Master. I've never felt that before."

"I have."

Sebastian looked up at him with wide eyes.

"Don't forget I let you fuck me *before* Hamilton gave me permission. Sometimes you just have to do it. I see that now. Remember it."

"You believe me though?"

"Promise me, you really haven't been fucking around?"

"Not even once, Master. I didn't think Dylan counted. I won't do it again. I know you have to punish me and it's okay, as long as you believe me. As long as you trust me."

"Is it because you don't have enough time with me?"

"Not really, I see more of you than I ever did of Hamilton. I'm just used to more sex than I've had lately. I let my body get the better of me. I know better. I'll be better."

"Well, Brad will be back in action tomorrow and our new rule is that you can come with him whenever you need to if I'm not going to be home that night, okay?"

"You don't need to change the rules for me, Master. I need to be better behaved."

"It's only fair. But, if I'm going to be at home you will only come for me, agreed?"

"Yes, Master. You're so good to me."

"I try to be. You have to help me though, remember?" Sebastian nodded and Alec kissed his tear-stained cheek. The little smile warmed Alec's heart. "Now we need to talk punishment."

"Whatever you wish for me, Master."

"I have a paddle, but I'll be honest, I don't think I could do it."

"Maybe you should try?"

Alec shuddered. The thought made him want to heave. He'd be okay paddling Sebastian for kink; he certainly hadn't minded dishing out the odd spanking he'd given him in the past, but not for real. It was a step beyond his comfort zone. "The only punishment I can think of is more likely to have you rejoicing right now, and that's an evening in the cage. We're going to the club later."

The tremble in Sebastian's body this time was one of anticipation. *Not a punishment at all then.* That left Alec stumped as to how to proceed. He couldn't leave it too long or the punishment wouldn't mean anything.

"I'd like you to decide on your punishment as the cage seems to be something you want but there is one other thing I need from you."

"Anything, Master."

"We're going to go into the bathroom and weigh you." Sebastian blinked a few times, not understanding. "I want you to bulk up a bit."

"*No.*"

"I'm serious. You're all bones, more so than usual and I don't like it. By the time I get back from Australia, I expect to see a marked difference, even if it's just muscle you add. Do you understand?"

"Yes, Master."

"Don't make me force feed you hamburgers and chocolate."

Sebastian looked ready to heave at the thought but he just nodded. Alec added it to his checklist of things to watch out for in the near future. Not that he'd know how to address an eating disorder but it couldn't be difficult to find professional help.

"Good. Now, will you be okay? I want to take my day out with Bradley and release him so he can have some fun at the club tonight."

Sebastian cupped Alec's face in his hand. "I love you, Alec. All this aside, I never meant to hurt you."

"I know, sweetheart." Alec kissed Sebastian's hair. "It just happens sometimes when we love someone, especially when that person loves us back." The anger he'd felt, grabbing Sebastian's hair, shouting and throwing threats he'd never follow through on. Alec suddenly had a glimpse of what life must be like for Hamilton every time Alec stepped too far away from him. It wouldn't have taken much more for Alec to lash out rather than just manhandle Sebastian. Food for thought in his already overcrowded and over-pressured mind. Australia couldn't come soon enough but before that he had to send Bradley away on vacation with Worthington and go to his parents. His birthday would fall when he was down under and his mother would never forgive him if he waited until he came back to visit.

His mother. *Fuck*. He hadn't told her about the ring. Alec stifled the sigh, not wanting Sebastian to think he'd done something else wrong. He took time to kiss Sebastian's lips, gentle, tender kisses that warmed and soothed. Alec wasn't the only one living through radical change. He'd known it, had been meaning to ask about it, but Sebastian always played so damn happy. "Is it too much for you?" he finally asked.

"Is what too much?"

"You were never twenty-four seven with Hamilton. Is it too much?"

"No, I love being with you this way."

"You can love it, and it still be too much. Just think about it for a few days. Really think about it."

"I will, Master."

Sebastian snuggled in and Alec held tighter. Of all the things in his life that kept changing, this one he didn't want to learn to live without. Besides, if Sebastian wasn't around, who would pick up the pieces after Alec's mother ripped him a new one for withholding important information? Life in the fast lane. He'd dreamed of it for so many years. He'd imagined it to be easier to navigate, easier to carve out the path he wanted but that was the thing with dreams, even when they came true there was always a catch. Alec hadn't anticipated having so many dreams come true together. They didn't clash but they weren't exactly compatible either and it made everything harder than it needed to be.

Sebastian shuddered and Alec stroked his back. "We'll find the balance again, Sebastian. I promise."

"I promise too, Master. Thank you. You can go and see to Bradley now. I have chores."

"And you'll be okay on your own?"

Sebastian beamed a glorious smile. "Yeah, I can work faster if I'm not tripping over you two. Shall I cook dinner?"

"A sit-down meal together would be nice before we go to the club. Not too heavy though, well, you know the drill. Which reminds me…" Sebastian's shoulders drooped. "Bathroom, young man. I want you on those scales."

"I'll sort it, Alec, but please, don't make me weigh in."

"Hard limit for you, huh? Okay, I have an idea." Alec patted the seat and Sebastian slipped off his lap and took the space next to him. Alec went to the wardrobe and searched through Sebastian's jeans, finding his favorite pair that he'd not seen him in for a while. He handed them to Sebastian. "Put them on."

"They're too big."

"I know. Put them on."

It was a slow, agonising process, but eventually Sebastian stood straight, with a hand holding up the jeans at his waist.

"How did you lose that much weight so quickly, weren't you wearing those in Cornwall?"

"I just overdid it getting back on track after all that junk food."

"You're sure that's all it is, you aren't sick or anything?"

"No, I just…" Sebastian slumped to the floor and covered his head with his hands.

Alec was there in a second, wrapped around him. So much of what was going on in that pretty blond head was completely out of Alec's range of measurement. How they'd come so far along the relationship road he had no idea, but was likely down to Sebastian's endless patience, which seemed to be wearing a bit thin in places. "I can't help if you don't tell me."

When nothing was forthcoming, Alec squeezed Sebastian's shoulders. "And as my boy, it's your duty to tell me everything that's bothering you. Do I have to remind you of the rules?"

"It's my thing," Sebastian said quietly, still not looking up. "I told you when we first moved in together. I used to be chubby. I'd be chubby now if I ate everything I wanted."

"And you think I wouldn't want you, or couldn't love you if you had a little meat on you?"

"You and Brad can eat whatever you want and you just turn it straight into muscle. It's not fair."

"I spend hours in the gym every week, we both do. It doesn't happen by magic. But you didn't answer my question. Do you think I'm that shallow, that I would kick you out if, god forbid, you're clothes actually fitted you?"

"No."

"Good, because if I get the feeling you're even thinking it I'll find the will to take that paddle to your ass and you won't sit down for a month, do you understand?"

Sebastian nodded his head. A shy smile lingered for a moment and slipped away.

Alec grabbed the waistband out of Sebastian's hand. "I want you back in these jeans by the time I'm back from Australia."

"But they were always big on me."

"You need to be able to wear them without losing them around your ankles every time you take a step. Sitting low on your hips is fine, if it'll make you happy. Deal?"

A real smile this time. "Deal."

"And you know you could always come to the gym with me."

"Can I?" The little bubble of excitement in his voice washed away some of Alec's stress.

"Five-thirty, Monday morning."

"What?"

"There's a gym in the basement. I go every other morning before you even think about opening those pretty little eyes of yours. I'll expect you up, bright and early." Alec left the bombshell to settle in for a moment. "Now, I'm off out. Don't forget we still need to negotiate your punishment. We can talk about it tomorrow."

"Yes, Master."

"Good boy. I love you, Sebastian." He kissed Sebastian's forehead. "I don't care how much weight you put on, you'll still be the same person and I'll still love you. That can never change."

"Thanks, I needed to hear that."

"Have more faith in me and don't bottle things up. I'll understand if you want time off, just say something."

"I do have faith in you."

"Thanks, because I needed to hear *that*. It certainly doesn't feel that way right now. So, punishment, dinner, talk, and jeans, yes?" Sebastian nodded. "Excellent. Now to go and unleash the horndog."

"It'll be nice to have him back in the bedroom."

"I'm looking forward to it myself. If only to stop him moping around the office all day."

A Punishing Schedule

There was something unnatural about seeing Sebastian in the flat with clothes on. He looked uncomfortable and fidgeted often but Alec couldn't back down from his decision in the same way he hadn't back down with Bradley's celibacy punishment. It was possible Sebastian knew it was almost as difficult for Alec and it looked like he was trying hard not to complain. The adorable pout however, he was unable to control, and it was eating away at Alec's cool. At least sex wasn't off limits with this punishment. Alec intended to make sure Sebastian's lips had much better things to do than pout as soon as bedtime came around. In the meantime, he tried to concentrate on the files he was reviewing for work.

"Dinner's ready, Master," Bradley called from the dining room.

"Thanks, we'll be through now."

Sebastian huffed. There were three conditions to his punishment. He would wear clothes from the time he woke until bed; he would forgo his favorite thing of serving Alec—whether that was food, laundry, or housework—and lastly no TV, all for two weeks. He was an avid soap fan and after four days was already tetchy about missing the life-changing goings on of various streets around the globe. But he mostly suffered in silence. It was heart breaking but necessary. Alec was sorely tempted to try corporal punishment next time. At least it would be over quickly.

The three of them settled around the table where Bradley served up a delicious looking meal of stir-fry vegetables and beef on a bed of noodles, accompanied by a side dish of asparagus and freshly baked bread.

"It looks great, Brad, thank you," Alec said, reaching over to squeeze his hand.

"Do you want wine or shall I just serve juice?"

"Juice is good for me, babe. You have whatever you'd like."

"I haven't given you much beef, Sebastian. I know you don't like to eat too much red meat."

"Thanks. My meal plan is shot to pieces anyway." Sebastian looked at Brad and smiled, or attempted to. "And you're a great cook. It's hardly a chore to enjoy it."

"Sebastian." Alec waited for him to look over. "What did we agree about your meal plan?"

He huffed again, and Alec was pretty sure he rolled his eyes. "Yes, Master, I *know*. But how do I implement a steady increase in protein and carbohydrate if I'm not allowed to cook anything?"

"You can start by toning down the attitude."

Sebastian flopped to the floor at Alec's feet. "I'm sorry, Master." Genuine at least. "I'm just grumpy at the moment. I feel like everything is spiraling out of control."

"Do you trust me?" Sebastian opened his mouth a few times but didn't say anything. He looked too stunned. "Well, do you?"

"Completely, Master."

"How can everything be out of control unless you don't trust me to be in control and look after you?"

A slow smile spread over Sebastian's face and he sighed contentedly. "You're so good to me." He uncurled himself from the floor and took his seat. "I feel better now, thank you."

"Make sure you tell me if you start to feel grumpy or shaky again, okay? Change takes time."

"Okay."

After dinner, Sebastian cleared the table for Bradley and loaded the dishwasher. It was the one thing he'd insisted on so he wouldn't feel pampered rather than punished. Alec could see there was something else on Sebastian's mind but figured it best to let it come out naturally. There was still tomorrow's schedule to review before he wound down into his own time so he went through to the small bedroom they'd converted to an office. It wasn't long before Brad joined him. The files revealed no surprises in store, always good news. They were just starting to wrap things up when Sebastian knocked on the door.

"Master, can I ask you something please?"

"Come on in."

"I'll leave you to it," Brad said, grabbing the last of the folders from the desk.

"No, you can stay. I …" Sebastian took a deep breath. "I wondered if you'd be interested in meeting some of my friends from work. Go out for a drink, perhaps. Both of you."

Meet friends from work? Bradley looked from Alec to Sebastian and back to Alec, waiting for him to say something. "I don't see why not," Alec said. "Is there any reason why you're asking now, anything I should know about?"

"I'm not fucking any of them if that's what you're asking."

"I beg your pardon?"

"Damn it. I'm sorry, Master. *That's* why." Sebastian flapped his arms in the air and huffed yet again. "I'm short tempered and ratty and I've been driving them up the wall the last day or so. They're worried about me."

"And you thought introducing me as the source of your bad mood would ease their minds?"

Bradley snorted, but covered the laugh with a hand over his mouth.

"I told them I was stressed about… stuff. They don't know how we are together but they know I moved recently. That I moved in with you."

"As my partner?"

Sebastian hung his head and nodded. "I didn't know how else to explain it."

Alec waved him over and pulled him onto his lap. "I'm more than happy with that." He kissed Sebastian's cheek and ran a thumb over the delicious pout that had resurfaced. "Tom and Chloe know I live with you, and to them you're my boyfriend. We say what we need to, to keep us safe. All of us. Do they know you live with Brad too?"

"No, but I'd still like Brad to meet them. If it's okay with you, Master."

"And what are you going to call me when we're out with your friends?"

"Whatever you want me to, Master."

"I'd say Alec is the best bet. So why don't you practice that for the rest of the night?"

Sebastian smiled. There was something cheeky going on behind the sparkle in his eye. Hopefully something hot, wet and naughty that involved those sweet lips over every inch of Alec's body.

Alec sighed contentedly and stretched out of the tangle of limbs. "I'm going to have to get a bigger bed if this is going to be a regular thing, boys."

Bradley slipped under his arm and took a moment to suck on Alec's nipple sending a rush of spine tingling shivers directly to his already sated cock. It twitched briefly but gave up any further attempt at rousing.

"How can it not be regular, Master?" Bradley smiled. "We live with you after all."

"True, but that shouldn't mean three in a bed is the normal sleeping arrangement."

Sebastian's head surfaced from the other end of the bed. "Don't you like us in here with you?"

"You know I do. But we're slipping out of master/boy into free-for-all orgy. Don't think I didn't catch you playing with my ass, Bradley."

"Just following your body, Master, and it was Sebastian who fucked you." Bradley stroked a hand over Alec's stomach and slipped it lower to cup his balls gently. "I wouldn't do anything you didn't want me to."

"Sebastian, why don't you go and start breakfast."

"Yes, Master."

Bradley kissed his way across Alec's chest. "Is there something in particular you want from me this morning, Master?"

"Just a little one-on-one. Remind you who's in charge around here."

"No doubts on that count for me."

Alec rolled them over and settled between Bradley's thighs. His cock had given up playing dead and was swelling nicely. Accompanied with the sight of Brad laid out before him Alec was soon rocking with a fresh need to take the body beneath him. Not just any body, Brad's body. Since the celibacy punishment there was something special in the way Brad gave himself to Alec. Different to his service fucks.

Different to Sebastian. And it rocked Alec's world in ways he hadn't known were possible.

Alec felt the breath catch in Brad's chest as he pushed forward claiming Brad's body yet again as his own. Such a rush. A body so powerful yielding so completely to his touch. So much he'd missed out on for so long, but no more. He was making up for it and then some and he'd never have enough. Not enough of Brad, not enough of sex, not enough of this feeling. And there it was again, the perfect opportunity. Alec paused his long tortuous stroke and smiled.

Brad squeezed Alec's hips between his thighs, stroked soft fingertips over Alec's chest. "You want me on top?"

"I want to take a time out from being master and have my ass reamed by a sexy co-worker. Does that work for you?"

"Don't do it just because you know I want it, Alec."

"Oh, I want it just as much, make no mistake about that. Have for a while." Alec squirmed under Bradley's roving hands.

"Why so long?"

"Why are you still talking?"

Bradley grinned and reached for the lube. He shuffled around between Alec's legs and wiped a covering of lube over his cock. Alec lifted his knees and Bradley moved into position, butting his cock head against Alec's pucker. "Are you sure?"

"Just fuck me already." Alec groaned as Brad pushed forward into his unprepared hole, loosened only a little from Sebastian's fucking a few hours previously.

Brad paused. "Okay?"

"I'm hardly a virgin. I think I can take the stretch."

"I ..." Bradley draped himself over Alec and sought out his lips. Hot, frantic kisses ensued that took Alec's breath and scattered his thoughts. He'd been expecting a slow, leisurely morning fuck. He was getting heat and passion he'd never known Bradley capable of. They moved together, every motion teasing his senses and drawing out his need. Sweat pooled and their bodies slipped over each other until a strangled sound escaped Alec's throat. The orgasm caught him out and he grabbed hold of Bradley's shoulder. "Fuck, fuck."

"I'm coming." Brad's words so soft, as he buried his head into Alec's neck and stilled. Neither of them moved, just breathed into the silence.

"Hey," Alec said, after another moment passed and Brad still hadn't moved. "Everything okay?"

"Yeah, I just…" Brad pulled out and settled next to Alec, pushing a stray lock of hair out of his eyes. "I haven't had sex like that since I was a teenager." His focus was distant, his body still trembling slightly against Alec's side. "I'd forgotten it could be like that."

"How is it usually?"

"Different. Choreographed I guess. That was… I didn't have to think, we just…"

"Brad, if you ever need to take time out to find more of that, you just have to ask."

"Why would I need to look for it elsewhere when I have it right here?"

A knock at the door disrupted the uneasy feeling in Alec's stomach. "Breakfast is ready, Master. Thank you, for letting me serve you."

"Serve? Damn. I'm so crap at this punishment thing. Sebastian, you should have reminded me."

"Yes, Master. Sorry, Master. I thought perhaps your mind was on things it was better I didn't interrupt." Sebastian's killer grin made Alec blush and Bradley chuckle.

"Yeah, yeah, Bradley got a taste of my cherry. I think I'd like my master hat back now, if that's okay with you two treasures?"

"Your wish is our command, Master."

"Oh, I'm sure it is. The fact you dangle the carrot and I fall for it every time doesn't come into it, right? I'm getting in the shower. Brad, use your own bathroom this morning, please."

Alec saw the hurt in Bradley's eyes but he couldn't take it back. He needed space; the walls of his massive apartment were closing in on him. He high-tailed it to the shower room and actually closed the door.

What the hell was going on? Alec let the lukewarm water flow over his head. The sex had been good. Scratch that, it was great. He'd come without even touching his cock. He'd wanted it, despite the echoes of a set up so what was wrong? Why did he feel so… odd?

They were all quiet over breakfast. Alec couldn't find anything to say and the boys looked wary of his mood. How could one fuck change the dynamic so much? And how was it possible for good sex to leave such a bitter taste?

"Will you be home for dinner this evening, Master?" Sebastian asked as Alec prepared to leave.

"No, I'm spending the night at Hamilton's. It's his birthday tomorrow; I wanted to wake up with him."

"Does that mean I can cook for Bradley?"

"It means you and Bradley are free to entertain yourselves." Alec glanced at Brad who dropped his gaze quickly to the floor.

Sebastian reached for Alec's chin and pulled his face round to look at him. "Is everything, okay?" It was an unusual enough action from Sebastian that Alec acknowledged everything was far from okay.

"It will be. Just give me a little time."

"It's me isn't it?"

Alec looked at Bradley. There was something in his eyes that hadn't been there before. Alec wished he knew what it was.

"I've messed it up."

"No you haven't. We'll talk about it later, okay? The car's waiting." Alec kissed Sebastian and grabbed his briefcase. It was a busy day. Lots of service clients, and far too much fucking. Would he be able to sit back and watch old men plowing into Bradley after this morning? Alec shuddered. Of course he would. Nothing had changed. They still had a job to do.

But something had changed and Alec needed to figure out what it was. And preferably before lunch.

The morning was difficult. Alec skirted around Bradley, leaving the office whilst he serviced Mr. Ketteridge, returning only to shake the man's hand. Bradley was already in the shower and fully dressed by the time he emerged.

"Are you ready to talk about this?" he said, sitting on the edge of Alec's desk.

"I don't know what it is," Alec said, honestly. "I'm sorry I pushed you away this morning."

"It's what I said, isn't it, about not needed to look anywhere else."

"Partly."

"It makes you nervous, that you might be my 'one'?"

"Hamilton shares me enough. People say they love me when they don't really, but it still hurts him."

"It wasn't meant like that." Brad smiled. "I do love you, but not in that way. Shit, am I making this worse?"

"I want to know what you think."

Brad moved to the sofa and patted the seat next to him. Alec obliged and Brad grabbed his hand, taking up a stroking motion over his fingers. "I had a crush on this guy when I was a kid. Couldn't think of anything else. After about a month of stalking his every move he gave in and the sex was crazy hot, all passionate and deep, like this morning. It sparked the memory for me, that's all."

"Then why do I feel like something's different?"

"You just filled a gap I didn't know I had in my life. Again. I'm not out to put my own ring on your finger if that's what you're worried about."

"But you feel it's different too, right?"

"Sure, but not in the way you seem to. I'm not expecting anything else from you. Alec. The occasional teenage shag will be great, but I was happy with the way things were before, and I'm happy now."

Alec stared deep into Bradley's eyes searching for a label to pin on what he saw there but nothing was forthcoming. "So I'm fretting over nothing?"

"I don't know, are you?" At least Brad's killer smile was still the same. "How do you feel about it?"

"Too early to say. Not sure what's spooked me." Definitely spooked. Behind the easiness was an awkward silence waiting to surface and it was itchy, crawling under his skin and making even the touch of Brad's hand feel strange. Out of place.

Brad sighed and placed Alec's hand back in his lap. "Guess I'll be in my own bed from now on then, unless you want me to stay with Hamilton?"

"Now you're being daft. I didn't say I don't want you around."

"Would it be easier if you just fucked me, set the balance straight?"

That did seem like a good idea. Maybe it was an authority thing, needing to own Bradley's ass, but then he'd just given it to Mr. Ketteridge.

"Don't want to fuck me either, wow, this is serious. Perhaps I do need to worry."

There was a moment's pause in Alec's thought process before he accepted how stupid he was being. Stupid and cruel to torture Bradley for his own hang-ups. It was Jasper all over again. Time to reassert some boundaries of his own. "Lock the door and get your kit off," Alec said, pulling at his tie. "I can soon put you in your place, if that's what you need."

"What I need, or what you need, Master?"

"Does it matter?"

Bradley rose smoothly and started to strip. Once naked, he locked the door and took his place at Alec's feet. "It's my greatest pleasure to serve you, Master. I am yours."

Seeing Bradley so poised, eyes to the floor, posture perfect, sent a rumble of possessiveness through Alec. "You are mine. I like that."

"Would it please, Master, for me to service him?"

Alec nodded his head and Bradley shuffled closer, unzipping Alec's fly and taking a long, slow lick along the underside of his cock. Alec sat back and let Bradley get to work, reveling in his expertise. Once he was good and hard, he positioned Bradley over the desk and fucked him hard. It felt good. It felt good and at the same time wrong. Alec paused and Brad lifted his head to look back. "I want you to fuck me, Master, to own me."

"And I love fucking you but what I want now is for you to fuck me." Alec slipped out and pulled Bradley off the desk into his arms. "We can still have a balance. It works with Sebastian. It can work for us. I just need to get used to it."

"You think it'll make it better to do it again?"

"I think it's the best option for sorting out my messed up thinking."

Bradley didn't seem sure but he did as requested. The fucking was no less sweet and Alec felt better for it. It still wasn't right, but it was better. A few more good fucks from Brad and he'd be back in balance. In the meantime, closing shop to new lovers seemed like a sensible idea. It was the only thing to do to stop it happening again. At least until he figured out how to separate having a cock inside of him from his feelings. A strange turn up for the books. He'd fucked and sucked nameless guys and never once felt anything beyond his own physical pleasure. Why was *being* fucked so different? If anyone could show him how to maintain the balance, it was Brad, Sebastian too for that matter. Still so much to learn, to discover about himself, about sex and ultimately about love. Thank goodness he was surrounded by friends who could help him piece together whatever the fuck this was going on in his head. It didn't make life easy but it did make it a little less complicated.

Birthdays and Bombshells

The finest smoked salmon served with scrambled quails eggs, sliced strawberries, and a sprinkle of dill. Warm bread coated with a layer of pure honey. A pot of freshly ground Australian Basalt Blue coffee and a glass of mango straight from the juicer. Hamilton's favorite breakfast. Alec was proud of himself for not having to call Sebastian over to help. All he had to do now was make it to the bedroom without throwing it all over the floor.

He set a single pink and orange rose from the balcony garden on the side of the tray and smiled. Hamilton would never see this coming and Alec loved nothing more than to surprise the man who thought he knew everything.

The room was still dark. Hamilton snored gently somewhere beyond Alec's vision but he found his way to the window and set the tray on the dresser. So peaceful. It was times like this Alec recognized how lucky he was to have found such a wonderful guy who brought with him such a great life. He opened the blinds to let in the early morning sun and slipped on to the bed, taking a few minutes to kiss the line of Hamilton's jaw until he stirred. "Morning, birthday boy. The breakfast fairy has brought you something delicious."

"Mmm." Hamilton kissed back. Slow, sloppy morning kisses with the echo of last night's sex. "Just the way I like it, warm and naked. You are naked aren't you?"

"Of course. But first, I made you breakfast."

Hamilton pushed himself up onto his elbows, a quizzical look taking over the sleepiness. "You made breakfast?"

"Sit up and get comfortable, Master. I'm here to serve you."

"I won't argue with that."

Alec collected the tray, placed it on the bed and perched next to a be-mused Hamilton. "I hope it's not cold, already." He lifted the first forkful to Hamilton's open lips and watched as it slipped past them onto Hamilton's tongue. He waited as Hamilton chewed, trying not to think about slipping his cock in next.

"Are those quail's eggs?"

"I know they're your favorite."

The way Hamilton's face lit up made the torture of being in the kitchen at such an ungodly hour worth the pain. Hamilton opened for the next mouthful and Alec obliged. It was a slow, sensual process clearing the tray of its contents, sharing strawberries and kisses, trying not to wander too far into stroking and caressing. By the time breakfast was over, Alec was practically panting but it wasn't time for that just yet.

Alec stole back to the kitchen with the dishes while Hamilton busied himself in the bathroom. A few minutes later they were back in bed, Hamilton stretched out to his full length. "You know how to spoil me," he said, stroking Alec's hair. Alec made his way over Hamilton's stomach with a line of kisses, nipping at the skin and covering the marks with long wet licks.

"It's my job, Master."

"It's a long time since you've called me that. I like it."

"Things may change around us, but you'll always be my master, first and foremost." Alec sat astride Hamilton's hips and leaned forward to whisper in his ear. "Now for your gift." With a little maneuvering and making sure to grind his ass over Hamilton's growing cock, Alec pulled the parcel he'd hidden from the bedside cabinet and presented it.

Hamilton shook off the lid and did a double take. A slow smile spread across his face as he lifted out the thick leather cuffs. "Are these for me or you?"

It took a moment for Alec's brain to regain its focus. *Hamilton in handcuffs. Lord, that is a powerful thought.* "Those are custom made for me," he said, his voice rough and dry from the places his mind was wandering. "But hearing you say that brings a whole new vision to mind."

"One minute I'm you're master, the next you want me in chains. Which is it to be?"

Alec stretched Hamilton's hands over his head and smiled. "Both. Not at the same time. But definitely both and besides, you in chains was your fantasy not mine. I'm just willing to make it happen for you."

"I'm sure you are. In the meantime, do I get to play with my gift?"

"Turning the tables on you is very tempting, but as you're the birthday boy, your wish is my command."

Hamilton rolled them over and the box tumbled to the floor. "Just as it should be," he said, nuzzling into Alec's neck. "Let's see how well these cuffs fit, shall we? So I can chain you to my heart."

"You don't need cuffs for that, Master. I'm already yours."

The low growl that escaped Hamilton sent a thrill through Alec's eager body. It seemed such a long time since Alec had given himself completely to his master. Too long by far. Caught up with day-to-day trivialities, his own boys, changes at work, and Hamilton's reluctance to take too much control after his outburst at Harrison's, had left the special bond between master and boy lost somewhere in uncertainty. The cuffs, Alec had decided, would be a fun way to ease back into their former dynamic without resorting to overly long discussions about finding themselves. Bondage play was something they'd not explored together. Alec had a little experience from Sebastian's growing interest in straps and chains and had been on the receiving end of some interesting experiments. Interesting enough to repeat with Hamilton.

If anyone was going to make restraint work for Alec, it was he. So many things, simple things, were different when Hamilton was on the other end of them. A kiss behind the ear, a firm stroke of the thigh, even a squeeze of his hand brought Alec to an incoherent haze of need. Things he could shake off from everyone else when instituted by Hamilton broke through Alec's cool and hit the buttons directly linked to his cock.

Much like now.

Automatic reflex had him trying to bring his arms down for protection from the teasing fingertips and kisses over his stomach. The tug against his wrists from the cuffs looped through the bedframe sent an extra jolt into his squirming body and his cock twitched, standing straight up like a mast.

"Oh, you like that?"

"Master, please, *don't* tickle."

"What if I want to tickle you?" Alec's knees jerked upward and bucked Hamilton, sat astride his thighs. "Feisty." Hamilton's chuckle echoed through Alec's brain. This was not what he'd had in mind when he ordered the custom-made handcuffs. Hot, naughty sex, yes. Slow, sensual lovemaking, yes. Torturous tickling, not so much.

He closed his eyes to the onslaught of sensations drilling into his calm, noted the sweat beading on his forehead, the slickness of Hamilton's lips as he brushed them lightly over Alec's hipbone. Words of pleading formed on his tongue ready to spring forth when tight, wet heat engulfed his cock and stopped their progress. Everything else fell away to the ecstatic groan that slipped from his mouth. Still it wasn't enough. Not enough friction, not enough speed to get anywhere. Hamilton continued to play, pushing Alec to the edge before dragging him back with soft puffs of air around his balls and the base of his shaft. A slow, torturous lick along the length, around the circumference, and under the head. A forceful dip of his tongue into the slit before swallowing Alec's cock once more.

"Please, fuck, fuck … I can't … I need …"

"What do you need, Alec?" Hamilton sucked in the length of Alec's cock, his lips tight.

"Oh, *god*, please let me come."

Hamilton laughed. "God isn't the one giving you a blowjob, darling."

They stared at each other, Hamilton with a half-smile. Alec couldn't get his brain around the meaning of the words. Why had Hamilton stopped? Was he waiting for Alec to say something?

"You're out of practice. What happened to coming only when I allow it?"

"I didn't, I haven't, have I?" Alec stretched his head forward. His cock stared back at him, still swollen to bursting, a smear of pre-cum glistened at the tip. Definitely didn't miss the orgasm. "Master?"

"There was a time you could go for hours with me teasing you like this and then I'd leave you for a few more before giving you release. Now, after just a few minutes you're almost past the point of no return."

"It's the cuffs," Alec lied. "They heighten the sensations. Not being able to move or respond to your touch." He was out of practice. It was embarrassing how quickly he'd lost that control, the ability to respond more to Hamilton's voice than his wicked caress.

"You need to be reminded of your role as my boy."

"Yes, Master."

"I'm going to fuck you but you will not come. Do you understand?"

Alec shuddered at the tone in Hamilton's voice. Pure ecstasy pumped directly into his veins and his cock twitched. The edge of danger was back in those dulcet tones. The issue of an almost impossible challenge. Comply or face the consequences. Alec had never been one for punishment as kink, but right now the thought cranked up the adrenaline, dragged the air from his lungs and made his body shiver in the best way. He managed a breathy, "Yes, Master."

"When I've had my fill of your body I'm going to plug you and send you to work."

Holy hell in a hand basket. The bastard. Alec grunted a nonsensical response.

"You will not engage in any sexual activity with anyone until I release you."

"Yes, Master, I understand." Alec closed his eyes, trying desperately to ignore the firm hand sliding up and down his cock. Closer, closer. *Fight it, damn you.* Hamilton let go and Alec let out a breath. Overthinking. At times like this, Alec appreciated his ability to overthink, to be consumed with random thoughts and keep the prospect of falling over the edge at bay.

Hamilton reached across the bed for the lube and settled between Alec's thighs. "Lift your knees." Alec pulled his knees to his chest and Hamilton dribbled lube over his pucker and worked it inside with his fingers. Alec tried to focus on the features of Hamilton's face and ignore the pressure, the slip of fluid. "I have clients today," Hamilton said. "I may call on you for service. Remind you of your place."

"Whatever you require of me, Master. I am yours."

The bottle of lube clunked as it hit the floor. Alec was still wondering whether it would spill when Hamilton speared him with one thrust. The sudden stretch made his eyes water, his back arch, and a strangled sound escape his throat. A frantic pace ensued and Alec bit down hard on his lip to take his mind off the rising tide in his body. He gripped the chain connecting the cuffs, tried to count the links that held him bound but his mind wandered back to the fullness, the friction, every thrust poking at the fire in his gut threatening to send it crashing through his body. This was the Hamilton he remembered. This was the Hamilton he needed to hold the balance in his crazy life, and this was the hottest damn fuck in history. He'd have to make breakfast more often.

Alec struggled to hold on to his sensibilities. *Fuck, don't come, don't come, please, please, please don't fucking come.* Over and over he repeated the mantra in his head interspersed with forced thoughts of interest calculations and yield forecasts, letting the sensations of the pounding wash through him without building to anything. It wasn't working. The heat started to pool at the base of his spine and he knew he was going to lose the fight, knew he was in trouble, just a little more and he'd be lost to it.

Hamilton pulled out, his face flushed, sweat dripping from his forehead. He was grinning. "Am I going to need to punish you, Alec, for disobeying me?"

"No, Master. Not yet, anyway."

"That's good. Turn over."

The cuffs made it awkward but Alec managed to make it on to his stomach, arms crossed over his head. Hamilton slapped his ass and moved him into position with his legs curled underneath his body. A moment later the pounding continued. Alec's cock lay trapped between his legs and his stomach. Every thrust brought unbearable friction and pressure that resumed the ache in his balls, the throb in his cock, the loosening of control. Right to the very edge and Hamilton stopped again.

He smoothed over Alec's back. "You are so beautiful. Beautiful always, but like this you're magnificent."

The intermittent fucking continued in various positions until Alec lost all track of time and reason. A peace settled into his bones, a lightness in his thoughts, until the constant hammering became background noise, secondary to the deepening of pleasure that buried into his soul and stoked the fire that burned there, then it was gone. It took a moment to register before his body ached with the loss.

"Shower and return to me for a plug. It's time for work."

Alec wanted to fight, argue, beg for more, but no words formed. Hamilton released him from the cuffs and it was all he could do to sit, let alone stand. Hamilton took his hands. "I'll help you."

Brain activity returned under the spray of water. Hamilton scrubbed him roughly but thoroughly. "You fucked me senseless," Alec said, turning at the pull of his hip. "I literally couldn't think."

"I noticed." Hamilton smiled. "Welcome back."

"And my ass is sore."

"Oh, darling." Hamilton kissed the tip of his nose. "It'll be worse with a plug. Best make it a small one."

"My cock aches."

"Good. It'll help you remember me on my birthday." Hamilton turned him again and slapped his ass. It smarted against his wet skin and he jumped forward. "Steady, don't want you falling over." Hamilton turned off the water and wrapped him in a towel. "Dry off and return to the bed."

Everything floated by in a hazy cloud until Alec found himself in the car heading to work. The butt plug chaffed and his arousal was still on simmer. Every dip and bump in the road shot sparks through his sweet spot. By the time they arrived at the office Alec was nursing a painful erection, his body trembled with every brush against it and a fine sheen of sweat covered his brow. Hamilton kissed his cheek as the elevator climbed. "Remember your orders, Alec. And send me your schedule. I'll call you for coffee."

"Master, please." Alec gripped Hamilton's arm. "Can I come with you now?"

"Alec." Hamilton's voice was laced with warning that tickled over Alec's skin and stoked the ache with its promise. "I'll call you when I'm ready."

The elevator chimed to announce Hamilton's floor and Alec could only nod as he watched his torturer disappear. It was all Alec could do not to run after him, throw himself at Hamilton's feet and beg for release.

Damn the man for being so unreasonable, so enticing, and so downright sexy.

"Alec, are you okay?"

For the first time, Alec acknowledged Brad's presence. "Coffee. I just need lots of coffee."

Every minute dragged. Alec couldn't concentrate. It was a good thing Bradley was as talented with real negotiating as he was on his back otherwise Alec would be in trouble. He watched as Bradley took over the table discussion with, what was luckily a very flexible client by the name of Witherstone. The man seemed a little confused by Alec's lack of contribution but once Bradley got down to the blowjob, his concerns seemed to dissipate.

Witherstone was young compared to their usual clients. No more than forty, for sure. Quiet and overly geeky, Alec wondered whether this was the only sexual contact the man had open to him. Every tempered groan that slipped from his tight lips took a bite out of Alec's cool and threatened to undermine the ounce of control he was managing to hold onto.

After what seemed like an age, Witherstone jerked and stilled, panting ever so slightly and wiping his brow. He looked startled, or perhaps it was starry-eyed. Alec couldn't decide.

"You're very good at that," he said to Bradley.

"Thank you, sir. Would you like me to help you clean up?"

"I can manage, thank you. Will I … uhm, do I see you again?"

Bradley looked at Alec. Alec knew he was supposed to step in and say something but all he could think about was the stray drop of cum on Bradley's chin. Alec wanted to lick it off before pinning Bradley to the floor to carry out all manner of depraved acts on his prone body.

"I'll schedule an appointment for you in a few days, Mr. Witherstone. Alec will discuss your service contract in more depth at that time."

"As soon as that? How wonderful." Witherstone shook Bradley's hand. "Oh, you have a little …" He pointed to Bradley's chin before reaching out to wipe off the evidence with his thumb. "Thank you, again. You've been most … uhm, helpful."

A moment later, the door closed behind Mr. Witherstone and Bradley flopped onto the sofa. "What the fuck is going on with you, Alec? The guy just tossed you a five-million-pound deal and you barely acknowledged him."

"Has Hamilton called for me yet?"

"Alec!" Bradley slammed his hand on the coffee table and Alec jumped. "Are you listening to me? Witherstone's service contract. Am I going to be fucking the guy as a regular or what?"

"Service contract, right. What are the details again?"

"Never mind. I'll write up a proposal and get you to read it when you get back from whatever fucked up place you're in right now. For goodness sake, find your wits for this afternoon. Viera and his cronies are booked for two-thirty and with you like that he'll have you stripped and fucked before you manage to say 'good afternoon, gentlemen.'"

Viera. *Holy hell.*

Alec sobered a little. "Have we requested Fraser for Earl what's-his-name?"

"All arranged. Now are you going to tell me what's going on and why you're so desperate to see the lord and master?"

"Butt plug."

"And that explains what, exactly?"

"Early morning torture, topped off by a butt plug. I'm seeing stars. And after I made him breakfast in bed, too."

The penny dropped and Bradley roared with laughter. By the time he pulled himself together his eyes looked damp. "Poor Witherstone wasn't sure what to make of you and frankly, neither did I. I was worried. Why didn't you just ask me to deal with it for you?"

"Not allowed. Have to wait for him. Can you check to see if he called when you were dealing with Witherstone?"

"Sorry, Alec, no calls waiting. I can see that from here."

"What the hell is he playing at making me wait so long?" Alec loosened his tie and went to the window hoping the view would clear his head. The tinted glass sheltered the office from the early fall sun already high in the sky. Outside, the world carried on its business unaware of Alec's growing desperation. He could see cars and people in miniature scurrying around and wanted to be one of them, wanted to breathe real air rather than the dry air-conditioned kind and feel a breeze on his skin, but he daren't leave the office. Too risky. He might miss Hamilton and then where would he be?

"Alec?"

He turned to see Bradley with the phone in his hand. Alec hadn't even heard it ring. Judging by the grin splitting Brad's face, it was the call Alec was waiting for.

"Mr. Hamilton would like to see you in his office. Do you need five minutes, or shall I tell him you're on your way?"

"Ha-bloody-ha." Alec clipped Bradley's ear as he walked past him and heard a quiet chuckle. Cheeky sod. He'd make him pay for that later.

The elevator was too slow; it would have been quicker to take the stairs. But that would have left him more flushed and breathless than he was just by putting one foot in front of the other. Four flights of stairs with the plug grazing his sweet spot would have been too much.

The open office of the eighth floor financials section was louder than he remembered. Had it really been that long since he'd called in to Hamilton's? Chloe caught his eye and waved but Alec managed to bypass her and make it safely to the door. He knocked and waited to be called in. He could hear laughter inside and remembered Hamilton had mentioned service. Just the thought of getting to his knees at Hamilton's command to suck nameless cocks had a tightening effect at Alec's groin. Back to the early days, and not a moment too soon. Whether he'd be as good as he used to be was something else. It surprised him that he'd missed this so much but it made life easy. No service contracts to negotiate, no power meetings with hungry executives desperate to get in his pants, and no multi-million-pound deals to screw up because he was so horny he couldn't think straight.

Alec opened the door at Hamilton's call and closed it behind him.

"Lock it please, Alec. There's a good boy."

"I say, Hamilton, is this your service boy?"

Alec turned to see Hamilton smile. "Not my regular boy, but I thought you would appreciate something special. Alec is my personal house boy."

"A very pretty package. Do we get to see him naked?"

Alec surveyed the room, trying not to make eye contact with his clients, and made his way to kneel at Hamilton's feet. Four men, all over fifty, very plain looking for the most part, except one. He stood out from the group with un-styled shaggy blond hair and piercing blue eyes that made Alec feel naked already.

Hamilton lifted Alec's chin and kissed him tenderly. "I've been waiting all morning to do that. Are you ready to serve me, Alec?"

"Yes, Master. Always."

Another kiss, lips barely touching. "Good boy. I'd like you to undress and take your position. Our friends are due the services of that delicious mouth of yours."

Alec smiled. Those words held such comfort, gave him value beyond his ability to read markets. He started to undress, hanging his jacket and folding his clothes neatly.

"I'm sure the rest of this boy is as delicious as his mouth, Hamilton. Don't we get to play with the full package? He looks the type to enjoy putting on a show." The bohemian addition to the group. Eyes as pale as glaciers sent a chill to Alec's bones but he didn't flinch. He wanted to, but he kept his cool and stripped out of his boxers and socks, coming to rest before the coffee table in the required position—on his knees, back straight, head bowed, hands resting in his lap.

"Your contract doesn't warrant full service, Harrison." Alec glanced up at the mention of the name. Is that why the guy looked familiar? A relation of Edward. No, he'd have met any brothers of Edward's already.

"He's your personal boy. How about we forgo business for the moment and I have access as an old friend."

"Emphasis on the *personal*," Hamilton said. Alec noted the touch of steel that had slipped into his voice. If Harrison pushed it, he'd likely end up with a black eye. As things stood, right now, Alec was so horny he'd happily fuck the four of them as long as Hamilton finished off with the *personal* attention Alec craved.

"Are you his master, or not?"

Hamilton lifted Alec's chin and stared deep into his soul. "How are you feeling, Alec?"

"Happy to be with you, Master."

"And what do you think of our friend's request to fuck you?"

"Whatever you want me to think, Master."

Hamilton's smile lit up Alec's world. "My beautiful boy." Alec gasped at the touch of his lips, wanted to hang on to that kiss and ride it all the way to the finish line. Alec dropped his gaze when Hamilton turned back to their audience. "And that, Henry, is why I don't hand out Alec as a party favor. I'm sure you understand. But there's no need to ruin our get together."

Henry Harrison. Alec would remember the name and ask Edward.

"Now, Alec, perhaps you should see to our friends two at a time."

Alec moved between two of the seated men, cocks already on display, and sucked first one then the other. It had been a while since he'd alternated more than one cock at a time but he soon fell back into the rhythm of things, keep one going with his hand as he sucked and tongued the other. Before too long he was moving on to the next pair.

Henry Harrison stroked Alec's hair and smiled and at that moment, Alec saw the family resemblance. Henry's eyes crinkled just like Edward's, their brows the same. Alec often remarked on the brightness of Edward's blue eyes; it seemed it was a family trait, though Henry's were much lighter in color, Edward's more intense. The conversation carried on over Alec's head as he got to work in earnest. He was soon on his knees at Hamilton's feet where he belonged with four happy and contented clients crowing his praises. At least his arousal had remained on a low simmer. For the moment. Though his cock bobbed, semi-erect as he shuffled to get comfortable.

"If you ever change your mind, Richard, make sure to call me."

"You'll be waiting a long time. Alec rarely gives oral service nowadays. I'm not likely to consider expanding his repertoire at this stage."

"What stage is that? Are you going to be replacing him?"

"No, Henry, I'm going to be marrying him. We've been engaged for a while now."

Alec shot a glance to Hamilton towering above him. *Married. For real married. As in sharing the rest of their lives together married.* Alec felt faint. It was the proposal all over again. Thank goodness he was already on his knees. The men offered their congratulations, insisted on attending the ceremony and made preparations to leave all before Alec took another breath. Hamilton's fingers carded Alec's hair and Alec moved into the touch, nuzzling Hamilton's cock. Surely, Hamilton would reward him for being so good. He wouldn't leave him any longer, he couldn't, it would be cruel, wouldn't it?

"Present yourself, Alec."

Auto-response kicked in, Alec turned on his knees and pressed his shoulders to the floor. He felt the cool dribble of lube over his pucker and Hamilton wiggled the plug, eliciting a low moan from Alec as he tried to keep focus. A few pumps, in and out, and Hamilton removed it altogether. It felt strange after so long but Alec didn't move.

"That hole needs filling," someone said behind him. "What say you to a little extra play?"

"I'm sorry, gentlemen. Alec and I will be conducting the rest of this session in private. I shouldn't tease, but it is my birthday, after all."

Alec stayed in position as Hamilton escorted the men to the door. He locked it again behind them and returned to Alec's side.

"What would you like from me, Alec? Say it and it's yours for being such a good boy."

"I just want you, anyway you like, Master."

"You aren't sore from the plug?"

"Not for you."

Minutes spread into what seemed like hours. Alec was strung out on Hamilton's focused attention. Every nerve in his body was a tightrope, every cell begging for release. When the orgasm finally rushed through him, it was bordering on painful, his body spasming for seconds before slipping into the come down. Peace settled around him. He'd come full circle to the moment just before waking Hamilton this morning with his breakfast.

The only move he could make was toward the stroking caress of Hamilton's fingertips over his back. His body shuddered with an aftershock and Hamilton kissed his neck. "I love you more than anything, Alec."

A contented sigh was all Alec could muster in response.

Uneventful summed up the meeting so far with Viera. Alec had been expecting fire and passion and whispered promises but so far Viera had been on his best behavior. Not that Alec would have had much energy to respond after the marathon Hamilton had put him through. Had he known Viera was in town? No, it had to be a coincidence. Hamilton didn't keep track of Alec's appointments. He'd been frisky because it was his birthday, not because he was staking his claim before the Stallion turned up.

And here it comes. Alec straightened his posture as Sal Viera slipped up behind him and pressed against the length of his body.

"Alexander. I find myself unfulfilled after our last discussion. Tell me, have you thought anymore about the potential we have for fireworks?" Viera's hot breath rolled across Alec's neck and he smoothed a hand over Alec's butt cheek. "I still remember how you taste."

A quick glance over to the conference table confirmed everyone else occupied. Alec spun in Viera's arms and claimed his smooth-talking mouth in a passionate kiss. Viera responded enthusiastically and Alec stepped up the heat, slipping his tongue past Viera's lips and grinding their hips together. Viera kneaded Alec's ass in his hands and for a moment Alec imagined what it would be like to let go and just let it happen. There was no doubt the guy would be a talented lover. But Alec's passion was an act. His body was still pleasantly sated from his lunchtime frolics with the love of his life. The last thing he wanted or needed was a dose of sleaze. This was merely to poke Viera's buttons, remind him Alec was no push over.

Viera pulled away, breathless and smiling. "You want to take my offer. Very wise. But not here. We should celebrate with something special."

"Your offer? I thought you were taking mine, offering me the man rather than the money." Viera's smile faltered. Alec pressed closer into his body and grabbed a handful of ass for himself. "Will I be your first, Sal? I'll be gentle, make it special for you."

"And there is no other way, nothing else I can give you that will allow me to taste of your body, heart and soul?"

"There is nothing else I want or need from you."

Silence hung between them and Alec wondered what form the rebuff would take. Viera's body stiffened momentarily before molding to the contours of Alec's own. "Very well, Alexander. If that is the price to be paid, I will give myself to you. I only ask that it remain between us. Our secret. And I request your company for the whole night to celebrate fully our union."

Fuckity, fuck, fuck. That was unexpected. Now what was he supposed to do? "Sal, I—"

"You have broken down my defenses, Alexander. What more can you ask of me?"

"Nothing, it's just..." Just what? Alec had asked for the impossible and Viera had agreed to give it. What was there to do but go through with the ruse and fuck the man stupid before receiving the favor in kind? "Will I be your first?"

"Not my first. As a young man, I had many sweethearts. But now, now it is very rare, and not for a long, long time. But you, I sense, will be worth the discomfort."

"I won't hurt you."

"You may not hurt my body, but I sense you will unsettle my heart. The hunter has become the hunted and I am already trapped in your snare."

This time the kisses were sweet and gentle. Alec didn't know what to do next, how to proceed. It had to be another scam, a cheesy set-up that would lead to Alec being left in the lurch like so many others who thought they were finally getting through to the modern-day Casanova. Guilt maybe? He'd make Alec feel so guilty that he'd agree to be first and Viera would disappear before the tables were turned. He wouldn't be falling for that trick.

Viera slipped to his knees and released Alec's cock, nuzzling into his crotch. "Tell me how you like to be sucked, Alexander."

"Not here." Alec glanced back to the others. Still caught up in their own games, oblivious to the goings on in his corner of the office.

"But I want to show you I am serious about our arrangement." A long, slow lick solidified Alec's cock enough for Viera to get a good grip on the head and suck it into the tight heat of his mouth. Hell, the man had talent. Alec closed his eyes and rocked back on his heels. So much for not playing into Viera's very capable hands. The unexpectedness, accompanied by the audience, albeit not paying much attention, and Alec found it difficult to hold back the tide. Within minutes he was spilling his load into Viera's willing throat.

Viera smacked his lips and smiled. "You have a very distinct flavor. I like it very much." He tucked away Alec's spent cock and got to his feet. "Now, when do we fuck?"

"I'll have Bradley schedule an evening meeting. Sal, you don't have to do this."

"I want to. I want to see you trembling in my arms, begging for my cock. And I want to feel you working inside me to ferry me to climax. We will have a lot of fun, you and I." He leaned in to whisper against Alec's neck. "And I have plenty of toys for us to play with. I think you must like leather or maybe steel, yes?"

If Alec hadn't just emptied his balls, he would have at hearing those words roll over his skin. His cock attempted to show an interest but gave up, leaving him with an empty feeling that needed plugging, And after being plugged so thoroughly already today. So much for taking a break from new lovers.

Viera continued to stroke Alec's ass and turned his attentions back to Bradley and Fraser. The action had reached a critical point and the boys were holding each other, sharing kisses, as their bodies rocked from the individual activities. The men finished up, leaving Brad and Fraser huddled together, hard and needy on the table. Alec couldn't bear the thought of sending them to the shower in such a state.

"Shall we watch the boys finish together, gentlemen?"

"Wonderful idea, Alexander," Viera said, squeezing a handful of Alec's ass. "I'd like to see this blond one fuck Fraser."

Brad wiped his brow before crawling over Fraser and grabbing a condom from the box, always at hand in such meetings. The boys shared touches and smiles, a few heated kisses, before Brad revived the action in earnest.

With the men's attention firmly on the conference table, Alec let his mind wander with Viera's hands. His pucker smarted as Viera's finger brushed over it. Alec had no idea his pants were loose enough to accommodate a hand inside them, especially with his cock growing by the second.

"I will take you much like your boy is taking Fraser," Viera whispered. "Slowly, tenderly, making sure to answer every need that arises in your body until you are ready to give yourself completely. I will love you so thoroughly you will think of nothing else for years to come."

Smooth, enticing, but hardly all-encompassing. Even with Viera's finger in his ass, Alec was thinking of Hamilton. Of how he'd taken so much care to feed Alec's need, to know his heart and his mind and work his body to breaking point. Those were things that came with time, experience of one another. Viera was no match for that. For all his purple prose, Viera was nothing more than a one-time shag, or at least he would be.

Fraser was the first to go, spurting pearly strings over his stomach. Brad followed close behind. The rest of the group didn't seem interested in afterglow cuddles and were already collecting jackets and briefcases.

Viera extricated his hand from Alec's pants. "I will stay again and taste you one more time before our date, yes?"

"That won't be necessary. I have to see the boys cleaned up and back to work. Bradley will be in touch."

Viera looked confused, pissed that his charms hadn't had the desired effect. But Alec wanted to get on and get home not waste time nursing Casanova's ego. He bundled Brad and Fraser into the shower and the clients toward the door.

Viera grabbed Alec's arm and pulled him to one side. "When will I see you, Alexander?" There was an edge to Viera that hadn't been there before. It leaked from him like a bad smell and tipped Alec into defense mode.

"It'll likely be toward the end of next month. My schedule is kind of full."

Alec backed into the wall as Viera stepped closer. "Why so long, what about the weekend?"

A quick side step and Alec maneuvered past him back into the room. "I have plans this weekend and I'll be off for a month soon. There will be time when I'm back."

There was a relaxing of Viera's shoulders, a sign of defeat, or perhaps disappointment. "I see I have yet to capture your imagination as you have stolen mine."

"Please, don't take it personally, Sal. Remember I have a fiancé. As exciting as what you offer maybe it can't outshine the pleasure of an evening at home with the man I love."

"He is a very lucky man to have such commitment from you. I only hope he has the sense to cherish it as I would even with half that attention."

"Another time then?"

"Maybe," Viera said, shrugging his shoulders. "Or maybe I will have other games to play by then."

Alec kissed Viera's cheek and smiled. "So be it. Have fun, Sal."

"Goodbye, Alexander."

What a day. Considering it was someone else's birthday, Alec had sure had his fair share of surprises, from abstract promises of real marriage to offers of fucking the seemingly unfuckable, and tonight would be no exception. A few hours tied up making preparations for tomorrow and then off to the select gathering at Hamilton's to finish off his birthday celebrations. Brendan, Dylan, Sebastian, Bradley, and Alec, all there to cater to Hamilton's every need. With entertainment like that on tap, why would Alec ever be taken in by the tales Viera tried to spin? Admittedly agreeing for Alec to fuck him had been a shock, but even that wasn't enough to compete with the simple things Alec's everyday life had to offer. And especially not the events that arose from breakfast in bed.

A Day of Nothing Much

Thank goodness for a quiet day. Alec went through his morning ritual of going over his schedule. One early morning appointment, lunch with Hamilton, and a single afternoon meeting. Bliss. After such a heavy workload for the last week with back-to-back meetings and preparations running into his own time, Alec was ready for a day of nothing much. He was still tired and achy from Hamilton's birthday bash a few days previously and the thought of stretching out on the couch for an hour before getting cuddly over lunch looked perfect.

Bradley placed his coffee on the desk and perched on the edge, somewhat of a morning ritual in itself. "Any special requests before your eight-thirty?"

Alec pushed back his chair and gave Brad a stern but appraising look. Sometimes he forgot just how gorgeous this particular slave boy was. The sun filtering through the blinds picked up golden highlights in Brad's silky locks and made his eyes greener than green. Behind those green veils lay purpose. He looked like a hungry cat ready to pounce on its prey. Alec had no doubts he was the intended victim. "You can't possibly be horny already. Only hours ago you were plowing Sebastian into the mattress."

"What can I say? I have a big appetite and a taste for something dark and brooding."

The look alone, Brad's desperately hungry eyes, had Alec shifting in his seat. "What are you after? And I don't brood."

Brad shrugged off his jacket and placed it carefully over the chair. "Why don't I crawl under there and give you some attention while you finish reading Granger's file? I won't be any bother, promise."

That smile could win awards. Alec sighed. It wasn't as if he could ever say no to Bradley, but keeping a cool head and working with Brad hanging off his pecker was going to take some effort. Alec nodded once and Bradley disappeared under the table. Moments later, Alec's cock saw daylight for the briefest instant before Bradley engulfed it in his very capable mouth. There was no point trying to concentrate on reading from that point on, Alec couldn't even keep his eyes open other than to stare down at Bradley's bobbing head every now and then. And he was teasing, taking Alec to the very edge before backing off the pressure, swirling his tongue, it was all Alec could do not to hold him in place and fuck his face off. Office decorum dictated otherwise. At home, Alec wouldn't have let him get away with it.

Alec found the will to clip Bradley's ear. The resulting chuckle resounded around Alec's cock sending a shudder through his body. "Finish it up, I'm dying here."

With a concentrated effort on Bradley's part, Alec was spilling his load, grasping the arms of the chair so tightly he had cramp in his fingers. He sat, still gripping the chair, as Bradley cleaned him up and tucked him away.

"And all before your coffee's cold."

"Huh?"

"Drink up." Brad prised Alec's fingers open and handed him his coffee.

The warm liquid facilitated the kick-start Alec needed to his brain and a limited function resumed. He took his time savoring the fullness of his favorite Guatemalan roast, the sweetness to the flavor, the hint of chocolate flowing over his tongue. By the end of the cup, he was fully functioning. "I'm going to get you back for that," he said, handing the empty cup back to Brad.

"I'll be waiting."

He didn't have to wait long. Granger was a huge brute of a man with a cock to match. Bradley was soon splayed over the sofa whimpering and grasping for something to hold on to. By the time Granger had finished with him, a light tremble had taken up over the entirety of Bradley's body and he was looking decidedly pale.

As soon as he packed Granger off, Alec went to find Brad in the shower room. "Are you okay? He looked a little rough."

Brad was still trembling under the spray of water and Alec felt guilty until Brad looked up at him. His eyes were glazed in the thoroughly-fucked-and-finally-sated way he usually had after a syndicate had nailed him six ways from Sunday. "I'm great," he said, grinning like an idiot. "Please tell me I get to do that guy again. He found every single spot that drives me crazy." He ran a soapy hand over his ass and winced. "I think I'm in lust."

"As long as you're okay. Do you need me to have a look at you?"

"Please, there's no way that guy was anywhere near the size of the Mighty H. I admit I'm a little tender, but it's all good."

"I'll check you over tonight if you're still sore. Just to be safe."

"Oh for fuck's sake." Bradley turned off the water and bent over, spreading his cheeks. "You may as well do it now as fuss over me all day long."

A quick inspection revealed a healthy, if overly abused hole and Alec left him to finish up. By the time he came back into the office, Bradley was looking fresh-faced and happier than he had in a while.

"He really hit the spot for you, didn't he? You're literally glowing."

Brad shrugged. "Just came at the right time. It's not like I don't get what I need from you."

"But you don't really. You can be honest with me Brad. I'm not going to be offended." *Much.*

Brad sat on the edge of the desk, carefully, and brushed off the knee of his pants. "I guess I like them big," he said, picking up a handful of paperclips. "Broad, muscular, football types. But you know I totally get off on you and Sebastian too."

"I'm hardly in the same category as Sebastian."

"I know." He started making a chain out of the paperclips and laying them across the desk. "You've got a good body. Sebastian's a little skinny, but he has that cute-as-a-button thing going on for him that makes him irresistible. But in an ideal world, I like the muscle-bound giants. Mind you, it's not often they have the package to match. The number of times I've got it on with a big guy only to find out his dick has shriveled to nothing from steroid use. Such a disappointment when you can jerk them off with two fingers."

"Well, thank you for that insight." Alec quirked a smile. "I'm afraid I won't be bulking up for you anytime soon."

"That's good. I like you, just the way you are." Brad plopped the paperclips back in their tray, kissed Alec on the forehead and turned to leave. "Anything in particular you guys want for lunch today?"

"A sandwich is fine."

"I'll divert calls to your desk while I'm out."

Muscles. No wonder Brad was always so horny; he rarely got a taste of what really turned him on. Was lots of average sex better than the occasional mind-bending experience where everything clicked into place? Alec had no idea. He had that special buzz in his life constantly and everything else was a bonus. How would he feel if all he had to survive on were the extras? It didn't bare thinking about. His life was great, no question about it, but to be without the icing on the cake? And again, Alec was grateful for having Hamilton in his life.

He was still musing about the benefits of his beloved when a knock at the door pulled him to his senses. A quick glance at his watch, Brad would be back any minute. Typical. He straightened his tie and jacket.

"Come in." *Holy shit.* Alec jumped to his feet and headed for the door. "Lord Wessex." *What the fuck are you doing here?*

"Caldwell. No need to stand to attention. I want your opinion. Three files outlining details of an investment I've been offered." Alec started to respond but Wessex held up his hand to silence him. "It's not in-house; you don't have to worry about stepping on any toes. Now, I know we keep you busy but do you have time to give them a once over now? A full report isn't necessary."

Alec fought the panic rising in his stomach and took one of the folders. He flicked through the first few pages. It was going to be heavy reading but nothing he couldn't handle. He took off his jacket and hung it in the closet before sitting at the conference table. "Can I get you anything? Coffee, lunch," he looked at Wessex and smirked. "Bradley?"

Wessex smiled. "You know me too well but a coffee will suffice. I'll find the boy, you look at those." Wessex placed the rest of the files on the table and left.

Alec put on his game face and tuned into the reports in front of him. It made for interesting reading. The question was why had Wessex brought them to him? His work spoke for itself; all his investments were over-performing against market trend. Was it a test, a trap, maybe? He pulled at his tie and opened the top button of his shirt. The room felt stuffy and cramped despite its size and the icy air blasting down from the ceiling vent. The uncomfortable tightening in his stomach only heightened his anxiety. It was possible his entire career hung on the way he played the next twenty minutes.

Wessex busied himself fondling Bradley—who thankfully had reappeared within moments of Wessex arriving—and drinking coffee, but it didn't hold his attention for long. After another ten minutes, he sat alongside Alec at the table. "First impressions?"

Alec sighed and sat back to face him. Crunch time. "You have doubts?"

"That much is obvious."

"Why bring them to me? Hamilton deals with your financials. It should be Tom or Fraser looking over this for you, or Rick himself."

Wessex patted Alec's knee. "We both know Richard isn't an investments manager per se. Besides, this is a personal matter. A *private* matter. And, I remember from our previous dealings this is your area of expertise. So, thoughts?"

"It's a scam."

The air puffed out of Wessex's chest and he cursed under his breath. "Explain."

"It's a very good one. Designed, I would say, to hand to clients who you have already lulled into complacency with a few choice financial titbits before. So they trust you and aren't going to take too close a look at the detail. Do you have stock tied up in this?"

"Tell me why. Is it illegal? False accounting?"

"Nothing like that. That's why it's so clever. You'd never be able to bring anything against the manager. All of the figures, that I've checked at least, look real enough."

"Then where is the scam?"

"In the details. For a start there are too many of them. The files are bloated with irrelevant information, far too much for a client portfolio." Alec flipped open one of the files to a page detailing potential growth. "This graphic is pretty impressive, right? But it only shows forecasts for the first three weeks compared to the other competing plans that show steadier growth for three years. The other high-yield graphics relate to investments not tied to the plan, just included to make it look pretty. And here," Alec pointed to a section of text toward the end of the last folder, "it actually states that long-term investment is not advised as profits drop off after the first month and yet it's being marketed as a long-term plan with a six-month tie in. By then you'll be lucky to come out with half of what you put in."

Wessex spent a moment reading the section Alec had highlighted. "It really does say that."

"With all the useless crap wrapped up in here I don't imagine many people would read that far. It was handed to you by someone you trust, who expected you to read the first few pages and assume everything was under control by the amount of detail given. Someone who would then shake his head and commiserate with you when you lost money together. Maybe try and convince you to reinvest with him."

"How do they protect their investment?"

"That's the other clever part. I suspect they can show proof of their own investment in the plan?" Wessex nodded. "My guess is they cash out as soon as you buy in, walking away with the short-term gains that might actually be realizable, though not as grand as proposed. On top of the commission they'd earn from your investment, it would be money well spent. A quick turn around with very little risk." There was a definite thinning of the lips going on. Alec thought for a moment about leaving it at that, but Wessex had asked so why not push. "Now tell me, do you need rescuing and if so, how much are you in for and for how long?"

"You can turn this around, even with a six-month minimom term?"

"I'd have to look at the fine print on the contract but I think so. How much?"

"It's not me. I've learned the hard way not to take anything on the word of another, even brothers in the Order. But Jasper has invested heavily."

"I'll need a copy of every single piece of paper he's signed as soon as possible. Even if it's electronic, email promises, texts, everything. Who was it? It has to be someone he's close to."

"Jasper isn't exactly conscientious. He's a sitting duck for schemes like this."

"He must still have known them not to run it past his broker or accountant."

"He did run it past his broker. The idiot gave him the go ahead."

"Then it's time for Jasper to find a new one." Wessex nodded once. "I'll need to keep these," Alec said, touching his pen to the folders. "Send everything else by courier as soon as you can. I'll get straight on it. It's unlikely I'll be able to get him out altogether but I should be able to minimize his losses. With a few prayers he may break even."

"I appreciate your time, Alexander."

"It's what I'm here for."

"And I can count on your discretion?"

"Of course. Perhaps Jasper should make an appointment with Rick. Tom is an excellent Account Manager. He'll be well looked after."

"Maybe you would see him?"

"I could, I guess, but my clients these days are usually consortiums or ..." *really, really, rich bastards with more money than sense.*

Wessex laughed. Actually laughed. "Jasper may be just a boy, but he's a Wessex. He has more than enough, even with this oversight, to qualify for your personal attention."

"I'm sorry, I didn't mean to imply ... anything. Shit."

"Don't even think about it. And your candor in this matter will not be forgotten." Wessex held out his hand. "Good day, Caldwell." Alec stood to respond to the gesture. His hand trembled as he took hold of Wessex's. He was pulled in for a brotherly chest bump and patted on the shoulder. "You're proving to be worth the investment."

Investment? What is that supposed to mean?

"I may transfer my own accounts to your office." And then he was gone.

Alec flopped back into his chair. *Fucking hells bells.* So much for a day of nothing much. He heard voices outside the door, raucous laughter and then it opened again and a flushed, slightly aggravated Hamilton walked in, closing it firmly behind him. Alec got up to greet him with a hug.

"What the *hell* was he doing here?"

"Private matter." The stare alone was enough for Alec to rethink his answer. The color Hamilton was turning sealed the deal. The last thing he wanted after such an amiable time of it was to reignite the green-eyed monster. Alec stroked Hamilton's hand and smiled. "He was filling me in on news of Jasper."

"Jasper a new fuck buddy now, is he?"

"If he is, it's your fault. You started it with him and you know very well I haven't seen him since the Davenports. Now stop being an idiot and kiss me."

There was the smile Alec was after. They both relaxed against each other. "So bossy lately," Hamilton crooned, pinching Alec's ass. "I might have to see to that."

"If you weren't being bratty, I wouldn't need to boss you."

"Touché." They settled on the sofa together and Hamilton angled himself to face Alec. All that was missing was the spotlight and the magnifying glass. "So why was he really here?"

"It *really* was about Jasper. I'm hardly going to lie to you. He wanted me to look over some accounts for him."

"For Jasper?"

"Yes, for Jasper. If it was for Wessex, he'd have come to you."

Hamilton's eyes narrowed and the look went straight through to Alec's soul. "What aren't you telling me?"

"Stop needling me about clients. It's lunch time and I want to spend it with you, not talking business."

Hamilton kept up the scrutiny a moment longer before relaxing again. "I suppose I can give into you this once. The tickets have arrived. For Australia. Three weeks today and we say goodbye to business for a whole month. I've booked a stopover in Singapore."

"That's more like it. I'll need to shop."

"Sebastian is taking care of it. For both of us. I hope you don't mind that I called him."

Alec poked Hamilton in the ribs and he feigned injury. "Just remember he's *my* boy now."

"I know. I do miss him though. That quiet way he has about him. We should have a party before we leave. Give the boys a workout to remind them to be good while we're away."

Alec prickled. "So you can fuck Sebastian without having to ask me, you mean?"

"I fucked him thoroughly just the other day. A birthday gift, if I remember correctly. I'd forgotten all those cute little noises he makes."

"If you're trying to make me jealous, it's working. Don't make me turn the tables on you." The heat rising in Alec's cheeks made him uncomfortable. The last thing he'd wanted was to start an argument. How had it turned around on him so quickly?

"I'm sorry, darling." Hamilton pulled Alec to him and kissed the end of his nose. "Teasing over, I promise. Cute noises or not, nobody turns me on like you. You've been my special boy since that very first day."

The apology felt good, soothed Alec's frayed nerves. He still remembered the first day too. "When you taught me how to fuck Michael."

"Mm, and he showed you how to suck cock." Hamilton touched his forehead to Alec's, their lips just an inch apart.

"And I got to kiss you for the first time."

"Oh, please," Bradley said, bringing in the tray of lunch. "I'm going to barf if you two keep up the smooch talk."

"Haven't you ever been in love, Bradley?" Hamilton said, squeezing Alec's hand and leaning forward to land the kiss that had been hanging between them.

"Nope, and never intend to be either. Looks too complicated to me. Just point me in the right direction and tell me who to fuck. That works for me."

"You don't really mean that."

"No," he smiled. "But I've better things to be doing than wondering if or when it'll happen for me. I figure it'll happen when it happens and not before. Until then, I'm content with the way things are."

"A very sensible philosophy to live by." Hamilton held up his coffee cup as though to a toast. "And if love can find the likes of me, then no one is safe. And I mean that in the best way."

"You two are obviously in one of those moods, so I'm going to find some lunch company with less *cheese*." Brad grabbed his sandwich. "I'll see you later. Next appointment is two-thirty, Alec."

There was barely time to say "thanks" before Brad was out the door.

"Do you think he's okay?" Hamilton said, looking for the world as innocent as a baby, all wide eyes and open mouth. A mouth Alec shouldn't want to plug with the swelling appendage in his pants.

"Brad is just Brad. He's an odd soul but he seems to work things out in the end."

"You like him, don't you?"

"He's a great PA. Always on top of everything, never put me wrong so far. Good eye for detail. And, yeah, I like him. He's fun and good to work with."

"And he's a good boy?" Hamilton picked up his sandwich and inspected it before taking a bite.

"Great with the clients. Fab at home. Pokes me when I need to pay more attention to Sebastian. Couldn't ask anymore of him."

"Will you take him with you when you go to the fourteenth?"

"I can't imagine working a bigger caseload without him. Though his choice of sandwiches is sometimes suspect." Alec picked the olives from his sandwich filling and put the pieces back together. "Why? Is it possible he won't be able to come with me?"

"It's not usual. But then you both serve Harrison and he's the one behind the move so," Hamilton shrugged, "maybe. I'll have those."

Well, that was a downer. They'd just got into a rhythm together. Alec didn't want to break in a new PA. "No you won't." Alec slapped Hamilton's hand as he reached for the discarded olives. "I'll be able to taste them on you after."

"You're monitoring my food now?"

"Aw, baby, you want me to enjoy kissing you, don't you? So no nasty olives for lunch, there's a good boy."

Hamilton's shoulders dropped like a spoilt child not getting his way. "I don't understand where I went wrong. You used to be so docile."

"You put a ring on my finger, sweetie, and promised to marry me." Alec chuckled and leaned in for a kiss. "See, much better without olives. Besides, you love it when I take over the little things, otherwise I wouldn't do it."

"True enough." Hamilton finished his sandwich and put the empty plate back on the tray. "It kind of reminds me of living with my parents. Very apt since we're off to visit them soon."

"But first," Alec said, speaking around his last mouthful, "you have to meet mine. They're here this weekend, remember? Best behavior from you. I don't want my mother asking after Sebastian every five minutes."

"I will try my best but I am what I am and that isn't really boyfriend material."

"I disagree and my parents are odd enough that they'll love you."

"Charmed, I'm sure." Hamilton emptied his coffee cup. "Is it too soon after eating to fuck? I'm feeling a little antsy."

What is it with the horny toads today? Must be something in the water. Alec couldn't say he was about to complain, though. "Lock the door, then. How do you want me?"

Alec hadn't seen Hamilton move as fast in a while as he dived to lock the door. "On top." He grinned as he started stripping off, making his way back to the sofa.

"Okay, sit down."

"No, I want you to top."

"Even better." Alec cleared the tray to the kitchenette and took off his clothes. Hamilton was already naked, with lube in hand, by the time he made it back to the couch. Definitely nothing to complain about. They'd come so far since that first day, and seeing Hamilton stretched out waiting for him was as tantalizing now as the very first time he'd taken him. Alec pushed to the back of his mind the fact it had only happened because of one of Hamilton's outbursts and concentrated on the beauty of it. "See, you do like it when I'm bossy."

"It brings out the boy in me." The mischievous grin Hamilton gave him went straight to Alec's cock. He ran with the thought and weaved a little magic and role-play into their intimate moment. They were both sweaty and more than a little breathless as they came to lie side by side on the rug.

"Time for a shower," Alec said, starting to stand. "But we'll need to be quick."

Hamilton pulled lazily on Alec's arm to look at his watch. "Cripes," he said, jumping up. "I have to be downstairs in five minutes."

A flurry of activity followed and Hamilton was out the door with no more than a kiss on the cheek. He patted Brad on the shoulder as he passed him.

"You two love birds are getting on well at the moment." Bradley dropped a file on the desk. "Your two-thirty."

"Yeah, it's nice when he's playful. It makes me think it could last forever, you know? Are you set for your trip next week?" Brad going to Bermuda with Worthington had come around too soon for Alec's liking but he was determined not to hold on too tightly. After their earlier conversation, it seemed even more important to allow Bradley a long leash.

"I've booked cover. Are you sure you're okay with it?"

"Why wouldn't I be? Peter will look after you and you deserve to be pampered."

"I appreciate it. I think it'll be fun. Oh, and the files have arrived from Wessex Jr. complete with a date request. Shall I bring them in?"

"Yeah, I'll get on to those as soon as this guy is gone. But Jasper will have to wait. I have my parents to deal with and the night on the town with Sebastian's crowd. When is that again?"

Bradley frowned with just enough of a sigh to make Alec feel guilty. "Tonight. Don't tell me you'd forgotten. I've been reminding you all week."

Alec had forgotten. Because he'd been trying to forget. It was one more thing with the potential to upset the apple cart of his pleasant life. Why would he want to meet people that had known Sebastian longer than he had, had probably fucked him on a regular basis before Alec called a halt to it? It rattled him, made him overthink every conversation with Sebastian since catching him with Brendan and Dylan, and a few before. "What time do we have to be there?"

"Sebastian is expecting us home no later than seven."

"I can do that." If he shifted his ass with Jasper's files. "Hell, what am I going to do without you, Brad?"

"Fuck knows, but I'm not canceling now." Brad picked up his favorite paperclips and started to arrange them over Alec's desk. Alec made a mental note to get rid of the pot while Brad was away but then thought better of it. "It will last though, won't it?" He looked at Alec with such soulful eyes Alec felt his stomach knot. "You and Hamilton. He loves you, you love him, why wouldn't it?"

"Too many reasons. I don't like to think about it. Day at a time and all that."

"And a month in Australia with the in-laws."

And not a moment too soon as far as Alec was concerned. "He's different when we're on our own. The icy façade drops, the jealousy goes into hiding." *Mostly.*

"That's how it is for all couples isn't it?"

"Don't know. I've never been half of one before."

"You never can tell what goes on behind closed doors, my dad used to say. Or something about airing dirty laundry."

"Our dirty laundry always happens in public. Anyway, like I said, I don't like to think about it."

"If you're planning to spend your life with the guy, perhaps you should."

The phone saved Alec from having to comment. Not that he had anything to say. It wasn't as though he hadn't had the same conversation with himself a hundred times or more over the last six months. No amount of contemplation or weighing pros and cons helped him move forward with the problems that lurked beneath the surface of his contentment. Today, he'd been able to head off Hamilton's jealousy at finding Wessex in his office. It could just have easily gone the other way. Definitely too much to think about. Alec put it from his mind and opened the file in front of him to recap before his meeting.

Witherstone? He'd seen this guy a couple of days ago. And then he smiled. Hamilton's birthday. The day he'd been too horny for Hamilton to think about anything but the butt plug wearing away his cool. With memories like that ready to spring forth, why was he worrying?

Brad replaced the handset and piled his paperclips back into the tray. "Your two-thirty is on his way up. Shall I send him straight in?"

"Yeah. I guess he's not your type, right?"

"If he qualifies for full service I have no problem fucking the guy. He's kind of cute, in a nerdy way."

"He does qualify. I should give him a call-in option too. You're sure you don't mind?"

"Alec, when have you ever heard me complain about the guys you need me to service? What's up?"

"Just thinking about you and muscles."

Brad touched a hand to Alec's cheek. "You're a sweetheart. I love that you worry about me but I enjoy my job. *Stop second-guessing and do what needs to be done.*"

Alec nodded and Brad left to greet Witherstone. Stop second-guessing and do what needs to be done. Wasn't that just a peachy life philosophy lesson? Alec may not be able to figure out what needed to be done for his own life but he knew for certain Mr. Witherstone was entitled to a six-week fuckfest courtesy of Alec and Bradley incorporated. Well, Bradley at least and that opened up yet another can of worms in Alec's mind. It was about time he expanded his team to support Brad in the service role. A few more contracts and the service commitments would be too much for one person, even someone as hungry as Brad. And now Alec found himself back at square one and all he could do was move forward one day at a time.

And Then There Was Dancing...

The evening wasn't going quite to plan. Sebastian had taken well to Chloe, Tom, and Fraser, but Alec was fighting the temptation to rip Carl's arm off as he watched him flirting and touching Sebastian. It didn't help that Sebastian was drinking and much more animated than usual. He'd been nervous about Alec meeting his friends from work and now Alec knew why. Carl was a letch. Older by a good ten years and just an all-round Mister Nasty. At least as far as Alec was concerned. He even looked like a miscreant. Long, greased back hair, a heavyset brow, and a distinct sneer whenever he looked in Alec's direction.

Alec had gone out of his way to be polite to him, and to Justin and Barbara. Barbara was a sweet lady and Alec could imagine her mothering Sebastian in the office. Justin seemed like a run of the mill guy, but Carl. Just seeing the way he looked at Sebastian made Alec's blood boil. And there was history. Alec could smell it. Carl was lusting after Sebastian from memory not fantasy. He was just about to make his move, to wrap Carl's wandering hands around his neck and strangle him with them, when Sebastian bounded over.

"Hey, you. Come dance with me?"

The unexpected counter tactic threw Alec's focus. The heat and closeness of Sebastian's body won over and Alec allowed Sebastian to drag him onto the dance floor. And boy, could Sebastian dance. The brush and grind of their bodies in such a confined space, hemmed in on all sides by shimmying limbs, left Alec hard and achy. He pulled Sebastian back against his chest, ground his hard cock into his slave boy's tight little ass, and wrapped his arms around him. His lips trailed over Sebastian's neck, nipped at the delicate skin behind his ear. Damn, why had they never done this before? Alec hadn't been dancing since... wow, since Hamilton had taken him as an apology for one of his crazy fits more than six months ago.

The thump of the music did things to Alec's body. Good things that made him want to be very bad. The temptation to peel away Sebastian's clothes, to spear him right there on the dance floor in the midst of the crush of bodies threatened to take over and Alec loosened his grip. Sebastian twisted in his arms and pressed himself in close, reaching up to nibble Alec's chin. Fuck, he was blistering tonight. Every movement from his taut little body teased Alec's unruly cock, pushed him closer to the edge of his sensibilities. But this was a public club and they needed to behave. There was no sex going on in corners, a little fondling maybe, but nothing like their favorite bondage club, Rapture, where the only rule was consent. There were no cuffs or collars, no cages or naked slaves tethered to fucking posts. All of those things were fun, but here, there was dancing. Hot, raunchy, tease-till-you-spurt dancing, and for some reason it was a fair trade.

Sebastian ghosted his lips over Alec's cheek and squeezed his hand. He was sure he whispered something but Alec didn't catch it. Sebastian drew him away from their den of iniquity, through the crowd, to the bar.

They found their little group and Sebastian, slightly unsteady on his feet, hooked his arm with Carl's. "Another drink, please, maestro." He beamed and rested his head on Carl's shoulder.

Tension rippled through Alec's body. "Don't you think you've had enough, babe?"

Carl glared at him. "Who do you think you are, his father? I'll get you one, Seb. You still on shots?"

"He's not my *dad*," Sebastian chuckled. "He's my—"

"Boyfriend," Alec interrupted. "Yeah, he's knows. Come on, I'll take you home."

"Aw, not yet. I'll be good, I promise." Alec grabbed Sebastian just as he looked set to slip to his knees and dive for Alec's crotch. It seemed Alec wasn't the only one thinking of Rapture's lack of rules. Sebastian wavered, looked confused, then leaned against Carl and smiled up at him.

The greedy look on Carl's face raised Alec's hackles. *Just you dare*, Alec thought as Carl brushed Sebastian's hair out of his eyes, casting a glance over his body in the process.

"You used to be good to me, Seb," Carl drawled. "What happened to that, huh? When are you going to see to me again?"

Alec grabbed Carl's hand as he moved to cup Sebastian's butt cheek. "I think you'll find that belongs to me."

Carl tensed his arm and snarled. "Last time I looked it didn't have your name on it."

"Just goes to show how long it is since you've been there." Alec let go and pushed him into the bar. "Now back the *fuck* off."

The sudden tension created a pool of stillness around them. They both stepped closer in a face-off and Alec pulled Sebastian behind him. He tensed automatically when a hand slipped over his shoulder followed by Brad appearing in his peripheral vision.

"Not worth it, Alec," he said, trying to rub away the tension. "Take Sebastian for some air."

Alec took the opportunity, hauled Sebastian to a quieter bar on the other side of the club, and ordered a couple of bottles of water. The anger rolled off him in waves. He settled Sebastian onto a high stool and force-fed him a full bottle, holding him in place by standing between his knees. Sebastian grinned a lot and kept trying to wrap his legs around Alec's waist and even though he didn't want it to, the bad mood dissipated. When Sebastian started simulating oral sex with his water bottle, Alec knew it was time to get him home, but he couldn't leave without the others and there was no way he was going to let Sebastian near Carl again.

He looked around, hoping to see Brad or Tom, and with a stroke of luck spotted Chloe making out with Justin. With the show they were putting on, Alec felt less guilty about pawing Sebastian on the dance floor. He managed to get their attention just as the first boob flopped out from her non-existent top. She giggled, tucking herself away, and ambled over to Alec's stool, grabbing Justin's hand on the way.

"Hey, boss. What's up?"

"I'm not your boss."

She pinched his cheek and giggled. "Yeah, but I like the way it wrinkles your supercool exterior."

"Any chance of you finding the others? I need to get Sebastian home before he strips off and humps the barstool."

"Aw, but I want to see that show." She leaned around Alec and ruffled Sebastian's hair. "We should strip together," she said, shaking her boobs at him. "Let it all hang out."

Justin, still holding on to Chloe's hips, pulled the edges of her top and her tits popped out. She gasped, giggled again, and turned to launch herself into Justin's arms.

Alec sighed. "Chloe, put the puppies away, I'm trying to talk to you."

She spent a moment attempting to squeeze them back under cover and straightened herself up. "Okay, listening."

Denied access to the upper echelons, Justin decided to zone in on the real prize and his hand disappeared underneath Chloe's very short skirt. She fidgeted, wriggled and gasped lightly, her lips parting. Alec tried to ignore her glazed expression and the slight rocking motion of her body. "Can you find Brad for me? Tom, Fraser? Anyone but Carl."

She toppled forward into Alec's arms and moaned. "Right now? We're having so much fun."

Speak for yourself. Stuck between a rock and a hard place, or rather a couple of randy nymphomaniacs. Sebastian clawed at Alec's hips trying to get him to turn around and in the end he gave up. Sebastian was chewing on his bottom lip when Alec faced him. "What is it, babe?"

"I'm sorry about Carl, Master."

"Call me, Alec, sweetheart, and you don't have to apologize for working with an idiot."

"But I used to let him fuck me all the time," Sebastian rubbed himself against Alec's chest. "Give him blowjobs at work, and you hate him. You won't hate me now will you, Master? You still want me." He managed to wriggle around to press against Alec's hip, his cock begging for attention. "Please tell me, you still want me."

Alec was putty when Sebastian pouted and right now, the pout was at an all-time super cute high. How could he be so insecure when everyone melted at the first sign of his distress?

Alec pulled him up to sit straight on the chair. "I'll always want you, always love you. I don't care about your past." He attempted a tender kiss but Sebastian latched on, throwing his arms around Alec's neck, and a leg around his hip. There was no fighting it. Alec leaned against him, letting their cocks butt together and ground Sebastian into the seat. The thudding of his heart drowned out the music and he grabbed Sebastian's ass and pulled him closer, devoured his mouth, nibbled over that cute little pout. Holy hell, dry humping hadn't been as hot since his days as a virgin. If he wasn't careful, one or both of them would end up in a mess.

A pair of hands on Sebastian's shoulders broke the kiss. It took Alec a while to register them as Tom's. Fraser and Brad had also materialized next to him at the bar. "Security's getting angsty." Tom nodded in the direction of a burly looking guy with a heavy gaze settled on them. Black t-shirt with SECURITY emblazoned on the front. Hardly subtle. But Alec knew that look. The guy may have been on the verge of coming over to caution their behavior but he was definitely interested in a private show.

Sebastian rocked into Alec again. "Please, I need you. A dark corner, bathroom, find somewhere?"

"I think I might have an idea." Alec untangled himself from Sebastian's clinch. "Keep an eye on him for a moment, Tom."

Alec headed straight for the security guard. The guy was taller than Alec had anticipated by the time he reached him. He was easily six-four, rugged looking but not too scary, and with nicely sculpted lips. Hungry lips that matched the look in his eye.

"Are you going to tell me off?" Alec said, cocking his head to the side.

"Just take it down a peg. Someone complained to the manager." Typical. Alec would bet a week's wages nobody had complained about Chloe's tits or Justin's finger fucking.

"It's the first time we've been here. Our usual club isn't so stuffy."

"Here we have rules."

"Shame, you looked like you were enjoying the show." A raised eyebrow with a smirk, but silence. "So, is there a back room or something?"

"For what exactly?"

"That's what you want isn't it—to watch us fuck?"

"Not much fun if all I do is watch."

That was a surprise; Alec had been expecting some denial to begin with, having to persuade the guy to participate. He looked over at Sebastian. Of course he didn't need persuading, Sebastian had never looked so fuckable. But tonight, Alec didn't want to share him. He wanted his alcohol-dazed little slave boy all to himself even if it was with an audience. "Brad's single," he said, gesturing in Brad's direction.

"Yeah, okay," the security guy snorted. "Like *he* would go for someone like me. Besides, he looks like he's pulled already."

"Nah," Alec looked over at Brad again. He was kind of close to Fraser, but he hadn't asked to mess around or take a time out. Alec turned his attention back to the man-mountain. "Frazer's a guy from work and believe me, you are exactly Brad's type." Alec leaned in closer. "All big and manly." The shudder was subtle but it was there. The man-mountain wanted to rumble. "Where do we meet you?"

"Out front. It'll be fifteen to twenty minutes after doors close before I can get away."

Alec slipped a business card into the guy's pocket. "We'll go for something to eat. Call me when you're ready."

He didn't give his name, just nodded and turned away into the crowd. Alec had never pulled a one-night stand in a club before, let alone for someone else. It felt good, made him feel powerful, in control, which counteracted the frustration brought on by Carl, and improved his evening no end. Now to tell Brad. And remind Sebastian that good things come to those who wait ... just a little longer.

Redheads and
Red Faces

Alec stared at the shadows passing across the ceiling. It was raining outside and he could hear the sound pitting against the large windows. Usually it would have lulled him to his dreams but tonight it drilled into his brain and fired up the synapses, keeping him alert. Of all the nights not to sleep.

Hamilton snored quietly next to him, a hooked leg pinning him to the bed. So possessive, even when unconscious, but this display at least made Alec smile. Things had been easier lately but the alternative was ever present, hiding just beneath the surface ready to surprise him. And he could never judge which things would send Hamilton over the edge and which he could brush away with a joke. One day it would be the big things that scratched, another something so ridiculous Alec wouldn't see it coming. The result? A sleepless night the day before his parents were due for birthday/engagement celebrations. There was no point counting the minutes, time to get up and do something.

He checked the time again. Almost three. He could grab some R&R with Sebastian. If that didn't make him sleep, nothing would. Slipping out from under Hamilton's leg, Alec kissed him on the shoulder. He shuddered and stirred. "Is it morning already?"

"No, baby, go back to sleep. I'm going to spend a few hours with Sebastian. Come over after breakfast."

"'Kay. Love you." And he rolled over and dozed back off.

Alec pulled on jeans and a t-shirt, picked up his shoes and crept out. He didn't breathe again properly until the front door clicked into place behind him. Alec took in the coolness of the hall and closed his eyes. Was it wrong to feel free? So many things were changing so quickly he couldn't keep up with his own thoughts and feelings. Everything felt so fragile and yet he knew he couldn't let go of Hamilton anytime soon. There was too much of him Alec needed; good things that were worth a little sacrifice.

Feeling stronger, Alec stepped away from the door and opened his eyes. He jumped almost a foot in the air at the sight of a hunched figure on the hall sofa, half hidden by the console table.

"Tessa? What on earth are you doing out here? It's three o'clock in the morning."

She didn't look up, but he could see her eyes were red-rimmed and puffy. She seemed so small and childlike, curled into a ball, knees hugged tight into her chest. "I wasn't expecting anyone to be around. I needed space from the flat."

"There's often traffic between mine and Rick's at stupid o'clock. Be thankful I have clothes on, I wouldn't normally at this hour." She smiled but it didn't reach her eyes. "I'm sorry, you're upset and I'm being an idiot."

"It's nice of you to try and cheer me up." This time she looked up at him. The sadness in her eyes tugged at something inside Alec's chest and he sat next to her on the sofa wondering if he should put an arm around her shoulder.

"Do you want to talk about it? I'm told I'm a good listener." She sobbed a little, her shoulders shaking gently. "Or I could leave you alone?"

"I try not to think about it but being out with my friends makes it worse and sitting at home… You don't want to hear me rambling on."

"Tessa, didn't your father tell you we were here for you if you need anything?" She nodded glumly. "Then come on in. I'll put the kettle on."

"I don't want to disturb the others."

"Brad's in Bermuda and Sebastian sleeps like the dead. It'll be just you and me." Alec stood and offered his hand. He pulled her to her feet and maneuvered her into the apartment and through to the kitchen. "Tell me as much or a little as you want. I know sometimes it's just the company that's important."

"I feel so stupid."

"Whatever it is, I guarantee I can top it."

She slumped onto the kitchen stool. "Men are so … argh." She looked at him, her eyes so wide and filled with hurt. "I thought he loved me, Alec. I thought we'd have a life together. I don't even know if that's what I wanted, but it seemed right at the time and now he's gone I keep convincing myself he was perfect and I blew it."

"Is this the guy I saw you with the other week?"

She nodded and Alec busied himself with cups and teabags. "Rory. We've been dating for a year, or were, I should say. He broke up with me because I'm … not what he wants, apparently."

"He's older than you?"

"Only by six months. We were at uni together. I just …" She picked at her fingernails. "It's embarrassing *and* annoying." The sadness was spiraling up a notch into something else. Something that made Alec nervous. He needed a containment plan in case things got shouty but he was out of ideas.

"He must be stupid to let a beautiful girl like you go." *Dumb, dumb, dumb thing to say.* She smirked at him, a glint of steel in her glassy eyes.

"You don't have to humor me, but thanks."

"I didn't mean it like that. Look at you; you're smart, independent, and clearly intelligent—outside your taste in men." She chuckled and Alec rubbed her shoulder. "From what I know of you, you're sweet and funny." The smile cracked and she sobbed. *Oh shit, wrong thing to say, again.*

"That's what *he* said. I'm sweet, childlike, but he wants a woman."

"Tessa, if he wants you to be someone else, something else, then it's better he's gone. Don't change yourself for some asshole who isn't going to appreciate your effort anyway."

"It doesn't stop it from hurting."

"Besides, who says that? 'I want a woman'. It's so … pathetic. It sounds like he's the one that needs to grow up."

"I know you're right, I do. But … oh, Alec." She threw herself onto his shoulder and sobbed. Alec patted her back, rubbed her shoulders, patted her back again, then gave up trying to console and just held tight. That seemed to work and she calmed down, releasing him from the death grip around his neck.

"Tea?"

"Please." She handed him one of the cups he'd set out and produced a tissue from somewhere to dab at her eyes. "I must look like a wreck."

"Bit puffy, but it's allowed." Her chuckle was delightful and Alec relaxed a bit. He'd never been much good at comforting. "Do you want to sit on the sofa instead?"

"Oh, I'd just fall asleep."

"That's fine by me. If you want to stay over, Brad's room is empty. The sheets are clean."

"You're such a sweetheart. But curling up in the bed where my dad regularly … well, you know."

"Ah, okay. I didn't consider that. He's actually only been here the once and I'm not sure the bed saw any use."

"Mm, I think I'll take the sofa. It's the thought of it rather than anything else even though I'm sure the sofa has seen much more action." She chuckled. "You have quite the reputation."

"Now *I'm* embarrassed."

"Don't be. It's one of my failings. It's why Rory left."

"I don't understand."

"He's thinks I'm naïve." She sniffled. "No good in bed."

Who was this guy, other than a complete jackass? But Alec knew how she felt. It had been his greatest fear and one of the reasons he'd found himself unable to cross the finish line until Hamilton had taken him in hand. The idea of being boring or no good in bed still tweaked a nerve inside his thoroughly oversexed body. Alec stroked the back of her hand, still filled with damp tissue. "It's just as much his fault if the sex isn't good. It takes two and all that."

"Don't let him hear you say that. He's convinced he tried to encourage and teach me but I'm not capable."

"Rubbish, And I'd say it to his face. Everyone can be scorching hot in bed; it just takes the right partner."

"I appreciate what you're trying to do, Alec, but considering your reputation, your opinion doesn't count."

Reputation. Again. No wonder Hamilton always assumes I'm up to no good. "I'm not sure what it is you've heard about me, Tessa, or from whom, but it seems you only have half the picture."

"Okay, I'll bite. What's the half I'm missing, Casanova?"

"I've been with Rick almost a year. But he was my first. I'd never done anything, no blowjobs, no hand jobs, just snogging and the occasional dry humping session if I was really brave."

Tessa narrowed her eyes. "A year ago you were a virgin."

"Yup."

"And what? Rick taught you everything because he's such a sex-god?"

The temptation to say yes, made Alec smile. But the truth was even better and one of the very real things that kept Alec going back for more. "He taught me some things." Alec made another cup of tea for them both and took his seat again. "What he really did was tell me it was okay, there was nothing wrong with me, and everything would fit exactly where it should, when it should. I was never under any pressure to perform. Not from him anyway." Hamilton had always kept him safe, away from the real wolves, the Henrys, Arlands, and Dickies—even though he meant well—of the Order. Allowed him the time and the space to figure out what he liked and wanted for himself. "The right partner at the right time allows you to discover your body. Once you know what works there's no stopping it."

She looked skeptical. "There's no stopping you, it seems."

Alec shrugged. "I know what I like. But there's still plenty I'm discovering all the time."

"Such as?"

"I'm a bit of an exhibitionist."

"Service boys do tend to be, or you wouldn't do it, would you?"

"That's true. But to go from virgin to service boy overnight was a bit of a fast track so some things Rick protected me from. Now I've found my confidence I can push the boundaries, try new things. Some were big no-no's for me in the early days." His cock twitched tentatively at the thought of some of those lines he was now willing to blur. It made him want to crawl back into bed with Hamilton or even better head to a club, but that was definitely not the direction for his thoughts right now. Or anytime during his parents' visit.

"I can't believe I've been having sex longer than you." Tessa slurped at her tea, and slammed the mug back on the counter. "And bad sex at that. I'm a Harrison for goodness sake. How is it possible that I'm rubbish in the sack?"

Now there was a loaded question. Harrison senior certainly had a gift and it was about much more than having a massive cock. He was an expressive lover, responsive to the mood of the moment. But then, experience did that for you. Alec understood that for himself already. The number of lovers he'd had over the year wasn't excessive, but regular sex with a handful of men had educated him to the fact that every one of them was different, with buttons in unusual, interesting places. It was part of the fun, the thrill of discovering another's body, how it worked. But he'd had to wait for it, pine for it, long for it, until the time came for him to finally graduate into the good sex club.

And there was Tessa, an Order child, who would have had access to any kind of sex she wanted from the age of sixteen and she was still getting it wrong. Harrison could have had different ideas for his girls, wanted them to stay away from the sex side of things. "You never used the service boys?"

She shook her head. "My brothers always made use of the service. I don't know if Arianne ever did. She's six years older than me, we've never been close."

"Didn't you want to?"

"It never crossed my mind. I've always been more interested in books. I had boyfriends at school. Lost my virginity at eighteen to a steady boyfriend. I've never done the casual thing." She shrugged. "I've never seen the point."

"There's nothing wrong with that." Alec could quite happily tick over with his regulars without needing to chase anything new for himself. Not that Sebastian and Brad would be impressed. "If you find the button that makes you go wild but you don't need to press it very often, that's fine. But, sweetie, you *have* to find the button."

"What button?" They both looked around to see Sebastian, strolling in to the kitchen butt naked, cock at half-mast. He kissed Alec's cheek and headed for the fridge. "Thirsty," he said, and poured a glass of juice. They watched him glug it down, rinse the glass, and head straight back to bed without a backward glance.

"Is he sleepwalking?"

And how was he supposed to stop himself from following that cute little butt and pounding it into the mattress? "No. He'll remember in the morning. I'm sorry about that."

"It's your house." The slight flush of color suited her, and she was smiling. Sebastian naked always seemed to cheer people up. "Why would he expect to find guests in the kitchen at …" she glanced at her watch, "gosh, it's nearly four-thirty. I should let you get to bed."

"You're welcome to curl up on the sofa. I'll grab you a blanket."

She nibbled her lip and looked at him with what were obviously well practiced kitten eyes. "Alec? Would you mind if I slept in your bed, with you?" Alec's mouth opened but no words came out. "At home I always crept into my brother Eddie's bed when I couldn't sleep. No funny business, I promise."

Alec sighed. Could his life get any stranger? But he'd never really been around for his sister so he figured it might be good to put in some surrogate time with Tessa before Lucy arrived in a few hours. Even if he was sleeping with her father. "Come on then. I'll find you something to wear."

She beamed and Alec sighed. He was such a push over. She followed him through to the bedroom and sat on the edge of the bed as Alec opened a drawer to find a t-shirt. He handed her the biggest he could find, hoping it would be long enough. "Do you want me to get a pair of Sebastian's shorts? They should fit you."

"This is great, thanks."

"Tessa, do you have an Uncle Henry?"

"You've met Henry Harrison?"

"He was in one of Rick's meetings, at work."

"He's one of my father's many cousins. His Grandpa was a bit of charmer. Lots of children out of wedlock." She smiled. "It makes for a very large family."

"They look so much alike; I thought he may have been a brother."

"It is a possibility. But daddy is usually very open with us about the unofficial family tree."

Unofficial, much like Jasper's story. At least he hadn't sucked off Harrison's brother, that would be weird. It was weird enough having fucked Hamilton's nephew and sucked off two of his uncles. "Would you like to use the bathroom?"

She nodded, and Alec showed her to the main bathroom along the hall. Could things get any stranger? At least it had taken his mind off his parents, if only for a while.

"Master?" Alec stirred to the faint whisper in his ear. Gentle fingers brushing back his hair.

"Sebastian? What is it?" He was kneeling on the floor beside Alec's pillow, his eyes wide as saucers.

"Why is there a girl in your bed?"

"What?" Alec sat up, and followed Sebastian's gaze. "Fuck. Is that…? Tessa." Of course it was Tessa. Slowly the events of the previous night filtered into his sleep clogged brain. "She broke up with her boyfriend." Alec collapsed back against his pillow and nestled in.

"So you had sex with her?"

"No, sweetheart. She just needed to be close." Alec lifted the edge of his duvet and Sebastian crawled under and snuggled into his side. So peaceful. Alec loved the quiet times before the day started with routines and rituals.

"It's funny," Sebastian whispered. "With you wearing clothes in bed."

"It feels weird, too."

"She's pretty. I like her hair."

Alec stared at Sebastian. There was a definite swelling going on against Alec's leg. "Are you getting a boner for her?"

Sebastian buried his head against Alec's shoulder. "Of course not. I'm cuddling you. You're the one making me hard, Master."

"That's okay then." There were plenty of odd things Alec was happy to deal with on a regular basis, finding out Sebastian had a soft spot for redheads, *female* redheads, wasn't one of them.

The slow rocking motion of Sebastian's body against Alec's leg sent a shudder and delicious tingles sweeping through him. Sebastian pressed his lips against Alec's ear. "I like it when you're jealous."

"I don't." They settled back down and Alec took to stroking Sebastian's shoulder. "Have you ever had sex with a girl?" Sebastian shook his head. "Would you want to?"

"Dylan used to talk about it a lot. He had phases of being a bit of a ladies' man. Brendan always complained about catching girl cooties."

"But you never wanted to try?"

"I had the opportunity at uni, and at clubs, but," he shrugged, "there were always guys I was more interesting in hooking up with. What about you?"

"I did think at one point I should try it, especially when man-sex seemed so elusive. But, I never found anyone I was remotely attracted to."

"What about her?"

"I'm her father's bit of fluff. It would be completely inappropriate."

Tessa rolled over to face them, a huge grin on her face. "And I prefer blonds." Sebastian flushed scarlet as Alec and Tessa laughed. She pointed to the bathroom door. "Can I avail myself of the facilities?"

"Sure, there are clean towels on the shelf if you want a shower."

"I'll shower at home. I wouldn't want you all to catch girl cooties. What do you usually do for breakfast?"

"Well, I usually have Sebastian but I'm sure we can find you something more traditional."

"I can cook, if you don't mind me raiding the kitchen."

"That's Sebastian's territory. I wouldn't dream of inviting you into his lair."

"Don't listen to him, Tessa. You're welcome to rummage around if you'd like. I'm Sebastian by the way; it's nice to finally meet you."

"Oh, we met last night," she said, winking at Alec. "You were thirsty."

Sebastian's head thudded against Alec's shoulder. "Why didn't you tell me?"

"And miss that look on your face when you figured it out? Why so shy all of a sudden?"

Sebastian kept his head down. "I'm not used to being around girls at home."

Alec could feel Sebastian's cock thickening again. "Especially pretty ones?"

"Master, stop it, please."

"I'll leave you boys to it." Tessa skipped from the bed with a backward wave. "Back in a jiffy."

"You'd best find something to cover up if you're going to be modest."

Sebastian's grip was surprisingly strong when he put his mind to it. Alec coughed at the squeeze around his chest. "You sure you don't mind?"

"Go find some shorts before I change my mind."

"And a t-shirt?"

"If you must." Talk about taking advantage of a situation.

"Thank you, Master. I love you."

After a good breakfast, Tessa looked much better, and seemed happy again. "Do you have plans for the weekend, Alec?" she said, clearing away the dishes and piling them up for Sebastian as he rinsed and packed the dishwasher.

"My parents are coming for a few days. I'll be off to pick them up from Paddington in an hour or so."

"Where are they coming from?"

"Penzance, they live in Marazion. I was going to drive down and collect them but they insisted on taking the train."

"I like the train." She picked up a cloth and started to clean the counter. Well trained in the art of domesticity it seemed. Alec never remembered to wipe down the sides. "And it's a nice enough journey from there. Bit long. I hope you sent them first-class tickets."

"I tried. They wouldn't have any of it. It'll take them the rest of the day to unfold after five hours in those tiny seats with no leg room."

"No different to being stuck in the car," Sebastian said. "Trains are cool. At least you can have sex in the toilets."

"I'm pretty sure my mom and dad won't be squeezing into one of those cubicles for a quickie, Sebastian. Not with my sister outside the door."

"Oh, I don't know." Sebastian grinned. "If your dad thought he could get away with it." He took the last of the dishes from Tessa and loaded them. "Alec's parents are really cool. But then, yours are too. I don't even care to remember mine."

"Mom loves you. That counts."

Sebastian smiled. "Yes, it counts a lot." He came to rest against Alec, and Alec buried his face in the warmth and homeliness of his blond mane, longer than usual at the moment and smelling of exotic fruits.

"Okay, well I'm going to head home." Tessa brushed off her hands and propped them on her hips. "Thanks for the company, boys. I really appreciate it."

"You're welcome any time, Tessa." Alec accepted a kiss on each cheek. "You can come over for boys' night if you like. We have them every few weeks. No funny business, just food, drinks, and sometimes a movie."

"I'd like that. Have a great time with your folks." She grabbed her folded pile of clothes. "Is it okay if I bring the t-shirt back another time?"

"No hurry."

Alec waited for the sound of the front door. "What do you think of our new friend and neighbor?"

"She's nice. I hope she doesn't end up in your bed too often though. I missed my morning cuddle and I won't see you later."

And there was the pout. Irresistible. "We can make a little time now." Alec kissed Sebastian's neck and shoulders; let his hand slip under the annoying t-shirt to tweak a nipple. It was by sheer chance he looked toward the door, thinking ahead to the bedroom. "Sebastian, go, now."

"What?" Sebastian turned around and stood face to face with a livid Hamilton, practically foaming at the mouth. Alec made a quick scoot around the room to put him out of harm's way but he dived back between them, grasping Hamilton's arm as he swung for Alec. "No!"

"This doesn't concern you Sebastian," Hamilton growled. "Stay out of the way."

"I won't let you hurt him. Just the same as I'd never have let anyone hurt you. Whatever it is you should at least ask him about it."

"About the whore I caught slipping from your apartment in one of his t-shirts? Not only am I sharing his ass with half of London, he's taken to fucking women as well."

Alec couldn't say anything. There were no words to counter the absurd accusation and even if there were, he couldn't be bothered to say them.

"Alec is *not* fucking Tessa Harrison," Sebastian said, still holding Hamilton back with a surprising amount of strength. "Not that he should have to explain it to you. What the hell has gotten into you lately?" Sebastian pushed back against Hamilton's attempt to move forward. "Nearly seven years I was with you and not once did I ever see you raise your hand to anyone in anger."

"I *said* get out of the way."

Alec could see Sebastian's grip on Hamilton tighten. "Don't make me hurt you, Rick. You know I can if I have to."

The anger drained from Hamilton as though someone had unplugged him from the mains. He stared for a long time at Sebastian then dropped his arm. "I'm sorry you had to see that."

"What the fuck were you thinking? His parents are coming today. How would that have worked, exactly? 'Hello Mr. and Mrs. Caldwell, I'm sorry your son has a black eye and a broken nose, but I'm a nice guy really.' Not the best introduction in the world."

When Hamilton finally looked at Alec again, his expression was full of remorse. "Alec?"

"I don't want to hear it. I need a shower."

Alec couldn't stop himself shaking as he stripped off the pajama bottoms he'd worn for his guest, and stepped into the shower. The hotter the water, the colder he felt, and yet he was burning up inside. When was it going to end? For the first time he wondered whether Australia was a good idea. A whole month alone with a guy who randomly flipped into a maniac and wanted to beat the shit out of him. It didn't sound like a sensible idea when you laid it out.

He closed his eyes and rested his head against the coolness of the stone tiled wall. The scent of lemony zest shower gel that would supposedly kick-start his day just made his stomach turn over. It was easier to push it to the back of his mind and forget about it than attempt to see a way forward.

A change in the sound of the water hitting the floor was the first indication he wasn't alone. He was expecting Sebastian's lips, soothing his troubled back muscles, but the press of the body against his back was taller.

"I know you don't want my apology, darling, but please, let me stay close for a moment." Hamilton wrapped Alec up in arms so gentle you'd never believe them capable of violence. Alec twisted in his arms to look at him. The sadness in his eyes was heart breaking. Alec wanted to fix it. Had to. As their lips met, the uncertainty of a moment ago washed away in the stream of water and the world settled back into place. This was the Hamilton he craved. If only there were a way to keep the alter ego from showing up.

Alec allowed himself to be coddled and caressed, and sucked to within an inch of his life. Hamilton dried him off in the biggest, fluffiest towel he could find and led him into the bedroom where he took time to massage his limbs with body lotion before choosing his clothes and helping him dress.

"Can I stay to meet your parents? I understand if you've changed your mind." Hamilton touched their foreheads together. Intimacy. Safety. How far beneath the surface was the tiger hiding?

"They're expecting to meet you. I don't want to explain why you've suddenly found somewhere else to be."

"I don't want there to be tension between us. I know I'm an idiot."

"And an asshole."

"That too." Hamilton stroked Alec's cheek, rubbed a thumb along his jaw. "Will you be okay?"

Alec swallowed around the lump in his throat, pushed past the swear words, desperate to escape. "How could you think I'd be fucking around with women?" The quietness of his own voice surprised him. "And half of London? That hurts, Rick. I can't tell you how much. It's going to take more than an apology to fix this one."

"I understand."

"And what if you'd hurt Sebastian instead of me?"

"Unforgivable. I know."

The peacefulness between them soothed Alec's frayed nerves and started the healing process but when it would be finished, Alec didn't know. He didn't want tension between them either. What he needed was a magic button. "What did he mean? Sebastian, that he could hurt you if he had too?"

"When he first came to live with me I enrolled him in a martial arts course. He was so little. I wanted him to be able to protect himself at college and if he was out on his own."

"So he's a secret ninja warrior?"

Hamilton chuckled. "Something like that. He'd have broken my arm easily. You may be his master, but today he was your protector." Training boys to look after themselves. That was Alec's Hamilton. The man he loved. Cherished. Worshipped.

"I need to see Sebastian." Alec squeezed Hamilton in a bear hug, almost to convince himself he still could. "Let him know I'm okay."

"Shall I stay here and start lunch?" Alec looked at him blankly. "While you go to the station?"

Station. Parents. *Fuck.* And just when he needed some space to think things through. One thing at a time. "That would be great. Thanks." Always one thing at a time.

The Truth Will Out

The station was busy, but strangely relaxing after his morning at home. For someone like Hamilton, who'd didn't have a monogamous bone in his body, the jealous outbursts were troubling to say the least. He could understand it to a certain extent. He'd felt that loss of control seeing Sebastian in the act, but Sebastian had broken the rules. Alec didn't have an exclusive clause with Hamilton anymore. Hamilton had no right to question Alec's sexual choices. Did he? And that was where good sense lost out to uncertainty. As Alec's master, as Alec's fiancé, did he have the right to be pissed off when he thought Alec was getting some after hours? May be he did, maybe he didn't. What he didn't have the right to do was knock Alec silly, period. And what he didn't have the right to do was spit wild and hurtful accusations or lose the plot. Why couldn't he just ask if he was concerned about something, like a regular human being? And there, Alec lost the thread again, because when was anything to do with Hamilton regular?

He checked the arrivals board for the platform number and wandered toward the gate. Time to shake himself out of contemplation mode or it would be twenty questions all the way back to the apartment on what was bothering him and why he looked so glum. Even Chris, the driver, had asked him if everything was okay.

"Alec!"

He barely caught Lucy as she jumped at him from nowhere, wrapping her arms around his neck and her legs about his hips.

"This is so cool. I can't believe you've lived in London this whole time and I'm only just getting to come and visit. Where's Sebastian?"

"Hello to you too." He placed her back on her feet and looked behind her. "He's at home helping Rick with lunch. Where are Mom and Dad?"

"Oh, you know what they're like. And they brought the biggest suitcase on the planet; neither of them can lift it."

"I should go and help."

"No need. Mom roped two lads into carrying it." She checked her makeup in a small mirror and reapplied some gloss to her lips. "It was so embarrassing. She just went right up to them and said they looked the type that needed to learn to help people. I nearly died on the spot. Told them in her day old people didn't need to ask, there would be a line of youngsters waiting to lift and carry for them."

"She's not even old. They're only fifty."

"Tell them that. On and on she went about the state of the country. I left them to it."

Alec took another look at the gate and sure enough about a hundred feet away, holding up the flow of commuter traffic, two lads were hauling a huge case behind them, followed by his mom and dad looking for all the world like royalty.

"Told you," Lucy said. "Last time I travel on a train with them, I'm telling you now."

"Alec, yoo-hoo." His mother waved. "There he is boys. Head for the tall, distinguished young man with my daughter. There he is look, George. I told you he'd be on time."

The two young lads pulled up to a stop just in front of him. They were looking a little worse for wear; probably from the good ear bashing his mother would have given them for clothes, hair, attitude, basic demeanor. The taller of the two, actually managed a smile. "She's all yours now, mate." He looked Alec up and down. "Can you manage the case, or will you break one of those manicured nails of yours?" It was a friendly smirk and Alec laughed. He pulled a couple of twenties from his wallet and handed them over.

"Run," he said. "Before she decides to put you on litter duty."

"Whoa, cheers, mate."

"Now just you wait one minute." All three of them dropped their shoulders and turned toward Alec's mother. "If you're going to take my son's hard-earned money, you can at least take that case to the car. Do you have the car, Alec, or are we taking a taxi? Please tell me we're not getting on the tube."

"The car's waiting, and I can drag a case a few hundred feet."

"I can't help you lift it into the boot, son," his father said. "Got a bad back at the moment."

"Chris is there. He'll help."

Alec's mother dismissed the two boys and Alec tipped the case back onto its wheels and headed for the exit. "What the hell have you got in here, a dead body? You do know you're not moving in don't you?"

"Excuse me, young man," his mother said, poking his arm. "Where's my hug?"

Alec settled the case on its end and crouched down to his mother's height for a bear hug.

"You looked so refined standing there. Makes me tear up, it does. My little boy, all grown up and a man in the world."

"Okay, you can let go now."

She released him from her grip and pinched his cheek. "So handsome. Now, who's Chris? I thought we were here to meet Rick."

"Chris is the driver. Now hurry up before he gets a parking ticket."

In the short space between the platform and the car his mother managed to regale him with the entire train journey, how proud she was he had a driver, the ecological consequences of too many cars on the road, and how she really wanted to see Buckingham Palace. She was still talking when he opened the car door and gestured for her to get inside.

"Take a breath, Mom. I'll be back in a moment."

His father gave him a suffering smile. "It's good to see you, son." They hugged briefly and his dad climbed in beside his mother. Lucy was already making herself comfortable.

Alec found Chris at the boot struggling with the case. "I don't suppose you'd give me a hand with this?" he said. "It's really heavy."

"I wouldn't expect you to lift it on your own." They heaved the case into the boot and Alec slipped into the car beside Lucy.

"Great car," she said, bumping his shoulder. "Do you get to ride a limo to work every day?"

"Not every day. But there are three of us in my building that work for the same company. If we're all due in together, we have the car. Otherwise I take the tube."

"It's not yours then?"

"Technically, it's Rick's. He lets me use it when I need to."

"Let's see it then," Alec's mother reached for his hand, and Alec obliged by showing his ring. "Oh, sweetheart. That's a beauty. He's rich then, this other boyfriend of yours?"

"I suppose. I don't really think about money anymore."

"All right for some," Lucy said, grabbing his hand. "By hell, look at the size of it."

"Language."

Lucy ignored her mother. "Is it a for-real diamond, not a fake?"

"It's real." Alec grinned. He'd missed Lucy. The previous evening with Tessa had highlighted how much of her life he was missing living so far away. The last year had domesticated him somehow and family suddenly seemed important. Perhaps it was just the idea of going off to meet Rick's family that was making him nostalgic.

The journey was sticky with traffic but it passed quickly enough discussing all the things they wanted to do and see on their short break. Lucy had never been to London before and wanted to see everything. His mom and dad had been when they were younger and wanted to see if the big attractions had changed any. There was no way they'd see everything in three days and they threw plans around for a Christmas visit for shopping and a show.

It wasn't until they pulled up outside the building and Alec and Chris had to fight the suitcase out from the car that a flush of tension ran through Alec's body at the thought of what would be waiting for them upstairs. Would Rick be his usual cordial self? Any sign of his alter ego would alert his mother and Alec would never hear the end of it. Everyone was unusually quiet in the elevator.

"You must be really rich," Lucy whispered, as the bell dinged for their floor.

"Um, not really. The flat comes with my job. I told you I moved up a few floors at work."

She nodded but didn't say anything else. The strange silence soon changed when Alec opened the door and Sebastian appeared in the hall to greet them. After hugs, kisses, and squeals of delight at the first glimpses of the apartment, Alec herded them all into the living room where Rick was waiting. Alec needn't have worried. He was his usual charming, adorable self, sweeping Alec's mother into the kitchen for a 'little glass of something special' before taking her and Lucy on a tour.

Alec enlisted Sebastian's help with the suitcase and took it through to Brad's room, closely followed by his father. They wrestled it onto the ottoman under the window so it was at a good height for unpacking. Alec started to unzip it.

"Oh no you don't." His father grabbed his hand. "Maggie will have me shot at dawn if I let you ruin your birthday surprise."

"Oh, hell. What's she done?"

"My lips are sealed. How about a nice cup of tea and a cookie. You do have cookies in this fancy pad of yours don't you?"

"We sure do," Sebastian said. "I remembered to buy your favorites or there are some homemade ones in the tin."

"As long as it's sweet and crunchy, I don't mind."

Sebastian kissed Alec's cheek. "Dinner will be about an hour. Do you want tea or coffee?"

"Coffee, I guess."

"You look to me like you need a nap," his dad said. "Not sleeping, son?"

"Didn't get much sleep last night. A neighbor just split up with her boyfriend. Needed a shoulder to cry on."

"As long as that's all it is."

Fuck. Alec should have known his father would see straight through everything to the bare bones. "What else would it be?"

Sebastian rubbed Alec's shoulder. "I'll go heat some water."

"So, are you going to tell me what's up or do I have to guess?"

"Not now, Dad. Let's gets you settled first, eh? Is anything in here Lucy's?"

"Your mother will sort it out later. Let's find that cup of tea then."

Lucy and his mother were smitten. Rick had them eating out of his hand with the personal attention If there was one thing he had in droves, it was impeccable manners. Alec was sure his mother would have liked to marry him herself. She cooed and fussed and sang his praises all afternoon to the point that Alec felt smothered by his perfection.

He slipped away to help Sebastian with the dishes and took a moment just to lean against him.

"You're doing great." Sebastian stroked his back and nuzzled into his neck. "You want me to stay longer? I don't think Brendan and Dylan will mind if I'm late."

"No, you should go and enjoy your weekend off. Don't worry about me. Everything's fine now."

"As long as you're sure." He popped in a dishwasher tablet and put the machine on. "The kitchen is stocked with all the stuff they like and Rick said he'll cook breakfast in the morning. I left a little present on my bed for Lucy. I hope she likes it."

"You're a godsend, babe, you know that, right?"

"I still like to hear you say it, Master." They kissed a little. Alec wanted to reach out and hold on when Sebastian stepped away from him. "I'll go and say my goodbyes. I'm only a few doors away if you need me. For anything."

Alec nodded. His heart hurt seeing Sebastian walk out of the room. Why had he arranged for him to stay at Hamilton's for the weekend when he needed him here? Because he hadn't expected he was going to need him for moral support in a stand-off with his own fucking master, that's why.

Alec could hear laughter filtering through from the dining room. He rubbed his face to try to get rid of his crabby mood. When he looked up again, his dad was standing in the doorway. "Got a minute?"

"Sure." Alec gestured to the breakfast bar and they both took a seat. "How do you like the place?"

"It's amazing. You've really landed on your feet, son. I'm proud of you."

"You know it's not all mine, right?"

"Still takes something to be in even a share of a place like this. I always knew you'd make good. Your sister will too, in her own way. But I always saw this for you."

"And how are things at home?"

"Are you sure about this marriage thing, son?"

"What, I'm not allowed to get married because Rick isn't a woman?"

His dad reached for his hand. "You know very well that's the last thing on my mind."

Alec did, and nodded guiltily. His parents had been nothing but supportive his entire life. It had taken him a while to understand not everyone accepted his kind. And they'd been there to nurse him through that too.

"You've got so much going for you, and what about Sebastian and that other guy you date? I thought you had a nice little arrangement going on."

"We do. We still will. But Rick," Alec sighed, "Rick's the one I really love, Dad. The rest is fun and … but I'd give it all up for him."

"And you're sure about him?"

"You don't like him do you? I could see it after about five minutes."

"He's polite, well mannered, has your mother wrapped around his finger already and that's no easy feat. But, no, I don't like him. I've nothing against him. He's just not for you."

"I don't know what I'm supposed to do with that."

"He's got a temper on him, hasn't he? Maybe you haven't seen it yet, but I can see it hidden behind that perfect mask he wears. I've seen men like him before and they destroy people. I don't want that for you, Alec."

"He's not like that." *I don't want to believe he's like that.* "It's complicated. I'm not the easiest person to live with."

"Put your hand on your heart, son, and tell me he's never raised a hand to you in anger, and I'll never bring it up again."

Alec looked at his shoes. The right one had a scuff on the toe. Must be from that bloody suitcase.

"I guess that means you can't. I'm not going to tell you what to do with your life. God knows your mother does enough of that for the both of us. Just promise me one thing." Alec met his father's concerned expression. "Find the line and stick to it."

"The line?"

"There's always a line. Promise me, if or when he steps over it, you'll walk away and not look back."

How was it possible his father could see what his mother didn't? What Alec wouldn't see? Alec had the very best of Hamilton, a side that nobody else saw; gentle with a subtle, submissive edge that rocked Alec's world when it peeked out from behind the mask. But with it, he witnessed the worst of him too. As hard as he tried to ignore it, he couldn't deny the potential for disaster. "What if I don't know where the line is?"

"You do. It's always there in the back of your mind. When he crosses it, you'll want to move it but you can't let that happen."

"How do you know so much about it?"

"Your Aunty May. She never held the line, Alec. Always pushed it further and further until the time she didn't get to come home from the hospital. Don't let that be you."

"I thought she moved to Ireland when we were kids."

Alec's father shook his head. "That drunken bastard of a husband beat her into a coma. She died a week later." His father sniffed. "I could have stopped it. Should have. She promised me she knew where the line was. I'm not around enough to keep an eye on you, son, but if you ever need to, you come back home."

They sat in silence for a while, Alec letting the information sink in even though he didn't want to carry it.

"Alec?" He looked up to see Hamilton walking toward him, every inch the angelic perfect boyfriend. "We were wondering where you were. Do you want to show Lucy to her room?"

Alec's father stepped down from the high stool and patted Alec's shoulder. "Find the line, son."

Alec nodded his head.

"What was that about?" Hamilton slipped his arms around Alec's waist and kissed his neck. "Are you sure you're okay? You've been really quiet."

"You know why I'm quiet."

Hamilton stiffened. "Is that why you're hiding in the kitchen? I did offer to stay away."

"I'm not hiding. I was catching up with Dad."

"I don't know why I said those things. Just know I love you more than anything."

"That's what makes it so hard. I know you love me. So to say stuff like you did. It doesn't make sense."

"The anger I feel at the time doesn't make sense either. It's completely irrational. I know that. Maybe I should leave. I don't want to ruin this weekend for you with your family."

Alec held on to Hamilton's arm resting over his stomach. "Don't you dare walk away from this, from me."

"Then give me space to make it up to you, sweetheart. Let me back in, please." The insistent nuzzling against his neck, the firmness of Hamilton's arms around him, pulling him back against his strong, warm chest made Alec cave. He twisted in his seat and their lips met in a crush of passion and longing that tasted so good Alec couldn't stop the groan that escaped.

Hamilton pulled his knees around and spread them, settling between and pressing his growing cock against Alec's crotch. "God, I want you. Do you think your parents will mind if we take a time out?"

"No, but I will."

Hamilton sprang away from Alec, and Alec laughed at the flush that colored his cheeks.

Lucy burst out laughing with him. "Chill, dude. I'm joking. I get you want to hump the pants off my brother every chance you get. You wouldn't have given him that bloody great diamond otherwise."

"Still," Hamilton said, straightening himself out. "I should have thought to hold back until we were behind closed doors. I'm sorry."

"I'm not." She grinned and Hamilton blushed even more. "He's different to Sebastian," she said to Alec. "I like him. He looks like he can keep you in line. When he's not fawning all over you, that is."

Interesting choice of words. Lucy had noticed the same thing as their dad but without understanding the potential undercurrent. Or maybe she was responding to the master in Hamilton. That was something he really didn't want to think about.

"Mom's unpacking. Is it okay to take over Sebastian's room now?"

"Yeah, he's made it ready for you. Anything you can't find, give me a holler."

"Will do. I'll tell Mom and Dad you two are taking a time out to catch up."

"No need. I'm coming through now."

"You won't be allowed in their room with the suitcase open."

"What it is?"

"Oh, I'm not telling. But don't worry it's not too embarrassing."

Alec groaned. His mother had a knack for brilliant gifts that you didn't want to show anyone else. She'd probably taken it on herself to buy him a set of dungeon toys or something equally ludicrous, given his unusual living arrangements.

With Lucy gone, Hamilton closed in. "Can we take a few minutes for ourselves?" Hamilton took his hand and led the way to the bedroom. There was something about having sex with your parents in the house that heightened the senses. Alec was ready to blow before Hamilton had stripped off their clothes.

"This doesn't get you off the hook," Alec said, squirming under Hamilton's attentions. Hamilton paused in his journey over Alec's torso and made his way back up to brush his lips.

"As long as you know I am yours completely, I'll hang off any hook you want me to." His tongue ran along the edge of Alec's upper lip and he was lost. Lost to the emotion in Hamilton's eyes; lost to the passion in Hamilton's lips; and lost to the momentum of Hamilton's body against his. When it came down to it, this was all that mattered. Moments out of time. Jealousy, anger and pain gave way to the ache inside, the overwhelming urge to connect, and the desire to be just for each other.

Girls, Girls, Girls

Now there was a sight for first thing in the morning. Alec watched from the doorway as Hamilton busied himself making what looked like an omelette for Lucy. She sat at the breakfast bar, chattering away to him about goodness knows what. A normal, family start to the day. Was it so hard to imagine that this could be a reality for them at some point?

"Hey, sleepy head," Hamilton said, slipping the omelette onto the plate in front of Lucy. "What do you fancy this morning?"

"Other than you?"

"Gagfest. Sister in the room." Lucy glanced over at Alec and screwed up her face. "And please, why so much skin? Don't you own a robe or something?"

Alec rubbed a hand over his chest. He'd put on shorts. What was the big deal? He joined Hamilton at the counter and kissed his shoulder.

Hamilton stepped behind him. "I'm sorry, Lucy. I didn't give a thought to put on a shirt."

"He," she said, pointing at Alec, "needs to cover up. Brother. Not cool." She grinned and winked at Alec. "You, on the other hand, are much better uncovered."

Alec roared with laughter and Hamilton slapped his ass. "She has a point, babe. I much prefer you naked."

"He may as well be." Lucy shoveled a mouthful of eggs and pointed her fork at Hamilton's crotch. "Those loose linen pj's don't cover *anything*."

"Oh, for goodness sake." Hamilton turned away from them both and Alec snorted another laugh. She was right again. The material clung to his ass cheeks showing every dip and curve, the faintest hint of skin peeked through the fine weave. Alec stepped around Hamilton and looked at him from the front. Oh, yes, there was his cock, nicely showcased. Alec covered his mouth with his hand to stop the giggles.

"I think you need to find a long shirt. She is only fifteen."

"It never occurred to me. Clothes are clothes after all. They shouldn't be see-through."

"Don't mind me," Lucy said. "Seen it all before."

They both looked around at her and she grinned, eyeing Hamilton's crotch again. He stepped closer to the counter to cover himself.

"What do you mean you've seen it all before?"

"Don't panic. I'm not having sex. Yet. But we get to see naked guys in Sex-Ed so, I … you know." She shrugged. "Different up close in real life though." She giggled and spluttered, trying not to choke on her eggs and Hamilton grabbed a drying cloth from the drawer and tucked it into the waistband of his pants like an apron. "Aw, come on, don't spoil my fun. Mom will appreciate it as much as me when she wakes up."

"That's it. I'm getting changed." Hamilton kissed Alec's cheek. "I'll make your breakfast in a moment, sweetheart." They both watched him walk out the room.

"Really nice body." Lucy slurped at her orange juice, freshly squeezed by the look of the juicer still on the side. "You've got him well trained. Cooks, cleans, entertains family members while you sleep in. What else does he do so conscientiously for you?"

Fifteen. Remember she's fifteen. "Not having sex *yet*? That sounds ominous."

"I've been horny for the best part of two years. You really think I'm gonna wait for Mister Right? Day after my sixteenth I'm getting a fake ID, heading for a club and finding me a nice piece of ass like that." She gestured toward the door where Hamilton had disappeared. "I look older when I dress up and without meaning to sound conceited, I know I'm pretty. We inherited good genes."

"Lucy, as your brother—"

"You should support me," she interrupted. "You're my brother, not my dad. Not that Dad would stop me anyway. So don't try and talk me out of it."

"Oh, lord," Hamilton said, returning in jeans and a shirt. "What is it now? I've already heard about the planned take-over of the local surf club. Your sister should go into politics."

"Lucy is counting down the days until she's legal."

"And you think she should wait?" Alec detected the hint of humor in Hamilton's voice. Funny though it may be, considering their history, it wasn't useful.

"I think she should be careful."

"I will be careful. It's not as if I'm looking for a husband like the rest of my friends. One-time thing. See what all the fuss is about. What's wrong with that?"

"I don't know. You just make it sound so... clinical." And easy. The years of torment Alec had gone through for the right moment, the right person and his sister was planning to just do it with little to no thought at all.

"What do you think, Rick?" Lucy paused with her glass of juice to her lips, waiting for his reply. There was a semi-pleading tone to the request.

"Don't put it all on Rick, Lucy. That's not fair."

She put her glass back down and squared up to Alec. "He's allowed to have an opinion, isn't he?"

Why had he missed her again? Oh yeah, little sisters were supposed to be cute, all sugar and spice. Somebody had forgotten to send Lucy that memo. There was definitely a big helping of slugs and snails in her genetics. And maybe a cactus or two.

Hamilton soothed Alec's back and he relaxed a little. "My personal opinion is that first times should be special. Not that you should hold out for true love necessarily, but that your partner at least knows you, respects you. It's important for your first time to be good or it can put you off for life, give you hang ups it's difficult to get rid of."

"So a stranger doesn't cut it. That's what you're saying?"

"Right. Experimenting with someone your own age, even if you're not going to date, is a much better idea. You'll both be new to it. It won't matter if you mess up, and it'll be fun finding out what feels good and what doesn't."

"And that's how you did it?"

"Lucy," Alec said. "I'm not sure that's an appropriate question."

"It's okay." Hamilton squeezed his hand. "I don't mind talking about it. Who else is there for her to ask?"

Alec sighed and reached for the bread. He wasn't going to win anything with these two, may as well carry on with breakfast. Hamilton took the bread from his hand and popped it in the toaster. "Sit. I said I'd make you breakfast."

Alec plopped on to the chair next to his sister and she chuckled. "Perhaps it's him who's got you well trained, eh?"

"Ha-bloody-ha, demon spawn."

"Angel feather." She poked her tongue out at him and they both laughed. "So, Rick, you played with friends to get you started?"

Hamilton looked at Alec. "I guess you'd say that." Hardly friends. Handpicked live sex toys courtesy of his father. Oh, and his only other boyfriend at the age of ... *fifteen*. Wouldn't it just be the way that Lucy would follow Hamilton's example and turn out to be some kind of sex-goddess.

"That does make sense. It's a few months away yet. I'll keep an eye out for possible candidates." She poured herself some more juice. "Any chance of toast for me too?"

With the conversation diverted, Alec felt more comfortable. Sex and sisters belonged in separate boxes in his world. He tuned out as Hamilton got back to cooking and quizzing Lucy about other aspects of her life. Summer camp. Surfing. Motorbikes. Husbands. "Hang on, what?"

"It's true," she said, stealing a piece of his toast. "Any marmalade?" Hamilton handed her the pot and a knife. "Ta. Charys and Daisy are both on the lookout for long-term blokes. I know it's daft. I keep telling them it is, but it's what they want. It's not for me to knock their dreams of a house on the beach and two point five kids just because it's not top of my wish list."

"What do you want to do?" Hamilton handed her a plate with more toast. "You take exams next summer?"

"Exams next year, yeah. Then I want to explore the world." Her face lit up as she wove a tale of adventure and excitement, full of animation and energy. "I want to study art and literature and music. Play *jazz saxophone*, live on the beach, and run naked in the woods with ribbons in my hair."

"Jazz saxophone? Do you play?"

Alec stared. After all that, how could Hamilton home in on jazz saxophone? Alec was more concerned about the running naked and beach-living parts.

Her shoulders hunched. "Can't afford the lessons at the moment. Or the saxophone. But as soon as I'm working." And the enthusiasm was back as she bubbled and fizzed about her favorite jazz artists, most of whom Alec had never heard. "Oh, and Candy Dulfer. She's fab."

"I've seen her in concert," Hamilton said. "I've been to a few jazz festivals in my time."

"No. Freaking. Way. That is so cool."

"You're into jazz?" Alec wasn't sure which one of them he was asking. It was a surprise on both counts. How could he not know that about either of them? They carried on chatting around him, ignoring the question, so he went back to his breakfast. Luckily, Hamilton could cook and talk at the same time and a full breakfast, with sausage, egg, bacon, mushrooms and beans soon landed on the counter in front of him along with a top-up of juice and a fresh pot of coffee. For that, Hamilton could talk about jazz all he liked.

"Please tell me you don't eat like that every morning?"

"Huh?"

Lucy was frowning. "All that processed meat."

"It's a weekend special," Hamilton said, settling down to a plate of the same. "Weekdays are usually fruit and cereal. I make sure he eats properly."

Alec didn't comment. He wasn't about to let on that Sebastian spoiled him most mornings with a cooked breakfast.

"You know Dad has high blood pressure, right? That plate there is a heart attack waiting to happen. And don't think it won't happen because you're young and fit. If it's in your genes, it's in your genes."

Alec looked at his plate and sighed. Why was it the things he loved the most turned out to be so bad for him? And why did family members feel the need to point it out?

"I'm vegetarian now," she continued. "Have to look out for what's important. Besides, the stuff they do to animals is gross."

"Let him enjoy his breakfast, Lucy." Hamilton topped up her juice. "Tell me about school. Are you staying on for the sixth form?"

Despite the warnings of impending doom, Alec did enjoy his breakfast, helped along by the constant babble of his sister's plans for world domination. She'd become very political and idealistic. An interesting turn of events considering it wasn't long ago her entire world revolved around the tides and swells at various local beaches.

Alec checked his watch. "Do Mom and Dad always sleep this late now?"

"Probably doing the deed. They're at it like rabbits for some reason. That's why Dad has a bad back. Tried some stunt or another involving the chest of drawers."

"Please, stop." Alec put his hand over her mouth. "There is such a thing as too much information."

She shook him off and wiped her mouth with a serviette. "I blame you. It's only been like it since you came home with all that talk of sex parties and three boyfriends."

He looked pleadingly at Hamilton. "Please save me from my family."

"I think they're charming. Nothing like I expected."

"I told you they were odd."

"That's what I mean. They seem perfectly normal to me."

Well they would, wouldn't they? Alec started to clear away the plates. Anything to release his mind from the thought of his parents "doing it" in Brad's bed.

"I know your parents wanted to visit the Tower and the Palace today, but after such an enlightening conversation with your sister I think we should reevaluate our plans."

"Are you taking her to Downing Street so she can start a demonstration?"

"Actually, I thought we could take her shopping for a saxophone."

"No. Way!" Lucy was off her chair and hanging around Hamilton's neck so fast she left a blur. "You are the best brother-in-law ever. *The* best."

"We should enlist some help." Hamilton pulled at Lucy's arms trying to relax her strangle hold. "I still need to apologize to Tessa. Do you think she'd like to join us, Alec? She can help Lucy shop for clothes and make-up and the like."

"I love you already. I can't wait to tell the girls." Lucy released Hamilton and hugged Alec briefly. "Got to text them. Back in a bit." She was gone in a streak of lightning.

"Why do you have to apologize to Tessa?"

"Don't worry; I didn't say anything to her. I just feel bad about assuming she was up to no good. With you."

"Don't you think you're overcompensating with Lucy? She's not a toy you can tweak to get you out of the doghouse."

"Okay, now it's your turn to apologize." Hamilton's stare was as hard as Alec had ever seen it. "I am not in the habit of using family members as leverage. I'm sorry if you think me wanting to see your sister achieve her dreams is a step too far along the road for our relationship."

Alec put down the last of the plates and went to Hamilton. He cupped his face and placed a kiss on each cheek. "You're right. I'm sorry. That whole thing yesterday messed with my head more than usual. I promise no more second guessing your motives."

"I've never had a younger sibling to spoil. I thought it would be nice for both of us."

"It will be." Alec wrapped his arms around Hamilton and squeezed. "I love you," he whispered. "Even when I'm being an idiot."

"I'll finish clearing up. Will you ask Tessa?"

"Sure. I'll go now. I'm forgiven?"

Hamilton smiled and kissed Alec's cheek. "Always."

Lord, could Tessa shop. Alec was completely exhausted and his arms ached from all the bags he had to carry. The girls had disappeared into yet another clothes shop when Hamilton spotted a coffee house across the road and dragged Alec toward it. They stocked up with coffee and cake and found a table. The relief of sliding into a booth and dropping everything in a heap at his feet was beyond perfect. "I can't take much more," he grumbled, as Hamilton slid into the seat next to him.

"We're nearly done. And I'm the one lugging the saxophone."

"It was your idea to buy it."

"You really don't like that I want to help her, do you?"

"It's not that, Rick. I'm just tired and cranky."

"Don't lie to me."

Alec sighed. It wasn't all of it. "I love that you want to make her life easier. It's just … I don't want Lucy caught up in my world."

"You mean *my* world. You think I'll be some kind of evil influence on her or something."

"I mean *our* world. The Order. I don't want her to see that side of our life; don't want her understanding the way it works. She has ideas about being able to make a difference. I want her to keep them and build a life with all that energy and attitude she has."

"Alec, I would never introduce Lucy to the Order life. Never. And if you'd asked me, I'd have advised you against doing the same. Sometimes I wonder if you know me at all."

You and me both. But Alec felt guilty. He leaned against Hamilton's shoulder. "I guess we're out of sync at the moment. How do we put it right?"

"I wish I knew." Hamilton sounded as tired and fed up as Alec felt.

Fear rippled through his body. Was this the beginning of the end already? It couldn't be. He wouldn't let it happen. All couples had to work at their relationships, it made sense they would too. The thought that Hamilton might think it wasn't worth the hassle suddenly weighed heavy on Alec's heart. Things had been so easy at the start. The relationship they shared now was worlds apart from those first tentative weeks together. And that gave Alec an idea, an idea that buzzed through his body leaving a trail of tingles and expectation. "Maybe it's time for you to put me in my place?"

"I thought me trying to put you in your place is the problem that led to this mess."

"We're not in a mess, are we? Not really. Rick, tell me you're still in this with me."

Hamilton took his hand and ran a finger over the ring that had seemed to cause so many problems. "I've never been more *in* anything, in my life.

That's why I'm such a disaster. I'm so afraid it's going to end. I can't lose you, Alec. You're the closest thing I've ever had to a real life."

"So, maybe it's time to put me in my place in the *right* way." Alec stroked his hand along Hamilton's thigh. "It's a while since we've done that."

"You think you're acting out because I've given you too much of a voice?"

"Not quite. I like that we're equal partners in our everyday world. I just think the dynamic that started this for us is one that works, makes the hiccups easier to deal with." Alec took Hamilton's hand and kissed it, looking up into his eyes. "I miss you, Master. I know you need me to see all of you, the real you, and I love what we have together. But I also need you to see all of me, and that means remembering that part of me will always be your boy."

"And I've been failing in that duty."

"I need you to keep me safe."

"And instead I've been the one you need saving from."

"Let me keep you safe too."

"I'm sorry you're so unhappy. And here I am making such grand plans to be part of your family."

"Stop that right now. I'm *not* unhappy. But if every time I try to talk to you about keeping us on track you're going to give me the 'woe is me, I'm so terrible' line, I soon will be."

"Alec, I'm trying here. It just seems like sometimes it isn't enough. I see you pulling away from me and ..." He rubbed his face and turned on a smile. "You're right. No complaining. We'll make time for some games this week. Lighten the mood."

"Are you feeling naughty right now? We can shock this Sunday shopping crowd by catching up on a little snogging."

That brought a genuine smile. Hamilton reached in and kissed Alec's neck, along his jaw to his lips. "My beautiful boy." A chaste peck ended the interlude. Alec didn't have time to protest. The shop door opened and in flew the tempest. Lucy had another three bags in her hand and the widest grin he'd seen from her yet.

"Tessa is just the best at finding cool stuff." She flounced into the booth, Tessa flagging behind her. "I am parched. Can we eat?"

"Caffeine drip required," Tessa said, dropping another bag and taking a seat. "I am all shopped out."

"You had me beat an hour ago," Alec said. He waved over the waitress and ordered another round of drinks and pastry for the girls. "I'm afraid to ask how much you've spent today."

Hamilton put up his hand to stop Lucy speaking. "Don't even think about it. I specifically said not to look at the price tags. It's not as though you see Lucy very often. You should spoil her while you can."

"Didn't I tell you he was the best, Tessa?"

"You're brother doesn't look very convinced."

Ouch. An innocent comment at just the wrong time. "Rick's better at dishing out the star treatment than me. If he says I need to lighten up, then I do."

"Ugh, they're going to get all kissy face and loved up now. Just when I'm trying to eat."

"Too right." Alec pulled Hamilton into a long, slow smooch full of apologies and promises, extra sweet from the cake and with a good kick of coffee. Perfect. Now all they had to do was fight their way home with a zillion bags and hang on to what Alec hoped was a brighter tomorrow.

Tension was running high with the imminent unveiling of the suitcase surprise. Alec was sure he was going to be embarrassed to some degree, and yet it was okay. Whatever it was he wanted to share it with Hamilton. He wanted him to be part of the family. He was family.

They gathered in the living room around the coffee table where two gifts sat. One was a birthday present for Alec and the other a house-warming cum engagement gift for both Alec and Hamilton. Similar in size, but easily distinguished by the wrapping paper. Both looked dangerous from where Alec was sitting.

"Which shall we open first?" Alec said, looking to Hamilton for support.

"If we start with the joint gift, the rest of the evening can center on your birthday celebrations."

Alec nodded. "You open it."

"Come now, boys, it's for both of you. One at each end." Alec's mother looked as nervous as he felt. Add to that the blush he was sporting at the thought of him and Hamilton being on either end of anything in front of his parents and it was no wonder his stomach acid was on overflow. He found he needed to swallow a large knot that had formed in his throat.

Hamilton tugged on the paper, tore his end open and waited for Alec to do the same. Alec pulled the rest of the wrapping off and they both reached for the lid of the plain box. Alec knew this was the heavy one, but he couldn't begin to imagine what it would be. Opening the box only revealed a layer of tissue paper. He pulled it back and paused. *Holy shit.*

"Oh, wow." Hamilton reached into the box with both hands and tried to lift it out but couldn't. He stood over the box. "Alec, give me a hand?" Together they pulled out a polished statue, possibly pewter judging from the matt patina. "Maggie, it's beautiful."

"I thought it would make an interesting addition to your home," she said, obviously pleased Hamilton liked it.

Alec didn't know where to look. Beautiful it was. It was also highly erotic. More suggestive, but still not the gift you'd expect from your parents. Two lightly muscled, naked men, with limbs entwined and sporting impressive erections stared at him with expressions of ecstasy. Hamilton moved the box and laid the statue across the table. It was big. More than two feet long, a foot wide and a foot high. No wonder it was heavy. What Alec couldn't picture was his mother in a shop that would stock something so explicit.

"Where on earth did you find it?" he asked, staring at his mother.

"Don't you like it?"

"It's amazing. It'll look great on the dresser in the bedroom, but I'm more interested in finding out how you bought something like this."

"You're not the only one with a liberal lifestyle, young man."

Hamilton was stroking the contours of the man on top and Alec placed a hand over his. "Sorry," he said. "It's so …"

"There's something else in the box." Alec's dad said.

Alec reached through another layer of tissue and pulled out a photo album. "You didn't?" Oh, yes they did. He opened the first page to see the goofiest picture of himself, age five, dressed as a lion for a school play.

"Let me see." Hamilton took it from his hands and chuckled. "Now that's a cute kid."

"Why would you do this to me?"

"You're building your own family now, son," his father said. "It's not just you in there. It's a collection of all our special family moments. Up to date ones of me, your mother, and Lucy, and lots of space at the back for the life you and Rick will build together."

"Starting right now," Lucy said, appearing from behind her mother with her phone, ready to take a picture. "Say cheese."

Hamilton put his arm around Alec's waist and leaned against him. The flash stunned Alec more than he already was. Hamilton kissed his cheek and the flash went off again. "Are you okay?" He whispered in Alec's ear.

Alec met his gaze. He looked so happy it made Alec smile. "I'm more than okay. He reached forward for a kiss, savored the taste of Hamilton's soft, rosy lips and ignored the flashes of light and his meddling sister's chuckle.

"Now for your birthday present," Hamilton said. A smile quirked the corner of his mouth.

Alec took a deep breath and tore the paper off the second box. He paused briefly before lifting the lid and the layer of tissue. *No, it couldn't be.* He dropped the lid and pulled at the tissue. "Where did you find these? I thought we'd lost them."

"I never lose anything," his mother said. "Just put it away for the right time."

Books. Alec's pride and joy from his dorky past. A full set of Harry Potter first editions, the first two signed by JK after a four-hour wait on a rainy Saturday. It'd been pure luck getting a copy of the first one. He'd found it for a pound at a car boot sale. At the time, he was just a kid looking for a good read, he hadn't realized how popular the series would become and how valuable his pristine copy would be. Hidden beneath the books, individually wrapped, lay his collection of mint condition Power Ranger action figures. "God, I was so obsessed with this show. Please tell me you haven't packed my White Ranger costume in here?"

"No, but I still have it. And the lion costume from the photo. Never know when you might need it again." Alec looked at her. "Lots of same sex couples have children these days." Alec opened his mouth but nothing came out. "Oh, I know you're young yet. I'm just saying. That's all."

Alec was aware of Hamilton's fingers digging into his thigh, he didn't know if it was to prompt him to say something or because he was rigid with fear and fighting the urge to run away.

"Way too early for baby talk, Mom. But thanks for bringing these. It'll be great to have them in the library."

"I hope you don't mind that it's nothing new."

"Really, this is perfect." Alec stood and kissed her, hugged his dad and Lucy, and returned to Hamilton's side. "How does it feel knowing you're engaged to a bookworm?"

"A Mighty Morphin Power Ranger bookworm?" Hamilton winked at him and Alec blushed. He stroked a hand over Alec's chest. "It feels great, sweetheart, and the photos are wonderful. Now, shall I serve drinks and dinner?"

"Thanks." As Hamilton stood up Alec hugged him tightly, fighting down a well of emotion that had sprung from some unknown place. "I don't know what I'd do without you, Rick."

"I'm not planning on going anywhere."

"Promise me," he whispered, holding on for dear life as though something would be along any minute and rip them apart.

"I promise, Alec." Hamilton patted his back. "Whatever it takes, we'll make it work."

Alec let go of him and Hamilton smiled, cupping a hand to his cheek. "Will you set the table for me?"

Alec nodded, blinking a few times to disperse the unshed tears threatening to spill. As long as they were in it together, it would work. But kids? His mom had gone out on a limb all on her own with that one. Living such a cock-eyed life between the two of them was one thing, dragging a kid up in the process was something else entirely. Certainly not part of the five-year plan. Or the ten-year plan for that matter.

Alec hoped quietly that the thought hadn't horrified Hamilton so completely that he'd be weird about it. He smiled warmly at Alec as they pottered in the kitchen. Perhaps he'd chosen to ignore it altogether. Just like Alec should have. *You're building your own family now, son.* His father's words echoed around his brain throughout dinner. What kind of family was he building with houseboys, office boys and regular fucks? Not a traditional one, that was for sure. But maybe it didn't matter. When it came down to it, they were happy despite the occasional hiccups. A few more laughs wouldn't go a miss. The air had been heavy, serious lately, and there was no need for it. Not really. It was an easy fix. Starting with the placement of an overtly erotic statue in his bedroom.

Boys and Their Toys

The sign over the mantle read "these hallowed halls." Hardly hallowed, more reeking of money and privilege. Alec couldn't complain. These men were his bread and butter. These *halls* housed the upper echelons of society in shrouded mystery from outsiders and ensured the survival of the richest. Alec wondered whether they ever really accepted someone of his standing into their clique or whether they merely tolerated him the way their Victorian ancestors had tolerated "new money."

On the other hand, he was instrumental in ensuring they remained the richest. He may be new money but his investment advice was sound and his track record impressive. Alec had made a name for himself and not just because of his abilities on his knees. Besides, what was a blowjob between colleagues?

He mixed much more easily these days. The month or so of new clients since his move to the twelfth floor had brought a new chapter to his working life. Occasionally he still serviced, but mostly he handed out favors and concentrated on the real business. Alec nodded at the appropriate place in the conversation, added a titbit of information to his captive audience and allowed them to continue their speculations over the impact of upcoming elections in some far-flung country on the global economy. Almost time. Another twenty minutes, a handful of signed contracts and he could leave.

"Alexander?"

Alec followed the sound of his name and met eyes with a familiar man on the other side of the room. The man gestured him over. Alec couldn't place him. He hoped the man wouldn't drop him in it with comments about his cock sucking abilities in front of this new circle of contacts who knew him only as a manager. Alec excused himself from his company and made his way over. Young, a little paunchy, receding hairline. Nope, not a client. He'd remember a younger guy; they were so rare.

"Alexander. Caldwell isn't it? For the moment at least."

"Forgive me, sir, have we met before?"

"Nathaniel Philip. We bumped heads briefly at your little engagement soirée. How is Richard?"

Light dawned. *Philip. Old school friend of Hamilton's. Classified dangerous. Fuck, no back up.* "Ah, I remember now." Alec offered a handshake. Philip lingered and Alec pulled his hand away.

"How long till you conclude business?"

"Thirty minutes or so."

"Good. Have Jenner show you through to my private chambers afterward. We have things to discuss."

Fuck, fuckity fuck. "I'll see you shortly." Alec turned to go.

"Alexander?"

The look in Philip's eye was nothing but predatory when Alec turned back to him. "Don't keep me waiting too long."

Alec nodded once and tried to smile. Tried, despite the sudden rush of acid into his throat. But fuck, if he couldn't deal with the occasional asshole on his own he didn't deserve to be walking the fucking hallowed halls without supervision. He straightened his posture and walked confidently back to his own party. It was a front, but he knew he pulled it off; he'd been doing it his whole life.

With business concluded, Alec shook hands with his new clients, bid them safe journey until their service meetings the next week at the office and filed the contracts immediately with the in-house courier service. He'd have to call on boys from the pool again to help Bradley out. Now to face the demon in his midst.

Jenner was a decent old stick. Much like Maurice, Alec imagined he had some interesting stories about the goings on behind the oak paneled walls of this particular establishment. He raised shrewd eyebrows when Alec asked to be shown through to Philip's private chambers. Private chambers—in this place—said more than Alec wanted to hear. Jenner paused before a large ornately carved door and looked at Alec. "It's not really my place, sir, but may I offer a word of advice?"

"I'd be glad of it, Jenner. You know I'm new here."

"Master Philip can be a touch impatient and a tad flexible with the truth. Be very clear about your wishes and remember you *always* have a choice."

"That sounds ominous."

"He's a good man, when he remembers to be." Jenner smiled and patted Alec's arm. "As are you. There is a bell pull near the fire if you need anything."

"Thanks. He's going to eat me alive isn't he?"

Jenner just smiled and knocked on the door before opening it. "I have Master Caldwell for you, sir."

"Excellent. Just in time for tea. See to it, Jenner, will you?"

"Of course." Jenner stepped to one side and waved Alec through. He smiled brightly and left. That had to be a good sign, the extra smile, surely?

"You are such a pretty picture. Take a seat, please."

Alec took the offered chair glad it wasn't a casting couch straight out of the gate. He cast his eye around the room. It still amazed him that places like this existed. He could easily have stepped through a time vortex one hundred years into the past. There were no visible signs of technology anywhere and the bell pull Jenner had mentioned was a sturdy looking rope affair straight out of a period drama.

"Don't look so worried, Alec. May I call you Alec?"

"Alec is great."

"And you must call me Nate. No need to be formal when we're alone." Philip sat in the chair to the side of Alec and angled slightly toward him. "So, I understand you report directly to Edward Harrison, is that correct?"

"Yes, sir ... um, Nate."

"And you are a service manager in training." Alec nodded. "On the twelfth, no less."

"That's correct."

"Your promotion, given your experience seems a little premature and

I understand you are scheduled to move to the fourteenth floor within the next six months."

"My account portfolios speak for themselves, do they not?"

"My concern is not with your success as an investments manager but your position within The Order."

"I don't understand."

"For such a meteoric rise I would have expected you to be either from a moneyed family or well and truly fucked by our highest ranking members. It seems you are neither."

Alec decided to stay quiet and wait for the next question. It would be too easy to fuck everything up in the next five minutes if he let his mouth run away with him.

"Tell me what you know of your role."

Alec reeled off what he knew of service managers so far and the different services offered.

"Very good. You only have one boy on your staff. How do you hope to service the increase in clients over the coming months?"

"I have access to the pool of office boys and often work with Hamilton's boy, Fraser."

"You were a boy yourself for less than a year. What experience do you have of supervising such service?"

"I have two house boys of my own."

"After Richard's own heart I see."

"More so. Rick's boys are only with him on weekends, mine live with me permanently."

"You don't live with Richard?"

"We live in the same building but in separate apartments." *Not that it has anything to do with you, asshole.*

There was a knock at the door and the conversation paused while Jenner served afternoon tea. Philip waited until Jenner left before reaching for his cup. "Let me tell you the real reason I'm poking around."

Thank fuck for that.

"I'm not sure you've been given an adequate introduction to The Order. You've been railroaded because you're fucking Richard and Richard quite rightly wants to keep you close. Are you fucking Harrison as well?"

"I'm a level one, you know that. Rick is my fiancé so of course we're fucking."

"Direct and to the point. I like it. Do you know anything about the structure of The Order other than service manager, office boy, and Harrison as your boss?"

Stumped. "No."

"Then let me educate you. Harrison is a senior corporate manager. Corporate managers are responsible for interdepartmental and intercompany relationships. They ensure members have access to the business services they need such as investments and underwriting that happen in your building, legal, media, public relations, finance, housing, travel, anything you can think of. Another corporate manager you will know is Peter Worthington."

"That's why they're the ones who arrange lunches and new business contacts."

"Well done. Now, service managers have various flavors. Entertainment," Philip gestured to Alec with a wry smile, "security, basic travel as in chauffeured cars, private planes, and risk assessment."

"So, where do you fit in?"

"I'm glad you asked." Philip's grin was nothing if not smug. "This country has twelve regions, each with a board of four regional managers and a regional head. I'm Regional Manager-Corporate, for London City."

Bloody hells bells. "You're Harrison's boss."

"I'm very impressed with how quickly you pick things up. I actually have ten senior managers from various companies reporting to me, each with a team of somewhere between ten and twenty managers across the disciplines reporting to them. That makes me a very handy man to know."

"And what does all of this have to do with me?"

"Your line of command leads directly to me, through Harrison. It's my business to ensure all of my order managers are adequately trained and correctly assigned."

"And you don't think I'm up to the job."

"I wanted to meet with you on a one-to-one, see if I can see what they see. Peter Worthington speaks very highly of you and I greatly respect his opinion."

Dear Peter. Alec could do with one of his hugs about now.

"I have no issue with your work performance as an investments manager. You should have been promoted out of Hamilton's team before you were inducted into The Order but I can't undo the past."

"So what's the problem?"

"You are a natural candidate for a corporate position. I don't understand why you've been designated service and certainly not entertainment. Risk Assessment, maybe, but a glorified pimp? Come on, Alec, you're worth more than that."

"My personal life suggests I have the necessary and, I've been told, rare skills required for Entertainment. Not everyone is comfortable ordering a colleague to fuck strangers and still maintain a good working relationship with them."

"That's very true. And where would we be without our Service contracts?" Philip's smile chilled Alec to the bone. There was more going on here than he could grasp. He felt it, even if he couldn't pull the details into his mind. Philip placed his cup back on the tea tray and folded his hands on his knee. "However," *and here it comes*, "I see no evidence of your ability to recruit and train new boys. You're practically still a trainee boy yourself and yet you're destined for the fourteenth floor. It's a different class of client, Alec, and they are known for their eccentricities."

"I'm only seven weeks into my training. In the coming months, I'm confident I'll receive everything I need to fulfil the role and you have no reason to assume otherwise."

"I understand security has been called to your office to contain a domestic disturbance."

Bastard. "It didn't interfere with business. No clients were present."

"And yet I know of it."

"I wouldn't expect you not to." Alec was starting to feel strung out by the quick-fire questioning. He could do with some whiskey in his tea.

Philip smiled. "I like you, Alec. You're smart and not easily intimidated by rank and power."

That's because you're a knob.

"I stand by my remark that you would be better placed elsewhere but for the moment I'll let the current plan run its course."

Thank fuck for that. Alec let out a slow even sigh of relief.

"There are conditions, however."

Of course there are, you pompous prick. "And they are?"

"You are to recruit your own office boys before you move to the fourteenth and one of them should be designated special service. I don't expect you to train a pain slut in such short time but he should be well versed in role-play and be a willing switch for light scenes."

Whatever the fuck that means. "Two more boys?"

"For now. I will inspect them personally, as I do all boys that service for floors fourteen and above. That will include your current boy, though Peter assures me he is suitable."

"Is that all?"

"Those are the terms of your promotion to the fourteenth within investments and underwriting. Should you decide to move into Corporate, I can offer you a position in any one of ten different companies within the City alone. Hell, I can offer you a job in any city in the world."

'Important men will offer you the world, Alec'. Who had said that to him? "I'm very happy where I am, thank you."

"Richard is very taken with you. He must be to have such a public outburst. I suggest you keep a tighter rein on your private life. You need to show you can keep control of your boys, after all."

"Thank you for the advice. I really should be getting back to the office."

"I won't keep you much longer. It's just a matter of my service now. I know Harrison has actioned a request that you not be commissioned for personal service. I don't know if that's for Richard's benefit or his own. Rumors are rife around you already. But in this instance, I think I'll override his ruling. Please," Philip gestured to a chaise along one wall, "I know you're a level one and I'll respect that if you insist, but I will ask you to strip. I want to see you naked while you suck my cock. If you are willing to be fucked, all the better. It can be our secret."

"I'm very sorry, Nate, but I'm going to have to disappoint you on both counts."

"That is unlikely. Remember your position, Alexander. More importantly, remember mine."

"I'm not just Rick's fiancé, I'm collared." Alec pulled his chain from inside his shirt and tie. Anger flashed across Philip's face and Alec swallowed back rising stomach acid before continuing. "My master, Rick, has forbidden me to submit to any sexual service requests from you. I understand that his will as my master overrules any Order entitlement or request."

"And he gave this order, when, exactly?"

"The evening of the dinner. After we left you."

"I see. And the order applies only to me?"

Alec decided to think on his feet, knowing Hamilton would back him up. "And any of the men that were with you that evening."

"Very well. I'm sure I can find plenty of cocks for you to service in this fine building of ours. You will take off your clothes and assume your position."

Alec flushed but he tried to keep his mind clear. There would be a way around this. There had to be. *Think, think, for fuck's sake, think.* He could see Philip's growing impatience at his inaction. *Got it.* "I'm sorry, Master Philip, but to service others at your command is still to submit to your request for service. I am unable to comply with your wishes."

"I'm sure Richard thinks he's very funny. But he won't be smiling when I'm ramming my cock down his throat for this insult."

Now to show *Nate* he wasn't the only one a little flexible with the truth. "You know, Nate, Rick wears my collar too. I have my own boys after all; it made sense to add him to the family. I'm sure you recognized he was a switch a long time ago. He just needed the right motivation."

The anger broke and a genuine smile swept over Philip's face. "Well played, Master Caldwell." He gave a quick snort of laughter. "You are going to be so much fun to have around." He stood and held out his hand to Alec. "Round one to you. I look forward to our next game."

Alec let himself relax and stood to receive the handshake. Philip pulled him close and whispered in his ear. "Just know I don't always play fair."

"Neither do I," Alec replied. "But I do like a good challenge." Alec really hoped he wasn't going to regret that.

Philip laughed again and let him go. "I knew you were wasted in Service. Come and work for me, Alec. Forget Investments, what about Mergers and Acquisitions?"

"Really, Nate, I'm flattered. But for the moment I'm happy where I am."

"Understood. I still want to test your new boys. As soon as I see the paperwork for your transfer I'll stop by for a taster session."

"I'll look forward to it."

Philip slapped him on the back and opened the door. "Let the games begin, my friend. Let the games, begin."

The shake in Alec's hands made it difficult to speed dial. He tapped his foot waiting for an answer.

"Alec?"

"Hey, Rick. Have you got a minute for me to pop in and see you?"

"I thought you were off to Tristan's tonight. Is everything okay?"

"Yeah, yeah. It's just that I have something I need to talk to you about and I'd rather not do it over the phone."

"Alec, tell me what's going on. Now."

"Fine, I've just had afternoon tea with your old buddy, Nate Philip."

"Fucking hell. What did he make you do?"

"Rick, please. Five minutes."

"I'm already at home."

"I'm on my way."

It seemed it was the day for overactive stomach acid. Alec couldn't remember the last time he'd been so nervous. Seeing Hamilton standing a foot away had sent Alec's confidence that he'd done the right thing somewhere three floors beneath them.

"Come on. You're shaking like a leaf. What happened? I'll have that filthy bastard's balls for this. It's a step too far."

"Nothing," Alec managed to splutter. "I didn't do anything for him."

Hamilton turned his shrewd gaze on Alec. *Fuck.* Ant under a magnifying glass. Considering the refocus session they'd had the day before, in which Alec had rediscovered Rick as his master on many levels, the next few minutes would be decidedly odd. Odd and yet fulfilling. It had taken an asshole like Nate Philip to show Alec the untapped potential with his own fiancé. Alec handed Hamilton the box. "I got you this."

"What is it?"

"For fuck's sake, Rick. Open the damn box."

Hamilton quirked a smile and opened the lid. He stared at the contents for a moment, looked up at Alec and opened his mouth to say something. He abruptly closed it again and looked back at the box.

Alec spilled the whole story to the speechless Hamilton. When he paused for breath, Hamilton shook his head. "I still don't understand. I know I let you rule the roost a little too much, but seriously, Alec, you're giving me a collar? And what the hell has that got to do with Philip?"

"He wasn't happy that I refused his service."

"I'm not surprised. I'd have loved to be a fly on the wall for that one."

"He said he was going to take it out on you, with his cock down your throat."

"It's a wonder he hasn't called already."

"He won't." Hamilton looked confused again. "I told him I'd collared you too."

The look on Hamilton's face was a mixture of horror and amusement.

"He'd already made a jibe about me keeping you in line with my boys. I figured I should play him at his own game of flexible truths."

"And it got you thinking that perhaps it's not such a bad idea after all?"

"You really are a prize idiot sometimes." Alec pointed to himself. "Country Bumpkin graduated from Oxbridge where I had to endure three miserable years with the likes of your poncy friends thinking they could get one over on the village idiot. I've told Philip you're collared. He congratulated me on my win and announced the games open. The first thing he's going to do is turn up in your office and check your fucking neck."

Hamilton laughed. "You're right. Damn, you really have outsmarted him."

"Not if you aren't wearing it."

Alec pushed the box closer to Hamilton's chest but he handed it back to Alec. "Oh, I think the honor should be yours, Master," he said with a grin and a slight bow of the head.

Alec snatched the box and pushed Hamilton to his knees. He'd had enough of smug bastards today and his patience was wearing thin. He walked behind, took the chain and threw the box on the floor. Alec's hands started shaking again as he reached around Hamilton's neck.

"I hope to god nobody else sees it," Hamilton said, bowing his head so Alec could fasten it. "I'll never live it down. They already say I baby you."

Alec paused, his fingers still on the clasp of the necklace that now hung around Hamilton's neck. "Would it be so bad?"

"What?" Hamilton started to stand but Alec held him on his knees and leaned in to his ear.

"For them to know you're mine. You are still mine alone, aren't you, Rick?"

"Alec, I—"

Alec fisted his hands in Hamilton's hair and pulled his head back. "I certainly don't remember you asking for permission to be fucked by anyone else." The shudder running through Hamilton's body, the slight swelling at his crotch suggested that there was more to the idea of him being a switch after all. "Well? Has anyone else fucked you?"

"No one but you."

"No one but me?"

"I swear, Alec. You know I wouldn't lie to you."

Alec tightened his grip, put an arm around Hamilton's chest and pulled him back. "You swear, what?"

"I …" The confusion slipped away and a smile quirked Hamilton's perfect lips. "I swear … *Master.*"

Alec released his grip and Hamilton fell forward. "That's better. Perhaps I should give you a treat. What do you think?"

Hamilton spun around on his knees and met Alec's gaze. The look was mischievous, challenging, but most of all it was fucking hot. He sat back on his heels, back straight, hands in his lap and lifted his chin. "I'd like that very much, Master."

The thought processes stalled in Alec's brain. Hamilton on his knees, calling him master. The stuff of dreams. He stepped closer. "Suck my cock."

Hamilton pulled at Alec's belt, unzipped the fly and took out his cock all without breaking eye contact. Alec's jaw dropped as Hamilton licked the length of his burgeoning member and smiled. He sucked in the head, swirled his tongue around the edge and then sat back, letting it pop from his mouth like a lollipop. "Tell me how you want it, Master." Voice like velvet stoked Alec's cock, hot breath over the wet head sending tingles through his body. Fuck, as a hot little slave boy Hamilton could give Sebastian a run for his money. Hamilton smiled such a naughty, gut wrenching smile and licked up Alec's shaft again leaving a wet trail. The slight drag of teeth as he reached the head accompanied by the wiggle of his tongue was too much and Alec shot his load with a groan over Hamilton's cheek. Hamilton lapped up what he could and chuckled.

"Damn." Alec grabbed Hamilton's shoulder for support. "That was… you barely touched me."

"I think I've been around boys long enough to learn a few tricks, Alec." Hamilton wiped his face and smiled. "That was fun. We should play that game again."

"Yeah, if you want me to spurt like a teenager."

"You were just as bad." Hamilton sat back and rubbed over his crotch. "Look, I have a wet patch. I'm going to have to change my pants." He stood and kissed Alec's cheek. "I am officially collared. Are you happy now?"

"Would it though?"

Hamilton dropped his pants and stepped out of them. "What?"

"Be so bad if people thought we changed it up now and then. I do have my own boys. It's obvious I can switch."

"I've never given it any thought. I guess it was the shock of seeing you hand me bands."

"Do you want me to see to that for you?" Alec stroked over Hamilton's leaky erection.

"You go on to your party. Make me wait like a good little slave boy."

"But you won't wait."

"Alec, I don't lie to you. If I say I'll wait, I'll wait. If I say I'm yours alone, then I am. Now go to your party before I *switch* to demanding master and slap your cheeky backside."

It was Alec's turn to smile. "I'm just doing my bit to take care of you. I love you, Rick."

"Yeah, go on. Off to your private shag fest."

"It's boys' night. No sex. Just food and chat and beer."

"Go. Don't forget to call in when you get home. You sleep in my bed tonight so I can fuck that attitude out of you."

"Yes, Master." Alec kissed his forehead and hightailed it out the door.

Too Much Green

"You look tired."

"For all the best reasons, Master."

Hamilton stroked Alec's cheek where he knelt. His favorite position, at Hamilton's feet. It had been a long day so far after so little sleep, but Alec wasn't complaining. He nuzzled Hamilton's thigh and sighed contentedly.

"Mm, we had fun, didn't we?"

"Much more than fun." So much more than fun. Rules, rituals, boundaries, didn't matter what you called them, they helped set things straight in the muddle of Alec's head. Every master/boy scene defined their relationship a little more. Even the ones that turned the tables. The band around Hamilton's neck had intensified the dynamic somehow. It was a statement, sure, but it was also a reminder of their deepening bond. A bond Alec knew he'd be exploring for many years to come.

"As much as I like you curled at my feet, it's time to get back to work. Are you busy this evening?"

Alec shook himself out and brushed off his pants. "Not if you don't want me to be."

"Dinner, then?"

"Alone? Or can Sebastian and Brad join us?"

Hamilton's eyes lit up. Fuck. He was thinking about Sebastian. Again. Had to be. Alec reigned in the urge to spit venom.

"I guess I shouldn't keep you all to myself so close to our vacation. Have you finalized things for their care while we're away?"

"All sorted."

"Alec, what's wrong?"

He didn't want to say it. Didn't want to own up to his jealousy but Hamilton would pull it out of him in the end. "You miss Sebastian being yours."

"I'm very fond of him, but I'm more than content, thank you."

"You're not fucking him tonight. I won't allow it."

Hamilton chuckled. "Is that for my benefit or his? I'm sure he's had more than enough of me over the years."

"He'd still be with you if it wasn't for Brendan. I was an easy solution for the best of both worlds."

Hamilton's posture stiffened, his expression changed to confusion. "What the hell are you going on about?"

Alec took a deep breath. Had he really said that aloud? And after things had been going so well. Trust his stupid insecurity to rear its head at the most inappropriate time. But it had been on his mind for a while. It was stupid, but it helped explain Sebastian's recent behavior. Alec didn't doubt Sebastian loved him in a sense, but he'd never replace Hamilton in Sebastian's affections. There was too much history, too much devotion. Sebastian saving Alec from Hamilton's anger had highlighted something he hadn't seen before—exactly how well the two of them knew each other—and now Hamilton was calling on Sebastian for chores and favors behind Alec's back, and it grated.

"Alec, you need to talk to me."

"It's stupid. Of course you still want him. I should get back to the office."

"You will stay right where you are."

Alec sighed, but he turned back to face Hamilton. "Rick, don't make me talk about this. It hurts."

"What does?"

"You and him. I'm just the spare part that lets you maintain contact."

"You are being completely ridiculous. Sebastian loves you. Asked to leave me for you. How could you think anything different?"

"I don't know. Maybe because you're always arranging things without me."

"You mean the vacation shopping?" Hamilton snorted. "A single request. As a surprise for you, because I knew you'd hate doing it. Please tell me you're joking."

Alec couldn't say anything. He stared at his shoes and shuffled. What he hadn't figured out was whether his jealousy related to Hamilton or Sebastian, or both. Probably both. A double whammy right in the chest.

Hamilton took out his phone. "You stand there and don't make a sound." Alec nodded and watched Hamilton place his phone on the table and speed dial. He put the call on speaker.

"Hey, Rick. What can I do for you?"

"Sebastian, how is the shopping coming along?"

"All done. I'll pack your cases this weekend. Not long now. Remember what I said." Sebastian's tone changed. Alec hadn't been privy to the touch of ice that edged his words.

Hamilton rolled his eyes. "You tell me every time we speak, Sebastian."

"And I'll say it again. If he comes back with even one bruise that wasn't there before, you'll have me to deal with and it won't be pretty."

"I know."

"You're on thin ground with me at the moment. I'm leaving him in your care. If you don't look after him—"

"You're going to have my balls, I *know*."

"I love you, Rick, but I won't stand for it. We will fall out if you don't pull it together."

"Got it."

"Will Alec be home for tea? I was going to make his favorite." The ice had melted and the Sebastian Alec knew and loved was back.

"You should call him and ask."

"I don't want to bother him. He'll call if he's going to be late. Well, sometimes he remembers to call."

"He loves you. Remember that."

"When he remembers me. He has no idea how much I'm going to miss him. Anyway, I need to go."

"Okay. See you soon."

Alec dabbed at his eye. Must be an eyelash or something. He sniffed a little trying not to catch Hamilton's penetrating gaze.

"How stupid do you feel now?"

Alec shrugged. Hamilton took the few steps and wrapped his arms around Alec's waist. He didn't say anything. Just held tight until Alec's body relaxed into the embrace.

"I'm sorry for thinking the worst."

"For some reason we both do it far too often." Hamilton kissed Alec's cheek. "Now you know I'm not lusting after Sebastian as soon as you leave the room, shall we get back to work?"

"I should spend time with him this evening. Can we rain check?"

"Alec, I'm going to have you to myself for a whole month. I can survive this evening without you."

"But what will you do?"

"What do you want me to do?"

"Other than be with me?"

"Okay, enough. You're not making any sense. You have dinner with Sebastian and Bradley. I will entertain myself."

"Can we still share the car home?"

"I'll call in for you when I'm finished here. I'll try to make it early. We can play a little before we head home so you have the best of both worlds. Now go, before I strip you off and fuck you senseless for being so sweet."

That seemed like a very good idea. Alec moved in for a kiss just as the comm chimed. "Mr. Hamilton, your next appointment is here."

"Thank you, Sasha. I'll be right there." Hamilton kissed the end of Alec's nose. "I have to go." He tapped Alec's ass. "Keep it sweet for me."

"Always."

Alec lingered outside Hamilton's office, watching for the moment Fraser disappeared inside and imagined him locking the door and stripping off. His chest ached and he sighed heavily.

"Alec, Are you okay?" Alec turned to see the concerned look on Tom's face. He brushed Alec's arm. "Coffee?"

Alec nodded and followed him to the break room. They settled into a quiet corner and Tom pulled his chair closer to Alec's. "You going to tell me what's up?"

How could Alec say what was up when he didn't know himself? Tom put a coffee cup in Alec's hand and waited. Alec took a sip and let the heat and flavor stimulate his thought process. He did know what was wrong; he just didn't like giving the thoughts breathing space. "How much time does Fraser spend in Hamilton's office?"

"Not as much as you used to." Tom sat back with his coffee. "Green-eyed monster rattling his cage?"

"Just a bit." More than a bit. Between thoughts of Hamilton and Sebastian, Hamilton and Fraser, Sebastian and everyone, the green-eyed monster was rampaging all over Alec's pretty little world. "Do you still fuck him?"

"Hamilton? You know I don't. It was just that one time." Tom watched Alec sipping his coffee for a few minutes. "I thought you guys fucked whoever you wanted?"

"Exactly. How do I know he isn't going to find somebody to replace me?"

Tom chuckled. When Alec didn't respond he sobered up and took on a more serious air. "It works both ways. What if you find someone to replace him?"

"I won't. There isn't anyone like him."

"I'm sure he feels the same about you."

"How can he? I'm just an office boy made good. One, in a long line of fucks. He's everything to me."

"You're really having a hard time of it, huh?" Tom stared into his coffee. Alec wished he could tune into the thoughts thrashing around inside his head. Tom had always been the practical one. Down to earth, steadfast. Alec needed that now, needed his objective view of what was fast becoming a very complicated landscape. Finally, Tom looked up and met Alec's gaze. "Go play the field for a while. It'll make you feel better. Take your mind off it."

"Seriously? That's your advice?"

Tom shrugged. "It's what I'd do."

Alec knew very well it was the last thing Tom would do. He was a one-woman guy and, other than his minor indiscretions with Alec, seemed content to stay that way. "And Emma?"

"We broke up. I've been seeing Fraser on and off."

"Trying on a boyfriend for size?"

"No, we just fuck. It scratches an itch. We're hardly soul mates. He's a great bloke though. Good to hang out with after work."

Hmm. Maybe Tom should join Alec's team as his new boy. But then Alec wouldn't be able to hand out Tom in the same way he did Bradley. It wouldn't seem right somehow. And he certainly wouldn't want Tom having to fuck Philip. Alec didn't want anyone fucking Philip. He'd have to think about whether to share Brad. He didn't want to, but it might mean Brad couldn't move with him to the fourteenth and that was even more unthinkable.

"Penny for 'em?"

"Where do you see yourself this time next year, Tom?"

"Same place I guess. A promotion would be nice but I'm a realist. There are no promotions in Hamilton's team without joining the fuck squad and that isn't for me."

That scuppered that idea. It was also phenomenally unfair. But then Alec had been stuck in Hamilton's team longer than he should have been. Who knows how much longer he'd have waited for the next opportunity without the Order behind him opening doors. "Transfer?"

"One day. For the moment, I'm racking up some good experience. You left me some major accounts when you moved. It's good for the CV."

"Would you consider working on my team?"

"On the twelfth? Sure. But I thought you were all about service. I couldn't do that. I don't have a high enough sex drive."

"What I actually need is an account manager. Brad doesn't have the experience to monitor and evaluate accounts. He's the best PA in the world, but I could really use you in the background for process. It'll look even better on your CV than what you're doing now."

Tom looked doubtful. "And you could swing that without me having to join your fancy club?"

"No harm in trying." Besides, how was Alec supposed to keep on top of the increasing number of accounts if all he had time for was supervising Brad's fuck diary? He needed a team around him to take care of everyday working routines to free him up for client research and Order business.

"Chloe would be mad, mad, mad."

"I can't poach two of you from Hamilton. I don't know if he'll let me have you." Chloe. She'd fucked practically everyone on the eighth floor. If it weren't for her lack of discretion he'd consider offering her the position of office girl. And wouldn't she just jump at the chance to get it on with Hamilton. It painted pictures in Alec's mind he didn't want to consider. "Do you think he's fucked anyone else on the team?"

Tom's jaw dropped. "Like who? Andy and Kean are straight as a die, and Jake is not his type. Besides, half of 'em are girls. Does he even *do* girls?"

Alec shrugged. "It's not a conversation I remember us having." Why would they? But then he'd had the conversation with Sebastian so perhaps Hamilton was hiding the fact his list of lovers was probably half as long again as Alec had ever imagined. He sighed. What a flaming idiot? He was getting as bad as Hamilton with all this speculation about what was going on whenever he wasn't around. It had to stop. They both had to stop, before things really got out of hand. Alec looked down at Tom's hand on his knee.

"Are you sure you're going to be okay, Alec?"

"It just runs away with me sometimes. I'm good, really. I'll be even better once we can spend some real time on our own."

"If you need me, for anything, I'm always here for you. You know that, right?"

Alec smiled. He didn't fail to notice Tom's hand slip further up his thigh. "Is there an ulterior motive behind your suggestion I play the field, by any chance?"

"I miss you. The team isn't the same anymore."

"So you thought you'd try for a blowjob?"

Tom pulled his hand away. He looked hurt. "Why would you think that? Not one of your precious boy wonders, am I?"

Alec felt guilty. He patted Tom's knee and grinned. "Come on, we'll head to the bathroom on the fourth. No fucking though."

"Alec, that's not what I meant."

"I know. I want to. I don't have much opportunity these days. My clients are only ever interested in Bradley or Fraser."

On his knees, with Tom's cock nudging against his tonsils, Alec could almost forget the last year. It had been a hell of a year, but stressful in so many ways. He took a moment to suck on the head and tongue the slit, relishing Tom's groans.

"Fuck, that's good," Tom murmured, before pushing deeper. Alec swallowed around the intrusion and felt the quiver of the cock and the shudder in Tom's body as he stilled and shot his load. Tom let his head fall back against the cubicle door and Alec sucked and licked his softening cock. "You're bloody good at that," Tom said, smiling down at him. "You want me to return the favor?"

Alec let Tom's cock slip from his mouth. "Not right now, but you owe me one."

"You betcha." Tom pulled Alec to his feet and met his lips for some serious snogging. They were both a little breathless by the time they came up for air. "I've always fancied you, Alec. Do I get the chance to fuck you one day?"

"Never say never, sweetcheeks."

"Damn it, I should have asked before you sucked me dry."

Alec hugged Tom close and pinched his ass. "Let's put a pin in it for another day. A day when we aren't squashed in a toilet cubicle."

"Oh, I don't know. The chance of getting caught adds to the fun."

"Out," Alec said, slapping Tom's thigh. "Time to get back to work." Before he promised something he wasn't sure he'd follow through on.

Clearing the Mind

The delicious waft of herbs and freshly baked bread drifted into Alec's path as he opened the front door. "Someone's been busy," Brad said, hanging up the keys in the key cupboard just inside the door and leading the way along the hall.

"Master." Sebastian appeared around the corner, barely covered by a very small apron around his waist, grinned, and dived into Alec's arms, wrapping his legs around him.

"Hey, babe. Smells good in here. I'm starving."

"Thank you, for coming home on time. I took the chance and cooked your favorite, roast lamb with all the trimmings."

"You are perfect, you know that right?" Alec took some time to knead Sebastian's ass cheeks, kiss his neck and face until he chuckled. A pang of something hit him in the chest as he set Sebastian back on his feet. He would miss him, of course he would. How could Sebastian think he'd forget about him? "How long before dinner?"

"Half hour or so. Can I take your jacket?"

Alec started to herd Sebastian along the corridor to the bedroom. "How about we take a shower and you can get me naked?"

"No complaints from me."

Alec wrapped his arms around Sebastian's body where he stood, arms outstretched to support himself against the shower wall, and increased the length of the strokes slipping into his perfect little body. There were times, like right now, when Alec couldn't imagine wanting anything other than this. The warmth of Sebastian in his arms, the feel of Sebastian's silky skin, the delightful sounds that escaped his plump kissable lips, the tightness of Sebastian's body dragging him toward climax. Perfect moments that stretched into a blurry haze of rising passion. If only he could hold on to it, pull the memory over the gaps where other things intruded. Serious things. Like Hamilton. Like Australia. Like leaving Sebastian for a whole month with free rein to fuck whoever he wanted.

Sebastian grasped at Alec's hip and pulled him closer. "Stay with me, Master."

"I don't want to be anywhere else." Alec kissed Sebastian's shoulder and sucked at the stream of water cascading over his back. "I love you, Sebastian. Always." Alec picked up the pace, adjusted the angle of his hips until Sebastian groaned. "Are you ready to come?"

"Yes, Master."

"Good boy. My perfect boy." Alec squeezed him and nuzzled into Sebastian's neck. "I'm ready for you." A few more well placed thrusts and Sebastian's ass clenched around Alec's shaft as he shot into the stream of water. Alec kept up his stroke into the tightness and soon followed with a strangled cry. He stayed deep inside, following through with slow, sensual movements as his cock softened. How many lovers would Sebastian have had by the time Alec made it home? Who would he turn to when he needed to be pimped out? Jasper? Brendan? Alec shook his head. He had to stop thinking about it; he'd drive himself mad otherwise.

He let his cock slip out and grabbed a squidge of shower gel. He washed Sebastian's hips and thighs, and along the crack of his ass, careful not to get too close to his pucker. He gave his own cock a quick rinse while Sebastian finished up and turned off the water.

"Are you okay?" Sebastian took a towel from the shelf and wrapped it around Alec's waist before reaching for another.

"More than okay." He raised his arms for Sebastian to wipe him down. "You?"

"That was a very pleasant surprise. I should check on the dinner. Unless... you want me to stay close?"

"I do want you close, but I want dinner too. I'm torn."

Sebastian smiled. He kissed Alec softly on the lips. "Dinner wins out. I'll leave you to dry off. Love you."

"Love you." Two words that seemed to say so much, but what did they really mean in Alec's world? He said it so often. To Sebastian, to Hamilton, even to Harrison. He toyed with the concept in relation to Brad, albeit in a different way, so what *could* it mean? It meant Alec would have problems if that person were suddenly gone from his life. He wouldn't be able to fill the hole they left behind. He'd feel sad and lost when he couldn't hug or kiss them, talk to them... fuck them. Was that a deep enough concept of love for a guy his age? The pang of sadness, the tightness in his chest when he thought of Hamilton or Sebastian not being there had grown exponentially in the last few weeks. He had to make more of an effort to be there for them. Hopefully it would be enough. In Sebastian's case, the next few days were crucial. He'd try harder to think ahead, to surprise him, to remember him. And it would have to be enough to carry them through, to ensure Sebastian would still be waiting for him when he came home.

A sleepy air had descended over the apartment after such a full dinner menu. Sebastian had out done himself with starters, full roast, and dessert, all washed down with copious amounts of wine. Alec was pleased to see Sebastian drop his birdlike eating habits and overindulge too. They all chipped in with the clear up and it was soon time to settle down for the evening. With no client meetings the next day, Alec could relax without having to head into the office for an hour, which always ended up as two or three.

Stretched out, with his head on Brad's shoulder and Sebastian at his feet, Alec was content. He had one hand smoothing over Sebastian's hair and the other stroking Brad's forearm where it lay across his chest. He didn't want to disturb the gentle peace that hung around them, but however content his body, and full his stomach, his mind was still racing. He turned to place a kiss on Brad's chest.

Brad kissed the top of his head in response and put his e-reader to one side. "Everything okay?"

"Just thinking about work."

"Anything in particular?"

"I was thinking of asking Hamilton to transfer Tom upstairs with us. I should start building a proper team before we get bogged down."

"He seems nice enough. You'd know more about his performance and what he's like to work with."

"He's a good account manager. And he knows about the Order so it would be easy. I hated that Hamilton's team knew so little about what was really going on down there."

"It's the same in all Order teams. The second floor was no different. Other than the fact Davis is a sleazebag."

Alec pulled himself up to Brad's level and adjusted the lightly snoring Sebastian over his lap. "I thought you liked working for Davis."

"I liked my job. I never said I liked Davis. I couldn't believe my luck when Hamilton started calling on me. He'd always used Mehmet or Michael. Lucky for me he decided you'd prefer a blond." Brad looked down at Sebastian and ruffled his hair. "Can't think why." He grinned and Alec blushed. He'd not thought about it before. Hamilton, Sebastian, and Brad were blond. Various shades, from Hamilton's sandy tones, to Sebastian's creamy locks, with Brad's surfer straw in between, but all blond. Harrison was fair. Or had been, before the encroaching gray silvered it up. How could he not know he had such a strong type?

"Tom's not blond. I've fucked him."

"I'm sure you've fucked plenty of guys that aren't blond. I'm just teasing."

"Jasper isn't blond. Nor is Danny Merrimont."

"Alec, stop." Brad chuckled. "I wasn't being serious."

Alec knew he was pouting. But the comment had thrown him. He liked blonds. He'd just never noticed how much until now.

"You overthink everything," Brad teased. "You're going to worry yourself into an early grave. Nobody cares that you have a thing for blonds. Lots of people do."

"I don't like being so predictable. There's something to be said about retaining an air of mystery."

"I never know what's going on inside that pretty little head of yours so don't worry about it. Your mystery is intact."

Alec settled back against Brad's shoulder. The brush of leather from the sofa at his back sent a sensual tingle running through his body. He wasn't just partial to blonds, he was partial to sofa sex with blonds. His cock stirred and he nestled closer to Brad's side.

"Hungry?"

Alec grinned up at him. "Always."

"You won't get up to much with that sleepy kitten draped over you. Want to move to the other sofa?" Brad said, tapping his hand on the arm of the neighboring couch, just as soft, just as sensual, but very blue and currently blissfully empty awaiting action.

It was tempting, but Alec didn't want to disturb Sebastian just yet. "Let him sleep a bit longer."

"While I have your attention, there was something I wanted to ask you." Brad shifted in his seat and Alec groaned inwardly. Whatever it was, he had a feeling he wasn't going to like it.

"Should I fill my wine glass first?"

"Don't be silly. Overthinking, again."

Alec waited but Brad didn't say anything else. A light thrum had taken up his body and he was tapped his foot. "For goodness sake, what is it?"

"You remember the security guy, Rob?"

"From the club?"

"He phoned. Asked me out." Alec sat up again and stared at Brad, but Brad didn't look around. "I would normally have just said no, but with you being away for so long…"

"You're leaving me?"

Brad groaned. "Oh, for fuck's sake, Alec, of course I'm not. What is wrong with you lately? Not everything is a conspiracy to leave you on your lonesome. I just thought, as you won't be here, I could hang out with him. We're not picking out curtains."

"Hang out with him?"

"Well, you know." Brad shrugged. "Fuck mostly."

"Oh."

"I guess that's a no then."

"Now who's being stupid?" Alec caught the flash of excitement in Brad's eyes. Damn it, he was really interested. Not everything was a conspiracy, but some things were.

Brad curled into himself as though he were an excited kid and pulled his knees up to his chest. "I've never really been on a proper date with a guy."

"I thought you were just fucking?"

He shrugged. "He wants to take me out to dinner. I'm guessing there'll be sex after. Won't there?" Brad looked uncertain and Alec laughed. Sebastian startled at the sound but didn't wake. "What's so funny?"

"You are precious, do you know that?"

"The whole dating thing kind of passed me by. I was too busy fucking everything that paid me the slightest attention. I won't know what to do if he wants to walk around holding hands."

"You really liked him, didn't you?"

"Fancied him, you mean." Brad nodded. "Massive arms. I love big arms on a guy. And he was powerful, fucked with abandon, but..." Brad squirmed in his seat. "He was gentle too. Bit of an all-around package."

"Well, as long as you aren't planning on picking out curtains anytime soon, I'm happy for you." Brad hugged him hard and he squeaked involuntarily. "And don't think you have to kick him into touch when I'm back. There's nothing wrong with you having a boyfriend for occasional dates. Just remember who you belong to."

"As good as that sounds, what are the odds it lasts more than a month? The whole relationship will have come and gone in that time. Besides who's gonna want to hook up with me on a more regular basis with my job?"

Alec contemplated Brad for a moment. He looked genuinely concerned. There was more going on than he was letting Alec see but he wasn't sure how to drag it out of him. "You know you'll always have a place with me, right? I know you think you're only here as a perk of the job but I do care about you, and I'll miss you the same as I will Sebastian."

"I know. It's just, I don't know. I can't see you and Hamilton wanting to keep all of us around once you think about moving in together." Brad looked at Alec, his eyes wide and sad. So sad, Alec wondered if he might tear up. "I'm nobody's favorite, Alec. If anyone gets the boot, it'll be me. How am I supposed to start over when my whole life revolves around you?"

"Not that I think you aren't talking complete rubbish, but let's say we plan around it? You have the next month to start carving out a life independent of me. Get back in touch with your friends; find new places to hang out. Once I'm back we'll make sure we don't slip back into the 24/7 thing. I know it's easy, we fit so well together, but you're right, it's not practical for either of us in the long term. Hamilton won't be impressed if I'm whinging for my Bradley and Sebastian teddy bears every five minutes."

Bradley chuckled and rested his head against Alec's. "I'm going to miss you."

"Likewise." They kissed a little. Then a lot. Alec let the heat build nice and slowly before backing off. Bradley humphed and Alec tweaked his cheek. "You should take proper days off from me and your sugar daddies. And if it doesn't work out with Rob, maybe take the odd night to go dancing. Brendan and Dylan go clubbing a lot during the week. I'm sure you'll get to know them much better over the next few weeks."

"I don't want to hang out with them. Brendan is such a brat. I have no idea how Dylan puts up with him."

"You put up with me."

"True." Brad winked. "It'll feel weird making arrangements to do things without you."

"Start small. Perhaps I'll have Tom come and keep you company on the twelfth while I'm away, rather than have that other guy keep an eye on things."

"Oh, god, yeah. Kirby is another guy I really don't like. Just like Davis. In your office, he'll have me serving him coffee naked and move the phone to the floor in the corner of the room so he can watch me crawling around for him." Brad shuddered. "There's a reason his boys are mostly Level Four."

"That kinky, huh?"

"Nothing kinky about it for me. From him it's just vulgar. And you can guarantee he's planning on fucking me several times a day, all under the guise I've done something wrong. He makes me feel dirty."

"Why didn't you say anything when Harrison suggested he step in for me?"

"Not my place."

"Fucking hell, Brad. Of course it is. You're *my* boy, first and foremost.

I'll leave instructions with Davis and Kirby that you're only to fuck your scheduled clients while I'm away. You're such an idiot sometimes."

Brad grinned. "Whereas you are completely lovely."

The kissing started again with Brad putting in a more concentrated effort. This time, Alec didn't want to leave things on simmer. "Move," he said, slipping out from under Sebastian. Brad stretched out on the empty couch and pulled Alec against him. Their cocks butted together as they moved. Good friction, but not enough. Alec reached for a sachet of lube from the table and ripped it open. He swiped a little over each of their cocks and used the rest on his own pucker. Brad raised his eyebrows and Alec gave the 'ssh' gesture, looking back briefly at Sebastian's sleeping form. Brad didn't fuck him often and never in front of others, but when he did it was always hot and fiery, with an edge of something Alec didn't get from anyone else. He straddled Brad's hips and settled over his cock, taking a long, slow descent. "You're mine," he whispered against Brad's chest. "And I'll only share you when you want to be shared."

Brad hissed, adjusting Alec's position and joining in with light, slow, thrusting. "I love it when you let me inside."

Alec rocked faster, circling his hips and grinding against Brad's body. "If ever there's someone you don't want to fuck, you tell me. Understand?"

"Promise."

"Whenever you want to fuck me, you tell me. Understand?"

Brad only nodded as he bit his lip to muffle the sound of his groans. Blistering heat, a swirling tide threatening to overtake him, and Brad's hand pulling at his cock, all served to eat away at Alec's cool. They were both close, tumbling toward the precipice, when Alec felt another set of hands on his back, soft lips on his shoulder, and more lube over his already stretched ass. He paused, turning to see a killer grin spread over Sebastian's face.

"Just hold still," Sebastian said, kissing Alec's shoulder. "I'm coming in."

Before Alec had a chance to register in his already lust-addled brain what Sebastian was talking about, he felt the head of Sebastian's cock butt against his ass. Sebastian put a hand over Alec's mouth before he could say anything and nudged forward. Alec actually saw stars as the ring of muscle around his hole started to stretch to accommodate the second cock. The string of expletives he let go was muffled and indistinguishable against Sebastian's hand. "That's it," Sebastian said, "Just hold still. Patience is everything." Sebastian pulled out a little and added more lube. "Slow and steady does it."

Alec looked down at Brad's shocked face, his eyes wide and hungry. Alec grasped his shoulders as Sebastian eased inside by what felt like an eighth of an inch at a time. Brad steadied his hips. After what seemed like an age and then some, of slow movements and increasing pressure, Sebastian paused.

"There, I knew you could take us both. Harrison's been good for you and I've seen the size of that dildo Rick uses on you."

Alec could hear the words but their meaning didn't register. When Sebastian started to move, he thought he'd actually pass out. Not from pain, though the stretch was definitely something to behold, but from the incredible, heady fullness that swept through him.

"Fuck us, baby," Sebastian said, stroking Alec's back. Alec started to rock back and forth slowly. Sebastian added more lube and the butting cocks slipped in further. Alec whimpered against Sebastian's hand but kept moving. The lack of air in his lungs was making him dizzy and he slumped forward over Brad's chest, pulling away from Sebastian's hold over his mouth.

"Fuck, fuck, fuck." The discomfort was easing with each thrust. Much like the first time Hamilton had taken him. Much like getting used to Harrison's full length. The stretch shifted into something deeper, the constant pressure over his sweet spot brewed the pooling heat in his gut, and the small movements he'd been taking lengthened. He hissed as he moved a bit too fast and a ping of discomfort hit.

"Slow and steady," Sebastian whispered, wrapping his arms around Alec's stomach and pressing against his back. "Feels so good. Take us with you, Master."

"It hurts." It didn't, much. A bit. The odd pinch.

"Want to stop?"

Alec shook his head and whined. Bradley chuckled and the extra movement was enough to send Alec crashing over the edge. He gripped Brad's shoulder, spurts of cum shooting between them. Sebastian was still moving. "Stop, stop. I can't ..." But Sebastian didn't stop and neither did Alec's cock as another jet erupted.

The next moment he was empty. Literally and figuratively. Draped over Brad's chest, he couldn't bring himself to move even though he wasn't sure either of the boys had come. Brad stroked his hair. Sebastian curled over his back. It was all he could do to keep breathing. Slow, steady breaths into the quiet place that had opened up inside his mind. He sighed contentedly and his whole body shuddered with a powerful aftershock. He closed his eyes and the room drifted around him. He could hear soft voices, felt warm, and safe, and loved.

Alec stirred to the gentle rocking of his shoulder. He opened his eyes to see Sebastian smiling. "The bath is ready, Master."

"Bath?" Alec started to sit up.

"Careful," Bradley said, holding onto him. "We're starting to stick together. Peel away slowly, if you can."

Sometimes messy sex was good but the aftermath, if it wasn't deal with it straight away, was clearly not. Alec winced as his ass finally hit the towel placed over the seat beneath him. *Damn, that's tender.* Not so far past pleasant to be painful, but he'd definitely feel it in the morning.

Sebastian pulled him to his feet and steered him through to the bathroom. Good job they had such a large tub. The three of them climbed in together and Alec sighed as the warm water enveloped him. These were the times he really appreciated the finer things his new life afforded him. A large stone tub, big enough for four men to stretch out. Fast-fill taps with constant hot water. Subdued lighting to sooth the mind and help restore calm to the body.

Within moments, Sebastian started washing him, beneath the water, with a cloth. His hand slipped between Alec's thighs but Alec grabbed it. "Ah, ah. Let it soak a while. It's sore."

"Do you want me to check it for you?"

"I'm fine. Just be gentle with me."

Brad cuddled into Alec on one side and Sebastian sat on the other, washing his shoulders. "Was it good?" Brad asked. Alec cocked open one eye and surveyed Brad's sheepish smile.

"It wasn't bad."

"You came loads," Sebastian said. "So it can't have been bad."

"Not bad at all. Full to the point I felt like I'd burst open. But definitely not bad. *You're* bad." Sebastian stopped his preening and looked up. "Putting your hand over my mouth so I couldn't stop you."

"Would you have stopped me?"

"No."

Sebastian grinned and carried on smoothing the cloth over Alec's neck and shoulders.

"That's not the point. Don't go thinking you can jump me whenever you feel like it. And expect me to turn the tables. On both of you at some point."

"Been there, done that," Brad said, matter-of-factly. "Never did get the t-shirt though."

Sebastian swept Alec's hair off his face. "I wouldn't normally do something like that without asking, but sometimes you have so much going on in that head of yours you don't know what you want. I thought it might give you some breathing space up there."

"It did that all right. It gave me a sore ass too."

Sebastian laughed. "And something to remember us by when you're away."

Alec certainly wouldn't forget it anytime soon. He shifted carefully and an ache radiated deep inside his body. Scratch that. He wouldn't be forgetting for a long while.

A Pause...

The heat felt glorious against Alec's skin. He was unusually sleepy for mid-morning; the long flight had eased its way out of his body along with the unrealized stress of constantly being on call for sex. There was also something oddly relaxing about not being responsible for other people's needs. Hamilton was there, of course, but in the ten days since they'd left England they had settled into a comfortable companionship that he imagined regular couples had together. It's possible they had more sex than most, but even that had developed into a more relaxed and playful mood. Not the vanilla nightmare of a Hamilton afraid to step over the line, but a real rollercoaster of stretching boundaries and uncovering hidden needs. Overall, it was fair to say Alec was enjoying his vacation.

He smiled at the slow creep of Hamilton's hand stroking his back. Not the familiar, everything's okay stroke, but the uncertain tease of the sexually hungry.

"You're tan is the most delicious color, darling," he said, kissing Alec's shoulder.

Alec turned his head, still resting on his arms as Hamilton slipped onto the sun lounger next to him. "You made it very clear when we arrived that this hotel would not appreciate our usual public displays, baby."

"It's not a display. I just want to be closer."

"Then perhaps you should stop stroking my butt crack, sweetie. Because right now I have a display in my shorts that will impress no one but you."

"Oh, god. I didn't even know I was doing it." Hamilton chuckled. His hand came to rest on the small of Alec's back. It didn't really help Alec's predicament. One touch with the right intent from Hamilton could turn Alec's cock solid—for a very long time. "Darling, do you miss them?"

"Sebastian and Bradley?"

"The other cocks. Do you miss Harrison's cock?"

Alec pushed himself up to lean on his forearms. Hamilton shuffled a little so that Alec was looking down into his face. He looked so young. Without the suit and the continual subservience around him, he'd melted into a stunningly handsome thirty-year-old, rather than the hard-nosed businessman everyone knew him as. Alec kissed his forehead and cheeks. Stuff the hotel rules. "I don't miss the cocks. I do miss their company. Before you, I didn't really have a social life. Now I'm never alone. Even my work commute is with you and Brad. It's nice to take a break from duty and responsibility." He grinned. "It's fantastic to have you all to myself. But, yes, I miss the boys turning up to give me a hug and rattle on about nothing."

"Do you hate not having any time to yourself? We could move Sebastian and Bradley back to your old apartment a few days a week. If you need more space it won't be a problem."

Arriving home to an empty flat wasn't something Alec was eager to reinstate in his life. There was something about Sebastian waiting, naked, to service his every need that made the day pass just that little more smoothly. He smiled at the thought, and was surprised not to feel a pang of sadness at the distance currently between them. "I like having flatmates. I have my own room. The boys don't bother me if I close the door. Besides, I wouldn't want to uproot Fraser; he's only just getting settled there."

"As long as you're happy."

Alec kissed the end of Hamilton's nose. "I'm very happy. What about you, do you miss the asses and the hot wet mouths around your cock, or ordering people to strip and fuck?"

Hamilton wriggled further under Alec and reached up to kiss. Young and playful for sure. Alec hadn't known he had it in him and it made him three times as sexy with the new edge of vulnerability. "What is there to miss when I have you, right here?"

"We should take this upstairs," Alec said, nuzzling into Hamilton's neck. He wanted to hold him naked, feel as much skin on skin as possible.

"It's okay. I just need to be close for a moment."

Alec lay back down, his head on Hamilton's shoulder, his arm resting across his chest. He resisted the urge to wrap a leg over him and instead placed chaste kisses against his warm skin and closed his eyes again. *Perfect.* Even more perfect was the hand that slipped under Alec's body to hold his cock, not to play with it, just touch it. It was reassurance, perhaps for both of them and Alec soon drifted off to sleep.

Family Jitters

The big day was upon them and Alec was nervous. In just over an hour, he would meet Hamilton's family; the family who'd given their sixteen-year-old son a slave for his birthday so he could learn the ropes of sex that seemed to pull the strings to power in their world.

Hamilton had explained, as part of Alec's manager training, it was a rare gift to be able to recruit office boys without finding yourself caught up in endless lawsuits for harassment. It took time to study a person without them knowing they were being watched. It was a skill to pick out certain tells that suggested they would be amenable to the various duties required. They needed to be hungry, but not power crazy. Honest and trustworthy to a fault. Open to instruction and even mild abuse by some of the less patient members of the Order, yet not a doormat. Hamilton's father had recruited for a time as a young man and he'd seen the potential in Hamilton as a boy, the way he mixed and made friends. Hamilton's father was a man who would cut Alec into his component parts within the first five minutes and spend the rest of the day analyzing his discoveries.

Then there was Hamilton's twin brother, William, who insisted on the use of his full name, and his girlfriend Constance, who refused to answer to anything but Tiggi.

Hamilton teased Alec about being nervous but he was just as bad. He'd tried on four different outfits and was tearing the closet apart to find something more suitable. He settled on a pair of loose linen pants in natural cream and a white linen shirt. He looked incredible. Alec also went for linen but in the form of a more tailored suit. The open necked shirt showed off his necklace. Hamilton's family would know immediately it wasn't a fashion statement and Alec was glad that part, at least, didn't need explaining.

"It's no good," Hamilton said, flopping onto the bed. "You're going to have to fuck me to calm me down."

"Again? I just got out of your ass an hour ago."

"If it were possible to keep you there, I would. Permanently."

Interesting. And this from a guy who hadn't bottomed in fourteen years of sex until he'd met Alec. "That can be arranged." Alec smiled. "Why don't you strip off those pants and get on the bed. All fours, please."

Alec couldn't quite get his head around the fact Hamilton didn't question him. It seemed the vacation, or maybe Alec himself, had tapped a hidden sub in Mr. Everyone's-Master-Hamilton. Alec went to the drawer where they kept the toys and lube. He chose the smallest finger-thick butt plug and smiled. It was the first one Hamilton had used with him when they'd shopped for bands what seemed like a millennium ago.

Turning back to the bed to find Hamilton's bare ass staring at him was an instant hard-on moment. He smoothed his hand over the pert muscled globes. Hamilton's hole belonged to him and him alone. How would he feel if he had to share it as Hamilton did with Alec? He pushed the thought from his mind but rather than lubing the plug, Alec lubed his cock and slipped inside. The groan from Hamilton sent shivers over Alec's skin. Only Alec drew that sound from him. It gave Alec strength and a peace difficult to rival.

He teased with slow, deep strokes, kneading Hamilton's ass cheeks as he moved. He wanted to say how much he loved him. He wanted to say how special this was, how much he wished he could stay right there, but instead he wrapped up the emotions and expressed them through the slow, sensual rock of his hips. It wasn't about climax. It wasn't even about sex. It was about being there for each other, whatever they needed to get through the days, a bonding of souls rather than bodies.

He pulled out slowly and kissed each cheek before lubing the plug and pushing it into place. He worked it a few times in slow motions as he had with his cock before inserting it fully. "Now you have me inside you for the rest of the day," Alec said, kissing the small of Hamilton's back. "Exactly where I want to be."

They dressed again in silence and held hands walking to the car. "Only you, Alec," Hamilton whispered, placing a tender kiss to his lips before moving around to the driver's side. Conversation bubbled to life for the rest of the journey, but a new peace existed between them.

Alec wasn't prepared for the huge estate they pulled into. His stomach was doing a strange dance and he felt small. No other word for it. He clutched at Hamilton's hand.

"Don't worry Alec, they are no different to anyone else you've met."

"They are, Rick, they're your parents."

"Believe me, my father is going to love you."

It didn't calm his nerves. It made them worse. When Hamilton's father decided he didn't like Alec, Hamilton would be upset and Alec would feel like a failure. Why had he suggested this?

Hamilton took his hand and kissed the ring on his wedding finger. "You are my partner, Alec. They will be curious, because I've never brought anyone to meet them before, but they will love you."

"My parents' house would fit in the fountain."

"You know how stupid that statement makes you sound."

"It's the truth."

"But you're saying it as though it matters."

Alec tried to ignore the towering stone columns, the overly precise gardens and the sheer size of the house. The people inside were just people, right? Hamilton dragged him up the few steps and straight through the double oak doors. A butler greeted them before Alec did a double take at the man who walked through the large arch to the side of them.

"Oh, fucking hell, that's weird." Alec fought the temptation to cover his mouth with his hand. Swearing within seconds of entering the house probably wasn't such a good idea. The butler raised an eyebrow but was obviously trying to hide a smile. Alec relaxed a little and bumped Hamilton's shoulder. "You didn't tell me William was an identical twin."

Hamilton winked. "William, Tiggi, this is Alec."

"Alec or Alexander?" William said, holding out his hand. His smile was different to Hamilton's, his face the same yet somehow different. Alec was safe. He couldn't think of anything worse than getting a hard-on for Hamilton's brother every five minutes.

"Either," Alec said, retuning the handshake. "It's lovely to meet you."

"Oh, my dear boy. It's *fascinating* to meet you. I was convinced the big lug was unlovable."

"Definitely not," Alec grinned. Tiggi smiled, shook Alec's hand, gave Hamilton a cursory peck to each cheek, but remained quiet. She was surprisingly plain considering her surroundings but she had presence. Even with her lack of words it was obvious who wore the pants in the relationship and for some reason it set Alec at ease. Maybe knowing that the Hamiltons could be tamed gave him hope for the future. It certainly gave Alec cause to smile.

The chat and introductions were brief. They were ushered into a further room where Alec found himself in the clutches of Hamilton's mother. A pretty woman, definite signs of enhancement against aging, but Alec could see reflections of Hamilton's face in hers.

"Mrs. Hamilton," Alec said, kissing each cheek in customary 'lovey' fashion.

"Call me Berry, darling, everyone does. Ah, here's your father."

Alec took a deep breath and turned to greet Mr. Hamilton. The man was the same height as Alec but his presence was commanding and he was handsome. Very handsome. The fairness of his hair covered much of the gray he was allowing to encroach naturally. He was an older version of his sons. Even his build was the same, though he was an inch or two shorter. Alec was looking at Rick in thirty years and he liked it.

"Alexander," Mr. Hamilton said, holding out a hand.

"Mr. Hamilton." The man gave no first name. Obviously not impressed then. Fuck.

"Richard." He pulled Hamilton into a hug. "You've been away too long. Now, tell me why you aren't staying here?"

Hamilton flushed. "Father, please don't start with this already."

"This is your home."

"And I am on vacation."

"We'll discuss it later. Alexander, have you been to Australia before?"

"No, sir." Alec felt his own cheeks color and was thankful for the squeeze of his hand in Hamilton's.

"I understand you're a country boy."

"My family are from Cornwall. Marizion."

"I know it. Not far from the Davenports."

Hamilton slipped his arm around Alec's waist. "Father, we've just walked through the door. Can we ease up on the interrogations, maybe sit, have some tea?"

"As you wish."

Hamilton took Alec's hand as they walked through a series of halls and rooms to end up on a terrace overlooking the ocean. The table was already set for brunch.

Hamilton pulled Alec's chair close and kept hold of his hand. The conversation centered on William telling Hamilton's boyhood secrets, occasionally drawing a gasp from their mother and a giggle from Tiggi. It was light, pleasant company but an underlying tension remained. Alec tried to concentrate on the incredible view over the landscaped grounds, on the dancing flickers of sunlight off the huge swimming pool, but he was far too aware of the intense gaze of Hamilton senior boring into his soul. It reminded him of his meeting with Nathaniel Philip. Alec shuddered. It didn't go unnoticed. Hamilton Senior raised an eyebrow, looking so much like Hamilton Alec found himself swallowing around a lump in his throat. Hamilton squeezed Alec's suddenly sweaty palm. "Are you okay, darling?"

Alec tried to smile. "Just a little warm."

William echoed Alec's thoughts and suggested they meet later; he and Tiggi were going to swim. As the company broke up, Alec excused himself and headed to the bathroom, led by the butler whose name he still didn't know. Hamilton Senior was waiting for him when he came out.

"Alexander, time for a chat."

It wasn't a request. "Sir." Alec nodded and followed him into an impressive study, light and airy but with a traditional feel. Books lined the walls from floor to ceiling. Large, over-upholstered chairs formed small reading nooks in the corners, and a huge honey colored desk sat before a wall of windows. The smell of aged leather and polish permeated the air.

Hamilton Senior closed the door behind them and took hold of Alec's hand, bringing it closer for inspection of the ring on his wedding finger." It's true then," he said, dropping Alec's hand. "You're engaged to my son and yet I'm only just meeting you."

Alec stared blankly. What was he supposed to say to that?

"Is there a reason it couldn't have waited?"

"Rick wanted me to wear the ring when I started in my new position, I—"

"Ah, yes. From office boy to manager in one easy step. You must be very pleased with yourself."

Alec bristled. He'd prepared himself for many things, but pompous prick wasn't one of them. "I'm sorry. I'm not quite sure what you're implying."

"Well, don't just stand there. Let's have a demonstration of your skills."

Alec continued to stare. He couldn't possibly mean—

"I'm second chair for the GC New South Wales and Victoria. I would say that places you on your knees to suck my cock, boy."

A snort escaped Alec's throat and he shook his head in disbelief. "I'm afraid that won't be possible." *You stupid, fucking, asshole.*

"I beg your pardon?"

"Under the circumstances, sir, I don't think it would be appropriate."

"What are you wittering about, boy? Come here and suck my cock before I decide to fuck you instead."

So that's what Alec could expect from his in-laws, to be treated like a sex perk. He was pretty sure Tiggi wouldn't have been subjected to such behavior. The disappointment bit hard in Alec's stomach and he fought the bile rising in his throat. "I'm aware I may not be what you were hoping for, Mr. Hamilton, but I love your son very much. There is no way I'll take part in any kind of sexual activity with you, or William, or any other member of this household."

"You've sucked Wessex and Merrimont. You've been fucked by that boy of his. Don't tell me you didn't know they were family."

How the hell did he know about Jasper? "Actually, at the time I didn't

275

and I was following Rick's orders. In fact, perhaps that's the best way to deal with this. If Rick tells me to suck your cock, I'll do it. But not before."

Hamilton Senior drew himself up to his full height and Alec attempted not to wither in front of him. "You *will* do it, or you'll forfeit your membership of the GC. And before you think one of your sugar daddies can bail you out, you should know I am still *very* influential in the City."

I'll bet you are, fucktard. Alec shrugged his shoulders. "So be it."

"What?"

"I was never interested in the GC, Mr. Hamilton. It was a bonus that came with loving your son, dating your son. You can have the apartment, the job, and the boys. What you can't take is the love Rick has for me." Alec turned to walk out the door.

"Alexander." Hamilton Senior placed a hand on his shoulder. Alec turned back but found he couldn't meet Hamilton Senior's eyes. He'd let Hamilton down, his father hated him. Hamilton Senior lifted his chin with a finger. He was smiling. "I had to be sure you weren't freeloading. My sons are very dear to me. I won't see them hurt."

"I don't understand."

"I was testing you. If you went to your knees too freely, you don't have the backbone you need to survive. If you went to your knees to retain your status, you don't have the honor to be with my son."

Alec tried to push down the anger that flared inside before it hit him, it was a classic Hamilton move. Chip off the old block. "I can see where he gets it from." Alec sighed. It explained so much. How many tests had Hamilton been subjected to growing up? No wonder he was such a basket case.

"Gets what?" They both turned to see Hamilton in the doorway. "I hope you aren't scaring him, father."

"Not at all. Just receiving the appropriate servicing from a GC boy."

The color drained from Hamilton's face. "Alec, you didn't?"

"No, I did *not*, thank you very much. What do you take me for?"

"Now, now, boys. No need to argue on my account. He fought his corner admirably, son, with his honor intact."

Hamilton was still staring.

"He was doing what you do," Alec said. "Setting me up when all he had to do was ask the damn question."

Hamilton Senior laughed, slapping Alec on the shoulder. "Good lad."

"Alec, you didn't touch him?"

"Of course not. Rick, how could you think—"

Hamilton flung himself into Alec's arms. "Thank you, darling. Thank you, so much. I feel sick." He turned on his father. "And *you*, how could you do that? Are you deliberately trying to drive us apart?"

"Richard, calm down. I was merely testing the boy's intent and resilience. If he's going to be a part of this family, he needs a backbone. It seems he has one."

Alec could see Hamilton's temper spiraling. He pulled him into a hug and gently squeezed his ass cheek, knowing the plug would move and focus his attention squarely on Alec. "Remember what's important, Rick. Let everything else fall away."

Hamilton rested his forehead on Alec's shoulder and pressed his body against him. "Love you," he whispered. "I'm sorry for being an ass."

"I'm used to it." Alec chuckled, kissing his cheek and letting his arms slip around Hamilton's waist.

"I'll leave you boys alone for a few minutes."

Soft, sensual kisses flowed with the gentle caress of hands over their bodies to reassure and reconnect. "My father is a bastard. I'm sorry he did that to you. Fuck, if he'd have touched you—"

"He didn't," Alec kissed over Hamilton's neck, smiling as he moaned and leaned closer. "So, stop thinking about it. Let's go back."

The rest of the afternoon went by without any issues. Hamilton Senior warmed to Alec and the atmosphere lifted. After another few hours, Hamilton had gravitated to Alec's side and was draped over him, practically sat on his lap. Alec stroked his thigh, noticing the slight tenting of his pants as he squirmed to get closer, kissing Alec's shoulder.

"Rick, what is it?"

"I need you," he replied, his breath heated. "I'm not used to waiting so long."

"Oh, fuck." Alec put a hand over his mouth. He really needed to watch his language. "I forgot. Do you want to leave?"

"We can go to my room."

"Won't they know?"

"I don't care. I'll end up humping your leg if we don't hurry."

"Lead the way."

Hamilton was already stripping off his shirt before they reached the door to his room. He dropped his pants just inside and was on the bed, naked, before Alec had closed the door. "Just take me," he said, panting softly.

"No. We're going to do this right."

"I don't have time for *right*."

"Excuse me." Alec slapped Hamilton's ass and chuckled as he jumped. "You will wait until I'm good and ready. Now, where will I find some lube?"

"In the bathroom cabinet."

Alec teased and tortured with a slow, languid fuck, keeping Hamilton on his back so he could kiss and nip and see the light in his eyes. Without any words or commands they came together and rested in a tangled heap of sweaty limbs.

"Worth the wait, baby?"

"Absolutely," Hamilton said, smiling. "Do it again and I'll skin your balls."

"Oh, I don't know. I think you have a slave hidden in you Mr. Hamilton, and I intend to find him and shackle him to my heart forever."

"You already have, Alec," Hamilton said, kissing his neck and shoulders. "I am completely yours."

"Do you mean that?"

"With all my heart."

"In that case, we're going shopping."

"For?"

"It's time you wore a band, Richard, and not just a pretend one."

"But I—"

"No 'buts'. You'll wear my ring and get used to it."

No words followed, just frantic kisses and another round of exquisite lovemaking.

"Feeling better gentleman?" Hamilton Senior said, as they made their way back to the deck for dinner. Alec pulled Hamilton close for a hug, whispering 'I love yous' in his ear until he squirmed. "Perhaps you should have stayed upstairs a little longer," his father said.

"We'll head off after dinner, thank you, father."

Hamilton Senior frowned. "Please stay, Richard. Just for a few days."

"We have our reservation until the weekend."

"Then come back here afterward. I'll arrange a party for you to introduce Alexander."

"So your cronies can all pull the same stunt you did? I don't think so."

"They would *not*. No son-in-law of mine would be treated in such a way."

Hamilton prickled. "By anyone other than you, you mean."

"Rick," Alec said, stroking his arm. "Your father has already apologized. You need to let it go."

Hamilton turned on him, narrowing his eyes and lowering his voice to almost a whisper. "You really don't have a problem with what he did to you?"

"Like I said, I'm used to it." Alec stroked Hamilton's cheek and pinched it playfully. "Do you want me to be mad at you for the Doctor or for Patrick?"

Hamilton slumped in a chair and pulled Alec onto his lap. He wrapped his arms around him and sighed. "You're too good to me, Alec."

"No," Alec said, kissing the top of his head. "I just love you."

Hamilton nuzzled into the crease of Alec's neck and he squirmed, trying not to giggle. "You're happy to stay a few days then?"

Alec held Hamilton's face in his hands and gave him a long, hard look. "I'm happy, Rick, as long as I'm with you."

And wasn't that the truth. The time away from the real world was a continuing revelation. Everything about Hamilton Alec had been unable to figure out made sense in the context of his family. The moods, the quirks, the odd routines, the mystery that was Rick Hamilton unraveled before Alec's eyes and presented him with a very interesting picture indeed. One he wanted to explore outside of their usual constraints. Alec couldn't deny the subtle ache growing inside him for a glimpse of Sebastian and Brad fooling around, or a slap on the ass from his old man, but the time away was proving to be much easier than he'd anticipated. After all the loose words and soppy confessions, it seemed Hamilton truly was his everything, right down to the occasional inability to communicate without painful games. It was possible the games, at least, had passed but Alec thought maybe they would be easier to stomach after such an invaluable insight into the making of Hamilton.

Families shaped you. Alec had often wondered how he would have differed had his family not accepted who he was. Sebastian and Vaughn came to mind, their stories similar in many ways. Alec and Hamilton both had the acceptance of their families; both had the support and encouragement to be exactly who they were and to become whoever they chose to be. Different stories, creating very different men, but it was becoming clearer to Alec that at the heart of it all there were striking similarities. Similarities that ultimately led them to wanting the same things, all be it from very different sides of the equation. It gave Alec hope for their future together.

All he had to do now was get through the upcoming schmoozing session with the local Order. He'd need the few days in between to turn the tables and have Hamilton take extra care to fuck the nerves out of him so he'd be sated and pliant, and prepared for any possible surprises.

Upside Down

The few days respite before heading back to Hamilton's parents wasn't long enough. Alec was starting to feel nervous at the reception he'd get from the Australian Order. If Hamilton Senior was anything to go by, it wasn't going to be good.

This time, when they pulled up at the estate, they were both dressed in tailored suits. Hamilton favored dark-gray pinstripes and had opted for one of his favorite Vivien Westwood white shirts and a dark-gray silk tie. Alec wore a more contemporary cut light gray suit with a dark-blue open-neck shirt.

"You look great, darling," Hamilton said, as he straightened himself out and closed the button of his jacket.

"Thanks. Harrison hates this suit," Alec chuckled. "I'm sure the old codgers here tonight will too."

"Well, I love you in it. Your ass in particular."

"Let's hope the only person to see my pucker tonight is you."

"That depends on whether you take up any offers you get this evening. There will be boys for service. If you want to fuck or have them suck you, it's likely you'll flash that perfect ass of yours."

Alec paused his stride. He hadn't considered the other side of the service role. Of course there would be boys on offer. And he would be expected to show he was a seasoned Order manager and partake of the delicacies gathered and prepared for him. But Alec didn't want to be the guest of honor at the all-you-can-fuck buffet. He was enjoying his time with Hamilton, one-on-one. Neither of them had touched anyone else in the weeks they'd been away and he liked it.

Hamilton had made his way to Alec's side and tweaked his cheek as though aware of Alec's growing uncertainty. Order politics would weigh heavy this evening. Why couldn't they forgo the nonsense for a little longer?

"What's wrong?"

"Do you think I should?" Alec grabbed Hamilton's hand and threaded their fingers together. "Use the boys, I mean. I don't want to offend anyone by saying no if they offer me service."

"If you fancy them, go for it."

"And you?"

Hamilton shrugged. "I'm not itching for anything else. I couldn't give a toss if I cause offense. I'm on vacation." He kissed Alec's cheek and led the way, up the stone steps and through the door.

They hadn't even made it into the reception room before Hamilton Senior bore down on them. He was wearing a dinner jacket and open necked white shirt. "Alexander, a moment."

He dragged Alec away and closed the door to the study. Alec felt Hamilton's absence through to his core. As much as things had eased with Hamilton Senior, being shut in a room alone with him hadn't been on Alec's list of wants for the evening.

"First of all," Hamilton Senior said, offering Alec a glass of whiskey. Alec took the glass and tried to relax. Whatever the old codger wanted, it couldn't be as bad as their first encounter. "Thank you for bringing Richard home. It means a lot to me."

"You're very welcome, Mr. Hamilton."

"Ah, yes. You can drop the formality now. Call me Henry."

"Thank you, Henry."

"I also want to give you a few pointers for the evening. You are not a service boy here, Alexander. You are my son-in-law and they should treat you accordingly. You do not offer services, nor should you be asked. If you are, you will tell me immediately and I will request the member to leave."

"I understand."

"Alexander, I want you to feel at home here. My son loves you very much. Richard doesn't love easily; in fact, I've never known it before.

With you he's…different, he's animated and alive, happy. But he belongs here, Alexander. With his family. I want you to bring him home."

"What are you asking me?"

"You're both still young men, but soon Alec, in a few years perhaps, you should make the move to Australia. Life is richer here. Freer."

"I don't know what to say. We have commitments in the UK, I have family."

"Bring them. Aunts and uncles, cousins, whomever you wish. I want my son to come home. Just think about it. A few years, but please, no more."

"Are you okay, Henry? I mean, health-wise is everything in order?"

Henry smiled. "I'm perfectly well. We all are. I just miss him, and William reminds me every time I see him that Richard is far from home. They are alike and yet so different."

"Yes, I'd noticed. Is William here this evening?"

"Heaven's no. He's always refused to have anything to do with the GC. I'm glad really. It's always suited Richard but William is shy and sensitive. Not a good match at all."

"I can't promise you anything, Henry. It's a lot to consider and we both have boys at home. But, as you say, maybe in a few years we'll be ready for a change of scenery." *If Hamilton hasn't kicked my ass to the wind for a new one.*

A fatherly pat on the shoulder and Alec was dispatched to find his fiancé. Here, at least, that was how they chose to see him. Alec still wasn't sure what his official ring wearing title was at home. It seemed to vary depending on whom he spoke to and Hamilton wasn't really forthcoming in offering advice or an announcement to clear things up. But it would be different at work after the vacation. It was going to be difficult to explain why they'd both been away for an extended time during the same period. It occurred to Alec, not for the first time since being away, that a more open declaration of their relationship was on the cards when they returned. What happened from there was anyone's guess.

Surprisingly, the evening was fun. GC, as they preferred to call it here, New South Wales was much like being at the Davenports. The men had brought their partners and boys. Sex was taken to discreet locations so you didn't have to get involved and the alcohol flowed sweetly.

Hamilton was drinking wine, but staying away from the whiskey. More than a little merry, he was very tactile but Alec noted with a smile, only with him. He'd never seen Hamilton around other Order members and not fuck. Tonight he stayed close to Alec and repeatedly turned down the offer of some really beautiful boys.

"Is there nothing we have for you?" A gentleman called Lewis, asked Hamilton. "You must like the look of one of our boys, surely? You could share with Alexander; keep one for the evening, or two."

"Lewis, I am more than grateful for the generous offer of your lovely boys and they are, every one, delightful. But this vacation is something of a mini-honeymoon. I really am more than content with the love of my life."

Honeymoon? Well, bugger. Alec brought Hamilton's hand to his lips and kissed tenderly. Hamilton's smile dazzled as he reached in to kiss Alec, and then kissed some more, and some more, and some more. "Time for you to be in bed I think," Alec said, breaking away.

Hamilton curled into his shoulder. "I'd like that, darling. Will you take me there?"

Lewis chuckled, patting Alec on the back. "Go and look after your boy, Alexander. He needs his master's touch this evening." Alec was left staring after Lewis as he walked away.

Hamilton nuzzled Alec's neck. "Take me to bed," he whispered. "I want you close."

Alec wrapped an arm around Hamilton's waist and walked him to their room. Hamilton stood grinning and Alec undressed them both and led him to the bed. "They think you're my master," Hamilton chuckled. "And you are for some reason. Since we've been here everything's upside down, like the country." He giggled. "But," he said, bouncing on to his knees on the bed, "tonight I am going to fuck you. And I'm going to fuck you so hard and for so long that you won't know which way is up." He fell back onto the bed. "Do you think you'd like that, Alec?"

"I would absolutely love it, baby." Hamilton pulled him down into a kiss, a hand trailing down his chest…and, he was asleep. "Typical," Alec mumbled. "And I really needed that fuck."

He pulled the linen sheet over Hamilton and sat in the chair opposite the bed. Everything was back to front here and Alec didn't know why. Perhaps it was Hamilton being near his family, or just being away from the office where everyone saw him in a certain way. Was this the real Hamilton? Alec had seen glimmers of it during their special weekends. It was nice and yet it was unsettling. Maybe Hamilton needed to refocus, just the way Alec did sometimes. One thing was for sure, if they were ever going to settle here, Alec had more work to do. He pulled on his suit and headed back to the party to schmooze. It wouldn't do for both guests of honor to be absent and it would take Alec's mind off the all-new Hamilton—sweet, sexy, oddly submissive and snoring loudly through his alcohol-dazed sleep.

Right Side Up

Their last few days together before heading back to the grind and grayness of London Hamilton pulled out all the stops. For the layover, he had checked them into an exclusive master/sub resort hidden away in a secluded tropical paradise. It had taken Alec nearly fifteen minutes to read the hefty confidentiality contract before a member of staff escorted them to their beachside villa and handed over the keys. They came with a reminder most of the buildings would remain off limits until they had both completed the guided tour.

"I'm afraid to ask how much this place cost," Alec said, looking around the main living area. Everything, from the floor to the walls to the furniture was finished in shades of off-white. Marble floor tiles, wispy curtains and bleached wood highlighted the lush greenness outside the floor-to-ceiling windows. A huge welcome basket full of exotic fruits and flowers sat on an extra-long chaise just inside the door and cast a delicate fragrance with the hint of vanilla.

"That's not your concern." Hamilton smiled and tipped the bellboy. "We'll be along shortly for the tour."

"Would you like someone to unpack for you, sir?"

"Not necessary, my boy will do it." The man nodded and left.

Alec slipped an arm around Hamilton's waist and pulled him back against his chest. "I'm your boy again now, am I? I like the idea of you taking back the reins."

Hamilton turned in Alec's arms and grabbed his ass, giving it a good squeeze. "I am definitely the master for this portion of our vacation. I trust I won't need to remind you of your place."

Alec slipped to his knees and nuzzled Hamilton's crotch. "My place is at your side, Master. Always." He unhooked Hamilton's short pants and retrieved his cock, already swelling nicely, and sucked it into his mouth. Hamilton carded his fingers through Alec's hair and relaxed into his ministrations.

There were several other couples at reception waiting for the tour. Alec felt overdressed. He was the only sub in the group with clothes on. A larger than life domme, in towering heels and a loose wrap around stole, accompanied a male and female sub chained together at the waist. An older man, probably in his fifties but looking very trim and fit, held the leash of a young woman with the palest skin and the reddest hair Alec had ever seen. Marks and bruises covered her body and Alec had to force himself not to stare. Lastly, two men stood behind a younger one, their ages were difficult to pinpoint. The young man wore a chastity device similar to the one Alec had used on Bradley. He smiled at Alec and one of his masters slapped him across the ass. He didn't flinch, just dropped his gaze to the floor.

"Ten lashes, for your insubordination," the man said, pulling the boy's head back by his hair.

"Yes, sir. Thank you, sir."

Alec stepped in closer to Hamilton's side and bowed his head. He didn't want to get anyone else into trouble.

Another male couple arrived a few moments later, the sub also naked with his hands cuffed behind his back. As they came to stand next to the rest of the group, the sub nuzzled into his master's shoulder. The master responded with a kiss to his forehead and a whispered word that brought a smile to the sub's lips. It was more the kind of pairing Alec was used to seeing and he relaxed a little. The hotel representative gave a quick count of heads and started the tour.

Alec continued to relax as they walked around. The hard-core guests were in the minority. Lots of nakedness, plenty of sex acts going on, but nothing along the lines of their fellow tour takers. He was looking forward to a touch of exhibitionism to round off their very private vacation. In the month they'd been away, neither of them had touched another person. It had been a strange time, with Hamilton relaxing to the point of slipping into the mode of a sub. He wanted Alec to be boss and to make the decisions. He wanted Alec to fuck him more than he fucked Alec. He was tactile verging on clingy. Alec remembered the relaxing of roles when he'd taken a few days in Cornwall with Sebastian. Alec had let go to the point he'd opened his ass to a number of new lovers on that trip. Maybe it was just something that happened sometimes. Not that Hamilton would be taking any cock up his ass other than Alec's, not now, or ever.

Alec was just getting comfortable, taking in the impressive facilities, appreciating the beautifully active bodies in every color, shape and size—who knew big people could be so flexible?—and then the guide announced they were about to leave the neutral zone. Alec grabbed Hamilton's hand. *That* was the neutral zone? The full-on orgies, the odd swing and fucking horse with multiple candidates waiting to fuck the subs, were *neutral* activities? He didn't want to walk through the large double doors looming bold as brass before them. Even the pictures from his limited imagination were too much.

"Don't worry, darling," Hamilton said, rubbing his back. "I just want to look. We'll stay firmly in the neutral zone for our visit."

"Thank you, Master." *Neutral zone my ass, staying in the apartment more like.* Alec had been expecting a little sex by the pool, not a full on twenty-four seven fuckfest.

"A pampered one," the master of the cuffed boy said to Hamilton. "I often bring Leo here for a pampering session. This time we're here for discipline training. Do you ever take the whip to him?"

"Not to this boy, but I do dabble on occasion."

"Leo has grown rather found of it over the last year. I booked this week as somewhat of a treat for him. You?"

"A refocus session without the usual distractions."

"It's the best I've found. We've been all over, but we always come back to this one. I find the coworkers have a little something extra and you can fuck any of them you know. Even the booking manager will cover his duties and bend over for you. I find it adds to the rush." He grinned, showing a dimple in his cheek and a gold tooth. Alec couldn't place the accent and there were no distinguishing clues as to his ethnicity. He looked powerful in body and character, and Leo was obviously smitten by the way he gazed lovingly at his master while he spoke.

"An interesting fact," Hamilton said, taking a quick look at Alec and quirking a smile. "Thank you."

The tour had moved through the doors into a much darker space. Thick gray fabric covered the walls and matched the color of the floor tiles. The only thing in the room was a manned desk at the far side next to a second set of double doors with smoky gray lights set above them. Two members of staff, one male, and one female, dressed in gray tunics, guarded the door. Alec certainly wouldn't mind bending *that* guy over, he'd pass for a runway model, all sleek lines and cheekbones.

"All zone changes have an anterior room and security to ensure you are aware of what lies beyond the doors." The guide ushered them through the next set of doors and into much riskier territory. They walked into a large circular lobby, in the same gray tones, with a dozen or so open-plan playrooms and what looked to be glass-walled rooms in a second semi-circle around them. Punishments and questionable bindings were abundant, along with moans and cries that pierced Alec's conscience. Alec didn't hide his discomfort and grabbed Hamilton's arm for moral support. It was Harrison's party on steroids, and this was only the first level outside his comfort zone. Hamilton spoke briefly to the guide and he led the group back to the neutral zone so Alec and Hamilton could leave the tour.

"The main thing to remember," the guide said to them, "is the whole resort is color coded. Neutral colors in the neutral zone," he waved his hand around the creamy walls of the lobby, "dark-gray to black, orange, and purple for the other areas. Our coding differs from other resorts. Know your zone and you'll have a lovely stay."

"Thank you," Hamilton said, "We know our zone already."

"The only other rules we have are on this." He handed Hamilton a small plastic card. "Enjoy your day." He gathered up the rest of the group and headed back through the double doors and out of sight.

"Thank you, Master," Alec said, squeezing Hamilton's hand. "I don't think I could have stomached anything heavier."

"This is our special time together. I don't want you to feel uncomfortable. Besides, that side of things only holds a passing interest for me. I was curious rather than anything else." He kissed Alec's cheek. "Are you hungry? I'd like to try the seafood restaurant."

"And we can study the rules?"

"Wonderful idea."

The rules were simple.

Full consent required at all times; there was a clause for subs entering the purple zones to sign away consent at the door of the forced fantasy suites. It made Alec shudder.

Keep activities within the permitted zones.

No photography or filming anywhere on the resort; even in private residences.

No sexual acts within areas designated for food services.

And lastly,

First names only. It was apparently to minimize the risk of anyone tracking a customer down in the real world.

Alec liked the rules. They were easy, comfortable rules, as long as he didn't think about what was going on behind the color-coded double doors around the center. And the thing he liked most was that he was here with Hamilton and they were still a whole hemisphere away from the rules and formalities they usually adhered to. They were free to explore each other any way they wanted without prying, questioning eyes.

The sun heated Alec's skin to the perfect degree, a light sheen of moisture but not so hot as to be uncomfortable. He sighed contentedly where he lay on a large floor cushion at Hamilton's feet and Hamilton reached over and fluffed his hair. They'd found their place at the center. A couple of different meeting places where things were very relaxed and light on sharing. Hamilton had spent the first afternoon teaching Alec the difference between using a feather for tickling and using it for sexual torture. He was so strung out by the time he climaxed he thought he saw stars and could do nothing other than curl up for a nap. When it came time for them to go to dinner, Alec was nervous but it had been a lovely evening.

They'd found a nice bar after and Hamilton had fucked him over the table, their first time in public in a long time, and it had felt great. Breakfast followed much the same pattern and now they mingled in a small alcove near one of the smaller pools with Hamilton chatting casually to another master about similar resorts in other countries.

Alec allowed his mind to wander. Christmas was just around the corner and he'd been with Hamilton nearly a year. The most amazing and eye opening year of his life. If anyone had tried to tell him the year before the direction his life was about to take he'd have laughed in their face. At times like this, he could still hardly believe it.

A movement caught his eye and he turned to watch a sub on the other side of the pool get into position on hands and knees. She shuddered, from what Alec was sure looked like pleasure, as a pale round man slid his cock into her. Alec watched them rock back and forth and his own ass felt empty. Hamilton hadn't let him come after their breakfast fuck and watching the action was having a noticeable effect on him. What he wouldn't give to suck on a cock now and have Hamilton plow into him as deep and hard as possible. Alec cleared his throat.

"Your boy looks needy, Richard."

Alec looked up at Leo's master standing over him. He hadn't noticed him approach. Leo peeked out from behind him and smiled at Alec. Hamilton chuckled and smoothed a hand through Alec's hair.

"What do you say to loaning him to me for a little while?" Alec perked up. He didn't know the guy's name but his cock was a good length, and fat. It twitched as Alec stared at it.

"I don't know," Hamilton said. "We've been keeping to ourselves the last few weeks and I have to say I've kind of liked it."

"Oh, come now. It's only for a short time. I'll pull up a chair right here if you'd rather keep an eye on him."

Hamilton looked at Alec. He really didn't seem sure. "What do you say, Alec?"

"As it please my Master," Alec said, nuzzling Hamilton's knee. Despite having enjoyed being just for Hamilton, Alec couldn't ignore the fact he really wanted that fat cock in his mouth. He could almost taste it already. He didn't want to think too much about what that meant for his dreams of a monogamous future. For the moment, he'd take the cock and be happy.

"Very well." Hamilton tweaked Alec's ear. "Pull up a chair."

Alec got to his knees on his cushion and turned to face Leo's master. The man pulled up a long stool and sat down, reclining slightly to give Alec better access to his cock. Alec looked at Hamilton, and Hamilton nodded. With his own cock already standing to attention, Alec shuffled forward and took the nicely swelling cock in his hand. It was the widest he'd ever seen aside from Harrison's.

"You can use Leo if you wish," the man said to Hamilton. "Though only his mouth, if you would. He's a little sore from training so I'm giving his ass a day off."

Alec tuned out the conversation and wrapped his lips around his new toy. A distinct flavor, not unpleasant and easy on the tongue. Alec played with the head inside his mouth before pushing his lips over the shaft; it was a real stretch for his lips to wrap around it. The man grabbed his hair and groaned. He wasn't rough and didn't hold Alec in place but a flutter of panic still ran through his body. He pulled off completely and looked at the guy. "You're doing beautifully," he smiled. "Very clever tongue." He smoothed Alec's cheek with the back of his hand . "No smile for me?" Alec gave a grin and got back to work. "Such a good boy you have, Richard. Lovely smile when he gives it."

Alec continued working, taking pleasure in the little noises the guy made. He held Alec's hair again and leaned forward to whisper in Alec's ear. "That's it, get me nice and hard so I can fuck that pretty ass of yours. I think it will be a nice tight fit, no?" Alec's whole body stiffened. He'd tried to pull off but this time the guy held him. "It's okay. I'm always gentle. Your master will be very proud of you."

Alec fought the panic and took a few steady breaths. The guy let go and stroked Alec's head. He pulled out from his mouth and spun Alec around on his cushion.

"Master," Alec said, pulling on Hamilton's knee. Hamilton patted his hand and continued talking without looking around. Alec jumped at the feel of cold lube over his pucker followed by two fingers pushing inside him. "Master, please," he whimpered. His mind was struggling for words;

his cock was so hard it throbbed painfully. *Fuck, fuck, fuck.* The man's fat little digits twisted and probed and Alec groaned and pushed back onto them. A war broke out in his mind. He wanted so badly to be filled and stretched—but by a stranger? And as nothing more than a toy? A shudder of pleasure ran through his body and the man chuckled, kneading Alec's balls in his hand and thrusting deeper with his fingers. Alec gripped Hamilton's leg trying to stop his body rocking into the motion but it was so hard. He was so hard. A moment of emptiness and Alec jumped again at the nudge of something thicker against his ass. He was torn. He wanted that fat cock so badly but Hamilton was right there. Should he take it without permission? Had Hamilton given his permission in some bizarre subliminal way Alec hadn't noticed? Oh, but he wanted it. Hamilton didn't control who fucked him. Never had. His fingers dug into Hamilton's knee with more force at the persistent push against his body. "Master, oh *fuck.*" Hamilton looked around just as the guy thrust forward with more pressure and speared Alec in one swift movement.

"Good boy," he said, stroking Alec's back. Alec whimpered again and gripped Hamilton. The cock was definitely wide. *Hell yes.* Stretching him more than he'd been stretched in a good while. *Fucking amazing.*

"What the hell?" Alec looked up into Hamilton's wide-eyed stare.

"He's tight, very nice ass."

"What on earth—"

"Master." Alec pulled at Hamilton. He didn't want him to stop it but he couldn't think what to say.

"Alec, I—"

"Cock, Master, please?"

Hamilton opened and closed his mouth a few more times, his gaze fixed somewhere over Alec's shoulder, he guessed at the cock pounding into him. Alec squeezed Hamilton's knee again and pulled at him until he shifted and Alec could reach his cock and wrap his lips around it. There was a strange air of confusion but Alec couldn't focus on it with any real effort. The heat was building in his body, the constant pressure, the feeling of fullness at both ends, and he was soon fighting back the rising tide. He couldn't come without Hamilton's permission. He couldn't. Hamilton's cock slipped from his mouth and he rested his head against his strong thighs, holding on for dear life. The thrusting escalated, teasing and twisting Alec's body.

"Master ... please ... need to ... fuck, fuck, *fuck*."

Hamilton pulled his head up to look at him. "Do you want this to stop?"

"Fuck, no. I ... come, I need to come, please, please, please." His voice trailed out to a whisper and Alec held on to Hamilton's arms, his desperation rising.

He was about to surrender to it, suffer the consequences of coming without permission when the pounding stilled, the grip on his hips increased, one last thrust and it was over. The guy rested balls deep for a moment, his cock still twitching in Alec's ass, then he pulled out and slapped Alec playfully. "Wonderful, Richard. Lovely boy."

Alec glanced up. Hamilton looked ready to explode, his face pink and slightly blotchy. Alec grabbed his shoulder and held on. "Thank you, Master, for seeing what I needed." He leaned forward, groaning as his cock slipped against Hamilton's leg throwing him right back to the edge. "Please," he whimpered.

"Are you okay, Richard?" Alec didn't look to see who was speaking. "You look a little shell-shocked."

"Excuse us, gentlemen." Hamilton stood up and pulled Alec to his feet. He held Alec's arm tightly and frog-marched him back to their villa without a word. Alec still felt dazed, his cock bounced with every step and his ass felt empty again. Hamilton only let go of Alec to fumble with the door. When it opened, he pushed Alec inside and slammed it. Everything happened so fast. Alec barely had time to register the possibility of danger when Hamilton threw himself to his knees and wrapped his arms around Alec's waist. "I'm *so* sorry, Alec. You have to forgive me, I didn't give you to him, I swear. I had no idea he'd fuck you."

Alec blinked a few times and patted Hamilton's head. All he could really think about was how close Hamilton's lips were to his needy cock. The temptation to push it against his lips was so strong Alec had to bite down.

"I should have stopped him." Hamilton looked up to meet Alec's eyes. "Please don't hate me. I just never thought—"

"What are you going on about?"

"I don't want you to hate me for not paying attention. I swear I didn't know. I didn't think… so *stupid*. Of course he'd think he could fuck you in a place like this." He squeezed Alec tighter. "I'd never do anything you didn't want, Alec. Please tell me it's okay? I could report him."

"Stop." Alec stroked Hamilton's cheek. "I'm not completely stupid. I wanted it."

"I don't understand."

"Rick, I'm not going to just stay on my knees in a public place while some guy assaults me. If I didn't want his cock up my ass you would have damn well known about it and so would everyone else."

"But I thought it was a hard limit for you, being fucked as a boy?"

"It was. It still *is* with us. I can't explain it."

"But you enjoyed it?"

"I'd enjoy it more if you'd finish me off." Alec thrust his hips against Hamilton's chest. Hamilton looked down at Alec's cock but didn't reach for it. "Rick?"

Hamilton sat on the floor and didn't look up. Alec sat next to him and touched his knee. "Are you okay?"

"I … not really, no."

Shit, Alec hadn't considered how Hamilton would feel about seeing him fucked by someone else. He'd been so caught up in his own pleasure, thinking only of himself as usual. "What is it?"

"I always thought, or tried to convince myself, that you fucked other people because you thought you should. It never occurred to me that you might actually like it the same as you would if it was me." Hamilton snorted. "Stupid when you consider my history, but for some reason I thought it was different with us." He looked up and the sadness in his eyes pulled at Alec's heartstrings. "I guess I thought I was something special to you. But I'm just another fuck. Better benefits maybe."

Irritation flared. "You are being completely ridiculous. You *are* special to me. For fuck's sake, Rick, if you can't see I love you then what's the point? Why did we even bother to come away?"

"To reconnect, focus on each other. Now all I can think about is that fat bastard fucking you senseless."

"You were hard as ever when I was sucking your cock. If you hated it that much you had a funny way of showing it."

"It was shock. At the time, it was hot. Unbelievable. Now, not so much."

"So what, that's it? You see one guy fuck me and now you can't touch me anymore?" Alec pushed himself off the floor and started pacing. "It's a fucking good job I didn't climb onto that doctor for you then isn't it. What would you have done then, kicked me out for giving me to some- one else and deciding you didn't like it?"

"Now who's being ridiculous? It's not ... I'm just trying to talk to you about what happened. If you're going to expect me to hand you out from now on," Hamilton sighed a long, heavy sigh, "I can't do it. I won't."

"Good, because I don't want you to." *Yet. Or at least very often.* "Noth- ing needs to have changed between us, Rick. I fucked some guy. So what? We do it all the time."

"*You* do it all the time." Hamilton's stare was icy. It cut through Alec's cool and made him feel a little sick. Way to initiate a guilt trip. "And what do I tell the next guy that asks for you? Now they've seen someone fuck you, they'll all want a go."

"And they will respect your decision as my master to say no. The same as they always have. I'm still happy to give out blowjobs for you. Just maybe be a little clearer next time."

A smile ghosted over Hamilton's face but it didn't stay. "I wanted to rip his head off. Or rather his cock and shove it down his throat."

"I don't think Leo would have been too impressed with that."

"Guess not."

The silence stretched on and a ripple of fear raced across Alec's skin bringing a chill despite the heat. "Rick, I'm sorry, I shouldn't have let him. I can see that now. I didn't think it would be a big deal for you. You've threatened to hand me out so many times and you do it with the boys."

"You've never been one of the boys Alec, you know that."

"Not unless you tell me. I still think you're going to wake up one day and decide you're bored with me, that you want a newer model."

Hamilton reached out his hand. Alec took it and Hamilton pulled him back to the floor and into a comforting hug. "Never," Hamilton said. "I can't choose to replace you anymore than I chose to love you in the first place."

"So we're good?"

"More than good. It's very clear to me that you are most definitely *not* just another boy. Now I have to reconcile in my mind that you are also not mine alone."

Alec let the words sink in. Was that a preliminary for "things are going to get bumpy"? They'd only just smoothed everything out. The perfect month, a rest from the world. The time for reconciliation was over they should be forging ahead with a new future not struggling to come to terms.

"We should think about food." Hamilton patted his knee. "It's way past lunch."

"If you want me to be just for you, Rick, I'll do it." Hamilton looked at him with wide eyes. "I won't lie and say I don't like having the odd fuck from someone else but you're more important. If you don't like it, I'll say no from now on."

"You'd really do that?"

Alec nodded. It would hurt, not having Sebastian and Brad, not having Harrison, but if there was one thing their vacation had shown Alec, it was that Hamilton would always be number one. "I've told you before, Rick. For you, I'd do anything."

Hamilton latched on and squeezed. He hugged so hard Alec thought he might actually pop a rib. "I love you so much, Alec. Thank you." The kissing started as the pressure of the hug released. Soft, gentle kisses that soothed and caressed Alec's troubled mind. He would do it for Hamilton without a second thought. Explaining the situation to Sebastian however, was not going to be so easy.

About Turn

The flight was busy and despite First Class comforts, Alec felt stressed. An impending cloud of doom hovered over his head and he couldn't determine the source of it. He wanted to put it down to going back to work after so long. The next week would be a long and arduous one. Too many hours at the office and not enough catch-up time, but he knew things were ticking over nicely in his absence. He'd kept in close contact with Tom and Brad, worked with Tom for an hour here and there on updates. The reviews would be heavy work but there were no issues to deal with. Tom and Brad had kept everything together, and Kirby had overseen the service contracts without any glitches, so that couldn't be what was worrying him, or not all of it.

He'd considered the possibility that he'd felt redundant but the reality was that, while the office ticked over without him, it didn't grow. Tom was an excellent account manager but Alec couldn't deny the edge he had over him for spotting higher-yield investments and the ability to feel in his bones the time to act. He still wanted him on the team full time, and that was top of the agenda on his return.

Sebastian was in good form, excited about the training plan he'd been working on, and keen to show off his newly sculpted body. Alec's family had managed to invade on his birthday with long-distance greetings so he wasn't in trouble there. Harrison and Vaughn were on a vacation of their own, skiing in some posh resort in the U.S. and he'd even kept in touch with Tristan and Tessa so there were no surprises waiting for him. Hamilton squeezed his hand and the knot in his stomach tightened. Hamilton. It was the only thing left to consider.

Alec took him in with a long, penetrating stare. So much had changed and yet nothing at all. They were both different, the way they were together was different, and there lay before them an unknown—going public at work with their relationship. Would it really be that much of a deal? Alec couldn't see anyone really caring, other than Chloe for being kept out of the loop. Ugh, and Chloe. She'd hate him forever when Tom moved permanently to his team.

"Everything okay, darling? You look a little peaky."

"I'm good. Just thinking about work. About us at work."

"Yes, we should think about that." Hamilton accepted a cup of coffee from the cabin attendant and placed it on the table to his side. "I'm happy to make a small announcement to the management team, if you're happy with that."

"To tell them what, exactly?" Alec waved off the offer of coffee for himself. He didn't need any extra stimulus; his brain was already working fifty to the dozen.

"That we've been away together and return as an official couple having exchanged engagement rings." Hamilton held out his hand and examined the new ring encasing his wedding finger. It had taken an age to find the right one, he was so fussy, but Alec had to admit he liked seeing it, staking his claim, advertising Hamilton was off the market to potential suitors. His cock twitched and his mind wandered to other ways of staking a claim. They should consider joining the mile high club. It was a long flight, after all, and they'd missed the opportunity on the way out.

"Are you happy with that idea?"

"Huh?" Alec let the fantasy slip away and smiled. "I love it. I want everyone to know. I always have." He kissed Hamilton's cheek. "It'll be nice not to have to sneak around."

"Alec, I've been thinking."

And here it comes. The muscles in Alec's shoulders tensed and his stomach churned.

"What I said about wanting you to myself." Hamilton was picking his fingers. Never a good sign.

"Go on."

"We've had a great vacation haven't we?"

"Rick, you're making me nervous."

"The last few days, after you said you'd go back to being just for me have been amazing. For me anyway."

Alec reached for Hamilton's hand and brought it to his lips to kiss it. "Me too, Rick, you know that."

"I don't need that from you, Alec. I want you to be free to do whatever you want."

"I don't understand."

"It was a knee-jerk reaction. I was in shock and didn't really think through what you were offering. The very fact that you would do that for me, did do that for me, shows I have nothing to worry about."

Alec was still confused. The words made sense but he couldn't draw the conclusion.

"I finally understand that you love me, really love me. That you're not going to run off with the first guy that offers you a better fuck because what we have is so much more."

Alec let out a half laugh, half snort. "You've only just figured that out?"

"I know you probably thought it was obvious, but not to me." Hamilton smiled. "But it is now."

"I still have no idea what you're trying to tell me."

"You can fuck whoever you want. You can set yourself up in a cage at the club on a Saturday night, take a regular lover with a cock the size of a marrow, it doesn't matter. I know you'll always be mine." Hamilton twisted in his seat and took hold of both of Alec's hands in his. "I don't want you to stop exploring because of my insecurities. I'd rather not have to listen to blow-by-blow accounts but for as long as you feel the need, I'm happy for you not to hold back."

"My ass is no longer off limits?"

"Not unless you want it to be. If you don't want other guys to fuck you I'll be thrilled, but I don't want you to make the decision based on my need rather than yours."

Well, bloody hell. It took another moment to sink in but when it did, Alec felt the first rumblings of the cloud over his head dispersing. A new wave of uncertainty gripped him. This was a good thing, right? There was no ulterior motive hidden anywhere. Alec studied Hamilton's face looking for signs of a *but*.

"You don't look convinced," Hamilton said. "Should I not have said anything?"

"You should always say what you feel, Rick. I just can't help wondering what the reason is for your change of heart."

"As I said, I don't need to keep you from other men to know you love me."

"And it's not because you want to start fooling around and trying out other cocks for size?"

Hamilton laughed and pressed a kiss to Alec's lips. "The thought hadn't crossed my mind. Hand on heart, Alec, for as long as you wear that ring I would never consider allowing another cock inside me."

"You're not even curious?"

"If I was even remotely curious do you think I'd have waited so long for you?"

"Why did you wait, or let me for that matter?"

Hamilton sighed and took a sip of his coffee. It wasn't a heavy sigh, more of an "I can't believe you're going to make me talk about this" sigh but Alec refused to feel guilty. It was something he'd wondered about, a lot, and he needed to know. It might even help unravel the last pieces of the mystery that was Hamilton.

"You have to remember the life I've led, or rather the sex life." Hamilton glanced around the cabin before placing his cup back on the table. When his gaze returned to Alec's he looked serious. "I've had sex with more men than I can remember, and I've been at it pretty much since I was sixteen."

"I know that. It doesn't explain why you wouldn't want them fucking you."

"Alec, I can count on one hand the men I've had even a passing emotional connection to with fingers left over. Growing up in the Order, you learn very quickly that there are too many men who want nothing more than to say they've had you; it's a status, a medal of honor to have fucked as many Order men's sons as you can before they're old enough to know better. Father was very clear about what I was to expect and it played out just as he said it would." He twirled his cup a few times and Alec waited. "He knew I was gay and wanted me to be able to separate my private affairs from Order sex. He saw it as the only way to keep from having my heart broken by men who promised me everything but only wanted to say they'd fucked a Hamilton."

"Rick, that's awful."

"It's the way it is. I'm nothing if not a realist. I could see what he was saying was true. So, when Father gave me Jesse and Mostyn dumped me, I thought it was best to get on with being an Order Legacy and fuck everything they put in front of me. I was still doing it when I met you. Having the boys meant I didn't even consider the fact I'd never had a real relationship. It's always been about sex. Very specific sex with little to no emotional involvement."

"But you love Brendan and Dylan, and Sebastian."

"Of course I do, but not in the way I love you. Theirs is a love born from practicality and repetition. Familiarity. We offer each other a particular dynamic that has nothing to do with romantic notions and ever afters. As much as I love them, sex is still a mechanical process that deals only with physiological responses, my need to control, and their need to be owned. Whereas with you ..." Hamilton smiled. "I've been making love to you since that very first night I wrapped you up in my bed."

Alec's eyes pricked with moisture and his voice cracked. "Why me?"

Hamilton pinched his cheek. "You were different. I knew it as soon as you wrapped those pretty lips around my cock. You've always been interested in *me*, Alec. I'm a real person to you, not some manager or faceless fuck at a party. You've always looked at what you can give me, rather than what I can provide for you. I've never had that before."

"But the boys—"

"All came to me out of their own needs that could have been met by any good master."

It was an interesting notion Alec was certain the boys would refute vehemently. For him, there had been no other options. "I'd fancied you forever by the time you noticed me."

"That's a nice thought."

"It's true. I was almost too embarrassed to work on your team because of the fantasies I'd enjoyed. You were my number one jack-off-bank image." Hamilton laughed aloud, gaining a few looks from the other passengers. "Coarse, but true," Alec said, smiling. "Even more so now I know what you taste and feel like."

"And that's why I'm not interested in expanding my repertoire of lovers. No one could match you, Alec. I don't see the point in trying. I've had more sex in the last fifteen years than most men have in a lifetime. I'll continue to have meaningless sex until I retire from the Order but everything else I need, I get from you."

Meaningless sex. Was Order sex meaningless sex? Perhaps Alec was still too new to categorize it in such a way. True, it wasn't emotionally taxing sex but the buttons it pushed were hardly what he'd call meaningless. Brad, Sebastian, and Harrison all elicited deep-seated feelings that did more than get him off and the rest was good old-fashioned fun. It certainly wasn't mechanical. Maybe he would think differently if he'd been at it for ten years. Worthington had said similar, talked of sex through obligation, but Alec just didn't see it that way.

"Who are the others?"

Hamilton cocked his head on an angle and looked puzzled. "What do you mean, others?"

"Other men you've been emotionally attached to. And why didn't they fuck you?"

"I ... don't know. I've never thought about it." He played with his cup again and Alec waited, again. A smile ghosted over Hamilton's lips followed by a frown. "Mostyn wasn't ready for us to get that involved otherwise I suppose it could have happened really early for me."

"You would have let him?"

"I think I probably would have. It was real between us. I liked him a lot. If he'd have asked or it had headed that way, I wouldn't have thought twice."

Alec really wanted to know more about Mostyn. The conversation paused while the flight attendant fussed over them offering food and more drinks. Alec willed him away so they could continue talking. Finally, after delivering a bowl of nibbles and a bottle of water with two glasses, he left them alone.

"I thought at one point there was something with ..." Hamilton bit his lip. "I don't want you to get the wrong idea, Alec. If I tell you this, promise me you won't brood about it?"

"Why would I? Whatever it is obviously didn't go anywhere."

"I had a few dates with Nathanial a few years back."

Fucking hell. Fucking, fucking hell. Alec seethed quietly. How could he not have figured that out? "But?"

"We wanted different things. He's too over-the-top ambitious. I found it exhausting."

"But he wanted to pursue it?"

"He wasn't very happy when I didn't want to make more of it. It was a long time ago."

"But you liked him."

Hamilton looked thoughtful. He crunched on a few crackers and fiddled with his heating controls. "We connected for a while. I fucked him a few times and it wasn't just office stuff. It was real with him. Or it seemed so at the time."

Only Hamilton could drop a fucking bombshell and be matter-of-fact about it. "You said you hadn't had a boyfriend since you were fifteen. That sounds to me like he was your boyfriend."

"He wasn't." Alec's chest tightened at the overly defensive tone in Hamilton's denial. "It was a handful of nights out," Hamilton continued. "It never progressed to anything more. I shouldn't have told you."

"You shouldn't have kept it from me for so long." Alec grabbed for Hamilton's hand and squeezed. "I don't care if you've had other lovers Rick. I just want to know who you've had feelings for."

Hamilton grinned, breaking the tension between them. "And you?"

Alec shrugged. "I've had crushes on lots of people. I've had boyfriends. I've told you about most of them."

"So why was I different?"

"You... you were a culmination of things. You gave me space to express myself. I'd wanted for so long, been afraid and embarrassed of my lack of experience but you waved it all away. You made everything I thought was wrong about me special. How could I not love you for that?"

"You are special." They kissed, tender kisses, almost chaste. Hamilton was smiling when he pulled away. "That's the sum of it for me. No one else comes remotely close."

"I'm glad you told me about Philip. I'll have to deal with him a fair bit over the coming months. It'll help me make sense of his behavior."

"For heaven's sake don't let on you know. He was paranoid I'd used him just to be able to say I'd fucked him. I think he'd fallen for a few of the traps my father warned me about."

"I'm sure part of his issue with me is that he's always thought I knew. Knowing makes him easier to handle. I don't need to rub his face in it. You will need to put your necklace back on for work though."

Hamilton chuckled. "I don't doubt you're a match for him, Alec. I just don't want you becoming like him."

"Hardly likely. I've never been power hungry. I can't see that changing anytime soon." He patted Hamilton's knee and Hamilton laid his hand over Alec's.

"We should try and get some sleep. Thank you, for understanding."

"I'll always try; you just have to give me the opportunity."

Hamilton smiled and plumped his pillow before fully reclining his seat. Alec depressed the button that changed his own seat into a sleeping lounger and took a blanket from the passing attendant, passing it to Hamilton and taking another. He had a lot to think about. The clouds may have dispersed but there was definitely still the rumblings of thunder about. He'd always known there was something more to the Philip story. Knowing he'd inherited the role of rival for more than just Order business added a new dimension to dealing with the slimy bugger. At least he didn't have to end Sebastian's world just yet.

For the first time since they'd stepped on the plane to fly away from the U.K., Alec let his thoughts stay with Sebastian. There was only so much they could say to each other in short calls and texts and Alec wondered what the time away from his master had really been like for him. Alec was relieved that the tension he'd felt about leaving Sebastian for so long didn't materialize. The fretting over how many lovers Sebastian would have had in the time he'd been away didn't even send a ripple of unease through his mind but he was looking forward to seeing him. Brad too, and Harrison, though that wouldn't be for another week or so. Alec settled back into his pillow, interested to find he was still more than happy with the idea of being just for the man by his side even though that probably wouldn't happen now. Sure, he'd have fun for a few more years, but monogamy was no longer a pipedream. It had substance and value, and for the first time Alec could look on Rick, not as a guy known to fuck anything that moved, but as a man who'd had less real lovers than Alec had himself. And that was truly something to behold.

Avoiding Square One

Everything was too bright and too noisy. How the hell did the cabin crew still look so perky and amenable after such a long flight? It took everything Alec had not to bark and snap as his fellow passengers pushed and jostled him. Surely the whole point of First Class was to avoid the cattle market, and yet Alec had the distinct impression of being herded. It didn't help that some faux celebrity Alec had never heard of had been on the flight and seemed determined to cause a ruckus and hold everyone up. Why didn't the woman understand nobody gave a toss who she was? After the luxury and service of Bangkok airport, including the pre-flight massage, the standards at Heathrow fell more than a little short. And he was freezing. England was damp and cold even inside the terminal.

The sky looked orange with the cast of the artificial lights against the early morning sky as he looked out the boarding tunnel windows. Alec had forgotten how miserable predawn December mornings could be. He shivered waiting for the baggage and Hamilton wrapped his arms around him and smoothed a hand over his back. "A good sleep is all you need," he said. Alec grunted and Hamilton smiled. "Perhaps we should get some coffee in you instead."

"I just want to curl up in bed." Alec broke into a grin. "With you."

"That can definitely be arranged." Hamilton rubbed his shoulder. "You should have kept a sweater out of the case. I told you it would be cold."

"I know." Alec sighed. He hadn't worn a sweater because he didn't want to be reminded they were flying home. There were too many things waiting to go wrong, too many variables beyond his control on too many fronts and the constant buzz inside his head was making him dizzy.

"Do the boys know where to meet us?"

"Yeah. Sebastian's just texted me. They're here already."

Hamilton loaded the last case onto the trolley. "Let's go then."

By the time they found their way to the main concourse and their meeting point, Alec was feeling slightly more human with a hint of excitement brewing in his stomach at seeing the boys. One minute he caught a glimpse of Brad, the next he was body slammed by an airborne Sebastian, wrapped in arms and legs, and deafened by the screech of his name in his ear. Alec dropped his bag and hugged back. The well of relief that flooded through him was unexpected and welcome. The warmth of Sebastian's body penetrated his jacket and he knew immediately he was home.

"God, I missed you," he whispered in Sebastian's ear. It hadn't registered how much until that moment with him playing limpet around his neck.

Sebastian nuzzled into Alec's shoulder. "Keep talking, I need to hear your voice some more." But Alec couldn't talk. He had no words for the emotions coursing through him. It was another few minutes before he could bring himself to let go and place Sebastian back on his feet. If Hamilton was pissed, he didn't show it. Alec stepped aside and let them have their own hug while he sought out Bradley. Their greeting was no less heartfelt and Alec wondered why he'd been so worried about coming home.

"It's good to have you back, Alec," Brad said, holding on to his hand for a moment.

"As of this moment, I'm officially glad to be back." And then just to make sure everything else was in order he slipped his hand into Hamilton's and squeezed. Brad grabbed his bag off the floor, Sebastian took over the baggage trolley, and Alec and Hamilton brought up the rear, still holding hands, as they made their way to the car.

"You can go straight home and catch up with them if you'd like," Hamilton said.

Alec felt a lump rise in his throat. He wanted to, but at the same time he wasn't ready to let go of the quiet space he had with Hamilton. "I want to stay with you. At least until we sleep off the flight. I've got all weekend to catch up and get back into a routine."

Hamilton smiled and bumped Alec's shoulder as they walked. "Just checking."

"I'm sure I'll have to pry Brendan off you once we get home."

"Probably. But he'll have to wait until we're settled for anything more than a hug. I'm not ready to jump straight back into being his master."

Alec's heart skipped. Hamilton wasn't eager to run off and fuck something else. That sounded promising. Very promising indeed. Perhaps more had changed during the vacation than he'd first thought. The meandering thoughts cut off during the crush into the lift and he remembered how tired he was. He stifled a yawn and leaned into Hamilton with a contented sigh, ignoring the disapproving stares from the couple next to them. Old busybodies shouldn't be looking if love offended their sensibilities.

"You didn't bring Chris?" Hamilton asked Bradley as they arrived at Alec's car.

"I didn't think to. Alec barely uses the Audi. I thought it could do with a run." He opened the boot and started loading the cases. "It's roomy in the back."

Alec opened the door for Hamilton to slide in and he climbed in next to him and snuggled up. "Wake me when we're home." He managed to kiss Hamilton's cheek before he yawned again and he let his eyes fall shut and the world fade to black.

Herded again. Alec was still groggy as Sebastian maneuvered him through the doors and halls and sat him at the dining table in Hamilton's apartment. "Food and bed for you." Alec took a moment to look at him. He was positively glowing and it warmed Alec's heart to have him close. He also noticed the jeans Sebastian was wearing, his favorite, and looking distinctly snug over what looked to be a newly formed and very pert ass. The lack of jagged edges and bony shoulders that usually poked through his shirt made Alec smile.

"What's the goofy grin for?"

Alec turned and Dylan engulfed him in a hug. "Hey, you," he spluttered against Dylan's shoulder. It seemed like forever since he'd seen him.

"Missed you, buddy." Dylan kissed his forehead. "You look like crap."

"Nice to see you too. Just feed me and let me sleep for a week." Alec cast a glance around for Hamilton and found him trying to fight off Brendan's insistent pulling to the other room. They exchanged words Alec couldn't catch and a despondent Brendan let go and trailed Hamilton to where he joined Alec at the table. They leaned against each other for moral support. It was great to be home but it was awfully crowded. Had it always been like this and Alec just hadn't noticed? He listened to the conversation going on around him but let Hamilton field the questions. He was content to watch Sebastian potter in the kitchen and took comfort in the smell of bacon and the sound of its sizzle and pop under the grill.

"You're very quiet."

"Huh?" Alec looked up as Brad laid a plate down for him.

"Surely you can't be that jetlagged," he said, looking a little concerned.

"I'm not. I didn't have a good flight. I'll be fine after some real sleep."

He ate while the others chatted and then let himself be ushered through to the bedroom, undressed and tucked in next to Hamilton. Sebastian touched his lips to Alec's gently. "Sleep well. It's good to have you home."

Alec reached up for another kiss. "I'll be back to normal in a few hours."

Peace settled into his bones as the door closed behind the greeting party and Alec wriggled closer and spooned Hamilton, slipping an arm around his waist and stroking over his cock. "We should have joined the mile high club," Alec said, nuzzling into Hamilton's neck. "Those bathrooms were huge."

"Next time." Hamilton groaned as Alec continued to stroke his cock. "I love you," he said, twisting in Alec's arms and kissing his face and neck. All that willing flesh just outside the door and Hamilton still wanted him. Maybe he could find the energy for a leisurely fumble—he pressed himself against Hamilton's body—and maybe not. He sighed and Hamilton chuckled. "We should sleep."

"Will you stay close?" he mumbled.

"Whatever you need, darling." And Alec drifted off again.

Alec stretched and yawned. Not quite fully rested but he felt a lot better. Apart from the empty bed. He came to a bit more and sat up. He could hear the shower running and he smiled. A nice clean package being prepared. He padded through to the bathroom and froze in the doorway. The air escaped his lungs in a gasp as he took in the sight of Dylan and Brendan ... with Hamilton sandwiched between them. So much for staying close.

"Alec."

Alec jumped at Hamilton's surprised tone. "Sorry," he grabbed a towel from the shelf and wrapped it around his waist. "Didn't mean to interrupt." He backed out the room and stumbled against the door jam. Why did it hurt? He'd seen Hamilton with the boys a hundred times, a thousand.

"Alec, wait." He heard Hamilton groan and he turned and bolted. "Brendan, get off me," Alec heard as he slammed the bedroom door.

"What's up?" Sebastian said, as Alec stormed into the living room.

"I want to go home. *Now.*"

Bradley jumped up and grabbed the keys from the table. Alec ignored Hamilton calling him and ran across the hall and into his own apartment. He dashed through to his own room, into the bathroom and locked the door. The bastard. The *fucking* bastard. All that crap about Brendan having to wait, about staying close, and all the time he was just waiting for Alec to fall asleep. He jumped at the thump on the door behind him.

"Alec, open this door."

"Leave me alone." He cussed himself for acting like a sulky teenager. And why the fuck had he locked himself in the bathroom? His face flushed with embarrassment.

"Whatever you think you saw, you're wrong. Now get out here so I can talk to you."

"I can't." His body refused to move. His heart was hammering, his chest tight and his arms would only wrap around himself. He slipped to the floor and rested his head on his knees. What the fuck had just happened? He held out his hand in front of him and watched it shake. Muffled sounds from the other side of the door caught his attention. Raised voices, a slammed door and everything went quiet. The tension drained from Alec's body but numbness remained. And he was cold. Again.

You're being a bloody idiot. As usual. He picked himself off the floor and turned on the shower. In the daze that was washing and drying he tried not to think about what he'd done and how stupid he'd been. Of all the ridiculous things to do. Since when had he run away from emotionally taxing situations? Oh, yeah, all the time. Like finding Tom and Hamilton, or Harrison's party. *Bloody hell.* So much for breaking the old mold. He opened the door and stopped when he saw Hamilton pacing the room.

"Rick, I'm—"

"What the hell do you think you're playing at, storming out and refusing to acknowledge me?"

Alec flopped onto the bed. He listened as Hamilton ranted and a sigh shuddered through his chest. "Rick, I'm sorry. I don't know why I did it. Please…" Hamilton stopped in front of him and their eyes met.

"We were supposed to be over this stuff."

"I know, I—"

"Alec, I can't live like this. It's too stressful. If the time away did nothing to fix—"

Alec threw himself at Hamilton and mashed their lips together. He couldn't let him say it, didn't want to hear it, wouldn't *ever* let him think it. Hamilton responded to the clash of their bodies with a firm grasp on Alec's ass and a desperate, hungry mouth. Alec melted against him but Hamilton pulled away and with a growl, threw him on the bed. He pinned Alec in place, forcing his knees between Alec's legs. Alec opened for him, welcomed the ferocity, needed the heat and the passion to stave off the fear eating away at his insides. Hamilton pulled at both of their towels and threw them on the floor. He didn't reach for lube as Alec expected, instead he wet his fingers and pushed against Alec's pucker. Alec flinched at the friction but pushed down to accommodate him. With a bit more spit and a quick coating of his cock, Hamilton moved into position and thrust into Alec's body with gritted teeth. The fucking was frantic and raw. An outsider would think it was they who'd been apart for a month. Alec had never been so desperate to connect, to be claimed by Hamilton. No thrust was deep enough, no stroke hard or rough enough, and he didn't want it to end. Why couldn't they stay here, alone, for the next year or two?

Hamilton grabbed Alec's cock and fisted it hard and fast, skirting the edges of discomfort, to bring him off. Alec grasped at Hamilton's shoulders and clawed at his back trying to hold him closer until the heat took over and the wave of climax crashed over them within a few thrusts of each other. Hamilton shuddered and stilled, his breathing erratic, and he stared down at Alec. "You'll be the death of me, I swear." He pulled out carefully and plopped himself down next to Alec on the bed. Alec rolled over him and stroked his cheek.

"I really am sorry."

"Don't ever walk away from me again. You have no idea how much it hurt to see you turn your back on me."

"I won't, I promise." Alec kissed Hamilton on his chest. "Put it down to the bad flight."

"Don't patronize me. Tell me why."

Alec put his arms around Hamilton and held tight. "I thought we'd agreed to spend the first few hours together acclimatizing before catching up with the boys. When I saw you … with them … I thought you'd …" He couldn't say it. Because it was so ridiculous, he didn't know why he'd thought it in the first place. "Once I'd locked myself in the bathroom I realized how stupid it was but then I was too embarrassed to come out."

"As long as you do see how stupid it was."

"I do."

"I didn't invite Brendan and Dylan into the shower. I was trying to get them to leave when you showed up."

"You don't have to explain."

"And Sebastian tore strips off me for upsetting you."

"Can we just back track to the nice peaceful vacation and forget it ever happened?"

"And when I do catch up with Brendan and Dylan?"

"You should. I want you to. I'd just expected you to be mine until we'd at least showered and presented ourselves ready to return to the madhouse."

Hamilton held him close. "I don't know if I'll ever be ready to rejoin the madhouse. But for the moment I don't feel I have the option not to." He sighed and kissed Alec's hair. "I need a shower. And my cock's sore. No more fucking without lube."

They took their time, washing, caressing, and soothing their frayed nerves. Alec's ass was tender and Hamilton's cock pinker than usual. It would make the respective catch up's interesting but they were back on track. A minor blip easily washed away and hopefully forgotten.

"I don't have any clothes. I need to go home for a moment," Hamilton said, wrapping a towel around his waist.

"I'm okay now. You should go and spend some time with Brendan. He's probably fretting. Apologize to him for me."

"Only if you're sure."

"I am. And ... maybe it would be a good idea if we entertain in our own apartments for the weekend."

Hamilton seemed to ponder for a moment. "You're probably right. A little space would be sensible, if only to calm the boys." Hamilton pinned Alec in place with his stare. "I'll hate every minute of it, Alec. Even now, I don't want to let you out of my sight."

"We'll be okay. I might take the boys to a hotel."

Hamilton nodded and went to walk out the door. Alec pulled him back for a last hug and a deep kiss that he hoped said everything he couldn't. Hamilton smiled as they broke apart. "I'll text you tomorrow."

"Tonight."

Hamilton smiled again. It lifted his mood but he still looked stressed. "It's practically tonight already, but okay, tonight." He squeezed Alec's hand and left.

Sebastian poked his head around the door almost immediately. "Is it safe to come in?"

Alec grinned. "I'm okay now."

"You weren't okay when you stormed through here."

"I freaked out over something stupid. All is well." Alec took a deep breath and acknowledged his own stress, about being home, about work, about his too familiar almost-disaster with Hamilton, had evaporated. Just a crusty residue remained. It would itch, irritate a little, but the damage was done and the worst cleaned up. The storm diverted yet again. "Actually," he said smiling. "Everything is great."

Sebastian didn't look convinced but what else could he say? Sebastian would never understand how much had changed with Hamilton during their vacation. He'd never know the Hamilton Alec did and in a strange way, he'd never know the Alec Hamilton did. There was nothing to be done about that either. He sorted through the closet for some jeans and a sweater. Bradley had materialized by the time Alec finished getting dressed. "I thought we'd go to a hotel, outside the city."

Sebastian and Brad looked at each other then back to Alec.

"I swear everything is okay. I'm just not ready for London yet."

"The cottage is practically ready in Somerton," Sebastian said brightly. "I could pack up some food and we could go there for the weekend. All that's missing is a TV and a stereo. The builders have even had the heating on to run in the new furnace."

An escape. A refuge from … he wasn't sure what, his own idiocy probably, but he knew he needed to get out of the apartment and forget the list of obligations that came with it for another day or so. "Brilliant idea. You grab the food, Brad grab some clothes, and I'll pack the toiletries." Time to go cold turkey from his newly refashioned Hamilton addiction. Not that he'd ever get over it completely but he could remove himself at times like this when it sent him into a tailspin. And he had things to think about. The last twenty-four hours had revealed more to Alec about his relationship with Hamilton than the rest of the vacation put together. They'd come a long way, much farther than Alec could have hoped but it was still tenuous somehow, ethereal. Before he could sort through what it meant in real terms and ground it into daily life he needed to focus, to catch up with the more subtle changes that had been outside of his control. Changes in the lives of people around him; important people, who wove their own magic in Alec's life.

"And Sebastian…" He turned in the doorway to look at Alec and

Alec's chest swelled. "You look great. The work you've put in, it really makes a difference." A difference he had every intention of exploring, inch by inch, over the next twenty-four hours. A well of uncertainty bubbled in Alec's gut waiting for a response.

Sebastian beamed, lighting up the room with his smile, and all was well in Alec's world.

Thus ends Volume Three of the erotic adventures of Alec Caldwell.

Join Alec in 2017 for the fourth volume of tales in which Alec faces the challenges brought to the fore from his official engagement and another promotion within the Order of Gentlemen.

For details of Volume Four stop by my Goodreads author page or the blog, detailed below.

Casey K
X

http://theriseofaleccaldwell.blogspot.com
http://caseykcox.blogspot.com
Email: caseyk_cox@yahoo.com

The Rise of Alec Caldwell

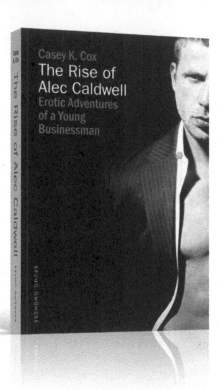

Casey K. Cox
THE RISE OF ALEC CALDWELL
Erotic Adventures of a Young
Businessman
208 pages, softcover,
13 x 19 cm, 5¼ x 7½",
978-3-86787-688-9
US$ 16.99 / £ 10.99
€ 14,95

Alec Caldwell has everything going for him. He's young, successful, and reasonably handsome. But at twenty-four, Alec is still a virgin. Almost as embarrassing as his virgin status is the crush he has on his boss, Rick Hamilton. Not a day seems to go by without Hamilton catching Alec staring or drooling. When Alec is called into Hamilton's office after the latest incidence of ogling he thinks he's going to be transferred. Instead he's offered the chance of a lifetime—to be Hamilton's personal sex toy at work. A whole new world unfurls as Alec is inducted into the exclusive Order of Gentleman that weaves through the rich and powerful corporate institutions of The City and beyond.

The Seduction of Alec Caldwell

Casey K. Cox
THE SEDUCTION OF
ALEC CALDWELL
Erotic Adventures of a Young
Businessman
208 pages, softcover,
13 x 19 cm, 5¼ x 7½",
978-3-86787-789-3
US$ 16.99 / £ 10.99
€ 14,95

Alec Caldwell is a successful investment manager, but behind closed office doors he's also a sex toy for his wealthy clients. As a new member of the exclusive Order of Gentleman, he finds himself immersed in a secret underworld of the rich and powerful. Doors to new worlds open before him and Alec's experience grows along with the importance of the men he services. But his newfound status puts the blossoming relationship with his boss and master, Rick Hamilton, under pressure. Alec is a hot commodity and temptation abounds. He finds himself questioning, not only the direction of his life and vocation, but the value of those he truly holds dear.